One Heart

that Beats for Two

ONE HEART

THAT BEATS FOR TWO

ROBERT W. ROSS

ISBN-13: 979-8497599374

Spartamac Publishing
Atlanta, Georgia
www.spartamac.com

I wish to thank my wonderfully sadistic Alpha readers without whose ruthless critique this book would not be readable. Given their complete lack of social graces, I understand why they wish to remain anonymous.

I would also like to thank all of my Beta readers for their thoughtful insights, suggestions, and corrections. I appreciate you all! Special thanks go out to Autumn, Charla, Garrett, Jocelyn, Keith, Keonah, Lindsay, and Nanci for going above and beyond!

Cover Illustration by George Patsouras

*To those who help work all things together for good,
and do so with open hearts, filled with love.*

Chapter 1

PROLOGUE

Caspian Lewis tightened the belt to his wool-lined trench coat, and hunched his shoulders against the cold as he walked across Loyola's campus. He glanced at his watch even though he already knew what he'd see there. Caspian was late...again.

What kind of person is late for the last lecture of their career, he thought to himself. "Apparently, I am," he said aloud. No one was near enough to hear the old man, or would likely have taken notice if they were. Caspian was known around the university as someone who often had lengthy conversations. "Sometimes other people are even involved," he laughed. Unfortunately for him, Loyola's virtually intelligent communications kiosks were still not aware of his idiosyncratic nature.

As he passed by one, it illuminated, and projected an anthropomorphic wolf avatar directly in his path. "Merry Christmas and a Happy New Year to you, Dr. Lewis. You just mentioned involvement. Do you need some assistance?"

Caspian pulled up short. "Oh, hello, Havoc. No, I'm fine, just late for class. Have to dash. I'm sure we can talk again later."

"That is unlikely, Doctor," said the holographic wolf-mascot. "Today is the last day of classes before the Christmas break, and I have no record of you teaching any classes during the Spring 2079 semester." Havoc T. Wolf shimmered for a second, then said. "You are retiring, Dr. Lewis. On behalf of the faculty, students, and staff of Loyola University may I offer you—"

1

Caspian walked through the projection, but called back over his shoulder. "Much appreciated, Havoc, but I'm late, I'm late, for a very important date. Have to dash." Dr. Lewis increased his pace and felt his heart thumping with effort. "Now wouldn't it be ironic if I dropped dead on my way to give a philosophical lecture on life?" he asked himself. The old man was still chuckling at his own mental musings when he turned the corner and spied a cluster of several dozen students. They were all huddled in small groups, he assumed for both companionship and warmth. Caspian could immediately tell that there were far more students assembled outside his classroom than were enrolled in his philosophy course.

Someone detached themselves from the crowd, and ran toward him. Caspian smiled at the young woman as she drew up beside him. "I know I'm late, Debra. No need to berate me," said Lewis.

She returned the smile, but shook her head. "What do I always say Doctor Lewis?"

"You're the grad student, I'm the professor," sighed Caspian.

"That's right," she laughed, "but this time I might berate you just a little. I did ask you to let me pair my phone to yours so I could unlock the auditorium, but you promised me you would be on time...for a change."

Caspian's eyes slipped off Debra's and to the mass of students. "Is that why they are standing outside, shivering like little bunnies? Oh no!" He immediately began patting his trenchcoat pockets, frantically searching for the telltale lump of his mobile phone.

Debra gently took hold of Caspian's arms, drew them down to his side, then placed both hands flat against his chest. "Stop," she said, with a smile. Debra slipped her hand into the zippered side pocket of the trench coat, pulled out the phone, then waggled it in front of Caspian. "I'll go unlock the door and get everyone settled. Don't run. We don't need you breaking something on your last day."

She turned to go, but Caspian stopped her, and asked, "Is it me, or are there more students than usual?"

Debra rolled her eyes. "I had to turn the last twenty away. It's a full house. Everyone knows this is your last lecture *and* I may have billed it as a philosophical pearl of great price." She shrugged. "Everyone loves you, Dr. Lewis, and who can pass up receiving pearls of wisdom?" Without another word, she started jogging toward the classroom, hand upraised and calling out, "Okay, I'm opening it up. No shoving!"

ONE HEART THAT BEATS FOR TWO

Caspian stared out over the midsized auditorium classroom. Each of the chairs were filled, and at least another twenty people were lined shoulder-to-shoulder against the back wall. Dr. Lewis felt his lips curl in a wry smile as he watched Debra scolding a few stragglers who tried to convince her there might still be standing room left. Finally, she turned, gave him a haggard smile, and offered a thumbs-up signal.

Caspian tapped on the lectern's microphone. A pop sounded throughout the room, and silence descended a moment later. Dr. Lewis removed his rimless eyeglasses and began wiping them with a cloth. They weren't dirty, but it was something he always did before a lecture, and he wasn't about to change. He held the spectacles out in front of himself appraisingly, then asked, "Can everyone hear me?" Immediately a chorus of affirmation flowed from the audience. Caspian nodded, then stepped around the lectern and walked to the center of the room's half-moon stage. He felt the crowd's eyes on him, as they watched in silence. An old stool rested in the far corner of the stage. Caspian walked over to it, picked it up, and set it in the middle of the stage. He sat down, hooked his feet around the lower rung, and smiled at the audience.

"So, none of you had anything better to do on a Friday night? I have to tell you, if this were 2022 instead of 2078, or if I was twenty-eight instead of eighty-two…" he chuckled, "*I* certainly wouldn't be spending my Friday night listening to me." Polite laughter rolled through the auditorium.

"Well," said Caspian, "seeing as how you have *all* made the dubious decision to fritter away one evening of your precious youth, I guess I should do my best to make it worth your while. What do you say to that?" Applause filled the room, and Dr. Lewis nodded. "So, before we get started, how about a little housekeeping. First of all, I know I'm old and forgetful, but I believe this course had one hundred seventeen students in it rather than what looks like over a two hundred and fifty. Just to confirm I haven't developed an advanced case of dementia over the last twenty-four hours, would everyone who actually took my Philosophy of Eros, Agape, and Philia 505 class, please raise your hand."

The professor nodded as dozens of hands went into the air. "Ah, good. At least you all seem to have managed to get the seats you paid for."

Dr. Lewis sat in silence for several seconds, then shook his head. "So, I have a good idea why so many of you are here, but it would be pretty embarrassing

3

if I got it wrong. Would one of you please let me know what you think tonight's lecture is about?" He grinned. "Or are you here to wish me well on my retirement?" No one answered, and Caspian shook his head. "Come now, this isn't going to work if everyone just sits there like bumps on a log. Let's try it again. What is my topic?"

Caspian stared at his silent audience, and waited. He was good at waiting. His wife was fond of saying that waiting was one of Caspian's core competencies. Finally, a young woman stood up, midway to the back. He locked eyes with the student, and smiled. "Why are you here, Miss…"

"Stewart," she replied. "Emily Stewart. I'm here because of what you promised."

"I'm with you so far, Miss Stewart," laughed the Professor. He saw how she suddenly looked uncertain, and gave her a nod of encouragement.

She squared her shoulders. "Professor there is a persistent rumor that you encountered something inexplicable after the pandemic of 2020. People say you sought the three forms of love, and that's why you teach the courses you do."

Caspian nodded. "Close. I wouldn't say I sought them as much as they found me, but maybe that's a distinction without a difference. Still, there has to be more to the story, because, so far, it doesn't seem worth filling a stuffy auditorium the last night before Christmas break. Forget rumors and stories, Emily. What brought *you* here?"

She paused for several beats, then said. "Supposedly, you experienced a tragic loss that resulted in transcendent joy. I can't reconcile the two. How is that even possible? Professor, I need to know."

Caspian nodded. "And that, class, is the true Miss Stewart. I just needed to coax her out a bit."

Emily stared directly at the professor and he could see the hunger in her eyes. All his best students had it. It was as old as humanity itself. It was the desire to know the unknowable, touch the untouchable, and experience the divine. Caspian Lewis had done all three, but never shared the story with any but those who had lived it with him. Emily Stewart's voice rang like a clarion bell as she said, "On your last day with the University, you promised to tell the story of One Heart that Beats for Two. That's why I'm here, Professor."

Caspian took a deep breath. "Thank you Emily." He nodded to her and she sat. "Is that why all of you are here as well?" A murmur of assent passed throughout the room. "Very well," continued the Professor, "a promise is a promise."

ONE HEART THAT BEATS FOR TWO

He stood. "Some will argue with me, but I believe philosophy is the study of life. Oh, I know our friends on the other side of campus say that life is the purview of biology. They are not wrong, but biology is the study of outer life, the life that can be seen, touched, and measured. Philosophy, at its best mind you, is the study of inner life, that which can never be truly seen, touched, or measured...only experienced."

Caspian walked over to the lectern, retrieved the bottle of water he knew Debra would have set there, then returned to his stool. He sat, took a long drink, then set the bottle on the stage floor. "There's a reason why I've never told this story before. You see, some stories complete a circle. All our lives are circles, some large, some small, and some with many concentric circles within them. For you, what I share tonight is just a story, for me, it is my life. I was one way in 2020. Two years later I was completely different." The professor lay his hand across his chest. "And the thing that happened in-between was one heart that beat for two."

Caspian smiled at all the faces, then glanced at his watch. "I will give everyone three minutes to change their minds and reclaim what I'm sure will be a wonderful Friday night. After that, I will begin, but trust me students, like the journey that changed me so many years ago, your hearing it may well change you. The choice to remain, is yours."

Professor Lewis watched as the students glanced left, then right. Some turned around as they heard others moving. Several left, but not many. Empty chairs were immediately filled, and exactly three minutes later, Caspian bent down, picked up his water bottle, then walked to the edge of the stage.

He opened his arms to the students. "My story, like so many, began in a small kindergarten classroom with a boy trying to impress a girl. That boy was me and that girl, well, she was an angel, and her name was Elizabeth Winters."

Chapter 2

CAS AND LIZZY, 2002

"Caspian Lewis, what do you think you are doing?" asked the kindergarten teacher.

The young boy looked up and smiled. "I'm telling and showing, Ms. Price. I know it's called *show* and tell, but that doesn't make sense to me. Why would you show something before telling about it? I mean, what if I brought in frog guts. Shouldn't I tell someone about—"

Laura Price did her best to try and keep a straight face, but finally gave up. She laughed. "I swear, Caspian, that impish smile of yours is not going to save you in the real world. Look at you. You are covered in grease. What am I supposed to tell your mother when she comes to pick you up?"

The girl next to him held up her hands. They, too, were black with grease. Laura's eyes went wide as saucers. "Elizabeth, what in heavens name? No! Don't wipe them on—" but it was too late. The young girl dragged her hands down her dress, looked at them, then wiped the remaining grease on Caspian's shirt.

In between the two children sat about a dozen pieces of plastic, one large metal rod, and a screwdriver. Ms. Price pointed at the parts. "Was that your dad's toy, the one you brought in to show everyone?" Caspian nodded. "Why did you break it?" the teacher asked in bewilderment.

"I didn't break it, Ms. Price. I took it apart. Lizzie wanted to see what was inside."

"I like seeing inside things," confirmed the girl.

"Caspian," sighed the teacher, "if someone asked you to jump off a bridge, would you do it?"

The boy furrowed his brow in concentration. "I don't think so," he said finally. "Well, maybe if Lizzie asked me." The two children smiled at each other, then Caspian gave his teacher a serious look, and said, "Lizzie is my girlfriend, so I might jump off a bridge if she asked me to...and it wasn't that high. How high are bridges?"

Her eyes flicked to the classroom clock. It showed 3:10. It was not uncommon for Caspian and Elizabeth to be the last children picked up in the afternoon. Still, their teacher tried to move the clock hands forward by sheer force of will. Nothing happened. She shook her head, then signaled to an older man who volunteered as the assistant in her classroom.

He stopped putting things away, and quickly crossed the room. "Need something, Ms. Price?" he asked, then looked at the pile of parts. "Lizzie, are you getting Cas into trouble again?"

"He wanted to do it," said the girl defensively.

"That was a classic toy," sighed the assistant. "I think it's called a ZoomerBoomer. You use it to wind up model cars. My son had one when he was little."

"Mr. Davies," began the teacher, "I'm going to take Lizzie to the bathroom and help her get cleaned up. Would you do the same for Caspian?"

"Sure thing," said the assistant. "Come on Edison junior, let's try and degrease you."

"Who?" asked the boy, but didn't wait for Mr. Davies to answer. Instead, Caspian pointed at the pile of parts. "I have to put the ZoomerBoomer back together. If I wash my hands now, I'll just get dirty again."

Davies and Price shared a look, then the teacher crouched down. "Caspian, are you telling me that you can fix that thing?"

The boy gave her an exaggerated nod. "Of course I can. Daddy says if you take something apart that you can't put back together, then you've broken it. He'd be pretty mad if I broke his ZoomerBoomer, Ms. Price."

She extended a hand to the young girl. "Come on, Elizabeth, let's get you cleaned up." The girl reached up, then pulled her hand back. Elizabeth stared at her black grease covered fingers, then showed them to her teacher. "It's okay," said Ms. Price, "You can take my hand. I'll clean us both up once we get to the bathroom."

ONE HEART THAT BEATS FOR TWO

Caspian watched as his teacher led Elizabeth from the classroom, then started laying the various ZoomerBoomer parts in a row. "Is your name Jack?" asked Caspian while he began fitting pieces together.

The assistant's knees popped as he sank to the floor beside Caspian. "My name *is* Jack, but I think we should stick with Mr. Davies," laughed the older man.

Caspian glanced up, confused. "I don't want to call you, Jack. You're old. My mom says you have to call old people by their last name. It's respectful. I was just wondering why Ms. Price doesn't call you Jack. Is it because you're so old?" Caspian pointed to one of the parts. "Would you give me that one, please?"

Jack handed the boy what looked like a long compression spring, then said, "It's a school thing, Caspian. Everyone here calls each other by their last name."

"Why?" asked the boy.

Davies shrugged. "Honestly, I don't even know why."

"Maybe it's because your real names are supposed to be secrets," said Caspian.

"Maybe," agreed the assistant, then said, "So, Lizzie is your girlfriend, huh?"

"Yep."

"You seem a bit young for a girlfriend," he chuckled.

"I'm almost six."

"Well, that makes a difference then," agreed Mr. Davies seriously.

"That's what Lizzie said, too. She was the one who told me that she was my girlfriend."

"Really?" asked the assistant.

Caspian looked up from his reassembly of the toy. "Really, really. I was just sitting here after Tell-and-Show, and she asked how the ZoomerBoomer worked. I told her I didn't know. You just push it up and down on the car, then the car zooms around. Once the zoom runs out, you ZoomerBoomer it again."

"I'm guessing that didn't satisfy her," said Mr. Davies

"Nope. She wanted to see how it worked."

"So, that's when you took it apart?"

Caspian shook his head. "That's when she asked me to take it apart. I told her no."

The assistant laughed again, then pointed to the dwindling pile of parts. "If you told her no, how come the ZoomerBoomer is in pieces?"

"Because she let me listen to her magic heart."

"She did?" asked the assistant with a smile. "I didn't even know Lizzie had a magic heart."

"She does," said Caspian, "but don't feel bad about not knowing, Mr. Davies. It's a secret."

"Oh, in that case, I'll be sure to keep it to myself," whispered the assistant. He pursed his lips. "How did you get to hear her magic heart?"

Caspian tapped his chest with one hand while reaching for more parts with the other. "She told me to put my ear right here, and that's when I heard the magic."

"What did you hear?"

The boy looked around, then whispered, "I told you. It's a secret."

Mr. Davies leaned close and spoke in a conspiratorial whisper. "You can tell me, Cas. I'm good at keeping secrets."

Caspian seemed to consider this for several long moments then asked, "Can I listen to your heart?" Mr. Davies put his arms behind his back, then nodded. Caspian scooted over, and rested his ear against the assistant's chest. After only a couple seconds the boy pulled back and said, "Nope, yours isn't magic. It's okay though, mine isn't either."

"What did my heart sound like?" asked Mr. Davies. Caspian tapped out a cadence on the floor. *Bump-bump, bump-bump, bump-bump, bump-bump.* "Okay," said the assistant, "and what did Lizzie's heart sound like to make it magical?" Caspian tapped again. *Bump-bump, bump-bump-bump, bump-bump, bump-bump-bump.*

"She has an extra *bump*," said Caspian in wonder. "That's why her heart's magic, and since I know about the secret, she said she has to be my girlfriend."

"I'm not sure that's how it works," offered the assistant.

"Of course it does, everyone knows that," said Caspian in a tone that made it clear he thought Jack Davies must know absolutely nothing about girls.

"Fair enough," said the assistant, his tone serious. "But Cas, I don't see how we got from Lizzie having a magic heart to your dad's toy laying on the floor in pieces."

Caspian set down the almost completed toy and stared at the assistant. "If your girlfriend asks to take something apart, you should do it. Everyone knows that."

"Oh, I'm sorry," said Mr. Davies. "I must have missed that girlfriend rule somewhere along the way."

"It's okay," replied Caspian. He fit the final two pieces together with a resounding click, then held up the restored toy. "You probably haven't had a girlfriend in a long time."

"My wife wouldn't like it," agreed the assistant.

Caspian considered this a moment, shrugged, then asked, "Should we go to the bathroom now?"

"Soon," replied Mr. Davies. He looked up as Elizabeth and her teacher reentered the classroom. "You hang tight here for a minute, Cas. I want to talk with Ms. Price before we get that grease off you."

"Okay," said Caspian, then fitted his ZoomerBoomer to the bottom of a race car and began pumping it up and down.

Jack Davies walked over to the teacher. Elizabeth smiled at him and seemed about to run toward Caspian when Ms. Price touched the girl's shoulder. "Elizabeth, don't get greasy again. Your mom is going to be here any minute." The girl nodded, then scampered after Caspian's race car, which had, quite literally, zoomed across the classroom floor.

The teacher sighed. "I think I'm done with show-and-tell for a while."

"You say that now," laughed Mr. Davies, "but you are a great teacher and know how much the kids love it. I bet it will be back, as scheduled, next Friday. Anyway, I just wanted to fill you in on my chat with Caspian, because..." Mr. Davies made air quotes, "his *girlfriend* might benefit from a bit of womanly wisdom."

"Oh no, what happened?" asked the teacher, her voice tinged with worry.

"It's okay. Just kids being kids, but I'm amazed at how early it starts."

She looked past him and watched as Elizabeth handed the car back to Caspian, who immediately began recharging it with the ZoomerBoomer. "Hmm, how early what starts?"

"Us being wrapped around a woman's finger," Mr. Davies chuckled. "She's the one who asked Caspian to take the toy apart." He paused, "because she's his girlfriend and that's why." He laughed. "Yeah, and men have all the power. I bet if Cas had asked Lizzie to take apart her Barbie's roadster, she would have told him to pound sand."

"Or, more likely, punched him," said the teacher. "Lizzie is a feisty one, that's for sure. Thanks for filling me in on how our fair Juliet is abusing her Romeo. I'll talk with her and let her mother know the backstory behind why her daughter's dress is covered in grease."

"I think she also has some kind of heart arrhythmia," said Mr. Davies.

Ms. Price arched an eyebrow. "Yes, she does. It's congenital but not dangerous. Her mom told me about it. How did you find out?"

"Romeo told me," Mr. Davies clapped his hands to get Caspian's attention, then motioned to him. The boy hopped up and started their way.

The teacher leaned in and snickered, "I don't even want to know how Caspian found out about Lizzie's heart, but do you think I should I tell her mom that the greasy dress was all *the boyfriend's* fault?"

"And so it begins," said the assistant as Caspian took his hand. "Isn't that right, Mr. Edison?" The boy shrugged. "Cas, just remember, it's always our fault."

"What is always our fault, Mr. Davies?" asked Caspian as the two left the classroom.

The assistant shot Laura Price a wink, then said, "Why everything, my boy, everything."

Chapter 3

EXPENSIVE FRIENDS, 2013

Caspian's eyes fluttered open. His bedroom was dark except for what little light seeped between the slats of his window blinds. His iPhone buzzed again, then was silent. He reached over and grabbed the device from his nightstand and pressed its home button...1:37 am. Caspian had been working in the yard all day with his father and was exhausted. He slumped back against his pillow, phone slipping out of his hand. Sleep had just about claimed him again, when he was shocked awake by another buzz.

This time he saw the text notification banner slide across the screen and his eyes few open. *Lizzie: Cas, help me. I'm in big...*

He immediately pushed himself upright, tapped in the unlock code, and his eyes scanned the entire notification. *Lizzie: Cas, help me. I'm in big trouble this time. I'm so stupid. Please answer me.*

Caspian's stomach turned somersaults as he saw the four previously missed calls, five texts, and a voice mail. Elizabeth never left voice mails. He didn't bother with any of them. Caspian immediately tapped her name and waited for the phone to make a connection.

"Cas?" came Elizabeth's frantic voice. "Cas, oh thank God." She started crying.

"Lizzie, what's the matter?" asked Caspian, but all he could hear was a few disjointed words separated by stuttering sobs. He took a deep breath. "Lizzie, I can't understand you. Try to calm down. Where are you?"

There was a pause. "At...at the old Smithfield cabin."

"What? That place is a wreck. Why in hell are you at that Blair Witch of a place at…" he glanced at his phone, "a quarter to two in the morning." He immediately regretted his words as he could hear Elizabeth start hyperventilating on the other end of the phone. "Okay, okay," he said softly, "Who is there with you?"

"Nobody. He fucking left me."

"Who left you?"

"Sean!"

"Sean Campbell?"

"No, Sean *fucking* Bean. They're filming another Percy Jackson movie up here. Yes, Sean Campbell!"

Caspian immediately slipped out of bed, and began looking for clothes. "Lizzie, I can tell you are freaked out…"

"What gave you that idea?" Came her near hysterical response.

"Two f-bombs in the span of thirty-seconds, for starters. You never—"

"You're right," she cried, "this place *is* exactly like Blair Witch. I'm…I'm going to get murdered and they will find parts of me, or they won't find anything and—"

"Lizzie, I'm not right. It's not anything like Blair Witch. Remember, I'm never right. You always tell me I am never right."

"You're never right," she agreed, then said it two more times, almost like a mantra.

"Exactly. I'm never right, but I am coming to get you." Caspian looked at his watch. "I should be there before four o'clock, okay?"

"Four o'clock? Wait, I think I heard something. No, it was just an owl. Cas, why four o'clock?"

He set his phone down, tapped the speaker button, then lowered the volume. "It's over an hour away, Lizzie, and that's with me ignoring every posted speed limit along the way."

"Oh God, will your parents even let you take the car?"

"They're asleep. All normal people are asleep, Lizzie. With any luck at all, I'll be home before they wake up."

There was a long pause, then he heard her inhale deeply. She let out a long sigh. It caught a couple times, but far less than before. "Cas," she said.

He looked over at his phone as he belted on a pair of jeans, "Yeah?"

"You're the best…really!"

"Thanks, Lizzie, but forgive me for not trusting your judgement right now, because Scott Campbell is a complete piece of shit. I've warned you about him."

"I know."

"He just wants one thing."

"I know," she said again, then her voice went hard, "and he didn't get it, so the fucking bastard just left me here."

Caspian finished tying his shoes, picked up his phone, and switched off the speaker. "If you give me an extra thirty minutes, I could stop by his house, wrap him in plastic, and shove him in the trunk of my dad's car."

Elizabeth barked a laugh. "You are my hero, Dexter."

Caspian smiled. "See, now aren't you glad I convinced you to watch those Netflix DVDs with me?"

She ignored his question, instead asking, "Will you stay on the phone with me while you're driving? You always make me feel safe."

He chuckled. "I may make you *feel* safe but I don't actually keep you safe. Remember when I taught you how to climb trees?"

"Three months in traction is hard to forget," she laughed.

"Exactly. Now listen to me. My dad has a car charger so I'll call you back and will stay on the phone with you except for when I go through Raven's gap. No coverage there."

"Wait, you're hanging up?"

"Just until I get in the car. I have to sneak out, and don't need to be juggling my phone at the same time. I'll call you right back, okay?"

"Okay…"

"I'm hanging up now."

"But you'll call back, right?"

"Yes."

"Okay…okay."

"And Lizzie…"

"Yeah?"

"Don't answer the door before I get there." Caspian made a *woo'ing* noise into the phone.

"Fuck you, asshole," she laughed.

"That's four f-bombs, and no thanks. I'm your friend, not Sean Campbell."

Caspian stared at his laptop screen in frustration as he struggled to write his essay on *Crime and Punishment*. "I swear Dostoevsky must have really liked that pocket watch. The dude took like ten pages to describe it, and I can't manage five pages to describe the whole book..." His voice pitched up. "...because it suuucked."

A second later, someone tapped at his door. "Caspian?" It was his mother's voice. "Caspian," she whispered, "are you awake?"

"I'm up, mom. Just writing a paper."

His door cracked open and his mother's face peeked in. "Hi honey. The swelling around your eye looks a lot better. How are you feeling?"

"I'm fine, ma." He grinned. "Like I said, you should see the door. It's a wreck."

"Yes, well unless the door has a broken nose and a black eye, I think it will be just fine. I have a mind to sue that mall. It's dangerous having automatic doors opening out that way."

Caspian shook his head. "Like I told you, it was my fault. I was looking down at my phone when the door smacked me in the face. Besides, customers aren't supposed to be in those mall back hallways. They're just for employees. I shouldn't have been taking a short cut. Aren't you guys always preaching to me about personal responsibility? This was *my* fault. Period, end of story, but I really have to finish writing this—"

"Elizabeth came to check on you," said his mother. "She's downstairs. I just wanted to make sure you weren't asleep." His mother smiled. "She brought you a present."

Caspian laughed. "I know that tone, Mom, but it's not gonna happen. We're just friends, but send her up."

"Friends for today," lilted her mother, "maybe more than friends tomorrow." She disappeared, closing the door after her.

A couple minutes later, another several taps sounded. "Entré," said Caspian.

Elizabeth opened the door, walked in, then closed it again. She was wearing a yellow ruffled summer dress with flowers printed on it. "You look like a vision of sunny loveliness," said Caspian. "What are those flowery things, they look like long pinecones?"

She looked down at her dress, then back at Caspian. "They are birds of paradise flowers, and you look horrible."

"Thanks," laughed Caspian, "I am retracting my *sunny* compliment for a description more in keeping with your outing last Saturday." He pretended to think while Elizabeth frowned. "Oh I know, how about this...you look like a d-list horror movie actress who gets impaled by a speargun."

"It's a bayou cabin. Why on Earth would there have been a speargun?" she asked flatly.

Caspian shrugged. "Bad writing. After all, you are a *D-list* actress."

Elizabeth raised her hands, and gestured toward him with the container she held. "I baked you cookies."

Caspian closed the lid to his laptop, and pulled his feet toward himself. Elizabeth slid onto the bed, then set the container of cookies between them. She popped open the lid, "They're chocolate chip with shredded coconut and walnuts in the batter."

Caspian grabbed one and took a bite. "Mmmm, yeah, that is what I'm talking about." He took another bite. "You must be feeling really guilty to bake me cookies."

"Actually, I felt really guilty on Sunday," said Elizabeth, then continued with her eyes downcast. "Then Sean Campbell showed up to school on Monday looking like he got sideswiped off his motorcycle and slid across asphalt...on his face."

"Huh," grunted Caspian, "that was oddly specific."

"Because that's what he said happened, Cas."

"He should be more careful. Motorcycles are dangerous," offered Caspian as he pulled a second cookie from the box.

"And you should be more careful about automatic mall doors that don't actually exist," grumbled Elizabeth. She finally looked up, her eyes filling. "What were you thinking? He's literally twice your size, and is captain of the wrestling team."

"But I'm wiry and quick," snickered Caspian.

"Your mom says he broke your nose."

"No, Mom says the Game Stop door broke my nose. My mother knows her son would never resort to violence." Caspian's voice lowered. "Even when faced with unrepentant assholes who try to blame girls for leading them on."

Elizabeth's eyes narrowed. "I never did anything to lead him—"

"Lizzie," interrupted Caspian, "you don't need to explain to me. First, you don't owe me an explanation. Second, I *am* capable of telling when a piece of shit is also a lying piece of shit."

She shook her head. "What did you do?"

Caspian shrugged. "I just went to talk with the guy. I told him what he did was uncool and way out of line."

"And he just hit you?" asked Elizabeth.

"No, I hit him," replied Caspian around a mouthful of his third cookie. "He might have called you a whore. I don't exactly remember. Right after that I cleverly blocked his fist with my nose. It broke. I totally distracted him by ruining his shirt with my blood. When he was looking down, I tripped him, then smashed his face into the asphalt. It's really all a blur."

The two sat in silence for several long minutes. Finally Elizabeth said, "So, your parents never found out you took the car, right?"

Caspian laughed. "I'm still breathing, aren't I?" She smiled. "I was afraid Dad would notice the mileage. He's only had the car a month. Oh, and I found out why Mom's keys weren't in her purse. She lost them." Elizabeth rolled her eyes. "Yeah," chuckled Caspian. "What are the odds that she loses her keys the same day I need to steal her car? If you ask me, it was very inconsiderate of her. Still, Dad's BMW does take the turns like it's on rails."

"You made it there in less than an hour, Cas. That was nuts."

"Says the girl who called me in the middle of the night, afraid that the Blair Witch was going to consume her soul."

Caspian reached for another cookie, but Elizabeth took his hands in hers. The two looked at each other. "I know I told you this when you picked me up, but I don't want you thinking it was just the emotions speaking. You are my best friend in the whole world, Caspian Lewis, and I love you."

He smiled. "I love you too, Lizzie." He motioned her closer, "now bring it in."

She rolled her eyes. "Really, are we still doing this?"

"Damn skippy we are," replied Caspian, "or do you want me making my way in the world without your magical protection."

Elizabeth pointed at Caspian's face with a finger, then moved it in a lazy circle. "I'm pretty sure my magic heart mojo isn't working."

"Oh contraire ma belle amie—"

"And now with the French," she laughed. "You know I almost failed French."

"Of course I know, you cheated off me. Big mistake, by-the-way, but I'll rephrase. To the contrary, my beautiful friend, your magic heart shielded me from a worse beating *and* enabled me to drive his face into the pavement." Caspian shrugged. "You know the rules, Lizzie."

"We were seven," she said incredulously.

Caspian ignored her. "The magic only works once, then it needs to be refreshed." He motioned to her again, and she slipped her hair into a scrunchy that she'd been wearing on her arm. With her hair pulled into a tail, Elizabeth slid close, then arched her back slightly. Caspian leaned sideways until his ear was pressed to her chest. *Bump-bump, bump-bump-bump, bump-bump, bump-bump-bump.*

After several seconds, he pushed himself back on the bed. "Am I still magic?" she asked with a laugh.

"Yep, still magic, and now I have another dose of Lizzie-luck to be used the next time either of us is in trouble."

"I really am quite a good friend, letting you have access to my magic luck," said Elizabeth, her tone serious.

"Ha, so you do still believe it," snarked Caspian, "but I thought it was dumb seven year old stuff."

Elizabeth gave him an imperious look. "I was just testing you, Cas. Fortunately, you passed."

"Oh thank God," sighed Caspian with mock relief. He sobered a moment later, then asked, "Do you remember what my dad says about friends?"

She pursed her lips. "That you can't make any new, old, friends."

Caspian nodded. "And that friends are emotionally expensive so no-one can afford to have too many, at least not real friends." He moved her hand, then snatched a cookie. "This is my last one. I need to make them last, because you might not do something this epically stupid for days, or even weeks. I'm serious, don't let me have any more, Lizzie. These are devil cookies."

She covered the box, then said, "I haven't heard this second part, just the part about new, old, friends. I love your dad's *dad-isms*."

Caspian nodded. "Yep, well this is another one of Dad's famous pearls of wisdom. Basically, he described it this way. Let's say a real friend knocks on your door at four AM, covered in blood, and holding a knife. What do you do? You ask, *is that blood yours?* Your friend says *No, it's not my blood.* Then you say, *Well shit, then we better bury that knife.*"

Elizabeth covered her mouth and started shaking with laughter. "Your dad should write a book."

"Yeah he should," agreed Caspian, "but his point was that you can't afford too many friends who show up covered in blood at four AM."

"Or call crying from Blair Witch cabins at one-thirty?"

"Or that," agreed Caspian, "Bottom line…when it comes to friendships, prioritize quality over quantity, which is exactly what I have done. And that is why you, too, are my best friend, Elizabeth Winters."

Chapter 4

AS TIME GOES BY

"Hey Lizzie, what's up? Fair warning, I only have a few minutes before I need to leave for class." Caspian did a sideways hop onto his dorm bed, then propped a pillow beneath his head. He laughed. "No, I cannot blow it off. It's my last class. Spring Semester, 2019, see ya! By the way, I've decided my grandma was right. You *are* a bad influence on me. Hang on, I'm going to put you on speaker."

"What if I have something private to say?" asked Elizabeth.

"My roommate has already left for the semester. I have the whole place to myself. So, Lizzie, what have you gotten yourself into this time?"

"Nice, Cas. Can't I just call my oldest friend-boy to chat?"

"Not really."

"You're such a jerk," she said laughing. "I haven't gotten myself into anything. If you are so smart, tell me why I'm calling, if not just to chat."

Caspian grinned at the ceiling. "Okay, well, there are several predefined Elizabeth Winters chat categories. First, there is the *I'm too stupid to ever be a doctor* category. That one is usually coupled with category two which includes fear of having failed a test that you invariably do well on." He paused. "How am I doing do far?"

"Still being a jerk, but go on."

"Okay, then there is the *I'm ugly and no man will ever want me* category. Granted, we haven't had one of those calls in almost a year, because…" Caspian affected a pompously British accent, "You've decided that Chadsworth Winchester the third is the second coming of Christ, thus *you* are no longer ugly."

"I know you don't like him," grumbled Elizabeth, "but you dislike everyone I date."

"True, but in my defense, you do have horrible taste in men."

"Chadsworth is very nice."

"Chad is a tool who constantly puts you down, and whose rare compliments you drink up like water from a desert oasis. I assume you're sleeping with him."

"We've talked about getting engaged after we both graduate next semester," she replied.

"I'll take that as a yes," said Caspian, "Thanks for helping perpetuate all those Catholic girl memes, Lizzie."

"Look who's talking, *Father Lewis,* at least I'm sticking with one man."

"I haven't been with any men," countered Caspian.

"You're such a dope," she laughed.

"Yes, but I'm your dope. Now where was I?"

"Category four?" she sighed. "How many are there, and when is your class?"

"This is the last one, and I still have thirty minutes before I need to leave."

"Fine, Dr. Freud, what's the last category?"

"It's the *I don't think I have what it takes to be a Doctor,* category."

There was a long pause, then Elizabeth asked, "How is that different from the first category?"

"Lizzie, it's completely different. This is when you talk about not being able to give people bad news, not having proper detachment, and not ever wanting to be a surgeon. Not for nothing, but just because your dad's a surgeon doesn't mean you have to be one."

"I hate the idea of putting people under and cutting them," she grumbled.

"Well, given that," mused Caspian, "I'd have to say you would make both a poor surgeon *and* a terrible serial killer."

She laughed. "You really are so dumb. I think I lose brain cells every time I talk with you. Do you know what I did to test my theory?"

"Which theory?"

"The *no-cutting-people* theory."

"No, what did you do? Did you try and cut up cadavers or something?"

"Eww, no. I became an organ donor."

ONE HEART THAT BEATS FOR TWO

This time it was Caspian's turn to pause. "Okay," he said finally, "I give up. How is that related?"

"It's related," she huffed, "because someone will have to cut me to get at the organs."

"But you'd be dead," he said.

"That's beside the point, Cas."

He laughed again. "It wouldn't be beside the point to me. I'd definitely want to be dead."

"I nearly threw up, just thinking about it," she said seriously, "then my mind went to all the other things surgeons have to do. I kept picturing myself walking into a waiting room, pulling off my mask, and giving that shake to people."

"What shake?"

"*The* shake, Cas. The, *we did all we could, but I'm sorry your loved one is dead*, shake of the head."

"Lizzie, you are cascading again. You haven't even graduated from premed yet, and you're telling parents their kid died on the table." He heard sniffling from the other end of the line. Caspian softened his tone. "What about the PA route? Remember, we talked about that a while ago."

"Chadsworth doesn't think being a physician's assistant will be very lucrative," replied Elizabeth.

"That from the dude who's getting a degree in native culture photography."

"Hey," said Elizabeth defensively, "a lot of those cultures are under assault by modern colonialism. The least we can do is ensure the native cultures don't disappear without a trace."

"Wow, he got you to memorize the whole brochure, Lizzie. I'm impressed. Look, I think native cultures are important too, but I don't think *Chadsworth* is doing fuck-all about it sitting in an air-conditioned Loyola classroom. If he really cared, he'd go and take some actual pictures rather than pontificating about the evils of colonization. Anyway, this isn't about him. It's about you. Physician assistants are awesome. I love my PA and do everything I can to avoid the doctor-doctor. Talking to him is like talking to a block of wood. Also, you were worried about the time and cost of medical school. You could be treating people and making a real difference in two years rather than four. Later on, if you decided to get your MD, you always could do that."

"Do you think my dad would be disappointed?"

"Hell no, Lizzie. The man thinks you hung the stars. He just wants you to be happy. For that matter, so do I."

23

"But Chadsworth said—"

"Enough with that or I'm going to harvest *his* organs, and I know just which one I'm gonna cut off first."

She laughed. "Will you wear a green henley shirt and carry a syringe?"

"Nice Dexter reference," said Caspian. He sighed. "I miss those days. Things were so much simpler then. All we had to deal with was rape-y jocks taking you to demonic cabins in the woods. Remember when we watched that movie."

"Cabin in the Woods?" she asked. "Yeah, you pointed at the blonde girl and said, that would've been you, Lizzie, if I hadn't saved you. Such a jerk."

"Stipulated, but you love me."

She sighed. "I do love you, Cas, and thanks."

"Sure thing, did I help?" No response. "Lizzie, you're nodding aren't you? I can hear the rocks rattling."

She snorted. "Sorry, yeah, I was nodding, and you did help. I'm going to do it. I'm going to apply to the physician's assistant grad program."

"That's awesome. I can't wait to hear what Chadsworth McStuffikins thinks about it."

"I think I'll hold off telling him until I get accepted. He's hinted at a special surprise after graduation, but before I would have started med school. I think he's going to propose."

"How wonderfully romantic," snarked Caspian. "Just be sure to have your guests crouch during the wedding, that way it will easier for him to look down his nose at all us plebs."

"I'll certainly consider it," she laughed, "all except for you. I want you to stand tall as my maid of honor."

"Nice one, but as much as I do love you, I'm not becoming a chick for ya."

"That's good," said Elizabeth, "because you would make a horrible woman. You will come for my graduation though, right?"

"Wouldn't miss it," he replied then glanced at his watch. "Okay, I have to get to class. Say goodbye, Lizzie."

"Goodbye, Lizzie," she echoed, and he chuckled as his phone screen went black.

Chapter 5

FRIENDS AND LOVERS

Caspian held his mobile phone with one hand while trying to plug his free ear with the other. "Hey Dr. Winters, it's Caspian. Sorry to bug you, but do you know where Lizzie is? My flight was delayed, didn't she tell you? Oh, well, I made it in time for the ceremony, but just barely. Yeah, I saw her walk across the stage, but was in the nosebleed seats. Anyway, she was supposed to meet me after the graduation ceremony, but I can't find her, and she's not answering her mobile. What? It's really loud here, can you say that again? She's at your hotel? Why is she at——? When did that happen? No, you won't. I'm gonna kill him for you. Huh? Well, sure I can come there, but I figured that you——. Oh boy, no problem. If Mrs. Winters wants me to come, I come. Can you text me the room number and address? Hang on, I'll check. Yep, got it. My phone says it will take about twenty minutes. What? Oh, hi Mrs. Winters. Yeah, he just told me. No, I've got the address. Dr. Winters just sent it to me. About twenty-minutes. Um, sure, I'll be there in fifteen…somehow. Yeah, I totally agree. I already offered to kill the little British puffball. No, I'll kill him later. I'm coming to you guys now. Yeah, bye."

Caspian disconnected the call, then immediately searched for a downtown cab service. After arranging to be picked up, he started sprinting across the Loyola campus. Several minutes later, he ran up to the waiting cab as it idled in front of the University's music complex. Caspian threw himself into the car,

25

and asked the driver to get them to the St. James hotel as quickly as possible. New Orleans had other ideas. Given that its streets were drawn in the early eighteenth century to accommodate horses rather than cars, what should have taken five minutes, took twenty. Caspian quickly paid the driver, jumped out of the cab and ran into the hotel. He maneuvered between a lobby full of guests, and slipped into an elevator just as the doors started to close.

"Five please," he huffed, then gave a grateful smile to the elderly man who tapped the requested button.

"Girl trouble?" asked the man as a wry smile played about his lips.

Caspian sighed. "How could you tell?"

The man shrugged. "You're young and you're in a hurry. It's always about a girl when you're young and in a hurry."

Caspian watched the floor numbers slowly increment as he said, "It's not like that. She's just a friend."

The old man laughed. "If you say so, son, but I was young once." The elevator chimed and the doors started opening to the fifth floor. Caspian stepped out, but the man called after him. "I never got myself into such a lather chasing after a friend." Caspian turned, but the doors had already closed. He saw his reflection in the polished brass. "Well, he's right about one thing. I definitely have worked up a lather." He grabbed a hand towel off one of the maid-service carts, and dragged it across his face. Caspian stared at the sweat soaked towel, then dropped it in the cart's dirty laundry hamper. "Ah, New Orleans in summer, what a gift," he murmured, then knocked on the Winter's hotel room door.

Caspian's eyes flicked right as he and Elizabeth stood in front of the hotel elevator. "I know that look," he said.

"I don't have a look," she replied. "There is no look."

"Okay," he said, "then the not-look you're wearing is very similar to normal people's *I don't want to do this* look."

She turned to him. "Well, I don't want to do this. You are forcing me to do this."

Caspian grinned. "See, you do have a look."

"Can we just go back to the room? My parents were being very nice about all this."

"Your parents were letting you wallow, and that's not what you need."

The elevator dinged, then opened. The two entered, and Elizabeth angrily punched the lobby button. "Okay, Dr Freud, then what do I need?"

"You need to not take those anger issues out on defenseless elevator buttons. What did the letter *L* ever do to you?" She stared at him with a flat expression. "Fine, what you need is for your best friend to take you to Pat O'Brien's for about four Hurricanes."

"That might be acceptable," grumbled Elizabeth. "Will this supposed best friend be buying?"

"He will," replied Caspian, then gestured toward the lobby as the elevator doors opened. A couple minutes later, the two of them were silently walking side-by-side on Canal Street.

"Thanks for not talking," said Elizabeth softly, then added, "or telling me what an asshole Chadsworth is, or saying *I told you so.*"

"I'm a professional, Lizzie. Professionals don't take cheap or easy shots."

"Meaning?" she asked.

"Meaning, it is obvious to everyone that Chadsworth is a complete douche canoe and you already know I was right." He lowered his voice. "Honestly, I wish I wasn't." Caspian looked at the street sign. "Do we turn here?"

"No," she replied. "We'll take the next right onto Royal street."

"It's freaking hot," grumbled Caspian. "How close is New Orleans to the sun? Wait, are we actually standing on the sun?"

"You're going to school in Orlando, Cas. It's just as hot there, and the bar's only six more blocks." She smiled at him. "Can you make it?"

He grinned back. "There's that award winning Elizabeth Winters smile everyone loves."

Her lips curved down. "Not everyone, Cas."

"Yeah, I know. Want to tell me what happened now or after copious amounts of alcohol?"

She snorted. "Both. Honestly, I should have seen the signs before now, but maybe I just didn't want to see them."

"I'm not great with signs myself," offered Caspian. "What do you think you missed?"

As the two chatted while walking along the uneven French Quarter sidewalks, Caspian could feel his friend's mood begin to lift. Her smile came more readily and lasted longer. She literally laughed out loud several times at Caspian's own romantic failures. Finally, the two walked up to Pat O'Brien's large double doors.

"Oh my God, air conditioning," said Caspian. "Remind me to avoid being sent to Hell, because I hate this sticky heat."

"Hey Cas," she said.

"Hmm?"

"Don't get sent to Hell." Elizabeth showed her teeth, then gestured to the bar. In less than five minutes, both of them were contentedly sipping on Pat O'Brien's famous Hurricane drinks. Caspian suddenly crinkled his nose, and groaned. Elizabeth frowned at him. "I told you not to drink it that fast, dork. You got brain freeze didn't you?" He nodded, then shook his head several times. "That won't help," she laughed. "Drink the water."

Caspian took several swallows of the comparatively warm water, then focused on Elizabeth. "So, Lizzie, here's the part I don't get. Why would the little British lima bean wait until today? Why ruin your graduation? I never liked the dude, you know that, but I never considered him downright evil. You decided you weren't going to Med school months ago." Elizabeth peered over her glass and murmured something. "What?" asked Caspian. "Take the straw out of your mouth. I can't understand you."

"I didn't tell him," she murmured.

"Dude!" exclaimed Caspian.

"I know!" she cried. "This is all my fault."

"Oh no, it's not," he said. "It's entirely *his* fault. Let me make that perfectly clear. Yes, you should have told him earlier, but if he broke up with you just because you weren't going to be a doctor, that's dickishness on an epic scale."

Elizabeth raised her hand to get the bartender's attention then held up two fingers. He nodded to her and she turned back to Caspian. "Chadsworth tried to convince me to change my mind."

"When, today?"

Elizabeth nodded, "Well, last night. He almost convinced me. I told him I'd think about it, then when he asked me this morning, I said no."

"And that's when he broke up with you?"

She nodded again, then spread her arms out. "He said he owed it to the world to be able to pursue his art, and couldn't do that if he was chained to some mundane job."

"He did *not* say that," groaned Caspian. Elizabeth drained half of her third Hurricane, then made an *X* motion across her chest. Caspian stared at her. "He really is a dick, but more importantly how did you just scarf down half that Hurricane without freezing your brain?"

Elizabeth lifted her chin. "You're not the only professional, Mr. Lewis. I've been training at this bar for four years and know what I'm about, sir."

He pointed at her. "Lizzie, you are drunk."

She pointed back. "Yes, I am."

"Maybe we should get some food, too," offered Caspian. She shrugged noncommittally, but he caught the bartender's attention, paid their tab, and they moved to a nearby booth. The two ate, drank, laughed and insulted each other as the hours ticked by.

"I'll have one more," slurred Elizabeth to the waiter.

"She'll have no more, and I'll have the check," said Caspian. The waiter gave him a relieved nod, then slipped the check onto the table. Elizabeth reached for it, Caspian was faster.

"I can pay for half," she said.

"I got it," as he scanned the bill. "Holy shit, Lizzie, how are you even alive? Do you know how many drinks you went through?"

She held up two fingers. "I only had three."

"You had six," he corrected.

"Then I should pay half," she said, then squinted at him. "Aren't you broke?"

"No, I took that consulting gig with McKinsey."

"But it hasn't started yet," she said, swaying slightly.

"They gave me a signing bonus. I'm good, and you are not good. We need to get you home. Dorm or your parents hotel?"

"Dorm, James," she said, then laughed at her own anachronistic reference.

The drive to Loyola's dorms only took a few minutes, but the driver seemed quite happy to have her out of his cab. Judging from how she kept sticking her head out the open window for air, Caspian tended to agree with him. Elizabeth started to stumble off in the general direction of her dorm when Caspian desperately tossed several bills to the cabby, then drew up beside her.

"Hello," she said.

"Hi, is that your building, there?" She nodded. "Room number?"

"Two fifteen. Come on, this way. The stairs are faster. These elevators came over on the ark."

Elizabeth leaned against the interior dorm hallway next to her door, as Caspian fished in her pocket. She giggled. "Why don't you carry a purse or something?" Caspian grumbled as he finally pulled her keys from the shallow pocket.

"I hate purses. I only carry one if I'm wearing a—" She broke off and stared at Caspian.

"What?" he asked.

"You need to open the door."

"I am opening it," he said.

"You need to open it, faster."

"Oh shit, hang on. Lizzie, cover your mouth." He twisted the key, and slammed the door open. Elizabeth bolted inside, then ran for the bathroom. Caspian only made it halfway there when she began throwing up.

He knelt down beside her, gathered her hair up and held it behind her head. "I want to die," she groaned in-between his flushing and her retching.

"That's just an abundance of Hurricanes talking," he said dryly. "Do you have any aspirin or Tylenol?"

She nodded. "In the cabinet next to the mini fridge."

"Are you okay enough for me to get you some water and enough pain meds so your head doesn't explode in the morning?"

She gave another nod. Caspian gently patted her on the back, then rose to leave. "Wait," she said, "would you grab me a tee shirt and shorts from my dresser. I think I got…stuff on these."

Caspian wandered around the dorm as he'd been doing for the past hour, then eyed the bathroom door for the umpteenth time. By dorm standards it was pretty spacious despite having clearly not been designed for privacy. There was a common area that contained a couch, coffee table, and small entertainment center. On one side, the living space opened to an efficiency kitchen, on the other, it led to the dorm's sleeping area which consisted of a pair of beds, dressers, and desks.

One of the beds had been stripped. Caspian assumed that was the one used by Elizabeth's recently vacated roommate. He plopped down on it, pulled out his phone and dialed. "Hey Dr. Winters, it's Caspian. I just wanted to call in case you guys were worried. Lizzie and I went to dinner and we're back at her place. Yep, she's doing much better." He looked up as the bathroom door opened. Elizabeth walked out in a vintage star wars teeshirt and running shorts. Caspian pointed to the phone. Elizabeth shook her head. "No, she's almost asleep," he lied. She made a tsk'ing gesture with two fingers. Caspian raised his middle one toward her. "Sure, I'll leave her a note to call you in the morning." Caspian laughed. "No, I didn't kill him…but tomorrow's another day. Brunch at Brennan's? Fine by me. I'll write that on the note as well. Yeah, I've got a room at the Marriott. Yep, you guys too. Sure, no problem. Bye."

"You just lied to my father," said Elizabeth with mock seriousness.

"No, I just passed along *your* lie," countered Caspian. "Why didn't you want to talk with him?"

She shook her head. "I don't want to deal with anything else. My head feels like it's filled with fluff and I'm seeing three of you."

"Lucky you," chuckled Caspian.

She moved to sit in front of him. "Yeah, which one is the real you?"

"The middle one," he laughed.

"The middle one," she said softly, then leaned forward and kissed him.

Caspian tried to pull away, but Elizabeth slipped her hands behind his head and pulled him deeper into the kiss. He tried to talk. "Lizzie, what—"

She pulled back just long enough to say, "Shut up, Cas," then kissed him again, this time pushing him down onto the bed.

Caspian's mind raced, as he sought some kind of mental traction. Elizabeth Winters was an empirically beautiful woman. If she was anyone but who she was, Caspian would have already tried to do with her what she was now trying to do with him. She broke the kiss, sat up while straddling him on the bed, and reached for her shirt. She had it half off, when Caspian's frontal lobe finally beat back the rest of his brain. He grabbed her hands, and pulled them down.

"Lizzie, no," he said softly.

She grinned at him. "Yes."

He shook his head. "No, not like this. Not with you."

Her nose began to redden. "Why not with me? What's wrong with *me?*"

He stared at her. "You're perfect, and you're my best friend, that's what's wrong with you." He sighed. "You also just had your heart broken and I got you drunk, so yeah, there's that."

She stared at him. "I love you."

He nodded. "I know. I love you, too."

"Then why can't this happen?"

Caspian smiled, then nudged her to the left. "Tell you what, slim, I'm betting this is the booze and heartbreak talking." He raised a finger. "However, if you feel the same way tomorrow that you do tonight, I'm willing to ignore centuries of good advice and throw caution to the wind."

She pursed her lips. "You aren't talking about sex, are you?"

Caspian shook his head. "Nope, not with you. In for a penny, in for a pound, Ms. Winters." Elizabeth cocked her head the way she did when considering. "See, you've already come to your senses," said Caspian.

"Huh, no," said Elizabeth. "I was just thinking about something. Okay, I'll sleep on it, and let you know in the morning."

"You do that," Caspian said, then started to roll off the bed.

Elizabeth sat up and took hold of his hand. "Where do you think you're going, mister?"

"To my hotel room?"

"Oh no you don't. You're staying right here. I'll grab a blanket and sheet for you."

She started rummaging through the dorms lone closet. "How do I know I can trust your intentions while I'm asleep?" asked Caspian.

She turned with bedding in hand. "I'll try to control myself." She handed him the blanket and sheets. "By the way, what exactly is this centuries old advice we'd be ignoring if we give this thing a run for its money?"

"Two nevers," said Caspian. He locked eyes with Elizabeth. "First, never date someone after a breakup. Second, and far more important, never make a lover of your best friend, you could lose both."

The two stared at each other for several seconds, then she helped him arrange the bedding in silence. He crawled underneath, and sighed contentedly as she did the same in hers. She reached over to thumb off the light, and saw Caspian's eyes were already closed. "I'm not going to change my mind, Cas."

"You're drunk. I'll believe it in the morning, Lizzie. Remember, in for a penny, in for a pound. Say goodnight, Lizzie." His voice trailed off at the end.

"Goodnight, Lizzie," she whispered, and the room became shrouded in darkness.

Caspian woke to the smell of coffee. His eyes fluttered open. Elizabeth smiled and handed him a steaming mug. He pushed himself into a more seated position, blinked, then accepted it. "So, how you feeling, slim?"

"Surprisingly good. I think your water, aspirin, Tylenol cocktail did the trick."

"Cool," he said.

Her lips quirked up. "Is that the only thing on your mind?"

He took a sip of coffee, then shrugged. "I can't think of anything else I'd like to ask."

"Okay," she replied. "Want to know a secret?"

He grinned. "Always."

Elizabeth leaned over and whispered in his ear. "Screw centuries of advice, I'm in for the whole pound."

Chapter 6

THE CALM BEFORE THE STORM

"Here they come," Elizabeth said excitedly, then slipped her hand beneath the Waffle House booth table. "Don't say anything, Cas, I want to see how long it takes one of them to notice."

"I'm not saying a darn thing," he laughed, "but if I were a betting man, I'd say less than thirty seconds before Jenny squeals."

"Or Michael," she said.

"He is a Jamaican squealer, that one," agreed Caspian.

Jennifer and Michael drew up beside the table. "Sorry we're late," said Jennifer, "David managed to get a speeding ticket coming over the bridge."

Caspian looked toward the Waffle House door. "So, where is he?"

"Parking blocks away like a damn fool," replied Michael in his rich Jamaican accent. "He says he can't afford two tickets in one day."

Caspian shook his head. "There were several spots left when we got here."

"And at least two remain," said Michael, then held up a finger, "but they are limited to one hour."

"So?" asked Elizabeth.

Jennifer slid into one side of the booth and Michael joined her. "So," she replied, "David says when all five of us get together we kibitz. Apparently, according to his particular take on Jewish conversation etiquette any good kibitz takes longer than an hour, especially for brunch. Personally, I think the speeding ticket traumatized him."

Caspian cringed. "He didn't try the whole Holocaust thing with the cop, did he?"

"He did, indeed," sighed Michael, "with no better luck than the last time he tried it. In fact, the police officer's name was Schneider, so I believe he may have taken the reference as a personal attack."

"I saw the cop's name badge," offered Jennifer, "I tried to warn him, but you know David, he was already off to the oppression races."

Michael laughed. "It might work better for him if he actually believed it. Also, his *Don't Blame Me, I Voted Libertarian*, bumper sticker is kind of a giveaway."

"Yeah," agreed Caspian with a smile, "I've yet to meet an oppressed Libertarian. Oh wait, speak of the Devil and he appears."

David arched an eyebrow at him, then tapped Michael on the shoulder, and said, "Scoot." Michael did. Their friend ran a hand through wavy dark hair, and sighed. "You won't believe what happened on the way here."

"You got a speeding ticket, tried to invoke thousands of years of perceived oppression as a reason not to pay it, failed, then freaked out over parking in a legit spot," said Caspian in a rush.

David stared at him. "Yeah, well, maybe you don't believe it, but it's not perceived oppression, dude. We've actually been——"

"Coffee?" said Elizabeth, interrupting David before he could really get rolling. She lifted the carafe with her left hand and began pouring into the first of the three extra cups that were on the table.

"Oh my God!" screamed Jennifer.

"That was less than two-seconds," said Caspian.

Both David and Michael had jumped in their seats, and now stared at Jennifer as she reached for Elizabeth's hand. "What's going on right now?" asked Michael.

"Oh my God, it's beautiful," gushed Jennifer. She slid the coffee carafe to the side, and held Elizabeth's left hand in both of hers. "When did he do it? How?" Jennifer's eyes slipped off Elizabeth and focused on Caspian. "Did you ask her dad?"

"Wait," said Michael, "You got engaged? Dude, you said you were going to do that next week. You made a big deal about it being the first day of Spring."

"You *knew* about this," yelled Jennifer, "and no one told me. *I'm* the best friend. *I'm* the maid of honor." She paused. "Lizzie, I'm still the maid of honor, right?"

Elizabeth laughed. "You are if you let me have my hand back."

"If I could get a word in edgewise," offered Caspian, "Yes, I wanted to do it on March twenty-first, but I got a notice from the travel agency that they are anticipating restrictions because of the Corona Virus thing that everyone's talking about." He shrugged, "So, we went to Grand Isle this past weekend and…"

"He hid the ring in an oyster shell and pretended to find it on the beach," said Elizabeth.

Jennifer's mouth dropped open. "And you opened it?" She squealed again. "Did you have any idea?"

Elizabeth shook her head. "I did think it was weird that there were oysters off the coast of Grand Isle, but you know what a great liar Cas can be." Everyone nodded.

"Hey now," objected Caspian.

"So, he told me that oysters are pretty rare because Lousiana's waters are so warm, but that the sand is so fine that what oysters there are almost always have pearls in them."

"Nice," said David, "the more bullshit the better. It keeps people distracted from the truth."

"That's what I figured," said Caspian.

Jennifer pushed both men roughly out of the booth, and reached for Elizabeth. "Come with me. I want to see it in the light, then you can tell me everything without the boys interrupting every two-seconds with stupid observations."

"But I'm hungry," objected Elizabeth, "and we've been waiting for—"

"Oh stop, Lizzie" said Jennifer as she pulled the other woman out of the booth. "They'll order for us. It's Waffle House, not Brennan's. Guy, please just text us when the food's here, we'll come back in."

Seconds later they were gone, and David said, "Well, now you've done it. You're out of the club."

"And what club would that be?" asked Michael, "Would that be the *I'm not marrying the hot girl who is also my best friend* club, because I don't want to be a member of that either. You are an idiot, David." Michael extended his hand across the table, and grinned. "Congratulations, brotha Caspian. You are a lucky, lucky man."

"Thanks, I think so."

"Yeah, I do too," agreed David. "I'm not trying to be a dick. It's just taken me by surprise, but now that you've done it, I am curious about something."

"Oh boy," chuckled Michael, "here comes one of Dave's super awkward questions."

"Shut up, Mike. It's a perfectly reasonable question. Cas, do you mind?" Caspian gave Michael a wink, but nodded to David. "Okay, so you've known Lizzie all your life right?"

"Well, not all," replied Caspian. "We met in kindergarten, but you knew that."

"Of course I did," said David, "but I'm trying to make a point here. Since Kindergarten, might as well be all of your life. Before that, we are basically goldfish. Anyway, isn't it weird knowing someone that long, and then, you know, sleeping with them."

"First, no, it's not weird. Just because you've known someone a long time doesn't mean you're attracted to them. Trust me, the vibe between me and my sister is nothing like what's going on between Lizzie and me. Second, we aren't sleeping together."

The two men shared a glance. "You mean, like not anymore since you got engaged?" asked Michael.

Caspian shook his head. "I mean like ever. You guys remember me telling you about her graduation last year, right?"

"Yeah, she jumped your bones after that limey asshole screwed her over," said David, then added, "You were the epitome of restraint and chivalry."

Caspian shrugged. "Wait," said Michael, "you guys never—"

"Nope," replied Caspian, "that was part of the deal we struck the next morning. *In for a penny, in for a pound.*"

"I don't get it," murmured David. "It's not like you were a virgin." His eyes grew wide. "Lizzie is a...no, she was with that other dude for a year, and he definitely wouldn't have waited."

"No, he wouldn't," grumbled Caspian, "but that's not the point. We both had pasts that we regretted, but decided that our future was going to be together." He grinned. "Lizzie says, we've been revirginized."

"I don't think it works that way," said David.

"It does for them," countered Michael, then said, "I think that's great." He laughed. "No wonder you moved up the date, brotha. You must be all kinds of backed up."

Caspian nodded. "You have no idea."

"Yeah, cause Lizzie is super hot," said David, "and I mean that in the most respectful and platonic way."

Michael sighed. "I don't think either of those words mean what you think they mean, because *super hot* sounds neither respectful or platonic, Dave." Michael took a sip of his coffee. "So, have you picked a date?"

"Lizzie has a couple in mind, but she's all freaked out about this Corona thing, says it's a novel virus, whatever that means."

"I heard on the news that they believe it came from China, maybe one of those wet markets," said David.

"Or they Frankenstein'ed it in a lab," offered Michael. "I read there was a secret lab in that Chinese town, Wuhan I think."

"You guys obviously know more about it than me," chuckled Caspian. "I just know that Lizzie is worried about setting a specific date until more info comes out." He shrugged. "I don't know why it matters, sounds like a flu of some kind, so what."

"Women can be peculiar when it comes to weddings, my friend," said Michael. "Best to just stay quiet and make yourself as small a target as possible."

Caspian pointed at his friend. "That was my thinking exactly." He raised his hand to catch the server's attention. "Now let's order some food before the girls come back and give us shit because they're hungry."

David craned his neck to look out the window. "Little risk of that, they both keep staring at her ring and hopping. I just don't get it. You know that carbon crystals are far more common than people think. I mean, diamonds weren't even that expensive until the Debeer's family created a false sense of scarcity in the early twentieth century."

"You tell that to your fiancé some day, Mr. Carbon Crystal," laughed Michael. "Then let us know how that goes."

The server walked up a second later. Caspian smiled at her. "So, my fiancé and her friend are outside, but we'll be ordering for everyone, okay?" The server nodded, then started scribbling on her pad.

Jennifer twisted Elizabeth's hand left, then right. She stared up at the sun as it peeked in and out of clouds. "Wow, it really is beautiful, Lizzie. It looks kind of vintage. Is it?"

Elizabeth shook her head. "No, he just had it made to look that way. Honestly, I didn't even want a diamond. I mean I didn't *not* want one, but it just wasn't a big deal to me."

"I love the little emerald chips around the side," said her friend. "How did he come up with that?"

"Green's my favorite color," said Elizabeth.

Jennifer squeezed her hand. "And he knew that…oh Lizzie, I hate you, and I love you. I'm so conflicted. You realize there are no good men out there, and girl, you not only found one, the one you found was your best friend."

"Still is," she said, then cringed. "Sorry."

"Oh shut up, I was just kidding. You know that. I'm thrilled for both of you." Jennifer's expression turned sly. "So, are you gonna do it now that you're engaged?"

Elizabeth barked a laugh. "No, we are not going to, *do-it*, as you so romantically expressed. We made a pact."

"Yeah, I know," said Jennifer, "Elizabeth Winter's legendary *Penny and Pound pact*. I bet Cas is sorry he didn't let you have your way with him that night at Loyola."

Elizabeth shook her head. "No, he's not, and that's part of why I love him."

Jennifer stared at her friend and felt her eyes begin to burn. "Oh, don't start on that or you're going to make me blubber. Tell me about the proposal. I didn't think oysters lived around Grand Isle."

"They don't," snickered Elizabeth.

"So how did he surprise you?" asked Jennifer then saw her friend's expression. "He didn't surprise you?" Elizabeth shook her head. "Oh, you are such a liar."

"No, not completely. I was surprised, until he mysteriously found an oyster that couldn't exist. Until then, I had no idea anything was going on."

Jennifer bounced. "Did he get down on one knee?"

"Yes, and I almost laughed, which would have been very bad."

"Why would you laugh?"

"Do you know how cold that water is, Jen? It's cold. I think his original plan was for us to go swimming and he would…" she made air quotes, "*find the oyster*. When he suggested a swim, I told him he was nuts. Anyway, he kneeled down in the surf and you know how much Cas hates the cold. His little lips started turning blue. He was adorable, but I almost laughed."

Jennifer shook her head. "Yeah, there's no laughing in proposals."

ONE HEART THAT BEATS FOR TWO

Elizabeth's voice cracked. "Oh, Jen, and he went to see my dad the night before." She fanned her face as tears filled her eyes. "Dad told me after, well some of it. He said it was," she lowered her voice, "man stuff, but that Cas actually managed to choke Dad up with how he promised to take care of me..and love me...and everything."

"Well, he was already supportive of you getting that graduate PA degree, unlike *some other person* who will remain nameless."

Elizabeth nodded. "I brought that up actually. I asked if he wanted to wait until after I graduated, but he said he was happy to support me while I finished my degree. He even told Dad, you know, 'cause they've been helping out with money. I think that's part of what got Dad misty, because he always took care of Mom so she'd be home with us."

"Have I mentioned that I hate you?" asked Jennifer.

Elizabeth cocked her head. "I'm not sure, have you?" Both women started laughing, then hugged each other.

Jennifer pushed back. "Wait, so have you decided on a date? I have so much to do. I'm in charge, right?"

"Down girl," laughed Elizabeth. "I don't know when yet. Cas would be happy if we just got some Catholic Priest drunk enough to do it tomorrow."

"I don't blame him," said Jennifer in mock seriousness, "the poor guy hasn't been laid in a year."

"Neither has the poor girl," retorted Lizzie, "and she's actually much happier for having been revirginized."

Jennifer shook her head. "I don't think that's a thing, Lizzie."

"Yes it is," countered Elizabeth, "Cas and I agreed that it was. Anyway, I've talked with some of my doc friends and they are really worried about this novel virus. It's called COVID 19, and could really cause problems."

"I thought it was just some flu from China," said Jennifer.

Elizabeth shrugged. "There's not a lot of information on it yet, but like I said, several doctor friends I trust and two of my professors, seemed pretty darn freaked about it. They said we should know more in a few weeks, so I'm just letting things ride until then."

"That sounds good...for now," admonished Jennifer, "but as soon as you have a date," she clapped her hands together. "I'm on the case."

The two women squeezed each other's hands, and bounced again. "I know you are, and that's why you will be the best maid of honor ever." Elizabeth glanced toward the Waffle House. "Looks like they are waving at us. Food must be ready. I'm so starved I could eat a horse."

"You better not," laughed Jennifer, "you have a dress to fit into, Mrs. Lewis."

Chapter 7

LIFE INTERRUPTED

"Caspian, are you sure you don't want a sandwich?" asked Elizabeth's mother.

Roger Winters eyed his wife over a mug of coffee. "How many ways does he have to say *no,* Mary? The man clearly doesn't want a sandwich. He's been driving Lizzie downtown for, what, over two months now. Has he ever taken you up on it?"

"There's always a first time," replied Mary with a smile that Caspian knew was for his benefit, and would mean trouble for Roger later.

For his part, Caspian decided to try and help his future father-in-law out. "It's my fault, really," he began. "I should have just told you that I'm not a big eater during the day. Lizzie says what I do is called intermittent fasting." Caspian shrugged. "I just call it being too lazy to make myself breakfast, and then too forgetful to eat lunch. I've been doing it so long that I really don't even get hungry until late afternoon."

Mary shook her head, then gestured to her husband. "You two, it's no wonder you get along so well. *He* just drinks coffee all day. It's not good for you, either of you."

Roger ran his hand through salt and pepper hair, then leaned forward. "I'm not bald." He patted his stomach. "I'm not too bad around the waist, and our doctor is envious of my blood pressure." He smirked at Caspian. "I think my coffee routine might just be the key to eternal life, besides didn't Lizzie say that the intermittent fasting thing was good for you?"

Caspian waggled his hand back-and-forth. "She's absorbing so much information at school that things tend to seesaw a bit, and that was before she started taking shifts at the hospital. Now, she has the hospital's practical stuff smashing into her university's theoretical stuff and," Caspian sighed, "I just worry she's taking on too much."

"I worry she's going to catch this damned COVID thing," huffed Mary, "and they are running her ragged at that hospital. How does she even have any time for her studies?"

"Loyola is giving her credit for three classes because of what she's learning on-the-job," replied Caspian, "and, well, a certain fiancé might just be writing the papers for her rather pointless medical administration class."

"Nice," chuckled Roger.

Mary seemed less sure, but Caspian said, "Mrs. Winters, you know your daughter even better than I do. Will she *ever* take a job where she's pushing papers rather than tending patients?"

Elizabeth's mother thought about it for a second, then shook her head. "No, that would pretty much be hell-on-Earth for Elizabeth."

"Speaking of Hell-on-Earth," said Roger, "Dealing with New Orleans rush hour traffic twice a day, then bringing Lizzie home at six in the morning sounds like its own kind of Hell." Caspian opened his mouth to reply but Roger, laid a hand on the younger man's arm. "I know what you're going to say, son, and you're right, she *is* worth it. I just wanted you to know that I appreciate how you take care of my little girl."

"I'm not going to have her driving home in the dark after a twelve hour shift," said Caspian in a matter-of-fact tone. "That's just not gonna happen."

"But when do *you* sleep?" asked Mary. "You have a full time job with that consulting company, what's it called again?"

Caspian nodded. "McKinsey, yeah, but COVID has us all on lock down, so my entire day is Zoom calls. Also, I really only need about six hours sleep. I hit the sack around ten, get up around four-thirty. Lizzie's shift ends at five. She's home by six. No worries."

Mary stared at her husband for a moment, then said, "Cas, your apartment is, what, fifteen minutes from the hospital." He nodded, and Elizabeth's mother shrugged. "You could just have Lizzie stay there, at least on the days she's working." She patted Caspian's hand, and gave a slightly embarrassed laugh. "We trust you, don't we, Roger?"

Before Elizabeth's father could respond, Caspian, said, "Thanks Mrs. Winters, but I don't trust me. The wedding is in less than three months." He smiled. "Lizzie and I met when we were five, right?" Both parents nodded. "Okay, so I'm twenty-four, which means I've managed to behave myself with respect to your daughter for nineteen years. Nope, I'm not screwing that up on the one yard line." He tapped the table. "She sleeps here."

"You're a better man than I was," murmured Roger.

"That's for darn sure," agreed Mary. Her husband smirked at her. "What?" she asked innocently.

"Don't give me that look, Mary Winters. As I recall, you—"

Caspian held up both hands. "Guys, if this conversation is going the direction I think it is, let's not."

"Let's not what?" asked Elizabeth as she breezed into the kitchen.

The two elder Winters smiled at each other. Caspian said, "Let's not... fight over my strange eating habits."

Elizabeth bent down to kiss her mother. "Mom, are you plying my fiancé with chicken salad again?"

"I offered, Lizzie. I didn't ply. It's what mothers do. God willing, you'll be a mother soon. Just wait, you'll do it, too."

"Ma, can I please get married before you start bugging me for grandchildren?" She turned to her father. "Daddy, I thought you were going to talk to her about this?"

Roger nodded. "I did talk to her."

"Well it didn't seem to take," lilted Elizabeth, "because she's still harping."

"I am not harping," countered Mary. "Caspian, am I harping?"

"Uh..."

"Do not answer that, Cas," said Elizabeth. "It's a trap."

Mary sighed. "It is not a trap. Your father told me what you said, and we both agreed that it would be unreasonable to expect any grandkids before next Thanksgiving."

"Daddy!" growled Elizabeth, "Thanks a lot."

"What did I do?" he sputtered.

She frowned at him. "What day is the wedding?"

"September 21st," he answered quickly. "See, you thought I forgot."

"No, I didn't think you forgot how long it is until the wedding, but I do think you may have forgotten how long it takes to make a baby."

"Nine months, right?" Roger looked to Caspian for confirmation, who nodded.

"Of the four of us," began Elizabeth, "who is in the last year of her medical studies? That was rhetorical, no need to answer. It's me, and it takes about ten months to make a baby, which, Mom knows very well. She assumed you were ignorant, which you are...no offense, and got you to agree that you two deserved a grandchild by next Thanksgiving. That means Cas and I need to—"

"I'm not in this conversation at all," interjected Caspian. Three pairs of eyes turned to him. He shrugged. "Just sayin', I've completely blocked the whole exchange."

Elizabeth frowned at her fiancé. "Thanks for the support, dork." She turned to Roger. "Daddy, you got played, but I love you." She kissed his cheek, then moved to kiss her mother. "You, Mom, are an evil mastermind with grandchildren-ous intentions, but I love you too."

Elizabeth started to hoist her small backpack onto one shoulder, but Caspian rose and took it from her. "I got this," he said, "The last thing you need is a torn rotator cuff." He glanced at Roger. "Have you felt this bag? I think she fills it with bricks."

"Or bio-technical engineering books that weigh the same as bricks," snickered Elizabeth. She raised up on her toes and kissed Caspian. "I read them during my break. It's only taken me twenty years, but I finally got you to carry my books."

"That's my girl," said Roger. "She plays the long game. Cas, you never had a chance."

"Tell me something I don't know," laughed Caspian.

"We have to go," insisted Elizabeth, then tugged her fiancé toward the door.

Her mother called after them. "Be careful on the drive home. That tropical storm is supposed to be coming through."

Caspian nodded. "Love you guys," said Elizabeth.

"Love you, too," replied her parents together.

Caspian looked at his watch for the third time. It was nearly five-thirty in the morning. He saw the security guard walking toward him, again. As he drew near Caspian lowered his window. "How much longer are you going to be?" asked the guard. "You're not allowed to park here." Lightning flashed, and both men stared up at the sky. Thunder cracked a second later causing the security guard to flinch.

"Look, I'm sorry," said Caspian. "My fiancé is volunteering here in the COVID wing. I'm giving her a ride home, so if you could—"

The security guard's entire demeanor changed. He shook his head. "Don't worry about it. You stay right where you are. What does she look like? I'll bring her down under my umbrella so she doesn't get drenched."

Caspian sighed, then gave a quick description. "Thanks, I appreciate it."

The guard pinched up his face. "Is your fiancé Dr. Winters?"

"Yeah," replied Caspian, "but she's actually—"

"I'll keep an eye out for her," said the security guard as he briefly scanned the entrance, then looked down at Caspian. "You hit the lotto with that one, bub. I've heard some of the senior docs talk about her. Brains, beauty, and a workhorse." He pointed at Caspian. "My advice...don't screw it up."

"Well, thanks," began Caspian, "I hadn't planned—"

"Oh wait, I think she's coming out now. I'll get her for you." He pointed at Caspian again. "Remember what I said."

The guard jogged around the front of the car. "Don't screw it up," murmured Caspian to himself. "Sounds like excellent advice. Good thing, too, because I was just thinking, I should screw up the best thing that's ever—"

The passenger door opened, then closed a second later. "Thanks Jim," said Elizabeth. "That was so sweet of you."

The security guard gave her a warm smile. "It's the least I could do, Dr. Winters. Thanks for everything you're doing here."

"I'm not a doctor, Jim. I keep telling you that."

He shrugged, then motioned to the hospital. "I don't care what they call you in there. You help fix people. I call you doctor." Jim's eyes slipped off those of Elizabeth and focused meaningfully on Caspian. He tapped the roof several times, and they started moving forward.

Elizabeth snapped in her seatbelt, then laughed. "What was that about?"

"What was what?"

"Cas, Jim just gave you the stink eye. What did you do to him?"

"I didn't do anything, Lizzie. Apparently, he thinks you are all that and a bag of chips, which you are. He also thinks I am undeserving of said chips." Caspian grinned, "Which, of course, is also true."

She leaned over and kissed him. "You are very much deserving of the entire bag of chips, Mr. Lewis." Several minutes later, they were heading toward the the I-10 onramp. "I'm sorry I was so late," sighed Elizabeth.

"No worries," replied Caspian. He glanced over. "Tough night?"

She nodded at him, eyes filling. "We lost almost fifty people. I feel like I'm useless, Cas. This shit is awful. It's bad enough that people are dying, but most of them are dying alone." Her voice fell to a whisper. "The lucky ones die with me, but who the hell am I?"

"I'm with Jim on this one, Lizzie. You're their doctor. You're the one putting your life on the line every night to help them."

"And you are putting your life on the line being boxed up with me in this car. What if I catch this thing and give it to you?"

Caspian shook his head. "How has that line of thinking worked with your parents?"

"About as well as it's worked with you, which is why I'm still living there." She stared at him. "What time did you get to bed?"

"I dunno," he replied.

"You're lying. I can always tell when you're lying."

"I know," grumbled Caspian, "and it's really annoying."

"What...time?"

"Around two, but—"

"Two? Cas, what the hell? You cannot function on less than three hours sleep. Why were you up so late?"

"I had a conference call with folks in India. It was the only time they could do it. Lizzie, can you please chill. I was sitting in a comfy chair staring at a web cam. That's nothing compared to what you were doing. I can still see the marks on your face from the masks you wear."

"Yeah, but I got a full night's sleep. Why don't we just stay at your place tonight?" She saw his expression, and laughed. "You sure do think a lot of yourself, Cas. Trust me, I can control myself..." Elizabeth grinned. "At least for one night."

"I'm not worried about you, Lizzie." He winked at her. "I'm worried about me. I mean just look at ya. Mask marks on your face. Armpit sweat on your scrubs. You are sooo sexah!"

Elizabeth lifted one arm. "And I smell like a wet dog. So, then your place tonight?"

"Nope," replied Caspian. "One wakeful night isn't gonna kill anyone. Remember, our *penny and pound* pact. I just suggested no sex. You are the one that said, no sleeping over."

"If I'm the one who amended the original pact, then I should be able to amend it again, right?"

"Contracts don't work that way, babe. Besides, we're almost to the bridge. Lean your seat back, go to sleep, and let your chauffeur do his job."

Elizabeth stared at him for several seconds, then sighed. "You are as stubborn as you are good looking."

"Nobody is *that* stubborn, Lizzie." His eyes flicked right, and Caspian smiled.

Elizabeth shook her head. "You are a dork, and I couldn't love you any more than I do at this very second. Is it September 21st yet? Because I'm ready to be Mrs. Lewis, right now."

"Not yet, but soon, and I plan to call you Dr. Lewis. It makes me feel more important."

Elizabeth shifted her seatbelt, then turned to snuggle sideways in her chair. "I love you, Mr. Lewis."

"And I love *you,* soon-to-be Dr. Lewis. Now, go to sleep."

Less than five minutes later, Caspian smiled to himself as soft snores began coming from the passenger seat. More lightning flashed. All the surrounding street and traffic lights flickered then went dark. Caspian adjusted his car's climate controls to dispel the fog that kept accumulating on his windshield. He tried to turn up the wipers, but they were already on their maximum setting.

Caspian slowed down as they approached the 510 interchange. Something flashed in his sideview mirror. Seconds later a motorcycle screamed past weaving in between two lanes of slow moving traffic. "What an idiot," growled Caspian. "People are driving slowly for a reason, moron."

"Who's a moron," murmured Elizabeth in her sleep.

Caspian cursed softly, then said, "Nothing, babe. Nobody's a moron. Go back to sleep. We'll be home—" He broke off as light bloomed just ahead of them. At first Caspian thought it was a lighting strike, but then he heard the shriek of metal crashing into metal. Cars began careening into each other. Parts of what might have been a motorcycle flew past the left side of his car. Caspian slammed his brakes, while unconsciously reaching over to press an arm against Elizabeth. He looked over as her eyes fluttered opened. "Cas? What's hap—"

The hood of their car caved in as the trailer of a jackknifed truck slammed into it.   Glass shattered, airbags began deploying from all directions, and Caspian felt the car begin to flip. There was a bright flash of white light, then darkness.

Chapter 8

WHAT DREAMS MAY COME

"Do you hear that?" asked Caspian.

Elizabeth turned off the stand mixer. "I'm sorry, I couldn't hear you. What did you say, Cas?"

"The beeping," he replied. "Do you hear it? I've been looking all over the house. Honestly, I feel like I'm going nuts. You don't hear it?"

She shook her head. "Could it be one of the smoke detectors?"

Caspian sighed. "No, I replaced all the batteries right after we closed on the house."

"Could be a bad battery?" she offered.

"Maybe, but it's not that kind of beeping anyway. It wouldn't wake you up, it's just kind of slow and annoying."

Elizabeth gave Caspian a kiss, then tapped his nose. "You go solve your beeping issue. I'm going to finish your birthday cake. The front number changing is a big deal, Mr. Old."

Caspian had started to walk away, but turned. "What did you say?"

She frowned. "I was just kidding. Thirty isn't old, and I'll be right there with you in a few months so—"

"I'm thirty?" She nodded, and he laughed. "What are you talking about, Lizzie?"

Before she could respond, two children bulled their way through the kitchen and toward a screened back door. "No running!" yelled Elizabeth. "How many times do I have to tell you little monsters that?" She grinned at Caspian. "Apparently, at least once more. It's amazing how selective their hearing is. Watch." Elizabeth walked to the screen door, opened it, then said in a normal voice, "Anyone want to lick the beaters?" Instantly there was a chorus of affirmation. Seconds later, a young boy and girl burst back into the kitchen. Elizabeth handed each one a mixing blade, then pointed to the table.

Caspian stared at her, eyes wide. "Who are they?" he asked.

Elizabeth cocked her head. "Okay, I'll play along. Those would be the twins. Your twins, well, our twins. I helped."

"But one's a boy and one's a girl," said Caspian half to himself.

"You noticed that too, did ya?" laughed Elizabeth. "I tried to send one of them back, but the doctor said no." She walked up to Caspian, draped her hands over his shoulders, and kissed him. "I love you," she said. "I'll always love you."

"I love you, too," he said haltingly.

Elizabeth nodded. "I know, but I have to go now."

Caspian felt his stomach twist. "Where are you going?"

"I'm...not exactly sure, or maybe, I am sure but just can't say right now." She shook her head. "It's all a little unclear. This was just a glimpse of what might have been." Elizabeth locked eyes with Caspian, and compassion showed on her face. "Oh, Cas, don't be afraid. Don't be worried. I'm fine. Come here." She pulled him close, hugging him. "The glimpse wasn't to show you what was lost, but what our love would have created." She turned to look at the table and smiled.

Caspian followed her gaze, as he did so the two children became gauzy, then faded. Elizabeth turned Caspian to face her. "Cas, my heart will always be yours." She pulled his head down. "Listen to my heart. Do you hear it?"

He nodded with his ear pressed to her chest. *Bump-bump, bump-bump-bump, bump-bump, bump-bump-bump.* Caspian started to lift his head, but she held him there. "Shhh, just listen. Listen, and remember. I love you. Look for me in all the things you love. I'll be there."

Bump-bump, bump-bump-bump, bump-bump, bump-bump-bump.

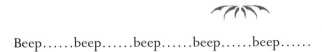

Beep......beep......beep......beep......beep......

Caspian's eyes fluttered open. He squinted against the glare of bright fluorescent lights, then groaned. Everything hurt. His entire body felt stiff and weak. He tried to move, but noticed an IV tube had been inserted into his right arm. His heart started beating faster, and Caspian's eyes locked on a machine standing to the left of the IV bag.

Beep..beep..beep..beep..beep..beep

A nurse sprinted into the room. She skidded to a stop, then her mouth dropped open. "You're awake." She rushed over to him, pressed a button on the side of his bed, then pulled out a small light. She flashed it quickly over both eyes, then let out a long breath, and smiled. "How are you feeling?"

"Like shit," croaked Caspian. "My throat hurts. Where's Lizzie?"

"Oh, um, well, you were intubated for, um, awhile and that's probably why your throat hurts. It should start feeling better soon."

Caspian nodded. "Okay, where's Lizzie?"

Before the nurse could answer another person walked in the room. She was much older, but had a kind face. She smiled at Caspian. "Hey, there, I'm Dr. Lisben. You got yourself knocked around a good bit, didn't you?"

"I guess, where's——"

"Just a moment," said the doctor. She turned to the nurse. "I need five milligrams of Ativan...quickly Mika please. So, Mr. Lewis, I want you to try and stay calm. We've needed to keep your heart rate low because of your injuries." She smiled. "You've kind of surprised us. We didn't think you'd wake up today."

The nurse rushed back in, and gestured with a syringe. Dr. Lisben nodded, and the nurse immediately moved toward the IV bag. "So, we're going to give you something to help you sleep a little bit longer, and I promise when you wake up, there will be some friendly faces to greet you okay."

"Okay," slurred Caspian as his voice trailed off, "but...but where's Lizzie?"

"Shit," said Dr. Lisben.

"Is he asleep?" asked the nurse.

"Yeah," she replied, shaking her head. "Mika, can you have patient services call the parents? Tell them to be here first thing tomorrow, and keep him sedated until then, okay?"

"Right away, doctor." The nurse left the room, and doctor Lisben turned as well.

She paused, looked back at Caspian, then shook her head.

"Caspian…Cas, it's Mom. Dad and I are here. Cas, can you wake up for me, baby?"

"Hi Mom," sighed Caspian. He opened his eyes. "Hi Dad."

"Hey, little boy," replied Robert Lewis.

Caspian snorted. "*Little boy*, wow, that brings me back. You only call me little boy, when——" His parents both glanced at the heart rate monitor *beep..beep..beep..beep..beep..beep..beep*

Rachel Lewis stared at her son. "Listen to me. You need to calm down a bit. The doctor said that you're not out of the woods yet."

"Mom, Dad, where is Elizabeth? Where is my fiancé?"

The two Lewis' shared a knowing look, and Robert silently got up, and walked out. "Cas, there was a car accident," said his mother. Tears filled her eyes. "Elizabeth is gone. We almost lost you, too."

"No!" he cried. "No, I was just talking to her." He grabbed his mother's arm as additional figures moved into the room, caught by his peripheral vision. "You're wrong, Mom. You're wrong," he said again, this time with both defiance and anger. "I was just talking to Lizzie."

Rachel shook her head, tears falling freely. "Oh Cas, I'm so sorry, but you couldn't have been."

His father sat back down next to Rachel and slipped an arm around her. Caspian look to his left. "Mr. and Mrs. Winters," he said, "thank God. What the hell is going on?"

Mr. Winters took a ragged breath. "Your mom's right, son. Lizzie's gone."

Mary Winters reached out and took Caspian's hand. She placed something in it. He looked down, opened his hand, and stared blankly at the engagement ring. "This can't be happening," he said. "This is a nightmare." Everyone around him nodded. Suddenly, Caspian pushed himself into a seated position. "No! I don't believe any of you. I want to see her. Where is she? Where is my Lizzie?"

The Lewis' and Winter's shared a long suffering look. Finally, Rachel said, "Cas, baby, it's been over a month. You've been asleep for almost five weeks. The doctors didn't know if we'd ever have you back."

Roger Winters leaned forward. "When you're better, we can take you to see her, Cas. It's a nice place, quiet and still. There are magnolias all around."

"Lizzie loved the blossoms," murmured her mother.

Caspian slumped against his pillow, and his voice lost all inflection. "How did it happen? I just remember the rain, lots of rain."

"Drunk driver," said his father. "He was on a motorcycle. He cut off a tractor trailer and it jackknifed. There were a lot of people hurt that day. It was all over the news."

"One of them was a patient of Lizzie's," said Mary, "She was pregnant, and had just been cleared from having COVID. She was trapped in her car, but the EMTs found her in early labor. They used the jaws of life, saved the baby, and they named her Elizabeth."

Caspian shook his head. "Is he dead?"

"Is who dead?" asked Rachel.

"The guy on the motorcycle."

Silence cloaked the room for several seconds. Finally Roger Winters said, "No, he's alive. He slid under the semi as it flipped, and ended up on the shoulder of the highway. He's been indicted on several counts including..." Roger paused. "...including vehicular homicide."

Caspian nodded. "That figures. Only the good die young, right? Lizzie is gone, and this asshole walks away from it." He gave a mirthless laugh. "Doesn't matter...this is all my fault anyway. She'd be alive if it weren't for me."

"No," said everyone at once.

"She suggested we just stay at my place in the city. I'm the one who insisted we drive to Slidell during a damn hurricane. If I had just listened to her, Elizabeth would be alive." ·

The two elder Lewis' shared an impotent look, not sure what to say. Mary moved to sit next to Caspian on the bed. She took his hand in hers, then whispered, "Those *if-only* worlds don't exist, Cas. Believe me, Roger and I have tried to bring them to life these past five weeks."

She nodded at her husband, who said, "You aren't the only one who wished they had done things differently that day. I knew the storm was coming. I could have told her not to go in to the hospital that day."

Caspian shook his head. "*Told her?*" he asked, "Lizzie? That wouldn't have worked, and you know it, Roger."

"Yeah, I know it," he replied, "just like you know you've been driving Elizabeth back and forth because you loved her and wanted to keep her safe."

Mary leaned down and kissed Caspian's cheek. "The last thing she would have wanted is for you to blame yourself."

Caspian stared up at one corner of his hospital room, as his eyes filled, then tears spilled over. He nodded. "I'm suddenly feeling really tired. Would it be okay if I rested now?"

There were nods and murmurs of assent, then everyone shared hugs, kisses, and offers of prayers. In less than two minutes, Caspian was alone. He looked out the large window and into a cloudy, Louisiana sky. He felt his jaw clench, as anger filled him. "She just lost her daughter," spat Caspian, "and she said she'd pray for *my* healing...mine!" He shook his head, then glared even more angrily at the sky. "I won't tell Mary this, because she's kind and loving, but I reject her prayers. I reject them, because I reject you." Caspian turned his back on the window. He closed his eyes, as tears fell down his cheeks, and words of a favorite poem came unbidden and unwanted. Caspian whispered them softly as if in prayer, "She was my noon, my midnight, my talk, and my song. I thought our love would last forever. I was wrong. Pour away the ocean and sweep up the wood. For nothing now can ever come to any good."

Chapter 9

A HEART OF STONE

"What do you mean, you're working?" asked Rachel Lewis, "Caspian, nobody works on Christmas day."

"Then I guess all the people at Denny's and China Garden are ghosts, Mom." No response. Caspian stopped typing on his laptop. He glanced at his phone to see if the connection dropped. It hadn't. He tapped the screen to make sure it was still set to speaker. It was.

After several seconds of silence Rachel Lewis said, "Your father and I went to Mass last night without you, because you told us you had to work. Now you are saying you're too busy to see your family on Christmas day."

"Mom...I—"

She cut him off. "Were you too busy to go to Mass today as well?" Caspian sighed. "You didn't go, did you?"

"No, Mom, I didn't go," he replied, more harshly than he intended. "I didn't really see the point."

"Elizabeth saw the point," retorted his mother. "You are lapsing back to the way you were before the two of you started dating. Elizabeth's faith had become important to her, Caspian. You went through pre-Cana together for heaven's sake. Elizabeth—"

"Is dead, mom. She's dead, and no Christmas Eve mass or Christmas day ham is going to bring her back. If God wanted me to go to mass so badly, he

55

could have paid more attention to hurricanes and drunk motorcycle riders." A rustling sound came through the phone. "Mom?"

"It's me, Cas," said his father. "Your mother handed me the phone."

"Is she all right?" asked Caspian.

"No, son, she's not. She just went upstairs, crying. Nice job."

"That's not my fault, Dad. It's one Christmas. I have a big RFP due, and the first company to submit theirs has an advantage."

"So, that's why you're working through Christmas?" asked Robert.

"Yeah, it's worth over five million dollars to the firm, and I'm the one who volunteered to draft it. If we win the bid, I'm a shoe-in for a promotion. Dad, I could make partner in less than ten years."

"Awesome," replied Robert, "I'll tell your mother. I'm sure that will stop her from crying."

Caspian pinched at his nose. "Dad, what do want from me?"

"Well, I'd like my son back, for starters. I don't know who you are, but you're not the Caspian I raised."

"I wish I could be that guy for you, Dad. Hell, I wish I could be that guy for me. But that Caspian is buried next to Lizzie." He started to feel angry. "Why can't anyone just accept that I'm different now? I mean, shit, a lot of parents would be proud of their sons for what I'm doing. McKinsey is *the* most prestigious consulting company in the world…the world, Dad, and I'm in charge of one of their most critical bids."

"Cas, it's not where you work that makes your friends and family proud of you. It's who you are. I understand you've suffered a terrible loss, but don't let it—"

"You understand!" yelled Caspian. "You understand. Do you really, Dad? Tell me the truth. What if it was Mom you got killed in a traffic accident?"

"Son, you didn't get—"

Caspian interrupted him. "What would you do?"

"I don't know," his father whispered, "probably something destructive and stupid. So, it seems the apple doesn't fall far from the tree in that regard." Caspian stared at his phone accusingly as his father added, "I would also hope the people who loved me would tell me I was being an asshole."

"I'm being asshole?" sputtered Caspian. "I am being an asshole! Why, because I'm working hard at my career?"

"No, because you've cut yourself off from all your old friends, your family, and when was the last time you spoke with Roger or Mary Winters?" Caspian felt his stomach twist, but said nothing. "It's been over six months, Cas. You walked out of that hospital room, then jettisoned everyone who ever loved you. You wanted truth, Caspian, well here it is. Elizabeth died. That's a horrible tragedy. Just because I said I understand what's happened, doesn't mean I understand what you're feeling. I don't. I can't. I also can't understand what Roger and Mary are feeling. I do know they love you. I also know you are hurting them, and they don't deserve it."

Caspian shook his head. "I'm nothing to them except a reminder that their daughter is gone."

"That's not how they see it," said his father. "They see you as the man their daughter loved. You're right when you said they lost her, but now you are making them lose you, too. You're not a father, Cas, so I don't expect you to understand this, but there are a lot of conflicting emotions that go through a dad's head when his daughter meets the man she wants to spend her life with. Three years ago, when your sister, Lucy, met Mathew, I was not thrilled. It had nothing to do with Matthew. He was a perfectly nice young man. Over time, I got to know him better, then I was like, okay, maybe I can deal with this. One day he came to me and asked permission to marry your sister. He told me they wanted to go through pre-Cana together, and get married in the Church. That's when I finally went from *okay* to *thrilled*."

"Well, you should have been," murmured Caspian, "Mathew is rock solid."

"You didn't let me finish," said Robert. "I was thrilled, *and* I was terrified. This man was going to take my little girl away. Hell, he was going to take my little girl away *and* take her into his bed. There's a reason why the father walks his daughter down the aisle, Cas. We give her away. We give her to another man. For twenty-two years, I was the number one man in Lucy's life. In the blink of an eye, when I put her hand in Mathew's, I became number two, and that's how it should be. But, Cas, there is only *one* way a father can make that moment feel right. He has to come to love his daughter's husband with the same fire he loves his daughter."

Caspian closed the lid to his laptop and picked up the phone. "Roger never said anything like this to me."

Robert gave a mirthless laugh. "No shit, Cas. It's a sensitive subject for dads, it makes us vulnerable to talk about it. Roger never brought it up, I did. We went to a bar, drank a lot of beer, and I told him about how it was when Lucy got married. Bottom line, when Elizabeth died, Roger and Mary didn't just lose a daughter, they lost a son as well. Now, despite what you keep telling yourself, you had nothing to do with them losing Elizabeth." Robert paused, "but as for them losing the son they came to love as much as their own flesh and blood, well, that's on you, Cas."

There was a long pause. Finally Caspian sighed. "I know something's broken in me, Dad. I just don't know how to put the pieces back together. Hell, I don't even know where all the pieces are. Work is comfortable. I'm good at what I do. It's controllable. I have this RFP. I'm going to deliver it first. I'm going to win the bid. I'm going to execute the work flawlessly, and I'm going to get promoted. I can draw a straight line from point A to point B, while controlling everything in-between."

"It must feel comforting having that kind of insight into the future," said his father softly. "You believe yourself to have an amazing amount of control, and we can't be hurt by what we control."

"Exactly," said Caspian, "Now, you are finally starting to get it, Dad."

"Oh, I've been getting it, Cas. I just play an idiot on TV. What I'm trying to tell you is the control you're grasping at, is just an illusion. Your family, your friends, that faith you've so casually tossed aside, that's real."

"Fine, Dad, I'll just stop what I'm doing and drive over. Will that make you and Mom happy?"

"No, and quite honestly, I don't want you to come. I love you, son. I will always love you, but I'm not liking you right now. Your mother has cried oceans of tears over you these past months since you got out of the hospital. I've held my tongue, maybe I've held it too much. David, Jennifer, and Michael have all come to talk with us."

"They have?"

"No, I'm making it the hell up!" yelled his father. Caspian winced. A sigh came from the other side of the phone. "Sorry, but yes, they came by several times. They are good friends, Cas. You know what I always say…"

"You can't make any new, old, friends," said Caspian.

"Right, and those three are keepers. Michael wanted to get you blackout drunk, and haul your passed-out ass to stay with his family in Jamaica until you came to your senses."

Caspian pinched up his face. "Wait, how does that even make sense? No airline is going to let Mr. Dreds drag me onto a plane unconscious."

"The very point I raised to him," chuckled his father. "Drug running stereotypes aside, apparently Michael has friends or family who have access to small private planes, the pilots of which don't ask probing questions. Just be glad I dissuaded him or you would likely be working for his aunt making curried roti right now."

"Fine, I'll call them tomorrow."

"No, Cas. They are planning something that I actually do approve of, and it's not until after new years. You may think I'm oblivious, but I'm not. I know what you are working on with McKinsey. You've told me. I listen. I've also responded to more than one RFP in my day. Once you win the bid, and I'm sure you will, someone has to pull together the statements of work, right?"

"Right..." said Caspian, surprised.

"There's that, *my dad's an idiot,* tone again, but I'll let it slide. Anyway, your friends are going to invite you to a beach house on the Florida panhandle. *You are going to act surprised.* You are also going to agree, because your mother also knows about this plan of theirs and it's the only thing giving her hope at this point."

"Dad, I really don't—"

"—want to take away your mother's hope," interjected Robert meaningfully. "I know you don't, son, which is why you will be acting both surprised, *and* accepting their invitation. That is what you were going to say, wasn't it?"

Caspian let out a long, slow, breath. "Yeah, Dad, that was exactly what I was going to say."

"I knew it was, son. I'm going to go check on your mother now."

"Okay, Dad. Please tell her that I'm sorry and I love her."

"I'll tell her you love her, but as for the sorry part, you need to show her, not tell her...and Cas?"

"Yeah, Dad?"

"Try to remember what this day is *really* about before you react to what I say next." There was a slight pause, then Robert said, "Merry Christmas, Son."

Caspian sucked in a breath, then nodded with the phone pressed hard against his ear. "Thanks, Dad. Merry Christmas to you, too."

Chapter 10

A REAL AND IMAGINED BEACH

Caspian dug his toes into the wet sand, then looked out at the calm, gulf, waters. "It's weird how warm the ocean is," he said, "I thought it would be freezing cold in January."

"It is," laughed Elizabeth.

Caspian turned to look at her. She wore a forest green, one-piece, bathing suit that seemed to highlight her slightly lighter green eyes. Her long blonde hair was wet, the water having made it look several shades darker than normal. "This is a dream," he sighed. She nodded. Caspian shook his head. "Everyone says I need to move on. How am I supposed to move on if I keep dreaming about you?"

Elizabeth slipped her hand into his, then looked out to sea, just as Caspian had done moments before. The two stood in silence for several minutes, with the only sounds being that of the lapping waves and seagulls calling to each other. Finally, Elizabeth whispered, "Everyone has it backwards, Cas." He turned to face her, but she continued looking toward the horizon. "It's not your dreams of me that are keeping you stuck. It's your being stuck that keeps calling me here." She sighed. "I love you, Cas. I'll always love you, and this isn't good for you." She locked eyes with him. "Caspian Lewis, I will not abandon you to grief."

"But you aren't really here," he said.

Elizabeth shrugged. "There are more things in heaven and earth, Horacio…"

Caspian sighed, "…than are dreamt of in your philosophy."

"More your philosophy, than Horacio's" snickered Elizabeth, "but you've got the sense of it."

"So you're really here? You're not a figment of my imagination?"

Elizabeth smiled at him. "We always loved playing word games, Cas. Think about it, would my answer to that question mean anything?"

He pursed his lips, then smiled back. "No, because if you were a figment, then it's just me talking to me. If you aren't a figment, then there's no way for me to confirm it. Logically, though, this is just my subconscious trying to work its way through the grieving process."

"How very Freud of you," she giggled.

"You hated Freud," said Caspian.

"I didn't hate him. I disagreed with him. He discounted the power of faith completely." Elizabeth's eyes flicked left, "Kind of like someone else I know, at least lately."

"No shit," said Caspian. "God and I aren't on speaking terms. He took you away from me."

"So you've separated yourself from everyone who loves you, including Him? Excellent plan, Cas. How is that working for you?"

"Not well, Lizzie, and these nocturnal lectures aren't helping."

"Because you won't let them," she countered, "but that's about to change in Florida."

Caspian narrowed his eyes. "Wait, how do you know about that?"

"Well, if I'm just a figment, then I know because you know, but—"

"But, if you're what, an angel, you came to provide some great insights?" interrupted Caspian with more heat than he intended.

"I'm not an angel, Cas. People don't become angels. You know that, or you did. Still, you're not completely wrong. The veil between worlds is gossamer thin when you're dreaming."

"Very poetic, Lizzie. How about I just walk into the ocean, sink to the bottom, then we can be together?"

"First of all, this is a dream ocean, so that wouldn't work. Second, if you really did something that epically stupid and selfish, we'd never be together. Now listen to me, Cas."

"I'm listening," he grumbled, "how could I not listen?"

She sighed. "Your friends love you. They are also desperately afraid for you, but have no idea what to do about it."

"There's nothing they can do."

"Not true," said Elizabeth. "They just don't know the doors to open. Fortunately, I do."

Caspian arched an eyebrow at her. "You do?"

She nodded. "I'm sending you on a quest."

"Now I know you're a figment," grumbled Caspian. "You always hated Dungeons & Dragons, and barely tolerated it when I ran quests on Elder Scrolls Online."

"True," agreed Elizabeth, "but this is different."

"Really?" asked Caspian, "How so?"

She laughed. "This quest isn't dumb. In addition, it will save your life and all those you love." Caspian eyed her. "It's your choice, Cas. It has to be, but if you take up the quest, you will meet me seven times in the waking world. If you don't take up the quest, well, then this is it."

Caspian pinched up his face. "Waking world? What do you mean, like as a ghost?"

"Something like that," she said with a smile, then pointed. "I've been granted a boon on your behalf. Depending on the choices you make, I will be given the ability to visit you up to seven times." She laughed. "Oh, and Cas, that last one, it's going to be a doozie."

"Wait, you know what's going to happen two years from now?"

Elizabeth shook her head. "I don't know, but I've been shown several possible paths, some good..." she sighed, "some not so good. I'm going to intercede where I can to help work all things to your good, Cas."

"And this quest is part of it?" he asked. She nodded. "Okay, I'll bite, what's the quest, Lizzie?"

She cocked her head. "Oh, Cas, I know you don't believe me, but while I can't offer any direct help with the quest, I can help with the disbelief. Look for Our Lady who weeps by the ocean. If you can explain why she's there or how she weeps..." Elizabeth shrugged, "then just write this all off as the delusions of a grieving mind."

"And if I can't?" he asked.

Elizabeth turned, and held Caspian gently by the shoulders. She stared deeply into his eyes. "If you can't, then ask your friends to help you find the three to whom my gifts were given. The first will help you see. The second will let you, once again, breathe without the shudders of sorrow."

"And the third?" he asked.

"The third will be the hardest to find, but in its finding, your broken heart will finally be healed."

Caspian stared at her for several seconds, then shook his head. "Why are you being so cryptic? This vagary seems designed to make all sorts of random things match when, in fact, it's all just wish-fulfilling bullshit." Tears began to fill Elizabeth's eyes, and Caspian suddenly felt sick to his stomach. "Lizzie, I'm sorry. I didn't mean—"

She shook her head. "It's okay, Cas. This is why I'm here. I'm just so sad for all that you have had to endure, and what is to come."

"Me," he sputtered, "I got *you* killed, and you feel bad for me. That's just like you, Lizzie."

She placed her hands on either side of Caspian's face, then kissed him. "Caspian Lewis, I tell you three times, you didn't get anyone killed. You blame God, but can't hurt him, so you hurt yourself instead." Elizabeth pulled back, then glanced over the ocean. "You're about to wake up, Cas. Tomorrow it all begins. I'm praying for you." She smiled at him. "I'm praying so hard. Take up the quest, please, if not for you, then for me."

Elizabeth started to fade from view. Caspian called out, then reached for her, but she was gone. He felt a buzzing on his wrist, but when he looked, his wrist was bare. It vibrated again. *Now, what the hell is going on,* he wondered, then the world around him grew dark.

Caspian groaned, opened his eyes, then glanced at his watch. It continued to flash an alarm indication and vibrate. 8:30 am. He sat up in bed, stretched, then said, "Hey Siri, what's the current arrival time for my trip today?"

The somewhat artificial female voice responded immediately. *You have one saved trip to Fort Walton Beach, Florida. Traffic is light and there are no construction delays. Total trip time is estimated at four hours and forty-five minutes.*

"This place is awesome," exclaimed David. "Give me a couple minutes. I'm going to get the wifi connected to everything."

Michael walked in from the condominium's balcony, and said, "I have to agree with Dave on this one. You've outdone yourself, Jen. Cas is going to love it." He gestured to the still open sliding glass door. "I mean we are literally right on the beach, there's nothing but sand and beach chairs between us and the water. How did you even find this place?"

Jennifer Landry nudged her rollaway suitcase to the left, then stared at the large living room in an appraising manner. She nodded. "I wish I could take credit for it, but actually it was a total freak accident."

"What do you mean?" asked David, as he began fishing endless cables from one of his bags.

"I got this message from Vacasa, you know the online vacation portal. It said, something like *Hello Jennifer, there has been a recent cancellation that we thought you would like to know about. As a valued customer, and due to pandemic restrictions, there will be no housekeeping services provided, but we are happy to offer this spacious condo seventy-five percent off.*"

"Yeah, but what made you think to contact Vacasa for our little Caspian intervention," asked Michael. "Don't get me wrong, Jen, it's bloody brilliant. He loves the beach. It just never would have occurred to me."

"That's what I was trying to tell you boneheads. I've never rented from Vacasa in my life. I even told them that when I called, but they insisted that I was..." she made air quotes, "*a premium guest*, so gave me the offer."

"Well, you're premium to me," said David absently, then added, "Wow, this place has blazing fast wifi. We're going to be able to stream 4k no problem."

"We did not come to the beach to watch Netflix, you nerd," laughed Jennifer. "We came to put a metaphorical defibrillator to our collective best friend and jump start his broken heart." She paused, then added, "But thanks for thinking I'm premium."

"Anytime, Jen," said David. "Okay, I have the Apple TV all set up, and the wifi code is on the entertainment center so you guys can connect your phones."

"What are the sleeping arrangements?" asked Michael.

"Well," began Jennifer, "I am painfully aware that without Lizzie, I'm the only chick in this sausage fest, so I'm taking the bedroom with the private bath."

"Don't lump me in with Dave," chuckled Michael. "Jen, you're too skinny for me, and too pale. In fact, I suspect your freckled skin will just burst into flame within minutes of stepping onto the beach."

She pointed at him. " I am not too pale. I am a porcelain goddess, thank you very much. You, sir, are an anglophobe. What were your people doing in Jamaica while mine were bringing culture and civilization to the world?"

"Probably hauling sugar cane for you *porcelain gods and goddesses* and getting whipped for our trouble."

"Damn, Jen, you really stepped into that one," laughed David.

Jennifer stared from one of her friends to the other. She frowned, then spun on her heels, red hair whipping around her. She caught the handle of her rollaway with one hand as she headed into the nearest bedroom. "I'm still taking the master bedroom. I don't trust either of you as far as I could throw you."

"We're not interested in peeping at you, Jen," laughed Michael. "You are a friend, not an object of lust."

She poked her head out. "That sounds very mature of you, Michael, but I've watched *When Harry Met Sally* about one hundred times, so I know that what you said right there, is complete bullshit. Men can't be friends with women. I'd prove it to you, but I'm far too shy to have you *accidentally* catch me hopping out of the shower. Just trust me on this. You're a man. You're under thirty, and I'd be naked. *We're just friends* is the last thing your reptilian brain would be thinking." She disappeared back into the bedroom, and closed the door.

Michael turned to David. "I believe we were just insulted, and what is *Harry and Sally?* Do you have any idea what she is talking about?"

David nodded. "*When Harry met Sally.* It's a movie. Kind of a chick flick."

"But you've seen it?" asked Michael, "Well that figures."

"Shut up, dude. It's a classic. Anyway, the point is that no man, under thirty, can be *completely* friends with a woman."

Michael shook his head. "And why is that?"

David made a knocking motion with one hand. "Because we want to hit that."

Michael pointed at the closed door. "You mean, Jen? She's a friend. I do not want to…*hit that.*"

David shrugged. "Did you not just hear what she said? It doesn't matter, what your frontal lobe thinks at this particularly moment. You actually do want to have sex with her, or at least part of you does. You just haven't thought it through. Given the opportunity, you'd totally do it."

"Let me use small words for you Dave. I do not find her attractive. I'm not saying she isn't attractive. Clearly she is from all the men who continually make runs at her, but she is not attractive…to me."

"Still doesn't matter, dude."

Michael shook his head incredulously, "So you want to have sex with Jen?"

"Well, not actively at this particular moment in time, but if I saw her naked in the shower, definitely and immediately."

Michael sighed. "I'm very disappointed in you, Dave."

"I don't blame you. I'm very disappointed in you, too," he replied.

"Me," sputtered Michael, "What have I done, except put my friendship above my libido?"

David smirked at him. "It's *why* you are able to do that, which makes me disappointed. There's only one explanation, and you already admitted it." David pointed at Michael, then did a bad Jamaican accent. "You're too pale." His voice returned to normal. "Sorry, dude. If you aren't tempted by a beautiful, freckled redhead with a slammin' bod like Jen, there is only one reason. Clearly, you're a racist." Michael stared at his friend for several beats. Finally David couldn't hold himself together any longer and burst out laughing. He pointed at Michael. "You should see the look on your face. Oh man, I wish I had my phone out."

"You are a dick, David Rushing. Tell the porcelain princess that my racist black ass has gone to Kroger to pick up the provisions she put in our shared note."

David was still laughing as Michael scooped his keys off the breakfast counter and headed for the door. "Sounds good," he said. "We'll text with any last minute goodies. Be sure to get extra bacon. Cas loves bacon."

The door had almost closed behind Michael, but he spun, then pushed it partway open. "Remember bacon? That's your contribution? Like I would forget that. Why don't you make yourself useful and figure out where we are taking Cas for dinner tonight. It needs to be on the water, outside, and they need to have crab cakes."

David offered his friend an enthusiastic thumbs up sign. The door clicked shut, and he started tapping on his phone.

Chapter 11

A CIRCLE OF FRIENDS

Caspian paused at the beach condo's door. He stared at the numeric keypad, then looked at his phone. Jennifer's e-mail, including the provided access code, caused what he knew was an irrational fight or flight response. *These are my friends*, he thought. *Yeah, but I bet they are going to treat me like some porcelain doll.* Caspian shook his head. *What the hell is wrong with me?* He barked a mirthless laugh, then murmured, "How much time do you have, Cas, 'cause this could take a while?"

A second later the door swung open, and Jennifer nearly slammed into him. "Oh, I'm sor—" Her face lit up with recognition. "Cas!" She threw her arms around him and squeezed.

"Jenny, I can't tell if you're happy to see me or pissed. Ease up a little before you crack a rib."

She released him, took a half-step back, then punched him on the arm. "I'm both, you jerk, and I didn't squeeze that hard. Your jet setting consulting life has made you soft."

"Stipulated," said Caspian, "but are you going to make me hang out on the stoop, or do I get to come inside."

Jennifer shook her head as if just realizing where they were standing, then stepped aside. "Of course, come on in, Cas. The boys are on the balcony, probably playing with the binoculars again. Can you believe this place actually came with binoculars?" She shook her head. "We found them resting on a birdwatching book. The only birds around here are seagulls. Those two idiots aren't fooling anyone. They aren't birdwatching."

"Boobwatching is more like it," laughed Caspian as he walked into the condo and dropped his leather overnight bag on the floor.

"Exactly!" agreed Jennifer, then yelled, "Dave...Michael...look who the cat dragged in."

The condo's sliding glass door made a scraping sound as it moved, and two familiar faces peeked through the opening. "Cas!" they cried out, as both their faces split into grins.

Within seconds, Caspian was receiving handshakes and backslaps from both his friends, while Jennifer looked on. Once their flurry of initial greetings had subsided, she jangled her keys. The three men turned toward her. "Okay," she said, "I'm picking up a few things from the store that Michael missed, any last requests?"

"I'd like a cigarette and a blindfold," chuckled David. Everyone stared at him in silence. "Hey, that was funny," he said defensively.

Michael shook his head. "Given that none of us are laughing, I must disagree."

"I don't even get it," said Jennifer.

"Any last requests," repeated Michael, enunciating each word.

Jennifer narrowed her eyes at David. "You are such a dork."

"No need to state the obvious, Jen," said Michael, then nudged Caspian. "We figured that we'd be going out for dinners the three nights we're here, but have stocked the place up for breakfasts and lunches."

"Sounds good to me," replied Caspian. "I'm sure I'll be cool with whatever we have." He paused half a beat, then asked, "What do we have?"

"Oh nothing much," lilted Jennifer. "Just all the fixings for pancakes..." Caspian smiled at her. "Waffles..." the smile broadened.

"Enough bacon to, quite literally, form our own makeshift pig," added Michael.

"Eggs?" asked Caspian.

"Dozens," replied Jennifer, "and cream cheese to blend into it. As you're so fond of telling us, there has never been a problem that can't be cured by breakfast food. Still your fav, right Cas?"

"Always and forever," he laughed, "but does this place even have a blender?"

"Yeah," replied David. "It's got everything. In fact, the wifi here is better than I have at home."

ONE HEART THAT BEATS FOR TWO

"Dork McDorkerson has been running speed tests, while we were on the balcony," said Michael with a sigh.

"What were *you* doing?" asked Caspian.

"Me? I was, uh, birdwatching."

Jennifer rolled her eyes. "Okay, that's my cue. You guys discuss the merits of Fort Walton's local..." she made air quotes, "...birds. I'm going to pick up the things Michael's XY chromosomes made him blind to us needing."

"Jenny's become a misandrist, Cas," said David with mock seriousness. "That's why we're all here. We need to have an intervention. She's out of control."

"Yeah, because why would we need salt, pepper, or more than one roll of toilet paper. Men, what a bunch of bastards. Okay, I'm out of here. Text me if you think of anything."

"Bourbon?" asked Caspian.

Jennifer called over her shoulder as she headed for the door. "Michael was in charge of booze, so I think we'll be fine, but you can quiz him."

The door slammed shut. "Caspian," began Michael, "Do not insult me by even asking. You know me. We have booze aplenty."

David reached into the massive communal patter of mixed seafood, pulled out several crab legs, then said, "I don't get it. You mean, people just hire you to tell them what they are doing wrong?"

Caspian had just taken a bite of crab cake, and gave his friend a noncommittal shrug.

Michael pointed with his fork. "Jen tells people they are wrong for free."

"Just you guys," she corrected. "For everyone else, I make them take me on a date first. Once they've paid for dinner, *then* I tell them everything they're doing wrong with their life."

Caspian swallowed. "And how's that working out for you?"

"I'm on track for becoming a nun," she said with mock seriousness.

"I'm not sure you're cut out for that," laughed Caspian, "but since you guys seem freakishly interested in my work life, no, clients don't just pay us to tell them what's wrong. We have to fix what's wrong too, or just replace it with what's right."

"Yeah, and how much does McKinsey charge for this fixing?" asked Michael.

71

Caspian laughed. "A metric shit-ton. I saw the bill rates once. It is insane, what clients will pay them per hour."

"You mean what clients will pay *you* per hour," said David.

"No dude. I meant what I said. They pay me well, but I'm making a fraction of a fraction of my bill rate. Heck, if I made what they bill me out at, I'd be retired in two years, tops."

"Seems like they expect a lot of you for all that," said Jennifer quietly.

Caspian took a drink from his beer, then shrugged. "No more than most jobs, I'd expect."

"All of us managed to make it home for Christmas," she murmured. Everyone stared at her. "Hey, I'm just saying that Cas' job must be pretty demanding."

Silence descended on the table and began to grow. Just before it became uncomfortable, Michael tapped his mug with a fork. "That sounds like more of a cocktail conversation than a dinner one." He looked around the table to see three affirming nods. "Good," Michael continued, "because I have done a spectacular job at stocking up our own mini bar, and will also be offering my unparalleled bartending services."

"Hopefully you bought enough for the five of us," said Caspian seriously.

David arched an eyebrow, then made a point of counting them out...one... two...three...and four. Both Jennifer and Michael started shaking their heads. "What?" asked David, "There's four, who's the fifth?"

"Go on, Cas," said Michael. "The uber nerd teed it up for you, slam it home."

"If you insist," laughed Caspian. "Hopefully Michael bought enough for the five of us, because I imagine he, and his ego, will each need their own drinks."

Michael made a show of grabbing at his stomach and pretending to laugh.

David shook his head. "That was a whole lot of set up for very little payoff."

Jennifer just raised her hand as the server passed by. "Check please."

Chapter 12

INTERVENTION

Michael held a glass out to Caspian as he slouched in one of the condo's deep club chairs. "Are you trying to get me drunk?" he asked.

"No," replied his friend, "I've already accomplished that. Now I'm trying to keep you drunk." He waggled the glass. "Take it."

Caspian squinted. "Which one is it?"

Jennifer pushed herself off the couch and mussed Caspian's hair as she passed by. "It's the middle one, Cas." David laughed and Jennifer shot him a wink. "I gotta pee. Don't you boys talk about anything important while I'm gone."

Caspian had managed to take hold of the offered drink, then laughed. "She makes it sound like she's heading off on a Lewis and Clark expedition." He pitched up his voice. "Don't you boys talk about anything important while I'm discovering the northwest passage." He laughed again at his own joke, then stared at his friends. "That was funny."

Michael collapsed into his own chair, then shrugged. "It wasn't *that* funny."

"I wanted another drink, too," said David.

Michael smiled at him. "Congratulations. The bar is right over there."

"But you made *him* one," countered David.

"True, but I *like* Cas. I just tolerate you, Dave, and that's a near thing."

Caspian air-toasted Michael. "Nice!"

"Thanks," he said, then offered a seated bow. "I try." A comfortable silence settled among the three friends, broken only by the occasional sigh or clink of ice against glass. Finally, Michael said, "Hey, Cas?"

"Yup..."

"I'm sorry it took so long for me to visit you at the hospital."

The mood of the room immediately shifted, and all three of them felt it. Caspian took a deep breath, then slowly let it out. "It's okay, dude. I was probably unconscious anyway."

"You were," agreed Michael, "but that doesn't matter."

"Yeah," interjected David, "there are studies that show coma patients reacting to the voices of family and friends. That's why a lot of people read to unconscious loved ones."

Michael stared at his friend. "Thanks, Dave. Very helpful. Maybe you should use the bathroom after Jen's done and shit out that encyclopedia you ate earlier."

"I'm just saying that visiting unconscious people can be helpful."

"I wish you were unconscious," grumbled Michael, then turned his attention back to Caspian. "Anyway, I wanted to tell you, that it wasn't for lack of caring."

Caspian waved his hand in a languidly dismissive manner. "Seriously, Michael, I didn't think that."

"I know, but still want to explain. It was one of my cousins. She got really sick right after her birthday. She'd just turned twenty-three, and it freaked the whole family out. Apparently it's something that runs in my mother's family and strikes in the mid-to-late twenties. My grandmother and a different aunt supposedly had the same thing happen to them. They both died around twenty-seven. Anyway, just a few days before your accident, my mom called me and said her sister's kid had been diagnosed with the same condition."

"Same condition? What condition?" asked Caspian.

Michael shrugged. "Mom was weirdly vague about it. I just got the 911 call that they had chartered a private plane to get Sara, she's my cousin, to the States. She flew into Austin, and I helped get her settled into a clinic there."

"Which one?" asked Caspian.

Michael shrugged. "Illumination something, no, wait, I remember. Illumination Medical Center."

"Never heard of it," said Caspian. "Austin has some amazing hospitals. I did work with Ascension Seton last year. Why charter a flight to take her to some rinky-dink clinic? What do they specialize in?" Michael gave another shrug.

"And you have no idea what was wrong with her?" asked Caspian. "That's weird, dude. Why didn't you ask Sara?"

"I did ask her," he replied. "She told me it was private, but I pressed her again. Then she glared at me, said it was women's stuff, and I backed off. You haven't met Sara. She's a force of nature. I didn't want to piss her off any more than I already had, especially if she was sick with some *woman* ailment."

"Probably wise," slurred Caspian. "There are some things we were just not meant to know, mon frer."

"How's she doing?" asked David

"Well, that's the good news," replied Michael, then took a long pull from his glass. "Apparently things were touch and go there for a while, but Sara's back in Jamaica now. Everyone says the danger has passed."

"Maybe she was lying about it being a woman's issue. Sounds like suicidal ideation to me," said David. "Lots of people kill themselves at twenty-seven, Jim Morrison, Kurt Cobain, Amy Winehouse, there are dozens more. I bet the place in Austin was some kind of inpatient clinic. Suicide and depression can definitely run in families."

Michael considered this for several seconds, then shook his head. "Against all odds, and despite his complete lack of empathy, the computer nerd may have the truth of it. Still, she always seemed so happy to me. Granted, I haven't seen her in a while, but maybe Dave's right."

"Even a blind squirrel finds a nut once in a while," chuckled Caspian.

"Yeah, but our blind squirrel is generally not very insightful," said Michael, half to himself. "Get this, my aunt asked me to arrange a massive bitcoin transfer to the clinic I mentioned."

Caspian pinched up his face. "Bitcoin? That's—"

"Weird," finished Michael. "Yeah, I know, and you've been using that word a lot."

"Sorry, when I drink, my vocabulary takes a hit, and *weird* is a really useful word."

"It's not weird to me," said David. "Bitcoin uses an encrypted blockchain that keeps things super private. Suicide and depression still carry a lot of social stigma in some cultures. What do Jamaican's think about it?"

"Oh we love both suicide and depression," snarked Michael, then heightened his accent. "That's why we smoka the ganja, mahn."

Jennifer walked back into the room. "Who has ganja?" Caspian and David pointed at Michael. Her eyes widened. "Have you guys been getting stoned... without me? I was gone five minutes."

"You pee, you lose," said David

Caspian nodded in agreement. "Yeah, Jenny, you just asked us not to talk about anything important. You didn't say anything about edibles."

Jennifer had unconsciously moved her hands to her hips in the universal stance of female disapproval, when Michael said, "Don't listen to them, Jen. They are just playing off hurtful stereotypes."

She smiled, then slipped into the last empty chair. "Oh good. I hate missing out on things."

"We know," said the three men at once.

Jennifer tried to frown at all of them simultaneously. "Hey," she snapped, "I had a dream you guys left me sitting at home and I missed out on the flight here so my concerns are totally valid."

"We drove here, Jen," laughed Michael.

David joined in. "Yeah, so your dream was dumb. It didn't need to add the flight, we could have successfully dumped you just by leaving you at home."

Caspian sighed then drained his glass. Three pairs of eyes focused on him. It took him a few seconds to register, then he said, "Sorry, I was just thinking about a dream I had yesterday."

"What was it?" asked Jennifer. Caspian shook his head. "Come on now, give it up. I just told you my pathetic abandonment dream."

He stared at her. "It was about Lizzie."

Caspian's friends shared a knowing glance. Clearly they had been looking for an opening, and he'd just provided one. Michael was the first to speak. "When you say it was about Lizzie, do you mean her or the accident?"

"Her," replied Caspian. "I used to have nightmares about the accident, but Lizzie was never in them. This one was...weird." Caspian looked up, realizing he'd just used the word for the third time, but none of his friends seemed to notice, so he continued, "I think the dream happened because we were all getting together for the first time since..." he paused for a beat, "since it happened. Anyway, she told me to have a good time, which I told her would be impossible. Then she said she was sending me on a quest."

"A quest?" asked David. "What kind of quest?"

"Wait," said Jennifer, "you mean a quest-quest. Like the holy grail kind of thing."

Caspian shrugged. "I have no idea. She just said if I went on the quest, I'd see her seven times in the waking world. Honestly, I like the sound of that, but have no idea what deluded quest my mind has concocted."

"Well, I think we need to figure this out," said Michael, "because your current approach, quite frankly, has been utter shit." He noticed how both David and Jennifer winced even as Caspian's brow furrowed. "Hey, someone has to say it, and I guess that someone is me. Cas, you've blown us off since the accident. That sucks, but I'll cut you some slack there. You've also blown off your parents."

Caspian opened his mouth to object, but David jumped in. "No, don't deny it. I talked with your dad. He said you didn't spend Christmas with them because you had to work on an RFP response. That's some grade-a bullshit right there. I've issued RFPs, man. No one reads those responses between Christmas and New Years." He shook his head, locked eyes with Caspian, and repeated, "No...one."

Michael nodded. "But that's not even the point. They're your parents. If you want to be inconsiderate and make your mom cry, well, sometimes we do that to our parents. Getting dumped on by your kids comes with the territory."

"Thanks," murmured Caspian, "so I get to be a dick to my parents, check. Not sure what your point is."

"I got this one," said Jennifer, and she moved to sit beside Caspian. She slipped her hand into his and squeezed. "This may be hard to hear, Cas, but what you've done to Lizzie's parents..." she shook her head, "...that's just not cool at all."

"What have I done?" he sputtered. "I haven't done anything to them."

"Or for them," said David.

"Or even talked to them," added Michael.

Caspian stared at his friends, each in turn, then his shoulders slumped. "I figured seeing me would just remind them of what they lost."

"Remind them, or remind you," asked Jennifer softly. "Cas, Roger and Mary love you. The way you've been these last months, it's like they lost a daughter *and* a son."

"Did they tell you this?" asked Caspian.

"Pretty much," replied Jennifer. "Elizabeth was my best friend, Cas. I've known her as long as you have. Heck, I even remember that ZoomerBoomer incident in Kindergarten, *and* when you got beat up defending her honor in high school."

"I didn't get beat up, exactly."

"Dude, I was there for that one," laughed David. "You totally got your ass kicked by…what was that asshole's name? The one that took Lizzie to the Jason Vorhees death house?"

"Sean Campbell," sighed Caspian.

"Yeah, that's right. Sean freaking Campbell, a complete dick if ever there was one. What's he up to now I wonder, probably selling used toupees or some shit. Anyway, the point is, Jen has the most history, and I have the second most."

"And I'm the most clever of the three of us," added Michael, then pointed to David and Jennifer. "So, my opinion matters just as much as theirs."

"That's debatable," said Jennifer, "but it's also irrelevant, because we all have the same opinion."

"And that is…" sighed Caspian as he stared longingly toward the distant tequila bottle. "Please, regale me with your joint wisdom, because this conversation has completely ruined the first light-hearted buzz I've had. Way to go, guys."

"I'm sorry, Cas," said Jennifer, "but you knew this was coming. You even said it when we invited you." She lowered her voice. "So, what is this, some kind of intervention?" Her voice returned to normal. "Well, yeah, it is. We all loved Elizabeth." She saw Caspian suck in a breath, then squeezed his hand again. "Maybe not as much as you, but we all loved her."

"She's gone, Cas," said Michael.

"A fact that has not been lost on me," growled Caspian.

Jennifer snuggled close to him. "But you are here. You are alive, Cas."

"In theory," he replied, "but in practice…I'm pretty much dead."

David snapped his fingers. "That's probably what your subconscious was talking about." Everyone stared at him. "The LizzieQuest. It was probably your brain giving you a roadmap out of the emotional quagmire you're stuck in."

"Maybe," murmured Caspian, "I'm not sure though. It seemed so real, and I've no idea what she was asking me to do. Honestly it was just…"

"Weird," said everyone at once.

Caspian nodded and David started rubbing his hands together. "Quests are my forte. I've finished every single quest in Oblivion and Skyrim. I did every side mission in all three Mass Effects. I even did every Zelda, Breath of the Wild quest, well except the golden poop one."

"Yeah, why would you want to do the golden poop quest," snickered Michael, then he rolled his eyes.

"Laugh all you want," said David, "but I'm a quest expert. Cas, tell us about the dream, and be as detailed as possible."

Jennifer sat up. "Wait, if we're going to start parsing Cas' vision quest, I need another drink. Anyone else?" She glanced around the room and made a show of counting. "One...two...three...and me. We are all lushes. Okay, I'll make a pitcher because I've a feeling we're gonna need it."

Michael turned the pitcher upside down, and shook it. Several margarita drops fell into his otherwise empty glass. He set the pitcher on the floor, then stared at his friends who all sat in stunned silence. "This is the dumbest thing, I've ever heard, and I've heard some pretty dumb things."

David dragged a hand down his face, and said, "I didn't even know Lizzie was an organ donor."

"I did," said Jennifer. "She signed up to do it during undergrad school. We were both supposed to do it, but I chickened out." Jennifer narrowed her eyes at Caspian. "How did you find out?"

"About her being a donor? She told me when she did it."

Jennifer shook her head. "No, I meant how did you find out what she donated? For that matter, why did you find out?"

He sighed. "It was because of the dream, Jenny. Lizzie said I needed to find the gifts she'd given. It kept nagging at me. I woke up with her words stuck in my head, like a splinter, so I called the hospital. Roger and Mary had me listed as next of kin, so they told me."

Jennifer shivered. "I'm sorry, Cas, but it seems ghoulish."

"I don't think so," said Michael, "It seems a very *Lizzie* thing to do. She's even helping people from the hereafter. I mean someone might be able to see because of her. I didn't even know there were lung transplants, but I imagine if you needed one, it probably would save your life. But, Cas, you said the hospital told you there were three donations. What was the third?"

He shrugged. "The chart was redacted, but the nurse said it was probably her heart."

"No way," said David. "Her heart would never have been accepted into the program. We all heard it, that crazy double beat it had."

Everyone nodded. Caspian stared into the middle distance. "I loved that crazy heartbeat."

Silence threatened to overtake them when Michael set his glass down hard on the granite countertop. "We don't need to know step three right now. It's enough we have the first two." Three pairs of eyes bored into Michael, and he casually leaned against the breakfast bar. "Obviously, I need to spell this out for you. DreamLizzie said that Cas needed to find the gifts she had given. Clearly, his subconscious knew she was an organ donor. Caspian gave himself this quest to bring closure and give meaning to his loss."

"Caspian hates being talked about in the third person," said Cas. "Beyond that, Caspian thinks you are full of shit." His eyes shifted from Jennifer to David, then he pointed at Michael. "You two can't be taking his Jamaican psychobabble seriously."

Jennifer shrugged. "You heard me earlier. I thought the whole thing sounded ghoulish, but the way Michael just put it, maybe not. I think he may be on to something."

David nodded. "I'm down for this you guys, but you do realize that absolutely no one is going to release donor related medical information."

"Of course they won't," said Michael, then locked eyes with David. "Which is why it's a good thing our newly formed Fellowship of the Ring has one of the world's most adept white hat hackers among its members."

"Uh, breaking into medical databases is not white hat hacking," said David. "It is, most certainly, black hat. It's also a felony."

Michael walked over, patted David on the shoulder, and said, "Then I suggest you don't get caught."

"Easy for you to say *rahsta-mahn*. Is hacking even a crime in Jamaica? Wait, do they have computers there yet, probably not? Anyway, I'm the one who would be putting everything at risk." He jumped up. "Still, since I obviously love Caspian the most, I'm willing to do it." David swayed slightly then snapped his fingers. "However, if we're going to form a true Fellowship, we need a ceremony of some kind. I know just the thing. I saw it earlier, and Lizzie would have loved it."

"Guys," began Caspian, "you all need to chill. I haven't agreed to anything. In fact—" Caspian's voice caught in his throat as David returned and set a small statue in the middle of the coffee table. "Where did you get that?" he asked.

"Huh? Oh, it was in a little alcove by the back bedroom," replied David.

"I'm sure the owner put it there," said Jennifer. "You shouldn't mess with their stuff."

Michael squinted at the statue and read the fine script at its base. "Our Lady of Fatima. I thought I recognized that statue. Yeah, dude don't mess with people's religious stuff. Would you like it if someone spun your dreidel without permission?"

David frowned at him. "Very funny, but I thought this was a statue of Mary not someone from Fatima."

"You're an idiot, Dave," snickered Jennifer.

"It is a statue of Mary," murmured Caspian, "and you're right, it was Elizabeth's favorite statue."

"See," said David, then set it down again. He extended one hand to Michael and the other to Jennifer. "Gather up guys. We'll form a circle and bind ourselves to the quest with this statue in the center. Come on, do it."

Caspian's eyes never left the statue as he slowly reached out to take Michael and Jennifer's free hand. She felt his tremble slightly, glanced over and asked, "You okay, Cas?" He nodded, but she saw the tightness in his jaw as Caspian's eyes remained fixed on the statue's face. She followed his gaze, frowned slightly, then looked up. "That's odd," she said, "is there a leak dripping from the ceiling?"

Caspian slipped his hand from hers, wiped his thumb against one of the statue's cheeks, then stared at the moisture he saw there. He gripped Jennifer's hand again, and closed his eyes. "Cas?" she said, voice tinged with worry.

He shook his head, and whispered, "Look for Our Lady who weeps by the ocean."

"What?" asked Jennifer.

"Nothing, just a phrase I heard recently." He took another breath, then slowly let it out. "I'm okay. I'm good, and you're right Dave. Lizzie would love us forming our little quest Fellowship around Our Lady of Fatima." He sighed. "Let's do this."

Chapter 13

HACKER

Caspian reclined on his hotel room bed, propped up by several of the provided pillows. He finished the e-mail he'd been writing and tapped the send button. His eyes traced their way to the top of the laptop screen, 11:55 pm. He yawned and was about to close the computer when a notification banner appeared.

David Rushing has requested a group FaceTime call, accept or decline. Caspian frowned at the screen, then shrugged and clicked *accept*.

Several seconds later, David's face appeared on the screen. He seemed to be in the living room of his apartment, and based on how the background continued shifting, Caspian concluded that his friend was pacing. "What's up, Dave? Is it just us, or—"

David's eyes locked on the camera. "Huh, oh...no, I sent an invite to Jen and Michael as well. She's connecting now. Not sure about Michael since this was all very last minute."

"Hi boys," said Jennifer, "forgive my face."

Caspian squinted at the screen. "Why is your face green?"

"Don't look at me that way. It's a face mask. I wasn't planning to be on camera tonight. I bet Dave appreciates it though. You know he always plays an Orc."

Caspian shook his head. "Wow, that's a flash back. How long has it been since we played D&D together?"

"A really long time, over two years I think," said David. He glanced at his phone's screen for a second. "You look more like an Orion than an Orc."

"Is that good?" asked Jennifer. "What's an Orion? I don't think anyone has ever played one before."

"Entirely different thing," said Caspian. "They are the green, generally sexy, humanoids from Star Trek."

Jennifer immediately struck a pose, head slightly tilted and lips pursed. "Dave thinks I'm sexy," she said in a sing-song voice. "He wants to kiss me. Because I'm an Orion hot-ty." She frowned then snapped her fingers at the camera. "Hey! Rushing. I'm making fun of you. At least do me the courtesy of paying attention."

"Huh, sorry. Where the hell is Michael? This is all his fault."

"I'll text him," said Jennifer.

"What's his fault?" asked Caspian.

David brought his phone closer to his face. "My spending the next umpty-ump years in jail, that's what."

"Michael texted me back," said Jennifer. "Actually, he dictated it. Apparently, he's driving but will be home in two minutes. He says, and I quote, *Dave, don't get your knickers in a twist.*" Jennifer's eyes swept from David to Caspian. "Okay, what did I miss?"

"Dave's going to jail," said Caspian.

"Really?" snickered Jennifer, "why this time?"

"Not funny," spat David.

"Dude," began Caspian, "you need to chill. Have you watched the news? People are burning shit down in half a dozen cities and no one is going to jail. What could you have possibly done to—"

"I hacked the organ donor database," blurted David.

"You what?" yelled Jennifer and Caspian together.

"Hacked," repeated David. "I hacked the—"

"We heard you," said Jennifer, "We just didn't believe you, or at least I didn't. Cas?"

"No, I didn't believe him either."

"Yeah, well, I did it," sputtered David, "and now I'm going to be arrested, tried, convicted, and jailed." He loosed a somewhat panicked string of laughter. "Look at me. I can't go to jail. I'll be someone's Orion slave girl in jail."

"You are neither green enough or good looking enough," said Michael as his face resolved in one of the FaceTime squares.

David pointed at the screen. "This is your fault, man."

"What did I do this time?" laughed Michael.

"Did you convince our good natured, but weak willed friend Dave to hack the national organ donor database?" asked Caspian. Michael cringed, and Caspian lowered his face into one palm. "Dude, we were hammered at the beach. Why would you follow-up on an idea we devised when...we...were... hammered?"

"First of all, it was David-Boromir-Rushing there who formed us into a Fellowship of the Ring, not me. In addition, you are still an antisocial workaholic who is ignoring his family and friends, so ultimately, this is really your fault, Cas."

"My fault? I answered Dave's stupid FaceTime tonight, didn't I?" asked Caspian defensively. "I also responded to every one of the texts you guys sent me."

"Eventually," muttered Jennifer.

"I'm busy,"

"Have you even gone on a date?" asked Michael.

Caspian narrowed his eyes at the screen. "It's only been nine months, dude, and I'm hanging up."

"No, wait," cried David. "I'm freaking out here."

Caspian sighed. "Fine, what did you do, exactly."

"I found Lizzie's donation record, well part of it anyway. Organdonor.gov has some kind of automated security that should only have been on the super high-security sites, you know, like the Pentagon and such. Damn it," yelled David. "The forums never mentioned organdonor.gov as being hosted on high-security servers."

"Probably because it's relatively tiny and no one would ever think to hack it," sighed Caspian.

David's eyes widened. "Oh shit, it *is* tiny, well, at least by comparison." He slapped himself on his forehead. "I bet they're using a multi-tenant structure. Oh shit, for all I know, I *did* just hack into the Pentagon."

"Dave I need you to relax a minute," said Michael. "This is really not a big deal."

David laughed hysterically "Says the Jamaican drug cartel family member."

Michael cocked his head. "Okay, that was pretty random, and more than a little insulting. My family has sugar cane farms and a distillery, but sure, we're all drug kingpins."

"Guys, stop," said Jennifer. "Dave's clearly upset. Can you at least try to not be dicks for two minutes?"

"Fine," replied Michael. "We'll take this one step at a time. Dave, which country was your VPN connecting through?"

David's voice fell to barely a whisper. "I thought the VPN was connected, but it wasn't."

"Oh boy," said Michael and Caspian together.

Jennifer's eyes went to each of the three men in turn. Finally she said, "What just happened? What's a VPN?"

"It stands for Virtual Private Network," said Caspian. "It's software that's designed to—"

"Keep me out of jail," sputtered David.

"—to mask your IP address," continued Caspian, then said, "Jenny, an IP address is—"

"I know what an IP address is, Cas," snarked Jennifer. "If you haven't noticed, I'm still teaching all my students using Zoom. Which, in case anyone is interested, really sucks."

He frowned. "Sorry."

Michael held up both hands toward his camera in a calming gesture. "Dave, what makes you think they even detected a breach?"

"My connection went down, dude."

"Okay, and did you check to see if you can get to any other sites?"

"Of course I did."

"And?"

"Nothing," yelled Dave. "I think the NSA took down my Internet. The men in black are going to put me in a dark hole somewhere, I just know it."

"What's your zip code?" asked Michael.

Dave blinked several times. "What does that matter?"

"Humor me."

"Fine, it's 70112." Michael started typing on his laptop. After several seconds he shook his head. David groaned. "What were you checking? Were you looking up police dispatch notices? I'm going to be arrested, aren't I?"

"There's a dispatch notice all right," said Michael with a grin. "I'll read it to you. *Zip Code 70112. Cox Communications apologizes for any inconvenience, but we are performing maintenance in your area. You may experience intermittent service interruptions starting at 11:00 pm, and continuing until 6:00 am.*" David's image shifted as he clearly had slumped onto a couch or chair. Michael continued. "So, Dave, when did you start poking around the donor database?"

"Around 10:30," he sighed.

"And when did your Internet go down?"

Another sigh. "About 11:10."

"Which means—" lilted Michael.

"I'm not going to jail," replied David with a relieved sigh.

"No, you are not going to jail. So, Dave, now that we've averted that crisis, I have two questions. First, did you get the recipient list so we can actually start on Cas' quest?" Michael's eyes danced with amusement as he continued. "And second, why is Jen dressed up as one of your Star Trek sex fantasies?"

⌒⁄⁄⁀⁀⁀

Michael tapped on his keyboard. "Well, it's certainly more than we had this morning, I'll grant you that, but next time, Dave, can you try to get more than just a name and town?"

There was a long pause as everyone stared at their respective screens, then David laughed. "Next time, oh, there isn't going to be a next time."

"Sure there is," said Michael, "but next time, you are going to use a weapons grade VPN with an embedded kill switch."

"How is that different than the one Dave didn't use this time?" laughed Jennifer. "I'm no techy, but this whole debacle seems like user error on Dave's part. I mean if you don't turn something on, it can't very well do its job."

"This one's always on, once it's installed," said Michael. "It will also automatically disconnect if the VPN tunnel fails."

"Those things are ridiculously expensive," said David.

Michael shrugged. "I just bought a copy and sent you a download link. Don't worry, I used my family's cocaine, pot, and heroin money."

David shook his head. "I was panicked. I didn't mean anything."

Michael just waved away the other's apology, "I know. Don't worry about it."

"Cas," said Jennifer. "You've been awfully quiet."

"Hmm, oh. I was just thinking about this Thomas Whittaker guy Dave found in the donor record. Are we sure he's one of the..." he paused, "recipients?"

David nodded. "One hundred percent on that. I was literally in Lizzie's medical file. Thomas J. Whittaker of Peak South Carolina. That's the guy."

Caspian nodded. "But there could be dozens of Thomas Whittakers. How can you be sure that he's the one who—"

"I've got that, Cas," said Michael. "My family ships stuff all over the world. We've got insanely detailed shipping databases. While I'm not an adept hacker like Mr. Rushing, I can research the hell out of things. I'll find this Whittaker fellow, filter out any duplicates, and make sure he's our man." Michael saw David's expression, then added. "By-the-way, I wasn't giving you shit just now. You *are* an amazing hacker. So, you screwed up your VPN. Big deal. You're a game designer who moonlights as a white hat hacker. You're not used to being at risk for someone tracking you down. The fact that you managed to get in, get info, then get out in less than an hour…damn impressive, Dave. I mean it."

David tried hard to keep his expression even, then gave up and grinned. "I'm with Michael on this one," said Jennifer. "We've got our first quest, thanks to you Dave. When do we go?"

"This still feels like a huge invasion of privacy," murmured Caspian.

"That's probably because…it's a huge invasion of privacy," said Michael. "Fortunately, you don't get a vote on this Cas. The intervention is still operative. I'll get a firm ID on Thomas Whittaker, then we'll figure out when we go to Peak."

"And what if he doesn't like us poking around in his life?" asked Caspian.

"I don't see that happening," replied Jennifer. "I did a bunch of reading about this after our Florida trip. The most frequent request of donor recipients by far is the contact information for donor families. They almost never get it, but lots of recipients go to crazy lengths. Think about it, Cas, wouldn't you want to thank someone for saving your life?"

He slowly nodded. "I suppose, but we don't even know if Lizzie saved this guy's life."

"Whatever she did was something big, and I'll bet my green Orion ass that he's going to be one happy guy to see us."

Caspian watched as both Michael and David nodded in agreement. Finally, he shook his head and sighed. "I can see that I'm not going to win this argument." Three heads moved side-to-side in an almost choreographed motion. Caspian laughed despite himself, then said, "However, since it is now after one in the morning and I have to be brilliant in less than seven hours, I am going to bed. Say goodnight guys."

He was greeted with a chorus. "Good night, guys."

Chapter 14

ROAD TRIP

"If I lose my job over this, you guys are going to support me for the rest of my life," grumbled Caspian.

"Drama much, Cas?" snickered Jennifer. "You aren't going to lose your job. You're a consultant. You can consult again on Monday. While we're hanging out in this airport, my class is being taught by a substitute teacher who doesn't know Zoom from Zydeco. God knows what kind of shit-show I'll be coming home to."

"Yeah, but teachers never get fired," grumbled Caspian.

"I work in a private school. We get fired plenty." Jennifer looked up as David approached. "Why do you look like someone just shot your dog, Dave?"

"Flight's been delayed. Some kind of storm moving down the east coast. We won't be boarding for another hour."

"Maybe this is a sign," said Caspian. "I told you guys I wasn't interested in doing this. I'm fine. I don't need any more," he made air quotes, "closure."

David and Jennifer both stared at their friend. "Dude," began David, "You are about as far from *fine* as anyone I've ever met."

"Yeah," added Jennifer, "your apartment was disgusting when we came to pick you up this morning, and that's after my making allowances for you being a man. How many pizza boxes do you think were laying around there, Dave?"

"At least twenty," he said.

"Well, they're not there anymore," lilted Caspian.

"Oh I'm sorry, were you collecting them, or maybe planning to play a giant game of cardboard Jenga?" asked Jennifer incredulously. "Wait, I know. You were going to make a GI Joe fortress out of them. Cas, you're lucky I was there because Dave would have just let them sit and rot, further stinking up your apartment while we were in South Carolina."

"Most of the meats are smoked or salted on pizzas, so I don't think it would have technically rotted," said David. Jennifer flared her nose at him, and he hastened to add, "but it certainly would have attracted bugs and whatnot."

"I might need the bugs," grumbled Caspian. "That's all I will be able to afford to eat when I'm fired."

David pinched up his face. "McKinsey doesn't fire people, because if they did, that would mean they made a mistake in hiring them. All you consultant-types have way too big an ego for that." He shrugged. "They'll just wait for you to quit."

"We had interviews to conduct today, and I'm the guy who wrote the questions."

David plopped down beside his friends. "They'll live." He looked around at the Admiral's Club lounge, then asked. "So, do we get free drinks in here, or just you?"

"Everybody," grumbled Caspian.

"What about that buffet stuff over there?" asked David hopefully.

"That, too."

"Oh, I thought we had to pay for both of those," chirped Jennifer. "Come on, Dave. Let's live like rich consultants for the day."

David laughed. "After you, Miss Landry." He saw Caspian's dour expression, then asked. "Want us to bring you back something?"

"Not hungry," he replied.

"Okay, what about a sneak peek at the game I'm working on? I bet that will cheer you up." Caspian fixed his friend with a flat stare. David shrugged. "Fine, I thought you were a Mass Effect fan, but if you're not interested—"

Caspian reached up and grabbed Dave's arm as he started to follow Jennifer toward the buffet. "What are you talking about?"

David smirked. "Oh, did I get your attention with something?"

Caspian leaned forward. "You didn't tell me you were working on Mass Effect."

He shrugged. "You didn't ask, and I'm not just working on it, I'm the technical producer." David saw the hungry look in his friend's eyes, and said, "There might just be a proof-of-concept mission on my laptop. Of course I couldn't show it to you. Top secret stuff. Still, we've known each other a long time. It won't be my fault if you figure out my password while Jen and I are chowing down on free lounge food." David winked, then turned and left.

Caspian watched him leave, then saw Jennifer pointing animatedly at something on the buffet. He eyed David's leather messenger bag. "Screw it, I'm still pissed at my ending options from ME3," he grumbled to himself. "They better have retconned the shit out of it."

━◝◟◜◞◝◟◜━

"I brought you a coffee," said Jennifer. Caspian didn't respond. Instead, he continued staring at the laptop screen. "Earth to Cas." She waggled the cup. "Coffee..." Still nothing. "Hey, isn't that Dave's laptop?" Finally Caspian looked up, then slowly closed the computer's lid.

He reached toward her. Jennifer handed him the cup. "Thanks," he said.

"Sure...why are you acting weirder than usual?"

David drew up beside her, and affected surprise. "Oh no...someone figured out my password. I hope he hasn't seen anything he should not have. Whatever will I do?"

Jennifer stared at him. "You both are so strange. Dave, why are you talking like a robot?"

"He let me see a prototype of Mass Effect 4," said Caspian.

David immediately looked around. "No I didn't." He snatched the computer off Caspian's lap, hissed, "Stop, thief," then slipped it into his messenger's bag.

Jennifer frowned at both of them. "You know, my grandpa texted me yesterday. He said that if you don't find your spouse by twenty-nine, you're likely to spend your life alone. If you, two, are representative of my pool of options, I'm screwed." David stared at her a beat, then shook his head. "What?" she asked.

Caspian sighed. "Your grandpa's probably right. I found my wife, well almost wife. What are the odds, I'll find another?"

David mouthed, *Nice going*, to Jennifer. She winced.

Before she could respond, her phone rang. She glanced at it. "It's Michael. I better take this. He was on an earlier flight, and may not know ours has been delayed. I'll ask him to rent the car, then we can just have him pick us up when we get in. Sound good?" Caspian didn't look up. She caught David's eye. He made an *I got this* gesture. She nodded, then accepted the call, and walked away.

"So, what did you think of the demo?" David asked.

"Graphics look good," murmured Caspian.

"No shit, what about the characters? Were you surprised?"

"A little..."

"A little..." repeated David, "well, then I guess you won't want to see the rest of it, when it's done next week?"

Caspian focused on David, who then raised both eyebrows. "Oh yeah, there's more." He sat down. "Come on, tell me what you think."

Caspian sighed as a smile spread across his face. "I was psyched to see Mordin...did you guys get the same voice actor? I love the way Mordin talks."

"Yep, same guy," confirmed David. "What about Liara? She looks hot doesn't she?" Caspian shrugged. "I know you don't like blue chicks, Cas, but throw me a bone here. I asked the designers to really give it their all."

"She looked good," he shrugged. "I was always more of a Tali guy."

"Tali," sputtered David. "You never got to even see her face."

"Yeah," agreed Caspian, "but she was russian, adorable, and I loved her accent." He paused. "Will we get to see her face this time? I mean really see it, not just in some stupid stock photo on Shepherd's desk."

David held up both hands. "That stock photo fiasco was before my time, dude. Don't pin that shit on me."

"Fair enough," laughed Caspian, "But now *everything* is on you, so my question is this. Will we actually get to romance Tali without her mask?"

"*You* won't," laughed David. "You're always a female Shepard and Tali doesn't play for that team, brotha. Now, if you break your long standing tradition of only playing female characters, I might be able to nudge the team toward a maskless Tali encounter."

Caspian grinned. "Male Shep...here I come. When do you think the game will be—"

"Okay," interrupted Jennifer. "I've got everything sorted with Michael. He's going to pick up the car, then will meet us at the arrival-departure lane. I told him we should be landing around three. Since we don't have to go to baggage claim, I can't imagine we'll be any later than three-thirty."

Caspian and David stared at her in silence. She eyed them, then shook her head. "You two were talking about something naughty weren't you?"

Both men shook their heads, glanced at each other for a brief second, then said "Nope!"

Michael beeped the horn of his rental car, then stuck his hand out the window and waved. He had to beep twice more before Caspian noticed where he was parked. After several more minutes Caspian, David, and Jennifer all drew up beside the large sedan.

Jennifer laughed. "A Cadillac? Who are you, Tony Soprano?"

"Yeah, he's the head of the Jamaican mafia," snickered David. "C'mon, Tony, pop the trunk."

Michael shook his head as he thumbed a button on the key fob. "Very funny, you guys. Did any of you numb nuts actually find Peak on a map? We're going to be in the car for hours over the next couple days, and Cadillac's are very comfortable. I love their seats. Now shut up, and put your damned luggage in the trunk."

"Hey," said Caspian, "is there supposed to be a body in here? I think it might be Jimmy Hoffa's grandkid."

Michael closed his eyes and slowly began to count. "I hate every one of you."

"What did I do?" asked Jennifer.

"What did you...Jen, you started the whole thing."

"Did I?" she asked with feigned innocence. "That doesn't sound like me at all." She flashed a smile, then said, "I call shotgun."

About ten minutes later they pulled onto I385. Michael sighed, pushed a few buttons, then lowered his hands from the wheel. "What are you doing?" whispered Jennifer.

"I'm driving. What does it look like I'm doing."

She lowered the sun visor and pretended to look in the vanity mirror. Caspian and David were both huddled around his laptop, and grinning like idiots.

She turned toward Michael who continued to stare straight ahead, while resting his hands in his lap. "Hey doofus, put your hands on the wheel."

"Why? The Caddy has SuperDrive. As long as we're on the highway, it drives itself. Look, see how it just slowed us down when that car changed lanes in front of us?" he glanced at Jennifer. "Pretty cool, huh?"

Jennifer frowned. "And do you think Cas will find your self driving car magical or..." she leaned left, then hissed, "terrifying. Put your damn hands on the wheel."

"But it doesn't need——"

"On the damn wheel...now!" she growled.

"What's going on?" asked Caspian.

"Mom and dad are fighting again," snickered David.

"He should be so lucky," grumbled Jennifer, then gave Michael a satisfied smile as he made a show of pretending to steer the car.

"So, how long until we get to Peak?" asked David.

Michael glanced at the car's nav system. "About three hours, give or take. Which of you guys made the hotel reservation? I just plugged in a generic Peak address, so I'll eventually need to adjust it."

"Reservations, not reservation," corrected Jennifer with a low chuckle. "I am not sharing a room with you barbarians."

Michael laughed. "It's not like we haven't all seen women-parts before, Jen. Honestly, we're just not that into you."

"Easy black Casanova, what you haven't seen of me is spectactular, and I'm betting Dave has only seen 3D models of women, elves, and orcs."

"Hey..." objected David.

"Anyhoo," she continued, ignoring David's outburst, "I'm not worried about you guys perving. I have three brothers. I know what it's like to live with three boys under one roof. In addition, Dave and I just experienced Cas' pizza box tower of roach terror. I had to put up with my brothers. I do not have to put up with you. Besides, Cas has a gazillion points. I used them to get two rooms. You guys have two beds and a pullout sofa."

"So, where are we staying?" asked Michael.

"Well," began Jennifer, "Peak is about as rural as you get in South Carolina, so our options were somewhat limited."

"Uh oh," grumbled Michael. "That doesn't sound good."

"It's not too bad," she countered. "Three point nine stars. It's a Holiday Inn. Those are usually pretty good, right?"

"Does it have breakfast?" asked David.

She turned to grin at him from the front seat. "It does have breakfast, and not just muffins. It says full American breakfast."

David shrugged. "Okay. I'm good then."

"When are we supposed to be meeting this Thomas Whittaker guy?" asked Caspian, his voice taking on an anxious edge. Jennifer turned to face front, and no one said anything. Caspian took a deep breath. "Tell me one of you called him."

Jennifer slipped off her shoes and crossed her bare feet on the dash. "Did you guys know that Quentin Tarantino has a foot fetish?" She drew smudges on the windshield with both big toes.

Michael looked over, and shook his head. "Stop smudging, Jen. They may charge me for excessive foot smudges."

"That explains a lot," said David. "I remember there were a lot of bare feet in that last movie of his. What was it called, I forget?"

"It was the hollywood one," said Jennifer. "I don't remember the name either but one of the crazy Manson girls had her feet all over the dash, just like I'm doing. Hey, maybe I'm going to kill all you guys in your sleep."

"So," began Caspian, drawing out the word, "I take all this bantery bullshit to mean that none of you let Whittaker know that Fred, Shaggy, Velma, and Daphne were going to show up looking for my dead girlfriend's organ donation?"

There was a long silence, then Michael said, "I'm assuming you are Fred in this scenario. I guess that makes me Shaggy."

Jennifer wiggled her toes again. "I'm definitely Daphne, which means Dave is Velma."

"No I'm not."

"Would you rather be Scooby?" asked Michael.

Caspian snapped his fingers several times. "Seriously, what was the plan. Were we just going to show up? Jenny, you told me that you guys talked this through and had it all planned out."

She lowered the sun visor again, and locked eyes with Caspian in the mirror. "We *did* talk it through, Cas." She gave him a sheepish smile, "We just couldn't agree on a plan. *I* thought we should call ahead."

"Yeah, and I asked her what she would say to the guy," said Michael.

"That's were we got stuck," sighed David.

"Thomas Whittaker has a woodworking business," said Jennifer. "I looked it up. He makes really beautiful furniture, both on spec and custom. He's got a large warehouse kind of place where he sells stuff in the front and works in the back. Since it's a public business, I figured we would just kind of check the place out."

"Then what?" asked Cas.

"Then something good would happen?" she said, voice rising.

Caspian sank deeper into the Cadillac's plush leather seats and sighed. "Well, at least we'll have a full American breakfast to get us started. I'd hate to meet Mr. Whittaker with only a lousy muffin in me. Oh, and for the record, ensuring plans aren't as crappy as what you guys have come up with…that's what we consultants do. Next time, ask me, okay?" Caspian leaned his head against the window and closed his eyes.

Jennifer smiled, and saw Michael glance at her. He shook his head questioningly. She leaned over and whispered, "He said, *next time*. That's a good sign, right?"

Chapter 15

THOMAS WHITTAKER

It was a bit before noon when their Cadillac pulled into a parking space on the gravel covered lot. Caspian had been dozing with his head against the car's window after not sleeping more than a couple hours the night before. For some reason, he found the pops and scratches of gravel beneath tires to be comforting, but then the car rolled to a stop and everything became quiet. He opened his eyes to find Jennifer staring at him from the front seat. He glanced left. David offered a weak smile. Caspian sighed, then noticed a pair of eyes watching him from the rear view mirror. "Oh for Pete's sake, you guys," said Caspian, "I'm fine. What are you afraid's going to happen when I meet this dude?"

"Demi Moore kissed Whoopie Goldberg when it happened to her in *Ghost*," offered David. He looked around, but saw no signs of recognition. "Oh come on," he sputtered. "None of you have watched that movie?"

"Hang on a sec," said Caspian, then pulled out his phone and tapped on it. He looked up at David. "*Ghost* came out in 1990. None of us were even born then."

"Whatever you guys," said David. "So, my mom may have rented *Ghost* a few hundred times with me in the room. That's not the point. The point is we should be prepared for weird shit, you know, just in case."

97

"I'll be sure none of us cross the streams, Dr. Venkman," snickered Michael as he opened his car door.

Jennifer and Caspian both laughed. David shook his head in disbelief. "Oh, so *Ghostbusters* references, those you guys get. *Ghostbusters* came out way before *Ghost*."

"Yeah," said Jennifer, "but Bill Murray is a genius and *Ghostbusters* is a classic, not some gauzy chick flick."

The four of them circled around the car and clustered together. David frowned. "Jen, you do realize that you're a chick, right?"

"Apparently, not as much a chick as you are, Rushing," she replied with a laugh.

"Oh, snap!" said Michael.

"Fatality," intoned Caspian.

David shook his head. "Screw you guys."

A scraping sound drew their attention, and all four looked toward a large pair of doors as they swung outward. The, now open, warehouse appeared to be of rough, but sturdy construction. Several windows were cut into the wood log framing, through which could be seen all sorts of furniture ranging from armoires to bed frames. Two men, one in his early fifties and the other at least twenty years older, struggled to carry what looked to be part of a dining room table. The old man stumbled, causing his end of the table to tilt toward the ground. Caspian was closest to him, and jumped forward to grab the polished wood before it struck the parking lot's gravel.

"Holy crap that's heavy," said Caspian. He tried to adjust his grip, then inclined his head toward Michael and David. His friends immediately jumped in to help, each taking a different side of the table.

The old man stepped aside, while the other nodded gratefully, and said, "Thanks guys. Normally my son is here to help, but his wife just had their first baby so—"

"So, you're a newly minted Grandpa," huffed Caspian as they continued to carry the table toward a large pickup truck parked nearby.

"Yep, and I'd be loving up the little guy right now if I didn't have a day full of furniture pick-ups to deal with. I'm Thomas, by-the-way, Thomas Whittaker. This is my favorite customer Joe Humphrey."

Caspian felt his stomach twist. He tilted his head to try and get a better look at the man, but the brim of Caspian's baseball cap was blocking his view.

"I really appreciate you boys pitching in," said Joe. "I don't know what we would have done if you hadn't showed up when you did." He paused a moment. "Hey Tom, I'm going to let down the gate of my truck."

"Good idea, Joe. You remembered to bring the packing blankets this time, right?"

"No, but Martha did," laughed Joe. "She says I'd forget my head if it wasn't attached. I'll go lay it out so everything's ready when you guys make it there."

Thomas gave Caspian and his friends a nod. "Joe has singlehandedly put two of my kids through college."

"Just out of curiosity," said Michael, "why didn't Joe back the truck up to your warehouse?"

Thomas chuckled "An excellent question, uh..."

"Michael."

"An excellent question, Michael, and one I probably would have asked if I wasn't running around all day like a chicken with its head cut off."

"New babies can do that to men," offered Jennifer, then added, "I feel kinda useless. Is there anything I can do to help?"

Thomas twisted his head toward Jennifer's voice, but she was too far behind him to see. "Oh," he laughed, "how many of y'all are there?"

"Just four," said David. "We flew into Greenville from New Orleans last night."

Jennifer glanced down the driveway and saw Joe struggling at the back of his truck. "I'm going help him with those packing blankets." Jennifer jogged off toward the truck while the four men continued heading that way as well.

"Y'all aren't picking something up are you?" asked Thomas, as he adjusted his grip on the table. "Joe was the last one on my list, and I planned to close up, so I could head to the hospital."

Michael fixed his eyes on Caspian who just swallowed, but said nothing. David tilted his head toward the furniture maker. Finally, Michael said, "Uh, no we aren't picking up, sir. We heard about your work and just wanted to take a look."

There was a long pause, then Thomas said, "So, you came here to browse... all the way from New Orleans?"

"I read about you, I mean your woodwork," said Caspian haltingly. "I just have a few questions. It won't take long."

They had finally reached Joe's truck and David slid to one side to allow the table top to be put onto the padded bed. He moved next to Caspian and everyone pushed. "Holy cow, this thing is heavy," said David.

"Mahogany's like that," offered Thomas as they all gave it one final push. He looked up briefly, caught Joe's eye and motioned to him. "Come on back into the shop and help me gather up the legs. They're too heavy for an old man like you to handle alone."

"Like us you mean," laughed Joe, "you aren't far behind me."

Thomas called over his shoulder and toward Caspian. "I didn't get your name, son, but I'd be happy to talk with y'all on Monday."

"Uh, it's Caspian, Mr. Whittaker, but we're only here through the weekend."

"Caspian, huh. Interesting name. Hang tight, or come into the shop where it's warm. We'll work something out. I just want to be sure and head out before..."

Thomas' voice faded as he and Joe approached the warehouse. "What did he say?" asked Caspian.

"Something about heading out," replied Jennifer.

David cocked his head. "Cas, I don't think squinting is going to improve your hearing. It's cold as a witch's tit out here. Let's take the guy up on his offer, besides, then he'll have to kick us out rather than just close the door in our face." David tapped at his temple. "See, I'm always thinking."

"This place is adorable," gushed Jennifer. "I don't think I've ever seen so much wood in one place before." She bent down to examine a coffee table, then murmured, "I wonder if he ships things."

"We do," came a voice from behind her. Jennifer rose, then turned around to find a young woman smiling at her. "Hi, I'm Madison Whittaker."

Jennifer returned the smile. "Oh, so you must be—"

"The daughter, yep. Youngest of three and the last indentured servant. I'm sorry, I didn't mean to eavesdrop, if you were just talking to yourself."

Jennifer waved away Madison's concern while casting an eye left and right. "Huh," she murmured, "that's odd."

"You looking for the guys you came in with? They're around the corner by the wood burning stove. We have free coffee if you want some." Madison saw the look on Jennifer's face and laughed. "You weren't talking to yourself, were you?"

"Not intentionally," replied Jennifer, "but apparently my boys abandoned me." She extended her hand. "I'm Jenny. Nice to meet you. Your dad mentioned that his son wasn't here because he just had a baby. I assumed that meant he was alone."

"Nope, I come in on Saturdays to stain pieces and do fine detail work, engravings and such." She waggled her fingers, then pointed toward her temple. "Small hands and better eyes, you know."

Jennifer nodded. "Your dad has eye problems?"

Madison's perpetual smile faded for a moment, then returned as a more neutral expression. She sighed. "Some, but things are better now." She shook her head. "So, you want me to tell you about the coffee table. It's really cool, and you have excellent taste because all that detail work is mine."

"Uh, yeah, what kind of wood is it? I know it's not pine, but that's about as far as I go."

Madison laughed. "No, it's not pine. In fact, it's about as far away from pine as you can get. That coffee table is made out of one hundred percent ipe wood, which is—"

"Maddie?"

The young woman turned. "Over here, Papa. I'm just helping this lady out with the ipe coffee table."

"Okay," he replied. "As soon as you're done, please pack up your stuff. I want to get to the hospital. I'm just running these table legs out to Joe's truck, then I'll be ready to go."

"Uh, Papa, there are a bunch of guys looking at things over by the stove, too," but her father had already disappeared out the workshop's front door. She sighed. "Well, I guess you know that he just became a Grandpa. It's pretty much the only thing on his mind, right now." Madison grinned. "Of course, that makes me an Aunt. It's very cool, but don't worry, I won't let him rush y'all. The baby will still be there in thirty minutes, am I right? So..." Madison ran her hand along the coffee table's wood grain, "Ipe is one of the hardest woods on the planet. A lot of time folks use it to make fancy decks because it's almost indestructible. You can't even nail through it. Because it's so hard to work, my dad didn't want to make this coffee table, but I convinced him. It's all tongue and groove construction. You could put your feet on this thing for a hundred years and it won't make a scratch." Madison nodded to where she indicated Caspian and the others had gone, "If your boyfriend leaves a drink on it—"

Jennifer held up a hand. "Not my boyfriend, none of them. More like brothers."

"Even better," said Madison, shaking her head. "Brothers are the worst for putting cold drinks on wood without coasters. You'd think my two brothers would know better, growing up as we did, but no, they are just as oblivious. Anyway, ipe wood laughs at water rings. Jenny, let me ask you something, do you have an apartment or a house?"

"Apartment," replied Jennifer, "in New Orleans."

"Really, I've never been to New Orleans. It looks so romantic."

"It can be," agreed Jennifer, "they call it the aging courtesan of America, but the old girl's still got it."

Madison's brow furrowed. "Courtesan…isn't that another name for a," she lowered her voice, "prostitute?"

"Pretty much," said Jennifer, "but with what it costs to live in New Orleans, she gets to be called a courtesan. It's fancier."

"So, I bet your apartment is kinda small then," asked Madison.

"Tiny."

The young woman gripped one edge of the coffee table, then lifted. "You're going to love this. It's hollow." Jennifer's eyebrows went up. "I know, right," laughed Madison. "Extra storage, boyfriend and brother proof, and perfectly rustic for a city called the aging courtesan of America."

Jennifer shook her head. "Please tell me you are going into sales, Madison, and I hope your dad has you on commission."

The young woman beamed. "Thanks, but I'm more artsy than business'y. Still, you gotta eat, right? So, if you want to buy it today, I can ship it to you for free. Normally, that would be about a hundred and twenty dollars."

Michael walked up a moment later, with David trailing slightly behind. He flashed a quick smile to Madison, then turned to Jennifer. "Whatcha doing, Jen?"

"Apparently," she replied with a final glance at the price tag, "I'm buying a coffee table."

"Really, well congratulations that's quite a commitment for you." He winked at Madison. "Jen doesn't have a whole lot of furniture, and none of it is nice." He held out a paper cup filled with a light brown liquid. "Just as you like it, one can't even call it coffee anymore, mostly just cream and sugar."

Jennifer accepted the cup. "Very funny."

Madison's eyes swept from Jennifer to Michael and back again. "Brother, huh? My brothers never bring me coffee…just sayin'." Jennifer almost spit out her first sip. Michael turned to David, but he simply shrugged in confusion. Madison extended her hand to the somewhat bewildered Michael. "Hi, I'm Madison. I love your accent. Where are you from?"

"Jamaica, and I like yours as well."

She shrugged. "I have an accent?"

David laughed. "Yeah, you do."

"Don't mind my friend," sighed Michael, "he's an idiot and your accent is quite lovely."

Madison blushed. "Thanks." She looked around. "Weren't there three of you?"

"Yeah, Cas was checking out some wood and leather trunk near the stove and coffee."

"Is Cas short for Castiel, like in the show *Supernatural?*"

Jennifer shook her head. "No, but he gets that a lot."

"And he hates it," chuckled Michael.

"His real name is Caspian."

"Oh, like the prince from Narnia."

Michael pointed. "Now that reference he *does* like. Prince Caspian!"

"You speak of the devil and he shall appear," said Caspian, then poked Michael in the ribs. "This place is awesome. I think I might want to buy that trunk, but couldn't find a price tag on it."

Jennifer laughed. "Go get him, Madison. There's blood in the water."

Caspian smiled at the young woman, and extended his hand. "Madison is it? Hi, I'm Caspian." She didn't move. "Uh, are you okay?" he asked. "You're looking kind of green about the gills all of a sudden."

Madison sucked in a ragged breath. "Di-did my dad see you?"

Caspian shared a look with his friends, then said, "Yeah, we helped him carry out a dining room table."

"But you were wearing that stupid hat," said David, then held it up. "You left it on a chair back there, by-the-way."

Jennifer moved toward the young woman, and gently touched her shoulder. "What is it, Madison?"

She pointed at Caspian, and shook her head. "I've seen your face. I've...I've touched your face."

Caspian raised a calming hand, but Madison stepped back. "Okay," he said lowering it. "I don't know what you mean, but," he smiled, "maybe I just have one of those faces."

"Maddie," said Thomas as he approached from the store front, "are you all packed up? I really want to get to the——" The elder Whittaker fell silent.

Madison slipped her arm around his waist, as the two stared at Caspian. "Papa, it's him. It's the man you've been seeing. Don't try and tell me it's not. I've etched his face a dozen times."

Thomas nodded. "That you have, baby girl, and you're right. It's him." Thomas' eyes washed over the four friends who had unconsciously moved toward each other. They all stared back with a mixture of confusion, concern, and alarm. Finally, Thomas said, "This may be a strange question, but does the name Elizabeth Winters mean anything to you?"

Chapter 16

A WOODWORKERS GIFT

Madison Whittaker paced back and forth, with her mobile phone pressed hard against one ear. "No, Mama, I don't understand it either. I've told you everything I know." She shook her head. "For the fifth time, it doesn't look *kind of like* the carvings. It looks *exactly* like them." She sighed in apparent frustration. "I don't know, Mama, but his friends are here. I'll ask them. No, he's talking with Caspian in the back room. Well, that's where the carvings are, so that's where Papa took him. Yes, of course. I'll have him call you as soon as he comes out. No, I don't think you should tell them. They should focus on the baby. Right. Yes, mama, I will. Okay. I need to go. I will. I love you too."

Madison tapped her phone, stared at it for a beat, then slipped it into her back pocket. She smiled at Jennifer, Michael, and David. "That went well, don't you think?"

Michael and David shared a look, while Jennifer cringed slightly. "I'm sorry," she said. "We thought about calling ahead of time, but—"

Madison arched an eyebrow. "Thought it might be weird to lead with, *excuse me, you don't know us, but we've stolen private health information that has led us to believe you recently received two corneal transplants from our friend's dead fiancé.*"

"Somehow," muttered David, "It actually sounds worse when someone else says it out loud."

Madison eyed him. "So, you must be the hacker, then." David gave an apologetic shrug, and the young woman continued. "I figured it was you. You're the nerdiest of the bunch."

Jennifer covered her mouth to keep from laughing. David glared at his friend, then turned back to Madison, "Hey, that's not entirely—"

She interrupted him. "It's not a bad thing. I like nerdy guys. My boyfriend is a total nerd." She lowered her voice and fake whispered, "Everyone knows the nerdy boys make bank, and since I plan to be the artist in my family, someone has to make money."

"I'm not a nerd, and I make a decent living," chuckled Michael.

"Fallacy of logic," countered Madison. "I learned that during SAT prep. All nerds make bank, but not all those who make bank are nerds." She shrugged and pointed at Michael. "That said, you're still a bit of an anomaly."

"So, what's in that back room?" asked Jennifer. "You mentioned to your mother something about carvings."

Madison nodded. "My dad had been on the cornea donor list for over a year. He finally had the transplant operation about six months ago. By that time, he was legally blind. He could see light and shadow, but not a whole lot else. Anyway, within a few days of the surgery, he started getting these weird…I'd guess you'd call them visions. It really freaked us out." Madison sighed. "My mom was worried something happened to him during the operation, you know, anesthesia stuff. When he was cleared from that, she and my brothers wanted him to go see a shrink. My dad didn't want to. He said he was fine, but kept having these flashes. He said it was like watching the movie of someone else's life. Anyway, since everyone in my family was going one way, I decided to go the other, and just be accepting of whatever he was experiencing. We talked for hours about what he saw. Finally, I suggested he describe the visions in detail so I could sketch them. That's how I did the board etchings stacked up in the back room. Papa did the bust himself, but that was of her, not Caspian."

Michael shook his head. "Hold on, what? Your dad was having visions of Elizabeth, too?"

"Not at first. Initially it was just Caspian. That's who I drew and etched into about twenty different boards, all different angles of the same face, your friend's face. My father would run his fingers over them after. As I said, almost everyone thought he was going nuts." She sighed. "Even I started to wonder, especially when he began to see…Elizabeth. My mother really didn't like him carving the bust of a young woman, that's for sure."

"There's a bust of Elizabeth in there?" asked Jennifer, pointing toward the closed door.

Madison shrugged. "No idea. I don't know what Elizabeth looks like. All I can tell you is that my father got obsessed with these visions he kept having of a twenty-something blonde woman. One night, he asked me to take him to the shop. He went into that back room and stayed there for hours. When he came out, he seemed better. I went in to look around. There was a wooden bust of a woman, freshly carved on his workbench."

"Did you take a picture of the statue?" asked David.

"It's just a bust," corrected Madison, "but yeah." She fished her phone out of her pocket, and started swiping. Without looking up, she asked, "Do you guys have any pictures of Elizabeth." There were murmurs of assent from all three, as each reached for their own phones. Madison glanced up, and waited while the others looked for a picture to show.

Jennifer was first. Madison held out her phone, and she watched as, first recognition, then tears appeared in the other woman's eyes. "That's Lizzie," Jennifer whispered, then held her own phone out to Madison.

"Oh my God," whispered the young woman, then looked up to see Michael and David each displaying different pictures on their phones. Madison shook her head. "She's so beautiful."

"She was," whispered David.

"Inside and out," said Michael.

Jennifer just rubbed at her nose, and nodded.

"I'm so sorry, you guys," said Madison. "I don't even know what to say. I mean, my father had something called Fuchs' dystrophy. He would have stayed blind without the transplant surgery. For us, it was an answer to prayer, but for you—" She shook her head, then made an expansive gesture to indicate the workroom. "Everything you see around us, he did since getting his sight back."

"It's okay," said Michael. "We are in completely uncharted waters here, and that was before hearing that your dad was having visions of Lizzie and Cas. We just came to help him get some closure. He's been a wreck."

"I can't even imagine," murmured Madison.

David had been shaking his head in silence, finally Jennifer lightly slapped his arm. "Stop that, you look like a bobble head doll. What's the matter with you?"

"What's the matter with me? Are you kidding? Am I the only one who is freaked out that Cas' dead fiancé has been haunting people who received donated body parts?"

"Is your neat little atheist world starting to crumble?" taunted Michael.

"No, it's not starting to—"

"What do you mean, people?" asked Madison. "Who else have you met with?"

"Poor choice of words," said Jennifer. "You're the first stop. We don't have any other names because Dave, I mean whoever hacked the donor database, only got your dad's info."

"But you *are* going to meet other people who, uh, received gifts from Elizabeth."

"Interesting choice of words," said Michael, "but that's the plan unless this one visit heals whatever Lizzie's death broke inside Caspian, which I highly doubt."

"Wow, you are really good friends to him. He's lucky to have y'all." Madison turned toward the closed door, and sighed. "I really wish I knew what was going on in there."

"Me too," said the others, all at once.

Caspian rubbed his temple with one hand as he stared in silence at the bust Thomas had carved. The likeness was uncanny. He shifted to look at it from a different angle, and felt his breath catch as the eyes seemed to follow him.

"I'm sorry," whispered Thomas for at least the third time.

Caspian shook his head. "Don't be." He reached out, ran a finger down the carved cheek of the bust, and whispered, "I just don't understand any of this."

Thomas sighed. "I didn't either, well, until about thirty minutes ago, when I caught sight of you." The woodworker rubbed at his chin. "You see, Caspian, I've never carved a darn thing in my whole life. I mean, I've whittled a bit and maybe carved a few rough toys for my kids..." he gestured to the bust, "but this...never."

"How did it happen?" asked Caspian.

Thomas shrugged. "At first, it was just vivid dreams. They started almost immediately after the surgery. My eyes were still bandaged, but I woke each morning with..." he pointed at the statue, "that face in my mind. I didn't really think much about it. My doctor said vivid dreams sometimes occur after general anesthesia. She said the dreams would pass. They didn't. In fact, once the bandages came off, they only became more vivid and intense. Then they started happening during the day. I'd be working on a project, and it was like a flash of lightning, but not really." Thomas shook his head. "It's so hard to explain. You know how, during a storm, there's a bolt of lightning and everything around you becomes bright as day for just a second?" Caspian nodded. "It's like that, except that instead of being surrounded in light, I became surrounded by hundreds of images."

"Images," said Caspian, "images of what?"

Thomas pointed. "Images of her, at first. They were all a jumble, lots of different ages from child to adult, yet somehow I knew it was the same person. Then, a couple weeks ago, I started seeing a new face." The woodworker nodded at Caspian. "Your face. I couldn't carve it like I did hers." He gestured to the bust. "I did that with my eyes closed. Maddy did all the other carvings. I'd sketch them into scraps of wood throughout the day, and she'd carve them in the evenings." Thomas took a deep breath, then slowly let it out. "Was Elizabeth your wife, son?"

Caspian felt his heart wrench within his chest. "Almost," he whispered. "We were engaged."

"It was a car accident, wasn't it?" asked Whittaker.

"Yeah. My fault, too. There was a storm. A bad one, and I shouldn't have been on the road." Tears filled Caspian's eyes as he stroked Elizabeth's statue. The wood felt warm beneath his fingers. "I didn't even get to say goodbye. I don't know if she was scared, or in pain, or called out to me." He shook his head, then stared at Thomas. "I don't know anything. I just woke up, and she was gone."

Thomas wiped at his eyes, then covered his mouth. He sat quietly for quite some time, then seemed to make a decision. "She wasn't in pain, Caspian."

"What? How do you know that?" He reached out to the woodworker. "Did she talk to you? Did my Lizzie talk to you? Can you—"

"No," interrupted Thomas. "It's not like that. She doesn't come to me. She's not..." he paused, gathering his thoughts. "She's not a ghost or anything like that, Caspian. What I experience isn't so much a visitation as a vision. I think I'm seeing things that Elizabeth either saw or that she experienced in a way that she then translated into images."

"I don't understand," said Caspian.

Thomas sighed. "I really don't either, and the explanation I just gave you isn't a very good one. What I can say for certain is that I saw you, in the car, after the accident. The images I saw also conveyed emotions, Elizabeth's emotions. She was scared, Caspian, but not for herself. She was scared for you. She saw you unconscious and covered in blood." Whittaker touched his forehead, then pointed at the same spot on Caspian. "You had a head wound?" Caspian nodded. "Concussion?" Another nod. "Yeah, she knew that, somehow. I remember an earlier vision where she saw herself in a mirror with a stethoscope around her neck." Thomas rubbed at his face with both hands then shook his head.

"There's something else, isn't there?" asked Caspian, "Tell me."

Whittaker chewed at his lip for a moment then said, "You asked if she was scared and I said not for herself, but that's not completely true.   Elizabeth didn't know how badly she was hurt, or at least I received no impression that she did.   I did get fearful impressions of her living a life without you." The woodworker reached out and laid a hand on Caspian's. "The prospect of that future is the only sense of fear I picked up."

"And now that's my reality," whispered Caspian. "Every, single, day."

"I think your reality is more than that," said Thomas. "Something miraculous is happening here. I mean, how did you even find me?"

"That's not a miracle," murmured Caspian, "that's just some twenty-first century hackery. One of my friends hacked the donor database." He shrugged. "Sorry Thomas, no miracle."

"Maybe not in the finding of me, but definitely in my recognizing you. Caspian, I've seen things that are impossible to explain." He narrowed his eyes at the young man in front of him. "And I think you have, too."

"Yeah," he said. "I have. She came to me too, but not like how you describe it.   It was in dreams, twice so far. My friends think I'm delusional, but I'm telling you, Elizabeth came to me. She talked to me. She sent me on this…" he waved his hands around, "…quest. Sounds ludicrous, I know."

"I was blind," said Thomas, "and now I see. A hundred years ago, that would have sounded ludicrous. For what it's worth, your friends don't think you're delusional."

Caspian barked a mirthless laugh. "You don't know them like I do."

"I don't have to," countered the woodworker.   "I know they are with you, here, today. I also know that the woman who gifted me back my sight, had a love for you that was stronger than death." Thomas reached up and gripped Caspian's shoulder until the younger man focused on him. "I saw you through her eyes. If, as you say, she's placed you on a quest, then it's because she loves you and wants something good for you." He sighed. "Look, I'm just an old furniture maker. The most miraculous thing I've ever encountered beyond the birth of my children is a tung sliding perfectly into its matching groove. So, take what I say next with that in mind, but I think you should embrace the task

Elizabeth has given you. Caspian, the woman you love has literally crossed over from death to deliver a message." He shrugged. "I think you might just want to heed it."

"She said I'd see her again, if I did."

Thomas' eyes grew wide. "If you did what?"

"I'm not completely sure, but I think she wants me to meet the other two people who..." Caspian made air quotes, "received her gifts. She said if I did, I'd see her one more time after that."

Whittaker smiled for the first time since they sat down together. "Well, son, if that's what she said, then I only have one question for you." Caspian arched an eyebrow, and Thomas rose, then extended a hand. "What the heck are you still doing here?"

Chapter 17

REVELATIONS ON THE ROAD

"Are we going to sit in complete silence the entire way back to New Orleans?" asked David.

"It's been, maybe, thirty-minutes," replied Jennifer. "Don't you have some kind of illegal hacking to do?"

"I haven't agreed to anything, Jen. I'm the one who goes to jail, not you."

Michael glanced in the review mirror until he got David's attention. "We know how to be more careful, now. You worry too much, Dave."

The young programmer shook his head. "There's that word again, *we*. As I just said, it won't be *we* who are incarcerated."

"How about if I put in writing, that I hired you to do it," sighed Michael. "That way I'd be an accomplice. Hell, I'll even send you an e-mail extorting you." His voice lowered, and took on an ominous tone. "David Rushing. I have pictures of you binging *Twilight* and reading fan fiction. If you don't hack the national donor database again, I'm going to release it to the Times Picayune."

Jennifer started laughing. "What kind of accent were you trying to pull off Michael? You sounded like some weird Jamaican mafioso."

"I thought it was pretty good, actually," he replied. "What do you think, Cas?"

Caspian had been staring out his window. At the sound of his name, he turned. "Huh? Sorry, I was kind of zoned out. What do I think about what?"

"About whether my dangerous accent is good, and whether Dave is a pussy."

"Well," sighed Caspian, "like I said, I wasn't paying attention, but if past is prologue, I'd say *no* and *yes*, respectively."

"Boom!" yelled Jennifer, then started pumping both hands in the air while rocking from side-to-side. "Cas gives a two-for-one slap down."

He turned partway around and gave her a wink, then said, "Just out of curiosity, why was Michael pretending to be dangerous and what did Dave do that made him a pussy…this time."

"Screw you, Cas," murmured David.

"He's waffling on hacking the donor thing again," said Jennifer, "Oh, and Michael pretended to threaten him."

Caspian nodded. "Ahh, then I'm with Dave on this one. I don't think we should poke around in that database anymore."

"Whoa," came a chorus from all three of his friends, then David added, "Dude, I did *not* say we shouldn't pursue it. I just said I didn't want to get caught and go to jail. We definitely should pursue it. I mean, this is like the first, and only, paranormal event I've ever experienced in my entire life."

"Same," said Jennifer, "but that wasn't the reason for my *whoa*. Cas, we have definitive proof that Lizzie has contacted you after…" Jennifer paused a moment, and lowered her voice to a whisper, "…after her death."

"And," said Michael, "we also have proof that the gifts she told you about are the organs she donated."

"We don't know that for sure," argued Caspian.

"Dude, are you being stupid right now?" asked David. "Since I'm the guy doing the hacking, trust me, I'm not the biggest advocate of this plan. However, let's call a spade a spade here. Lizzie appeared in two dreams, and talked to you about finding these mysterious gifts. Thomas Whittaker got a cornea transplant. He started having visions of both you *and* Lizzie, then carved a statue so realistic that if you sprinkled it with pixie dust, I think the damn thing would come to life."

"Yeah, and you almost left it there, you dumb idiot," said Michael shaking his head.

Jennifer flicked his ear. "Shut it you. I understand why looking at that bust is hard for Caspian right now. I even understand why he wanted to leave it behind, but, Cas, someday it's going to be one of your most treasured possessions. You can quote me on that!"

Silence filled the car like it was a fifth passenger. Finally, Caspian sighed. "What if it goes really wrong next time?"

Jennifer leaned forward as far as her seatbelt would allow. She draped her arms over Caspian's seat. "What do you mean?"

"I mean what if it goes really wrong. Thomas Whittaker was freakishly cool about this whole thing, as was his daughter. What if the next person gets pissed, or just is really put off. I can't imagine anything more personal or intimate that me wandering up and saying, *hey, you have my dead fiancé's kidneys and I was wondering if we could chat for a few minutes.*"

"Wait," said David, "when did we find out that Lizzie donated her kidney?"

"He was just giving an example, Dr. Einstein," chuckled Michael. "Remember, one of the records was redacted. We won't know what all three are until you hack the database again, which you are going to do."

Jennifer saw the look on David's face. She reached over and gave his thigh a friendly pat. "There, there, little one. Don't be afraid. If anything happens, I'll be sure to bring you a cake with a file baked inside."

"Hardy frakking har," replied David, then chewed on the side of his cheek. "What is it, now?" lilted Jennifer.

"Well, I'm just kinda curious, but am not sure if I should ask. You guys know how I sometimes ask things that are inappropriate?"

"Yes," said everyone at once.

"Thanks," David grumbled.

Michael flashed a smile into the rearview mirror. "You're among friends, Dave. Say what you want. It can't be worse than the *Lorraine* incident."

"Oh dear God," muttered Caspian. "The Lorraine incident. I almost forgot about that."

"You didn't forget it, Cas," laughed Jennifer. "You suppressed it just like the rest of us did. Still, you guys didn't have to live with her after. She was *my* roommate at the time."

"How was I supposed to know she wasn't pregnant?" sputtered David. "She *looked* pregnant."

Michael shook his head from the front seat. "I told you at the time, unless you're an OBGYN, you never ask that question."

"Even then," chuckled Caspian, "best to wait for the ultrasound."

"Well, now I'm definitely not going to ask my question," said David, then crossed his arms petulantly.

"Oh, don't be a baby," laughed Jennifer. "Ask."

"Yeah," added Caspian, "think of us as the sounding board you use to avoid situations like—"

"The Lorraine incident," said everyone at once.

"Fine," blurted David, "but remember you guys encouraged, me. I was just wondering what Lizzie's vision-ghost looked like. I mean old people sometimes look young, but she was already young. Then there was the car accident and—"

"Okay, maybe we were wrong—" called Michael from the front.

"No, it's okay," interrupted Caspian. "In fact, answering questions is the least I can do for you guys taking so much time out of your lives to quasi-abduct me, remove my ability for self determination, and generally sap my will to live." Silence descended for a brief moment. Caspian laughed. "I'm just kidding. You haven't sapped my will to live…at least not yet." He pulled down the sun visor and opened the vanity mirror so he could see David's reflection. "As I've said, she wasn't a ghost, Dave. She didn't actually visit me. I just saw her in a dream. I think what confused you was that she said I *would* actually see her in the real world, or as she called it, the waking world."

"Yeah, I didn't get any of that from what you told us earlier, Cas," said Michael.

"I'm with them," added Jennifer.

"So is she a ghost or not a ghost?" asked David. "I'm confused."

"What does it matter," asked Michael, "or do you want to hit her up for some lotto numbers?"

Caspian sighed. "I talked with Thomas Whittaker about this for a good bit. What happened with him was nothing like what I experienced. For him, it was like watching an old fashioned slideshow with interspersed movie vignettes. He said there was never any sound, and she never seemed to be speaking directly to him. In fact, whenever Lizzie wasn't alone, she was talking with me. I think some of what Thomas saw were her daydreams too."

"Really?" asked Jennifer. "What makes you say that?"

There was a long pause, then Caspian said, "Thomas saw our wedding."

"Oh Cas…" she murmured then moved to try and grip his left shoulder. The seatbelt wouldn't let her reach, so Caspian extended his right hand over his shoulder. She squeezed it.

"No," he said, "It's okay. In fact, it was kinda cool to hear him describe it. I mean Lizzie obviously told me about some of the things she wanted, but, wow, did she give Thomas *all* the details. He remembered them too, down to the cathedral decorations, my lifting the veil, the honeymoon suite before we left for Bermuda, the works." Caspian gave a half-hearted laugh. "Thomas said it's every man's dream to have a woman look at him the way Elizabeth looked at me in his visions." Caspian released Jennifer's hand and scrubbed at his eyes.

"Anyway, it was completely different when I saw her. She talked to me. She told me things that I could never have told myself."

"Huh?" asked Michael. "You lost me on that one."

"I accused her of being a delusion," sighed Caspian.

"What?" sputtered Michael. "You never do that to ghosts. They hate that shit."

"How would you know?" spat David.

"I'm from Jamaica," he said as if that explained everything. Michael quickly glanced around the car. "You guys are spoiled by me. Yes, I'm both handsome and sophisticated, but that doesn't mean I haven't seen my share of spiritual shit I can absolutely not explain. Jen, remember that voodoo shop we all went to in the French Quarter?"

"How could I forget. You idiots thought I needed to buy..." she made air quotes, "love potion #9."

"Right, that place. Oh, and you certainly should have used that potion, because the guy you were hot for at the time...what was his name?"

"Samuel," she sighed.

"Yeah, Samuel. You needed some love potion #9 to land that cat. He was so damn pretty I was about to ask him out. Anyway, that was not my point. My point was, think back about that voodoo shop."

"It creeped me out," mumbled David.

"I think it creeped us all out," said Caspian.

"Not me," countered Michael. "And do you know why?" He didn't wait for an answer. "It didn't creep me out because I grew up surrounded with all that stuff. I'm not saying it works. I'm also not saying it doesn't work. I'm saying, people *think* it works, and that's some powerful mojo just in itself."

"Is there a point hidden in there, somewhere?" asked Caspian.

"Yes there is a freaking point, Cas. You do *not* tell ghosts or visions of ghosts, that you don't believe in them!"

"I just said I thought she was a delusion."

"Which is even worse, especially after all the work she did to come and give you a message. Very rude, man."

"Okay, I'm an asshole," Caspian said with a shrug. "What do you want from me? I've already admitted that she couldn't have been a delusion because she knew things I couldn't have told myself...hence...not a delusion."

"You're lucky she didn't go all wet hair draped over her face angry, and scare the living shit out your disbelieving ass," said Michael. "You know, I hardly ever say stuff like this, but damn white people are a special kind of stupid when it comes to ghosts."

"Whittaker called it a vision," corrected David.

Michael glared into the mirror. "Whatever. Do you three remember when we watched the remake of Amityville Horror?"

"Yes," everyone groaned.

"Groan all you like, but the first time my house said, *geeetttt ouuuttt,* do you know what I would do? I would get the hell out. You people, you start checking out rooms, and grabbing steak knives. I mean what the hell is a steak knife going to do for you? It's a damn ghost."

"You are sounding a lot less Jamaican and a lot more Eddie Murphy right now," said David.

"He's stealing shamelessly," sighed Caspian, "but he's not wrong. Anyway, since we completed the first leg of Lizzie's quest, maybe I'll get another dream-vision. If I do, you guys will be the first to know."

Jennifer reached over and mussed David's hair, "And while you are dreaming, our intrepid hacker will be finding where we go next, right intrepid hacker?"

David's shoulders slumped in apparent defeat. "Yeah, I guess so."

"Good," said Michael, then pointed over his shoulder toward Caspian. "And what *won't* you be doing when next you are visited by a loving spirit."

"I won't tell her she's a delusion," murmured Caspian.

"No you will not!" agreed Michael. "He glanced at his navigation screen. Hey, there's a Waffle House on the next exit. Who's up for—"

"Me!" came shouts around the car.

Michael tapped the brakes, then clicked on his right blinker. "Scattered, smothered, and covered, here we come."

Chapter 18

A HOME FOR SARA

"Are you sure this is the right address?" asked Jennifer.

David tapped the screen of his car's navigation system. "It says we have arrived at our destination."

Jennifer stared at the nineteenth century garden district home. Its facade had a tetra-style, three-level entry porch with four round columns and ornamental iron grillwork. The first level columns were crafted in the Ionic order while the second and third level columns were Corinthian. To the right lay a hexagonal wing that included an elegant stained glass window. Above the third floor porch rose a stylized dormer with twin arched windows and a small steepled roof. Jennifer's eyes were drawn to the house's natural wooden slats, which sported what looked like fresh, white paint that spoke volumes about the care with which the elegant home had been maintained. "It's beautiful, but why on Earth would Michael buy a place like this?" she murmured.

"Because he's rich and wanted to buy himself a groundhog's day present," laughed David.

Jennifer turned and frowned at him. "He's *been* rich a long time, or at least his family's been rich a long time...all that Jamaican rum and sugarcane money." She gestured to the house. "He had an awesome condo downtown. Also, less than two weeks ago, we were together for how many hours during our South Carolina road trip? He didn't mention any of this."

Before David could answer someone tapped on his window. A large bald man wiped his face with a cloth, and smiled. "Hey buddy, I'm going to need you to move your car. When we back the trailer out, it would likely clip it. Can you back up just a little?"

"Oh, you guys are movers?"

The man cocked his head, then pointed at the *Crescent City Moving Company* badge on his work shirt. "We've got Mr. Thompson and the missus all squared away, but my crew and I are really hungry, so if you wouldn't mind backing up a bit, we'll be on our way. You can pull right up after us. Your friend has a really nice driveway. Pretty uncommon for this part of town too." He gave David's roof three quick pats, said, "Thanks, have a good one," then turned and walked toward the idling van.

David slipped his car into reverse, then backed up several car lengths. He turned to Jennifer. "Uh, did my brain glitch or did that dude just refer to Michael's wife."

"I heard it too," she replied softly, "So, either there's a glitch in the whole matrix in addition to your brain, or something crazy is going on." Jennifer opened her window and craned her neck out. "I wish those guys would hurry up and leave."

David furrowed his brow. "Why? What's the rush?"

She stared at him, eyes wide. "What's the rush? You are such a man, Dave. I know the guys bust your balls about your not being one, but that last question just proves the point. You *are* definitely a man."

"Great, Jen, thanks for affirming my *Y* chromosome, but what does it, or my testicles, have to do with your rushing the movers."

She shook her head. "Okay, Dave, listen up because I'm going to grant you insights into the female mind, or as Cas' dad would say, *a pearl of great price.* Are you ready for my pearl, Dave?" He gave her a flat expression. "I'll take that as a yes. Okay, here it is. One of my three best guy-friends has moved into a palatial, if obviously haunted, mansion-house. A move he never mentioned except briefly in a group text where he described it as..." she made finger-quotes, "changing venues a bit. An 1800s haunted house is not changing venues a bit, Dave. It's changing lifestyles. Also, as you mentioned, Michael apparently has a wife, that he failed to mention. A wife, Dave."

"Okay, I see your point. It's a little strange he didn't mention it, but maybe there's a reason. Maybe he got drunk in Vegas and Elvis married them. Maybe she's pregnant with his love child. Maybe——"

120

Jennifer pressed a finger to his lips. "That's my point. We don't know. I need to know, Dave. I need to know, right now. You want to talk chromosomes, okay. Both my *Xs* are screaming in my head right now. In fact, screw this, I'm getting out and—"

"Oh my God, relax a second," laughed David. "They are pulling out. If you try to hoof it up that hill, I'll beat you to the front door." He grinned at her, "Then, my *Y* chromosome will know what's what before either of your *Xs*."

Jennifer pointed at the back of the moving van as it pulled onto the street. "Go…driveway…now!"

⌒⁀⟨⟨⟩⟩⌢

"Surprise!" said Michael as he answered the door. He and David gripped each other's hands then bumped shoulders. Jennifer breezed past them and into the foyer. "Sure, Jen, come on in. Make yourself at home," chuckled Michael. She continued into the house looking this way and that but said nothing. He turned to David. "What's up with her?"

"I think you're in trouble," replied David, "but I'm not exactly sure why. Apparently, it has to do with chromosomes."

Michael pinched up his face as the two of them walked inside and he closed the door. "What are you talking—"

"Who's Sara?" asked Jennifer.

The two men looked at her as she stood facing the foyer with her hands on her hips. "I think you're right, Dave," began Michael. "I think I *am* in trouble."

"I told you," he agreed.

"Sara?" asked Jennifer.

"What about her?"

Jennifer started pointing at various boxes. "Sara—bedroom. Sara—personal items. Sara—bathroom. Who. Is. Sara? Did you get married by Elvis without telling me?"

"He didn't tell me, either," said David.

"Everything isn't about you, Dave," huffed Jennifer. She stared at Michael expectantly.

He started laughing. "Damn, girl. This really got your knickers in a twist didn't it?" He made a point of placing one finger aside of his chin. "Sara… Sara…the name does ring a bell. Now, where did I hear that name?" He shrugged. "Oh, I'm sure it will come to me. You guys want a beer? I need to give a you a tour of the house. The back porch is amazing and the place has a huge yard."

"It looks haunted," offered David, "but, sure, I'll have a beer."

"It's not haunted. We covered my complete intolerance for haunted houses on the way back from LizzieQuest, part one. Come on. I'll show you the kitchen, we'll drink the beers on the porch, then I'll give you the nickel tour after." The two men started walking deeper into the house when Jennifer stepped in front of Michael and placed both hands flat against his chest.

He looked down for a second, then locked eyes with her. "Something you'd like to add, Miss Landry?" Her nose flared in response and he laughed. Michael raised his hands in submission. "Okay, you caught me. I eloped to Vegas and got married over the weekend. Sara will be here on Friday."

"I knew it," said David. "I knew it. Elvis can cast a spell on people, even from beyond the grave."

Jennifer narrowed her eyes. "I know you Michael Thomson. I know your wily ways. You are lying to me right now, aren't you?"

"I am, indeed, and you deserve it. Both for being dumb, and for thinking I'd be *that guy*. I'd never get married without telling you all. Cas will be my best man, and you and Dave will both make lovely bride's maids."

"Screw you, dude," grumbled David, "I'll find the kitchen on my own, assuming some poltergeist doesn't possess me along the way."

Michael took a step to the side and started walking with his friend. "Also, how would I have managed to find, negotiate, buy, and close on a house over the course of two weeks?"

David glanced over. "Ah, now I get the part about us being dumb. It's a fair point. In my defense, I think Jen has been putting off some kind of insanity-inducing pheromone for the past fifteen minutes ever since the moving guy said you had a wife."

"Sexist much," muttered Jennifer, then said, "So if Sara isn't your—"

"She's my cousin, you guys. I remember mentioning her before." He pointed at David. "You were barely paying attention." His finger shifted too Jennifer. "And you were peeing. Anyway, that's not important right now. " Michael opened his arms and did a slow turn. "Check out my new kitchen."

David shook his head. "Wolf ovens. Subzero refrigerators. Holy cow, dude. This kitchen cost more than my car. I didn't even know you cooked."

He shrugged. "I don't. Well, I do, some, just not enough to deserve this kitchen. Sara cooks a lot. She worked at the restaurant attached to our main distillery back home." Michael affected a bad french accent. "She trained at Le Cordon Bleu, in Paris."

Jennifer shook her head. "Just how rich is your extended family?" asked Jennifer. "Did you say you went to boarding school in England before coming to the States for College?"

"Pretty rich I guess," replied Michael, "but I'm not exactly sure. It's a generational thing. My generation is just now taking over the day-to-day operational work, just like my father's generation is taking over the financial management of things. The whole boarding school thing, that hasn't been going on that long, it started with mine and Sara's parents going. Now, everyone goes. Our grandparents *said* it was to..." his accent thickened, "ensure the best education."

"And it wasn't?" asked Jennifer.

Michael shrugged. "I'm sure that had something to do with it, but I also think my grandparents wanted to shave some of the more melodious corners off our Patois."

"What's that?" asked David.

"It's what we speak back home," chuckled Michael, then pointed to Jennifer. "It's also called Jamaican Creole, so given how far back your family goes in New Orleans, there may be some similarities. Anyway, Patois is what happens when seventeenth century Irish and Scottish indentured servants teach Jamaican slaves how to speak english. It's musical, and personally I love it, but according to Grandpa, it wasn't sophisticated. So, what you get from me, or will hear from Sara, is, at best, Jamaica-light."

"And she's coming here to be what, your personal chef?" asked David. Michael and Jennifer stared at him with identical expressions of complete disbelief. "What?" he asked.

"You're a doofus, that's what," said Jennifer.

Michael nodded his head in agreement. "Sara isn't coming to be my cook. I helped her start an executive chef consulting service. She's already got contracts with Brennan's, Antoine's, and Commander's Palace."

"Wow," exclaimed Jennifer.

"Yes, and she is just getting started. I mean Sara's not even in town yet and she's been proactively contacted by Arnaud's, and Napoleon House as well."

"Wow," said Jennifer again.

"So, she can get us in those places without reservations?" asked David, "I've been using Match.com and——"

Jennifer pinched up her face. "Dave, please tell me you are *not* taking girls to any of those places on the first date. I swear, if you are, I may just throttle you. Do you know where my last date took me?" She didn't wait for a response. "Chick-fil-a." She raised a hand. "Don't get me wrong, I love *The Lord's Chicken*, and I'm not shallow. I don't expect much from a first date. I just want a guy who can engage in good conversation while staring at my eyes and not my boobs." She poked David in the chest. "But if you are taking your *match-chicks* to *any* of those restaurants on the first date, I may just have to scream blue-bloody murder."

"Chill, Jen. I'm not the Jamaican Rockefeller, that's him. I can't afford to take first dates to any of those restaurants, but by the time I get to a place where I *want* to take someone for a really nice night on the town, reservations are three weeks out." He grinned, "and that's how girls end up at Chick-fil-a."

Michael's eyes had been flicking back and forth between his friends as they bantered. He shook his head. "Two things. First, you guys should just date each other, then you wouldn't have these issues." They both crinkled their noses. "Okay, it was just a suggestion. And second, I will not let you use my cousin for access. She's a professional, not a vending machine. Now, do you want to see the rest of the house, or not?"

"I do," said Jennifer.

"Sure," agreed David, "but which rooms have the ghosts?"

"None of them," replied Michael, then started toward one of the kitchen's exits.

The three had just reached the house's expansive arcing stairway, when David snapped his fingers. "Wait, I just made the connection. Is Sara the cousin you were talking about at the beach, the one your family flew via charter to Austin?"

"Yep, that's her," he replied. "Come on, I'll show you the room she chose. I think she picked it because she figured I'd want the largest one, but honestly, hers is the best."

He started up the stairs. "Wait," said David, "did you ever find out what was wrong with her? Was it a suicide attempt?"

"What?" cried Jennifer. "Your cousin tried to kill herself? Your family flew her to Austin? How am I just now hearing about this?"

"You guys, stop," huffed Michael. He paused at the second floor landing, and pointed at David. "*You* are starting rumors. I still don't know what was up with, Sara. Both my mother and aunt told me to butt out." He shrugged. "However, I don't think it was suicide related." Jennifer opened her mouth to ask another question, but Michael shifted his finger in her direction. "As for you, Miss Microbladder, *you* were off peeing so you missed the entire conversation."

She ground her teeth in frustration. "I told you guys not to talk about anything important." Michael shrugged then started walking to his left. "So," continued Jennifer, "you have no idea what happened with Sara? It must have been serious if your parents chartered a plane. Is she okay now?"

Michael stopped and sighed. "You guys are exhausting with your questions. It wasn't my parents it was her parents, my aunt and uncle. I imagine it was serious, but you can't judge too much from the private plane thing. That side of the family hardly ever flies commercial. Finally, I still don't have any details, because, as I just said five seconds ago, everyone told me to butt the hell out, so I did. If Sara wants to talk about it, she will. If she doesn't, she won't, and neither of you are going to bring it up…right?"

"Right," they replied together.

"Don't sound so dejected," laughed Michael. "Now, you can fill in any salacious details you want. I'm sure the reality is far less interesting. My bet is some kind of eating disorder. Sara needs to eat some of the food she makes. The girl's too thin in my book."

Jennifer slipped an arm around Michael. "Yeah, but you think I'm too skinny as well."

"You are," he replied.

"I'm not," she snickered. "You just like your girls a bit juicer."

"Whatever," he said, "you can take your cues for what's normal from the modeling industry, but I'm not going to. I'm telling you, Sara did some modeling in her late teens, and I bet those bastards screwed with her head. From the ages of fourteen to sixteen, the poor girl wouldn't eat a single piece of roti." He pitched up his voice. "Carbs are from the devil, Coz. She actually said that to me."

"She's not wrong," said Jennifer as she walked into what would be Sara's room. "Carbs are from the devil." Jennifer turned her head causing her hair to whip across her face. It settled to reveal an impish smile, as she whispered, "but some of us like to dance with the devil in the pale moonlight."

"Hey, that's what the Joker said before he killed Batman's parents," interjected David.

"I know," replied Jennifer. Her eyes swept the room. "Oh my gosh, Michael, this room is fantastic. I can see why Sara picked it. Look at these floors. There are literally inlays in the hardwoods."

"I know," he said morosely, "that's why I wanted this room. It gets worse, for me anyway. Check out the bay windows."

"The glass looks defective," said David.

Jennifer shook her head. "You are such a doofus. That's what glass used to look like. It must be original."

"It is," confirmed Michael, "and apparently I know something that the walking encyclopedia there doesn't."

"That seems unlikely," joked David, "but give it your best shot."

"I will," countered Michael. "Glass isn't really a solid. It's a liquid. That's why it looks ripply and thicker at the bottom. Those windows have been dripping down like that for almost two hundred years." He gave a smug look toward David who just shook his head. "What?" asked Michael.

"Glass isn't a liquid or a solid. It's an amorphous solid."

Jennifer had moved to the bay window and was gently tracing her fingers along the panes. "A what?" she asked.

"Amorphous solid," repeated David. "Glass is somewhere between those two states of matter, and its liquid-like properties are not enough to explain why those window-panes are thicker at the bottom. We've found Egyptian glass vessels that don't show any sagging and they're thousands of years old."

"The realtor told me that glass moves, and she seemed pretty sure of herself," said Michael.

David nodded, then moved to lay on the massive four poster bed. "She's right, but mathematical models have proven it would take longer than the universe has existed for room temperature glass to rearrange itself to appear melted like that." David interlaced his fingers behind his head and grinned up at the bed's canopy. "Don't try to engage me in a war of wits, Bob Marley, because you are woefully unarmed. The fact is, glass atoms move too slowly for changes to be visible." He gestured to the window. "That's just shoddy nineteenth century workmanship that people now think is quaint."

Jennifer moved to sit at the foot of the bed. She folded her legs crosswise then licked a finger, pointed at Michael and made a hissing sound.

He frowned at her. "Okay, fine, but is it any wonder Jimmy Neutron, there, can't get dates without using Match?"

Jennifer barked a laugh. "You, two, are simply horrible to each other, and my girlfriends still don't get why I like hanging out with y'all so much. They just don't understand how much fun it is to watch boys interact with each other. The bonding is like a bloodsport, all the time." She sighed. "It does make me miss my wing-woman though. It's just not as much fun without Lizzie rolling her eyes with me."

"Sara arrives this weekend," offered Michael, but saw how Jennifer continued to stare into the middle distance. "I know she can't replace Elizabeth for any of us. That's not what I meant. I just——"

Jennifer smiled at him. "I know, and I didn't take it that way, Michael, neither would Caspian. Don't you worry, we'll take your little cousin under our wing and show her what's what, right Mr. Neutron?"

David shot Jennifer his most patronizing look, then said, "Right you are... Barbie."

Michael clapped his hands. "Okay, let's keep moving. We still have four bedrooms to check out, *and* the attic which is still full of a bunch of old stuff. I thought it might be fun for us all to go through it this weekend. You know how much Caspian loves old New Orleans stuff."

Jennifer rolled off the bed, and nodded. "Oh, yeah, he's going to love this place. Heck, he might want one of those rooms for himself."

David joined the other two as they left Sara's room. "I think you should give him the attic, you know, because that's where all the ghosts hang out."

"He can visit," said Michael, "He can even crash on a couch, but I've learned the hard way that friends make for bad roommates. Best friends make for worst roommates."

"Truth!" shouted Jennifer, and the three continued on their tour.

Chapter 19

THE BIRTH OF A CAMPAIGN

"I think this porch is my favorite part of the whole house," sighed Jennifer as she took another sip of her coffee. "Why don't more houses have wraparound porches. They're so wonderful."

"I'm just glad this part of it is heated," said David. "It's cold today."

Michael shook his head. "Heat was easy. I could have just used those propane space heaters. Ducting in A/C for the summer, that's another story. You guys have no idea how hard that was to make happen. The whole house, heck the whole district, is governed by historic architecture covenants."

"No idea what that means," murmured David, then looked up. "Oh, I know what each of the words mean. I even know, in general what might be entailed, but specifically, what did that mean to you?"

Jennifer stared at the younger man. "Almost none of those words were even necessary, Dave. Watch me." She shifted her gaze to Michael, furrowed her brow, and said, "Huh?"

He laughed. "Okay, it basically means I have to run almost everything by an architectural board which is part of the Garden District Historical Society."

"That's crap," offered David. "You own the house. It's your property. You should do what you want with it."

"Thus speaketh Ron Swanson from *Parks & Rec*," intoned Jennifer.

"Well it's true," grumbled David, "and Ron Swanson was an awesome character. I have a poster of his Pyramid of Greatness in my apartment."

"Well," began Michael, "I was aware of all the restrictions before I bought the place. I know you wear your libertarianism like a badge of honor, and that's cool, Dave. However, don't I also have the liberty to buy a house that I want, knowing full well the restrictions that come with it?"

"I concede the point," David sighed.

"Anyway," continued Michael, "I submitted a whole list of proposed maintenance and renovation items as part of my bid for the house. I also purposely included a bunch of stuff I knew they would reject." Jennifer gave him a quizzical look. Michael smiled at her. "Don't take this the wrong way, Jen. You're not naive, but you are nice. I sell booze for a living. I'm not as nice as you. Here's the deal, and I'm sure Dave will appreciate it. Bureaucrats love to say *no*. Saying *no,* is their super power. It's like superman being able to fly. Now, if you could fly, how often would you do it?"

"All the damn time," she replied with laugh.

"Exactly," said Michael. "So it is with bureaucrats and *their* superpower. By giving them some obvious things to say *no* to, I was able to shelter the things I really wanted to keep." He gestured around them. "Like this awesome heated and air-conditioned porch."

"You are an evil genius Michael Thompson," said Jennifer. "I want to be you when I grow up."

"You are far too pale, and not quite pretty enough," he replied with a chuckle.

Dave grabbed another handful of chips from a bowl in the table's center, then asked, "What were some of the things you told them you wanted to change but knew they'd reject?"

Michael grinned. "Well, I started with replacing the wood siding with Hardiplank, then—"

"What's hardplank?" asked Jennifer.

"Hardiplank. It's named after the guy who invented it, James Hardi. It's basically siding that looks like wood, but is made of cement and fibers. It won't ever rot, lasts practically forever, and termites can't eat it."

"So why can't you use it?" she asked.

"Because it's not wood, and the house was originally built with wood siding," replied Michael.

She laughed, "What if it was originally made of horse dung and straw, would they have forced you to—" she broke off as both Michael and David had started nodding their heads.

Michael pointed at her. "Now you're are beginning to get it, Jen. Anyway, I didn't mind having to use wood, so I stuck in the Hardiplank stuff. I also told them I was going to carpet the second floor, remove the dumbwaiter, decommission all three chimneys, *and* air-condition the entire wraparound porch by turning it into an expansive sunroom."

Jennifer nodded. "But you didn't want to do any of those things, did you?"

"Oh heck no. It would be a sin to put carpet over these hardwoods. I love the dumbwaiter, and I've already ordered three cords of split hickory for the fireplaces. Nope, all I really wanted was this one small area of the porch to be enclosed and air-conditioned."

"You can't even see this part of the porch from the street or the neighbors," said David.

Michael tapped at his temple. "The exact point I made when I tearfully gave up on *all* of my requests except the one where I said..." Michael clutched his hands to his chest and pretended to wring an invisible hat, "...please Mr. Rennovation-approver, please, let me just have this one tiny area of my porch enclosed. I'll withdraw all my other requests, if you just let me have this one thing."

"Definitely evil genius," said Jennifer flatly.

David shrugged. "I'll give him half of that, and it's not the genius part." He laughed at his own joke, then said, "You know what, I think we should use the attic for Dungeons and Dragons."

Jennifer slapped his arm. "Oh my gosh, Dave, that's actually a great idea."

"Don't sound so surprised," he snarked.

"No I mean it. That attic is a wreck now, but we could all come over and help spruce it up. Some of that old stuff could be placed around the house to give it even more of a nineteenth century vibe than it already has. The spinning wheel would look cool in a corner of the keeping room. The box of possessed-looking dolls definitely has go, though." She stood up and started pacing. "That creepy Amityville Horror window at the attic's front and the two dormers would let in plenty of light, but..." she paused and looked at Michael, "are you allowed to run electrical inside without getting permits?"

"Technically no," he replied, "but there's no way anyone can tell. I've got an electrician coming to fish a bunch of Cat 6 cable so all the bedrooms can have wired internet. These plaster walls are hell on wifi. Why did you ask about electrical, what are you thinking?"

"Well, first of all, are you cool with David's idea?"

Michael shrugged. "Are you kidding? I love our D&D nights, and it's not like I'd be using the attic for anything else. Besides, you know how Caspian's already started slipping into his workaholic doldrums, because *somebody* hasn't found a way to hack back into the donor database so we could plan our next trip."

"Hey," grumbled David, "I'll be ready in a couple days. I've put in a whole lot of safety measures. That way, I can poke around harder and longer. Cas won't even be back in town for almost two weeks. I'll have something for us long before then."

"It could be a double whammy," cried Jennifer bouncing. "We'll start our D&D campaign, which obviously will have quests, *and* Dave's hackery will have provided us our next real-world quest location as well."

"Triple whammy," offered Michael, then smiled at the other two. "Sara will be here. I'm the only one she knows in the city. Heck, I'm the only one she knows in the whole country. None of our family lives in the States and the only time she ever came here before Austin was to go to Universal Studios."

"Does she play D&D?" asked Jennifer.

Michael sputtered. "No. If you recall, I didn't either, until you nerdus-americanus creatures indoctrinated me into your cultic ways." He grinned at them. "We'll have to bring Sara into our fellowship. I think she'll love it."

"Will she play a wood elf?" asked David.

Michael glared at him. "I know all about you and wood elves. Do *not* lech after my cousin."

"Yeah," chimed Jennifer, then pointed at Michael's face while making a circular motion with one finger. "Don't you think she should play a...dark elf."

Michael placed both hands over his stomach and affected a fake laugh. "Oh, that's funny," he said, "You mean she should play a dark elf, because she's black. Oh you are so clever, Ms. Landry. Ha...ha...it is to laugh."

David shook his head in mock outrage. "Totally unacceptable. I don't think we should even let Jen play with us anymore."

Jennifer lifted both hands. "I know...I know. I'm a racist. Please cancel me. It's what I rightly deserve." She hung her head for several seconds then glanced up through a curtain of hair, and all three started laughing.

Chapter 20

SARA EDWARDS

"David Rushing, what do you mean you aren't meeting me there?" growled Jennifer. She glanced up at herself in the rearview mirror and frowned because she still had not mastered her own mother's impressive use of tone to convey both disappointment and frustration. For his part, David seemed immune to even her attempt at making him feel guilty.

"Jen, I've been working ridiculous hours because we're releasing the game's private beta in less than two weeks. Now, do you want me to help decorate our D&D campaign attic, or do you want me to hack the donor database, because I can't do both."

"It's not just the Attic, doofus," she grumbled, "Sara got into town two days ago and Michael wanted all of us to meet her tonight."

"I don't have a time dilation machine, Jen. Do you have a time dilation machine?"

"No," she replied.

"Okay then. I have to prioritize. I'll meet Sara another time, and this way the guy-girl ratio stays optimized."

"What are you talking about?" she asked.

"Without me there, it's just you, Sara, and Michael. That's two girls and one guy. In addition, Michael will likely just drink beer and critique what you and Sarah do. I'm sure you and she will put better touches on the attic than I ever could. You are girls after all."

"Sexist," she laughed.

"Better than being a racist…you racist," he shot back. "Anyway, tell Sara I'm really looking forward to meeting her."

"I'm going to tell her you are a convicted felon and have herpes," said Jennifer dryly. She pitched up her voice. "Bye Dave," then made a kissing sound and disconnected the call.

Jennifer still had a smile on her face as she wheeled her Mini Cooper S up the steep driveway and set the emergency brake. She hopped out, and walked up to the front door. "Huh," she said. "I think this is the first time I've been here by myself. I never noticed there's no doorbell." Jennifer reached up and took hold of the large lion's head knocker. She swung it up and down three times, with each strike creating a resonate boom.

After several seconds the door opened to reveal a young woman with dark skin, hazel eyes, and long twist-braids of coal black hair. Jennifer's face broke into a wide grin. "You must be Sara," she said.

The young woman smiled back causing dimples to form in both cheeks. "And you must be Jennifer. Michael's been going on-and-on about you. Come in. Come in."

Jennifer stepped inside, waited for Sara to close the door, then extended her hand to the younger woman. Sara shook it warmly, and her smile broadened causing the dimples to become even more pronounced. "It's really great to finally meet you, Jennifer. According to Michael, we're going to be best friends."

"Well," snickered Jennifer, "he said the same thing to me, so it just has to be true. And it's Jenny, or Jen. I just use Jennifer for work stuff."

"Jenny it is then," replied Sara, "but, I'm being a terrible hostess aren't I? Can I get you something to drink before…" she lowered her voice to a conspiratorial whisper, "…Michael puts us to work in the attic, which, by-the-way, has got to be haunted. Don't say anything to him though, he hates spooky things."

"Did you see the basket of old dolls?" asked Jennifer, as she let Sara lead her toward the kitchen.

"Oh my gosh, those dolls. They even scared me, but Jenny, I did something so mean that you may not want to be my friend after you hear it."

Jennifer squeezed Sara's arm. "You did something mean to Michael?" Sara nodded, while trying to affect a serious expression, but her dimples ruined the attempt. Jennifer's lips curved up in a wicked smile. "Well, now you *have to* tell me."

Sara motioned for Jennifer to take a seat at the kitchen table then asked, "Ok, I'll fess up, but first, what would you like to drink?"

"Anything's fine." Sara opened the refrigerator and Jennifer's eyebrows raised. "Holy cow, there's actually food in there."

Sara turned. "Yeah, it was almost completely empty when I got here. It's a sin really, a twelve thousand dollar refrigerator with nothing but about eight beers and a block of cheese. I'm a chef for God's sake, so we couldn't have that. I went shopping."

Jennifer joined Sara by the fridge. "I can see that." She pulled a bottle of capers from the door and waggled it back and forth. "No way, Michael bought these."

"A house without capers is not a home, Jenny. I told that to Michael. He gets a pass on that though because he's only been in the place for what, a month?"

"Less," replied Jennifer. "It's only been a couple weeks and he spent almost all that time modifying the porch and running wires for the Internet."

"Never let it be said my cousin doesn't have his priorities straight," chuckled Sara. "We might starve, but at least our laptops will work on the porch. Anyway, since you're up, what would you like?"

"I'd love a Coke," replied Jennifer.

"Good choice," said Sara as she retrieved a small glass bottle, then deftly popped the cap off against a corner of the granite counter. "These are Mexican Cokes. No corn syrup, all sugar."

Jennifer accepted the bottle, then took a drink. She grinned. "It has ice crystals in it. How did you do that?"

"Chef's secret," replied Sara. "Set the fridge to three degrees above freezing then put two or three bottles just where the air blows over the evaporator coils. Poof, icy Coke. It's magic, isn't it?"

"It really is," replied Jennifer, then made a vague gesture that encompassed the room. "So, what do you think of the house?"

"I totally love it," enthused Sara, "and I'd be a pretty crappy cousin if I didn't love this house, given what Michael went through to buy it." She noted Jennifer's blank expression, then said, "He didn't tell you, did he? That's so like Michael. Do something sweet and noble, then keep it a secret."

"Yep, all we got was, *hey guys, changing venues a bit, come check out my new place.* Then he texted us the address. I ribbed him about the whole thing after because this house couldn't *be* more different than where he was living downtown."

"I know," agreed Sara. "Michael did a video call with me from his condo." She pinched up her face. "As you might be able to tell from just the last ten minutes, I'm not great at hiding my emotions. Michael could tell I hated it. I felt horrible, too, because he was being so incredibly nice, opening up his home to me, introducing me to his friends, and helping my business get started." She shrugged. "Still, his condo reminded me of an open house from architectural digest, pretty, but sterile."

"That's an incredibly accurate description," said Jennifer. "So he could tell you hated it, but how did that lead to a man who's scared of ghosts buying an 1850's haunted mansion in the Garden District?"

Sara paused a moment to take in her surroundings. "Back in Jamaica, I lived in a large, colonial-era, plantation house with my family. This place actually reminds me a lot of home which—"

"—helps you feel right at home rather than a stranger in a strange land?" asked Jennifer.

"Exactly!" replied Sara, then shook her head slightly. "I have the best cousin in the world, don't I?"

"No argument from me," said Jennifer, "but then all my boys are sweethearts."

"All your boys, huh? You mean Caspian and David?" Jennifer nodded. "Yeah," continued Sara, "Michael can't stop talking about them, either."

Jennifer leaned back in her chair, and stared at the ceiling for a moment. "My boys. Let me tell you about my boys. Dave is a super-nerd, but incredibly smart and sweet. Don't ever tell him I said so. We have kind of a brother-sister pick-on-each-other thing going. I wouldn't want to mess that up by letting him know I think he's smart or sweet."

"Of course not," agreed Sara seriously.

"Then there's Caspian, our noble Narnian prince. His parents saddled him with one heck of a name to live up to." Jennifer sighed, "Still, he's somehow managed to do it. Have you ever heard the phrase, *a good man is hard to find?*"

"Jamaica isn't *that* different," laughed Sara, "In fact, if there were women on Mars, *they* would have heard that phrase."

"Well, Cas is one good man," said Jennifer seriously. "He's smart, loyal, loving, and drop dead gorgeous." Sara arched an eyebrow at this last, but Jennifer shook her head. "I had a crush on him once, but that was a million years ago. It lasted about a week because that's how long it took for me to realize his heart was already taken. Of course, it took another ten years for either he or Lizzie to come to the same conclusion."

"She was Caspian's girlfriend, the one who passed away last year, right?"

Jennifer sighed. "Fiancé, but yes. Her real name was Elizabeth, but we all called her Lizzie. She and Cas were in a car accident last May. He was in a coma for weeks, and Lizzie—"

Jennifer's voice trailed off, and Sara reached out to take her hand, but hesitated at the last moment. "I'm so sorry. I didn't mean to upset you. It was stupid of me to bring it up."

"No, you're fine," said Jennifer. "I'm glad you brought it up. Better you know the full story, now rather than trying to puzzle it out while we're all having dinner somewhere. I'm assuming Michael hasn't told you very much about it because—"

"He's a man," she finished, "and you're right. It's been like pulling teeth to get as much as I have from him."

Jennifer nodded. "Here it is in one paragraph. Cas and Lizzie were the founding members of our little band of misfit toys. We all three met in Kindergarten, but I wasn't formally admitted until third grade. David moved here in sixth grade and we adopted him shortly thereafter. Caspian defended Lizzie's honor in high school, which is a longer story. That's when I knew they'd end up together. Years later, some asshole really broke Elizabeth's heart, and Caspian rode in on his white steed yet again. That's when the scales finally fell from her eyes, and they were together ever since."

Sara was about to respond when both women turned their heads toward the stairs as Michael's muffled voice came from above. "Sar, did Jen get here yet? She said she'd be here by six. I swear that woman is always late."

Sara's eyes widened and she cringed a little. "It's okay," said Jennifer. "He's not wrong. I *am* almost always late. Heck, I was late today, just not as late as he thought I'd be." She held up a finger. "Watch this."

"I'm here Michael," Jennifer yelled. "Sorry, I'm late."

"It's okay," came the still muffled response. "Come on up. I want you to see —"

Jennifer interrupted, "Sorry about the stain. How do you get watermarks out of a table?" Jennifer gave Sara a mischievous grin as she continued to call out, "I only set the bottle on the table for a few minutes, but I think there's a ring."

They heard a door slam from above, then heavy footfalls. Finally, Michael called down again, this time from the landing above. "Where did you leave a bottle, Jen? We have coasters. Was it the dining room table?" Jennifer didn't respond, instead placing a finger to her lips, while Sara grinned back at her.

"That table is as old as the house," yelled Michael, "Hang on, I'm coming down."

Jennifer smiled at Sara who just shook her head, and laughed. "Remind me to stay on your good side."

"Oh that's easy, I only have a good side, but before your OCD cousin makes it down here in a huff, you never told me what *you* did to him."

Sara's dimples immediately appeared and she barely contained her laughter. "Okay, but you can't say anything." Jennifer made a show of pretending to lock her lips and throw away the key, as the younger woman continued. "Last night, after Michael went to bed, I couldn't sleep so I puttered around in the attic. I saw the box of dolls and I thought, wow, they really look creepy."

"Oh no," chortled Jennifer. "You didn't."

"I absolutely did," replied Sara with mock seriousness. "I set each one of those dolls in a line facing toward Michael's bedroom and leading from there up the stairs——"

"Toward the attic?" asked Jennifer.

Sara's eyes seemed to dance with mischief as she nodded. "He screamed like a girl when he woke up."

Jennifer burst out laughing, took Sara's hands in hers and squeezed them. "First, remind me to never get on *your* bad side, and second, Michael was absolutely right. We *are* going to be best friends."

Chapter 21

THE SECRET ROOM

Caspian stepped out of Jennifer's Mini and stared up at Michael's house. He turned and placed both arms on the car's roof. She smiled at him. "Go ahead, ask."

"Okay, why did Michael buy a replica of Disney's Haunted Mansion?"

"Dave and I already went through all this," she replied, then circled around the front of her car. "Come on, I want to show you something."

"Jenny, I've seen haunted houses before. I don't want to see this one. Hell, my dreams are already haunted. If I'm going to deal with spirits, I'd just as soon take a nap and hope Lizzie visits me."

Jennifer eyed him. "Cas, you've been home a week. Each of us have tried to get you over here. You've always had some excuse. Bottom line, your excuse *and* napping privileges have been summarily revoked. Last night was the third time you turned us all down. That's why I was dispatched to, literally, pick you up, today." She showed her teeth. "Don't make us do another intervention."

Caspian shook his head. "I texted with Dave on my flight home. According to him, he's run into a dead end on the hacking front. The quest is over. Why can't you guys just leave me to lose my mind in peace?" He sighed. "The more I talk, the more I just want to go home. I shouldn't have let you talk me into this."

Jennifer slipped her arm around Caspian's waist. "Don't flatter yourself, Mr. Lewis. I didn't talk you into anything. I threatened to go over your head to a higher power, and you know your Mom would be on my side, too." She started tugging him reluctantly toward the front door, then asked, "Anyway, what do you mean you're haunted and losing your mind?" Caspian mumbled something as they climbed the stairs leading to the house's expansive front porch. "What?" she asked, "I couldn't hear you."

Caspian closed his eyes for several seconds, then whispered, "I'm still seeing her."

Jennifer had raised a hand toward the door's knocker, but lowered it again. She turned to face him. "Cas, it's perfectly normal for you to dream about Elizabeth. It hasn't even been a year. Dreams don't mean you're haunted or losing your mind."

Caspian shook his head. "You don't understand. I actually *saw* her in the waking world, Jenny." He watched his friend grimace, and gave a mirthless laugh. "Yep, I'm a schizophrenic nut job. Now, can we just leave quietly before anyone notices?"

Jennifer leaned against the door, and crossed her arms defiantly. "No, we are not leaving. What do you mean, you *saw* her?"

He shrugged. "It's happened three times now. The most recent was in Chicago, by the lake. I had just gotten off work, so it was maybe ten at night." Jennifer frowned. "I know, I know," huffed Caspian. "I'm working too much. So, I was walking back to my hotel, and thought it would be nice to see some of the lake-effect snow. I was about to sit on one of the benches, when I suddenly felt a chill, then I saw her out of the corner of my eye. It was only for a second. When I turned, she was gone."

"You felt a chill?" asked Jennifer. Caspian nodded. "Well, that *is* a supernatural event. Imagine, feeling a chill, by Lake Michigan…in February. Cas, you were probably just thinking about Lizzie, and *thought* you saw something." She shook her head. "That's not nuts. The broader situation we're all involved in, well, that's another story. It definitely *is* nuts. Caspian, both you and the woodworker have been having dreams of Lizzie. Whittaker knew things that would be impossible for him to know. Heck, he carved a perfect likeness of Elizabeth without ever having met her." Jennifer smiled at him. "Occam's razor?"

Caspian smiled despite himself. "Don't use my logical constructs against me Ms. Landry."

"I will when necessary," she replied. "All things being equal, the simplest answer, even if inexplicable, is most often the correct answer. So, which answer is the simplest given that we know beyond the shadow of a doubt that *something* supernatural is going on? One, you've suddenly developed a case of schizophrenia, or two, the woman you loved has been given the means to communicate with you via dreams."

"And appearances," he added, "You're completely ignoring what I just told you happened in Chicago."

Jennifer glanced at the door a second then motioned to one of several rocking chairs that were scattered across the porch. Caspian arched an eyebrow, but Jennifer shook her head. "I'm always late. They won't even begin to wonder where we are for another thirty-minutes to an hour. Sit." Caspian did. "Okay," said Jennifer, "tell me about these appearances. Was it just her or were there also spectral kids like in the dream?"

Caspian rubbed at his temples. "No, it was just her. The first time was about four weeks ago. I was in town just for the weekend and my folks drove into the city to see me. Mom tried to maneuver me into attending Mass with them."

"How'd she do that?"

"You know my mom, it's one of her superpowers. She arranged everything perfectly so I was left with two choices, either go with them to Mass and keep the peace, or not go, and expose the truth."

"Which is?"

"I have zero interest in ever going to Mass again, which is exactly what I told her."

"News to me," began Jennifer, "Why don't you want to go? You and Lizzie loved going to Mass."

"Yeah, I *did* love going *with* her, but I have no interest into going to worship a God who would let Lizzie die." Caspian looked down, but Jennifer stayed quiet. After several long moments he looked back up, and said, "Screw Him. I'm done with all that."

"So, you're joining Dave's atheist club?" she asked.

"He's not an atheist," corrected Caspian. "He believes there's some kind of architect out there, but that whoever architected everything, doesn't give a shit what happens."

"And that's where you are, too?"

"Oh no," laughed Caspian. "I believe there is a God *and* He is active in some people's lives. He just didn't give a shit to save Lizzie, so at risk of repeating myself, screw Him!"

Jennifer considered this for several seconds. Finally she said. "Look, Cas, I'm practically the poster girl for lapsed Catholics. *I* certainly wouldn't take advice from me, so you probably shouldn't either. However, I am also pretty observant, so let me give you a few observations. First, Elizabeth's faith is one of the things that bound you together. I mean after the Chadsworth incident, her priorities really shifted. I know you guys were never, you know, intimate with each other. We all thought it was amazing that you both decided to wait."

"Dave didn't think it was amazing," murmured Caspian.

"Yes he did, but he was too much of an idiot to actually admit it."

"And that's another thing," said Caspian, shaking his head in frustration. "I don't even have that to hold onto. Memories of…" he looked down again, "us being together."

Jennifer took a deep breath, then slowly let it out. "I won't insult you by saying I understand how you feel. If you didn't go to Mass, I'm sure your mom will—"

"Oh I ended up going," said Caspian. "You forgot how we got on this tangent. That's when Elizabeth first appeared. I had just hung up with Mom, made her cry because I yelled, and was being a general asshole to her. I threw my phone onto the couch, then stalked into the kitchen. I think also I let out a string of colorful curses. That's when I noticed how cold it was in my apartment. I saw my breath, Jenny. It got so cold, I looked to see if somehow I had left a window open. When I turned around, Elizabeth was sitting on a barstool staring at me."

"Holy shit," whispered Jennifer.

He pointed at her. "*That* would have been a reasonable thing to say. I just screamed like a frightened toddler, then looked around the room, as if there were going to be more ghosts showing up."

"So did she do anything, or say anything?" asked Jennifer.

Caspian shook his head. "At first, she mostly just sat there, then motioned for me to take the stool next to her."

"Was she translucent?" asked Jennifer.

"Are you going to keep interrupting?"

"Sorry," Jennifer said, then made a zipping motion across her lips.

"So, Lizzie pointed at the stool next her, and no, she wasn't translucent. I'm telling you, it looked exactly like herself. Solid, full color, just like the last time I saw her. I even tried to reach out and touch her face." Jennifer's eyes widened, but Caspian shook his head. "She leaned back out of reach. That's when she spoke to me. She asked me not to touch her, so I didn't."

Caspian pursed his lips then pulled at them with a hand. "Finally, Elizabeth said, *You made your mom cry, Cas. She loves you and doesn't deserve it. She especially doesn't deserve you making her feel that way in my name.*"

"Ouch," murmured Jennifer.

"No shit, ouch," sighed Caspian. "Then she said, *I've been interceding for you, Cas, but I can't do anything if you won't let me.* Lizzie got this really sad and serious face, then she implored me to stop blocking her. What she said next is burned into my freaking head. *Please, Caspian, let me help. It's your choice, but if you don't, this will be the last time I can warn you. I told you this in the dream we shared. Accept the path you're on and I'll visit you five more times. Deviate from it, and I won't be permitted to come again.*" Caspian barked an unexpected laugh that caused Jennifer to actually rock back in her chair. He waved a hand at her. "Sorry, I was just remembering what she said next. She told me to call my mom back, apologize, and go to Mass."

"Did you?" asked Jennifer.

"What do you think?" snarked Caspian. His voice softened as he said, "I would have done anything for Lizzie while she was with us, so if my delusion of her tells me to apologize to Mom and go to Mass, well, then I'm gonna apologize to Mom and go to Mass."

"I don't think she's a delusion, Cas," said Jennifer quietly. "I think you've been given an amazing gift. I just hope you don't squander it."

"Well, we're about to find out whether it's a gift or a delusion," he said standing.

Jennifer joined him. She arched an eyebrow. "How are we going to do that?"

"Because I wasn't going to come here today, remember."

Jennifer nodded her head slowly, then her eyes widened in surprise. "Lizzie?"

"Yep, visit number two of seven. I was sitting on the floor of my apartment swiping through pictures on my iPad, and feeling pretty desolate."

"Odd word," interjected Jennifer.

"I agree," said Caspian, "which is why I took note of it when Elizabeth appeared in front of me sitting on the floor. She locked eyes with me and said, *You're feeling desolate. I've come with consolation.*"

Jennifer's nose reddened and her eyes filled with tears as she held her hand to her mouth. "Oh my God, Cas."

"Yeah," he replied softly, "it could be God, or it's the other guy, just torturing me. Anyway, she said, *I've come with consolation and good news. Dave has found my second gift. Meet with our friends tonight, then go find the young woman who received my gift.*"

Caspian grasped the door knocker, drew it back, then gave a sidelong glance to Jennifer. "So, if Dave hasn't magically found a way to safely hack the donor database in the last twenty-four hours since he told me he thought it might be impossible, then I'm a deluded schizophrenic." He slammed the knocker down three times, then winked at his friend. "Of course if he *has* magically discovered recipient number two, then we've definitely passed through the looking glass."

The door opened, David squeezed out, then shut it again. He eyed Jennifer, and looked at his watch. "You're early, well, for you." She opened her mouth to respond but he shushed her. "Listen, I only have a second and want to make sure you both keep your voices down. Sara doesn't know anything about our little quest." David shifted his attention to Caspian. "You know Sara right?"

"No," he replied. "Well, I mean I know *of* her, but we haven't met. Dude, I've been traveling. Why did you answer Michael's door, and what's with all the cloak and dagger bullshit?"

"Shhh," hissed Dave. "Michael's keeping Sara occupied. She's a nice girl and he doesn't want her caught up in all our felonies."

"Still not making sense," intoned Caspian. "What felonies are we talking about now?"

David leaned in. "I realized why I couldn't crack the donor database a second time. They moved it to be a tenant on a more secured server. Probably some Congressional mandate to save money even though it wouldn't actually save money because——"

"Dave," interrupted Jennifer, "I'm going to strangle you."

"Fine!" he whisper-yelled. "Here's the deal. I cracked it. Dude, I found out who got the second organ donation. LizzieQuest is back on!"

All the color drained from Caspian's face. He looked at Jennifer whose eyes, once again, filled with tears. She reached out and pulled her friend into a fierce hug. "Oh Caspian," she whispered in his ear. "I may be a horribly lapsed Catholic, but even I remember the Song of Solomon. *Set me like a seal upon your heart, like a seal upon your arm; for love is as strong as death.*"

Michael entered the foyer from a side room with a big smile on his face. It faded as he took in Caspian's expression. The Jamaican narrowed his eyes at David. "What did you do? All I asked was that you answer the door." He made an exasperated gesture in Jennifer and Caspian's direction. "She looks like someone just shot her dog and he looks like he's seen a ghost."

"I didn't do anything," replied David defensively, then looked around, and lowered his voice, "I just told them I managed to crack the donor database... again." He pointed at Jennifer. "She went all waterworks and hugged Cas. He went even whiter than he looks now. Oh, and neither of them took a moment to appreciate how amazing it is that I managed to get into those systems. It's like a freaking—"

"Miracle," said Jennifer with a final sniff.

"Yeah," replied David slowly. "That's what I was going to say. It's like a freaking miracle, except that I don't believe in miracles." He grinned. "So, absent that, I must just be a steely eyed hacking missile man."

Michael leaned forward a little and locked eyes with Caspian. "You okay, man?"

"I'm fine," he replied. "I'll fill you guys in later. Right now, I'm just processing." He forced a smile. "Besides, I was abducted here against my will to see some amazing attic." Caspian looked around at the house's fine millwork, and snickered. "The attic seems a strange place to start, given how cool just the foyer looks, but it's your house. I don't know why it's your house, but apparently it is."

"I'll give you the full nickel tour after we show you the attic. It was a team project."

Caspian arched an eyebrow. "And it's more impressive than the rest of the house?"

Jennifer slipped her arm around his waist. He looked at her, and she smiled up at him. "Not more impressive, just more, well, us. Come on, we'll show you."

They all started moving toward the widely curved stairway that led to the house's second floor. "Hang on a minute," said Caspian, "What about this cousin I've been hearing about? She's the whole reason we even have an attic, because apparently the attic came with the house, that you bought for her."

"Very funny," snickered Michael as they began ascending the stairs. He cocked his head. "She's in the shower. I can hear it running. My ears have become finely attuned instruments to the sound of running water. We, uh, had some pipe issues. All fixed now though. Anyway, I'll introduce you guys before she heads to work."

Caspian glanced at his watch. "It's almost seven. Where does she work that she's going in after seven at night?"

Michael shrugged. "I forget where it is tonight, Commander's Palace maybe."

"She's a chef?" asked Caspian.

"Executive chef," chimed Jennifer.

"Actually, she's the food equivalent of you," said David. "She's a chef consultant."

They'd reached the second floor and followed Michael though a series of doors until they were faced with a much more narrow staircase that led up into darkness. Caspian squinted into the gloom. "That place looks scary."

"It's a two hundred year old New Orleans attic. It's supposed to look scary," said Michael. "Come on *Miss* Lewis, I'll go first."

Caspian shook his head. "Wait, before I forget. I don't want to insult your cousin by being an ignorant dork."

"Half of that simply can't be helped," laughed Jennifer.

"Very funny," said Caspian, "but I'm serious. What exactly does a chef consultant do?"

Michael gripped his friend by both shoulders and grinned at him. "What do you do?"

Caspian furrowed his brow a moment, then said, "I go into places that have problems or could be better and either fix things or simply make them better."

Michael patted Caspian's cheek. "And that's what Sara does, just with food."

"She also gets paid stupid dollars for doing it," said David, "so you guys have that in common as well. Of course, I'm sure what she does is totally worth her hourly rate." He shrugged. "I'm far more dubious of your value, Cas."

Caspian rolled his eyes, and pushed past his friends. He started up the stairs, but said, "And you guys wonder why I'm always away at client sites. If I'm going to be abused, I'd rather be paid my stupid dollars, as David calls them. Y'all just torment me for free."

"In fairness," said Jennifer, "If you were around more, we'd give it to you in smaller doses."

"This stairway goes nowhere," grumbled Caspian, then turned to face his friends. They all smiled up at him. "What are you smiling at? It's a wall. The stairway ends at a wall."

"Does it?" they all asked as one.

Caspian blinked. "Really? Are you telling me there's a secret door?"

"Everyone loves secret doors, Cas," said Michael seriously. "Now don't get cranky, just because you can't figure out how to open it."

"I can figure it out," Caspian snapped back. He pulled out his phone and tapped its screen. A second later the flash illuminated allowing him to look around. He frowned at a light switch set into the right wall, then flicked it to the on position. Instantly, the entire stairway was bathed in a soft, warm glow. "Well, that's stupid," grumbled Caspian. "Why wouldn't you have a light switch at the *bottom* of the stairs?"

"No reason at all," answered Michael, "that's why there *is* a light switch at the bottom of the stairs. You just didn't turn it on."

They all watched as Caspian turned his back on them to stare at the seemingly dead end. He ran his fingers along the edges. He tapped on it with his right hand while placing his left ear against the wood. As he did so, Caspian's eyes rested on the light sconce mounted just before the stairs seemingly dead-ended. He turned to his friends and smirked. They grinned back. Caspian reached up and gently tugged on the sconce. It bent forward silently on well oiled hinges, then an audible click sounded from the nearby wall, as it slid sideways to reveal an open doorway. "It's a pocket door," whispered Caspian. "I love pocket doors."

"Who doesn't," laughed Michael. He brushed past his friend and took a step into the attic room, then turned. "The pocket door was always here. The secret release mechanism was Jen's genius idea." Jennifer affected a curtsey, which was entirely ruined by her cotton button-down shirt and jeans. "David built the actualators."

"Actuators," corrected David, enunciating each letter crisply. "They actuate the door." He winked at Caspian. "It also has bluetooth, so we can pair it to our phones."

Caspian's eyes grew wide. "So the secret door will just magically open when we get near it."

David nodded. "As the saying goes, any sufficiently advanced science is indistinguishable from magic."

"Oh shut up you two," laughed Jennifer. She grabbed Caspian by the arm. "Come on. I want you to see what we've done to the place. It's amazing!"

Chapter 22

DUNGEON MASTER

"Wow!" exclaimed Caspian for what must have been at least the sixth time. He peered through the large round window that looked out onto the front yard and driveway. He pointed to the latch. "Does this open?" Michael nodded, and Caspian tripped the latch. The window swung outward with a slight squeal of the old hinges. He raised up on toes, then poked his head through. "You can see everything from here. The city, the French Quarter... everything." Caspian closed the window, reset the latch, and turned around. "Dang, Michael, when I heard you bought an old Garden District house, I thought you were nuts, but all I've seen is this room and I'm sold."

"Like I said," began Michael, "I can't take credit for the attic. That was all Jen and Sara."

"Yeah," said David, "when we first came up here, the place was a mess. There were things scattered everywhere, and the floors were all covered in something dark and greasy. I'm also pretty sure some of the stuff we found up here was cursed."

"It did look a bit like a *Warehouse 13* annex," snickered Jennifer.

Caspian knelt down to run his hands along the polished hardwoods. "What a great show," he mused, "Do you guys remember when we used to watch that together the summer between our junior and senior years?"

"Of course we remember," laughed David. "We're not even thirty yet, Cas. We remember things. Besides, it's burned into my memory how Lizzie and Jen would always make fun of you and me throughout the show."

"You deserved it," said Jennifer. "You and Cas would totally be the first ones to touch something that definitely should never be touched." She started laughing. "I remember Lizzie saying that Cas would cradle a knife wielding doll named Chucky and teach it to use a Ouija board." Jennifer raised her arms in mock surprise. "*What could possibly go wrong,* she'd say." Jennifer suddenly noticed how both Michael and David were looking at her with tight expressions, and she sobered. "Oh, Cas," she said. "I'm sorry. I wasn't thinking. It's just—"

Caspian stood, and smiled at her. "No, Jenny. Don't be sorry. It's a great memory. And Lizzie was right, my cursed object detection skills are complete crap." He noticed how their expressions remained ones of concern, and sighed. "Is that what I've become?" Caspian asked. He didn't wait for a response, but continued on. "I'm the sad sack that everyone has to guard their tongue around, right?"

"No, Cas," began Jennifer, "it's not like that. I mean it's only been—"

"Nine months or nine years, Jenny. It would make no difference. I'm always going to love Elizabeth. I'm always going to miss her. It's probably always going to hurt. Don't get me wrong, I'm still a complete mess, but you guys do *not* need to treat me like some kind of porcelain doll, well, unless it's a cursed porcelain doll with a knife and a Ouija board." He grinned. It took several seconds, but finally each of their faces split into broad smiles.

"Wait," said Michael suddenly. "Since Cas doesn't have to be the center of our attention and concern for the moment, I'd like to point something out." Everyone stared at him. "I have no idea what Warehouse 13 is and you are all very insensitive for making me feel left out. If you don't remember, I didn't know *any* of you before college."

"I didn't even know you *in* college," said Caspian. "I was just visiting Jenny and Lizzie at Loyola and there you were." He shrugged. "I just figured they were looking to..." Caspian affected his best Jamaican accent, "score a bit of ganja man."

"You are a piece of shit, do you know that?" laughed Michael, then thickened his accent to a ridiculous degree. "Besides, everyone knows we only sella the ganja to white girls because we want to take them home."

"Oh that's just lovely, Cuz," came a voice from the other end of the room. Everyone turned to find Sara standing near the attic door. She wore a crisp chef's uniform and a disapproving frown. Sara shook her head at Michael. "Perpetuate stereotypes much?"

"It was a *joke*," insisted Michael, "now take that wooden spoon out of your butt and come over here so I can introduce you." Sara walked over and Michael put his arm around her shoulder. "Sara, this is Caspian Lewis. He's an awesome guy, and probably my best friend except when something's wrong with any of my computers, then it's Dave."

"Nice to be appreciated," murmured David.

"Cas, this is my cousin, Sara Edwards."

Caspian pointed to the embroidery on Sara's culinary uniform, then extended his hand. "Nice to meet you, Chef Edwards."

She grinned and dimples appeared in her caramel colored skin. "You don't have to be that formal, Caspian." She paused a beat, then said, "You can call me Chef."

Caspian shook her hand, but glanced awkwardly at Michael for a second, then back to Sara. "Really?" he asked.

She laughed, then turned to Michael. "And he's the smart one?"

Michael shook his head. "No, I said he was the pretty one. David is the smart one. However, Cas is also a more patient teacher, which is why he's the one who will be showing you the ropes during our first Dungeons and Dragons campaign."

Caspian's eyes widened as the entire room took on a different meaning within his mind. He turned around. "You renovated the attic into a D&D campaign headquarters?" Caspian tapped on the center of the room's octagonal table. "Is this..." He paused, then crouched down to look beneath the table. Caspian's head popped up a second later. "It is. This is absolutely a Majestic Designs table." He stared at Michael with his mouth open slightly. "Dude, where did you get a Majestic Designs table?"

"Surprisingly," said Michael, "I found it at Majestic Designs."

"In England?" asked Caspian, incredulously.

"That is where they keep the tables, Cas," chuckled his friend.

"But there's like a three year waiting list." Caspian began running his fingers along the intricately carved wood. "It doesn't even look like any of their designs."

"It's not," said Jennifer. "I designed it to match the house. I sent them sketches."

"I've never seen someone so in love with a table," observed Sara. "Maybe we should give Caspian and his table some alone time."

"Nice!" exclaimed David.

Caspian shook his head in wonder. "Holy cow. She's known me all of thirty-seconds and I'm already getting shit."

"In my defense," said Sara with a smile. "Mikey *has* told me all about you, Caspian." She shrugged. "So I feel like I've known you for years." Her expression turned sheepish. "Sorry if I overstepped."

"Pffft," blurted Michael. "Cas, don't be taken in by that pout of hers. She deploys that look like a super weapon. Just don't look at it, and you'll be fine."

"Well, *Mikey*," chuckled Caspian. "I'll take your word for it." He clapped his hands together. "So, when do we have our first D&D campaign and who's going to DM it?"

"First," began Michael, "don't you ever, and I mean ever, call me *Mikey* again." He pretended to scowl at Sara. "That name isn't to be used outside of Jamaica, and I'd prefer if it was wasn't used there either. Second, it's my house, thus I will be your Dungeon Master. I'm better at it than any of you. In addition, we need to keep the number of girls and boys balanced. Besides, Cas, as I already told you, someone has to teach Sara how to play. I do not want that someone to be me." He fake whispered. "She's a horrible student, and really quite slow...mentally I mean."

Sara shook her head. "Well, cousin, as much fun as this has been, I have to get to work. I can almost hear the sound of irate customer voices rising and soufflé's falling." She smiled again at Caspian. "It was really nice meeting you. I look forward to playing this dragon game. One thing though," her lips shifted to form the same pouting expression she deployed earlier. "Please be gentle and kind with me. I've never done anything like this before." She winked, gave the room a wave, then spun around and left the room.

Everyone remained silent for a beat, then Caspian barked a laugh. "Mikey, you were right. Her pout is a superpower."

"Weapon," he corrected. "I said it was a super weapon, and don't call me Mikey."

Chapter 23

INTO THE MATRIX

The doorbell rang to David's apartment. He peered through the security viewfinder, then opened it. Jennifer smiled. David did not. "You're late," he grumbled. She held up two four packs of beer. David eyed them. "You brought St. Barnabas, number twelve?"

"That depends," she replied. "Am I late?" She tilted one of the four packs back-and-forth in front of David's nose. "Am I late?" she asked again, this time with a lilt to her voice.

Before David could respond, Michael came up from behind, nudged him aside, and deftly plucked one of the bottles from its box. "In my opinion, anyone who brings good Belgian beer is never late."

"Come in," sighed David, "I'll give you a fifteen minute grace period per four-pack."

Jennifer's eyes widened. "Wait, that means I'm something like ten minutes early." She pitched up her voice in a childlike manner. "Should I come back when it's time to hack the big, bad government computer?"

David opened the door wider. "Shut up and put those in the fridge." He grabbed a bottle as she passed, then added, "keep one out for Cas. He's in my home office, hopefully not touching things he doesn't understand."

"Got it," she replied. There was a clink of bottles, then several pops as Jennifer opened them with the magnetic bottle opener David kept attached to his refrigerator. Another click-hiss-pop sounded as Michael's beer cap joined Jennifer's in being captured by the opener's powerful magnet.

David gestured toward the hallway leading from his open kitchen-living area. "Come on, let's get this show on the road."

Caspian spun his chair around as they entered the relatively small room. It consisted of a rather expansive L-shaped desk with a large hutch attached to one side of the L. On it rested three monitors arranged in a semi-circle. Beneath the desk to one side, sat a gleaming silver box with dozens of strange holes cut in the front of it. "How much did you spend on this computer?" asked Caspian.

David shrugged. "I think about ten grand." Both Jennifer and Caspian shook their heads. "It's a MacPro, and once I bought it, BioWare let me work from home two days a week. Prior to that, I had to go in all five, which sucked. I hate the traffic."

"What traffic?" asked Michael. "You live downtown and their office has an in-town address. How far could it possibly be?"

"Too far to bike, especially in summer, and I *really* hate traffic," replied David defensively.

"Yeah," interjected Jennifer, "but everyone is working from home now because of COVID."

"Well, excuse me for not predicting a pandemic," snarked David. "I bought the Mac literally two weeks before they locked us down for fifteen days."

Michael laughed. "Don't rub it in, Jen. Besides, with the vaccine being released, I'm sure folks will be back in offices soon."

"It's going to be months before we're eligible to get it," she replied, "and I'm not sure I even want the thing. I read it can alter your DNA."

Caspian shook his head. "You need better sources, Jenny. I assume you're referring to the mRNA version. I watched a super-cool documentary on that one. It was fascinating, and I think this will be the future of vaccines."

She pursed her lips, clearly doubtful. "If this mRNA stuff is so awesome, why is it just now being used?"

"Money," said Michael.

"Money? Money how?" asked David. "It's all going to be free isn't it?"

Caspian laughed. "TANSTAAFL, dude."

"There he goes," grumbled Michael. "Now he's going to grace us with another litany of Heinlein quotes, way to go, Dave."

"No I'm not," said Caspian, "but if I was, you'd be lucky. Heinlein quotes are awesome. Anyway, my point to Comrade Rushing there was…TANSTAAFL…

there ain't no such thing as a free lunch, even in your socialist utopia. Yes, the vaccines are going to be..." he made air quotes, "*free* to us, but these companies spent billions making them."

"Which the government paid," said Jennifer.

"Not all of them," countered Caspian. "A few turned down the money because they didn't want any government bureaucracy looking over their shoulders. If their vaccines hadn't worked, they'd have been epically screwed." He shrugged. "But they do, so now those companies are going to make huge bank, which they should, well, within reason. Anyway, Michael was right that it's all about the money. Take the mumps vaccine. It's been around for years. It's cheap and it's shelf stable, so can be shipped anywhere without refrigeration. What's the incentive to make an mRNA version of something cheap that works." Caspian saw his friend's blank faces. "Okay, think of it this way. Would you start a company, and invest one billion dollars to develop a mousetrap that will sell for $200 when there have been effective $1 mouse traps in market for years? No, you would not. Well, David might, but—"

"Frak off, dude. I built the entire credit system for Mass Effect 4. When you've built a legal-tender and bartering mechanism between alien species, then you can give me crap."

"Anyhoo," continued Caspian, "RNA is completely different than DNA. Nothing can change your DNA. If it could, then we could change our eye color or turn ourselves into butterflies."

"Gamma radiation alters DNA," said David.

Caspian sighed. "Yeah, by blowing it to pieces. It doesn't turn you into the Hulk. It turns you into a corpse."

"I know that," spat David. "I was just making a point. Now, get out of my chair." Caspian stood, allowing his friend to take the seat. David looked up and pointed. "Jen and Cas, grab a chair. Mikey, you can either pull a folding beach chair from the hall closet, or just lean against the wall looking vacant and pretty."

Jennifer and Caspian sat, with the latter crossing his feet on one corner of David's desk. For his part, Michael just gave an expansive sigh. "You feeling strong my friend," he said, pointing at David's back. "Call me Mikey, one more time."

"Nice *Elf* reference...Mikey," chuckled David. "I didn't think they had Christmas in Jamaica. Does Santa wear a speedo?"

"No, he wears a bobsled uniform," grumbled the other. "Aren't you supposed to be hacking? That *is* why we're here, isn't it?"

"I'm confused about that, too," said Jennifer. "When we were at Michael's yesterday, you told Cas and me that you'd already hacked the donor database."

David didn't turn around. "I've broken in, but I didn't extract any data. I want you guys here with me because I'm not sure what I'm going to find and will only have a limited time to parse through what I do find. We're going to need to make decisions fast with respect to which records we want to examine."

"Wait," said Caspian. "How short a time? For that matter, why is there a time limit at all? I thought you hacked the thing."

David spun his chair around. "Dude, how much detail do you want, because I don't think you've taken the prereqs for Dr. Rushing's Cyber Security 705 course."

"Did he just call me stupid?" asked Caspian.

"Yep," replied Michael and Jennifer together.

David sighed. "Look, I told you the donor database is now a tenant on a homeland security server. It has active defenses. I can get around them in query mode for a while, but when I download something, it's going to freak out and put the whole system into lockdown until it figures out if I'm legitimate."

"But you aren't legitimate," said Jennifer.

"Thanks Jen," he snarked. "I *am* aware. Point being, by the time the active defenses start probing me, I want to be headed for the virtual exit, not looking for more information. I'm going to bounce my connection off five different proxy servers in as many countries, but I really don't want Men-in-Black showing up at my door so—"

"Okay, I get it," interrupted Caspian. "We need to pick our targets quickly."

"Target, not targets," corrected David. "This is a lightning thrust into a highly secured system. We're going in, making a quick call what to grab, then we're getting out. My goal is for this to be so fast that any sys-admin who looks over the logs will assume the intrusion alert is just a false positive."

"I feel like that girl in the hacker movie you made us watch," laughed Jennifer. "What was it called, *Warhammer?*"

David let out an expansive sigh. "*Wargames*, Jenny, not *Warhammer*. It's only *the* iconic hacker movie of all time." He spun his chair and grinned at her. "*That girl* was played by Ally Sheedy, and if you're her, that would make me Matthew Broderick." He gave Jennifer a wink "the looove interest."

"In your dreams, nerd-boy," said Jennifer, "but I'll buy you lunch if you actually explain what you're doing because, against all odds, I'm finding it fascinating."

"I'll chip in on that," offered Michael. "I've never seen an actual hack except, you know, in movies."

David interlaced his fingers together, then cracked his knuckles. "Okay then boys, and girl. Strap in, because you're about to get a Master Class. Two things, though. First, no questions. I need to pay attention to everything all at once. Second, when I find a target, I'm going to ask which one you want me to grab. I'll need you guys to answer immediately. Majority rules. Understood?" David glanced at his monitor's reflective surface and saw three heads nodding. "Okay. Here we go."

He started tapping his keyboard. A small window popped up on the right screen. "I'm initiating a VPN. First proxy server is in…Singapore. See that green light, that means it's active. To the world, I now look like I live in Singapore." He moved his mouse. "Connecting to second proxy now… Sydney, Australia."

"Why did you skip over the Russian ones?" asked Michael.

"What part of *no-questions* did you find confusing?" asked David. He shook his head. "I skipped over Russia because, as you may recall, this is a homeland security server. I won't be using proxies from any adversarial countries. Okay. Now the Aussie one is green as well. Moving on to…Greenland, then to Stockholm, and finally Nairobi."

"So you're in?" asked Jennifer.

David sighed. "I haven't even started yet. That was all prep."

"I don't get it," she said.

"I do," offered Caspian. "He's created layers of, I don't know, anonymity shields. Right now it looks like he's in Africa. If these active defenses Dave mentioned break through that first layer, it will appear like he's in Sweden, then Greenland, Australia, and finally Singapore."

"And then New Orleans," added David. He tapped some more keys and a sphere illuminated on the right screen just beneath the VPN. New Orleans was positioned at the center of the sphere. Surrounding it were five colored bands each annotated with the countries he'd just mentioned. David tapped the screen with a finger. "I've programed my incursion software to automatically disconnect if the defense bots get past Sydney for any length of time. You'll be able to see a visual representation using this security sphere I created. Hopefully nothing will notice us at all and we'll exit with all five layers intact."

"Hope isn't a strategy," murmured Caspian.

"Shut up, Cas," lilted David. "Okay, I'm initiating the remote login now, so seriously, no more questions." He tapped his keyboard. A large login window emblazoned with the Department of Homeland Security's logo appeared on his center screen. David tapped on the keyboard, and a complex series of letters, numbers, and special characters populated the login box's name and password fields. He took a deep breath, then tapped *Enter*. Nothing happened. Caspian, Michael, and Jennifer all looked at each other. After several seconds, Michael took a breath and was about to speak. David's right hand shot up. His eyes remained fixed on the center screen, but he made a close your mouth motion with thumb and fingers. Michael closed his mouth. Less than two-seconds later, the login panel flashed *Access Granted*, then vanished. It was replaced with some kind of systems-administration panel. At the same time, a new window appeared on David's left screen. Long strings of letters, numbers, and characters began streaming down that panel.

"Those are the active defenses," he said. "Nothing to be alarmed about... yet. They're always running. My program is just watching them to see if they get agitated by anything I do here." He pointed at the center screen. "This is where you guys need to focus."

"Terrorist threat assessments," whispered Jennifer. "One of those menus says terrorist threat assessments."

"Yeah, and we won't be touching that one," said David. He pointed his mouse toward the bottom of a menu tree, and clicked on something labeled *HHS Data Storage*. Another menu appeared. He clicked *National Donor Database*. David glanced at a sticky note on his desk, then tapped in an eleven digit number that Caspian immediately recognized as being Elizabeth's social security number. The screen flashed again, this time a large warning displayed in red letters. "Authorized Medical Personnel Only. HIPAA restricted information. Violation carries civil and criminal penalties. Continue: Yes or No."

"Shiiit," murmured Michael.

David spun his chair around. "Last chance. I click this button, and we're all felons."

Everyone stared at Caspian, whose eyes remained locked on Elizabeth's, still visible, social security number. He nodded. "In for a penny. In for a pound. Let's do it."

David spun back around, and mashed the enter key with far more force than was required. Instantly, the first layer of the globe on his right screen shifted to yellow. A pleasant sounding female voice with a scottish accent said, *Active defenses engaged. Fifth proxy being probed. Breach in approximately ninety-seconds.*

"Who's that?" blurted Michael.

"It's Shannon, my little AI assistant," said David, "oh, and Michael, please shut the hell up. We were detected a lot faster than I expected." He glanced at the left screen, where the streams of characters continued to flow, then leaned forward. "Damn, they are good."

Jennifer turned to her left and spoke directly into Caspian's ear. "Do you see anything different on that left screen than before?"

He whispered back. "No, but apparently David can read that like Neo can read The Matrix."

Several seconds later, Elizabeth's driver's license picture appeared at the top of an information dense screen. Caspian felt his stomach twist as he read one of the first lines. DOB: 1/15/96 — DoD: 5/17/2020. Jennifer reached over and gripped his hand. He looked at her. She nodded and gave him a closed mouth smile. "I'm okay," he whispered.

David's fingers flew across the keyboard. "Okay, I'm looking for the donor information. That should lead us into the database itself."

"Holy shit," said Michael. "Aren't we even in the correct place yet?"

On the right screen the outermost band flashed red then disappeared. Shannon's slightly artificial voice came through the speakers. *Proxy five has been breached. Proxy four is being probed. Breach in approximately seventy-seconds.*

"Damn," murmured David. "Seventy-seconds? I was afraid of this. It's getting smarter." He continued tapping while intermittently glancing at both left and right monitors.

Proxy four has been breached, said Shannon. *Proxy three is being probed. Breach in approximately thirty-seconds.*

"Fuug," groaned Jennifer, and Caspian felt her grip on his hand tighten.

"I've got it!" yelled David. "Three organs were donated." He pointed at the screen. "Cornea, Lung, and..." David squinted at the third line item. "What the hell? It's redacted just like the hospital report."

Caspian pointed at the screen. "It says Redacted by FBI. Why would the FBI have any interest in—"

Proxy three has been breached, said Shannon. *Proxy two is being probed. Breach in approximately fifteen-seconds.*

"No time!" yelled David. "Which file do you want me to take? The lung one or the FBI redacted one?"

"Redacted," said Caspian.

"Lung," cried Michael and Jennifer together.

David clicked the file icon for the lung donations.

Shannon's voice said, *Downloading 256 bit encrypted file. Download complete.* Half-a-second later she continued. *Proxy two has been breached. Proxy one is being probed. Breach in approximately five-seconds. Disconnect protocol engaged. Disconnect successful.*

Four exhalations of breath all happened at once. David's chair creaked as he leaned back, hands rubbing his face. "Holy shit! What a rush."

"I'm gonna be sick," groaned Jennifer.

"I think you crushed my hand," said Caspian.

"Oh, sorry, Cas." She released him, and he began flexing his fingers.

"Did we get it?" asked Michael.

David nodded. "Oh yeah, we got it, all right."

"Well what's it say?"

David stared at his friend. "I don't know, Michael. Do you happen to have the encryption key? No? I didn't think so." He sighed, then turned back to his keyboard. After several more taps, Shannon's voice, once again, filled the room. *Voice commands active. What can I do for you, David?*

"Decrypt file called *E.Winters.zip*"

Understood. Please provide the private key?

"I don't have one."

Brute force decryption will take approximately six thousand, four hundred seventy-two years. Would you like me to start a brute force decryption? Yes or No.

"No," said David. "Shannon, access private key recursion program RushingViolence."

File accessed.

"Shannon, what is the estimated time to decrypt the file using RushingViolence?"

Indeterminate. Two decryption outcomes exist. Would you like me to describe the two outcomes, yes or no?

David cringed, then looked at his friends, and said, "Yes."

Option one, RushingViolence recursion program successfully generates the required private key. This will take approximately seventy-two hours. Option two, RushingViolence fails to generate the required private key. This would result in a null response. Decryption time estimate is between seventy-two hours and infinity.

"Is she joking?" asked Michael.

"Shannon never jokes," replied David. "Basically if she can't decrypt it in about three days, she never will."

Everyone sat in silence for several seconds when Shannon's AI voice, once again, came through the speakers. *David, are you still there?*

"Yeah," he said.

Shall I attempt decryption, yes or no?

"Yes."

Initiating RushingViolence recursion and applying first generated private key to encrypted file. Incorrect key. Generating second private key. Applying second generated private key to— David tapped on his keyboard. *Discontinuing voice prompts*, said Shannon, *Engaging all CPU cores, hyper threading at 4.4GHz.* The fans on David's MacPro began to spin up and a timer appeared on the screen. It displayed 71 hours, 57 minutes, 17 seconds, and continued counting down.

David turned his chair around and sighed. "Well, what you think, fellow felons?"

"I think I want to know what our odds are that this file gets decrypted," said Michael.

David considered this a moment, then said, "I give us two chances in three. I wrote that private key recursion program in college, but it's never failed me yet. Then again, I've never done something this spectacularly stupid."

Jennifer raised her hand. "Uh, I have a question. Why do you have a hot sounding Scotswoman in your computer, and did she name this program *RushingViolence* or did you?"

"Really?" asked David. "We just committed half-a-dozen felonies and that's your question?"

"I'm kind of curious, too," offered Caspian. "I also want to know why you guys didn't want access to that FBI file?"

David shook his head. "Both of you have very warped priorities. I named Shannon after a character in one of my favorite book series, okay. She's Scottish because the character was Scottish, so sue me."

"I didn't want the FBI file," began Michael, "because it adds another layer of complexity. I understand why someone might need a lung transplant. The FBI thing...who knows what that's about."

Jennifer smiled. "His answer is better than mine. I just freaked out and didn't want anything to do with the FBI. But Dave?"

"Yeah?"

"As the only woman here, let me tell you that if you keep making artificial girls in your computer, you won't meet any real ones." She crinkled up her nose. "I'm almost afraid to ask, but what other services does this Shannon provide?"

"Ha…ha…ha," said David, in a completely flat tone. "For your information, I have a date this weekend."

"Yeah," laughed Michael, "and your toaster is really excited at the prospect. It told us all about your date when we were putting the beer in your fridge."

Everyone started laughing. David just shook his head. "I hate you guys."

Jennifer leaned down and kissed his cheek. "Oh we love you, nerd-boy. Now, tell me about this date. It's a human girl right?" David gave her a long-suffering sigh, and Jennifer laughed. "Lighten up, and tell your big sis, Jenny, all about her. I'll give you some pointers."

Chapter 24

DRIVING MISS SARA

Caspian's eyes focused on his car's infotainment screen as a Bob Marley ringtone sounded. He grinned at the thumbnail picture of Michael that took up the left half of the screen's display. David had photoshopped a picture of their friend and added a ludicrously sized joint in Michael's mouth, while also surrounding his head in a haze of pot smoke. Their entire friend-group used the same ringtone and contact image. For his part, Michael made sure everyone knew how much he hated both. Of course, that just ensured they all would continue using it forever. Caspian thumbed the *accept* button on his steering wheel. "Greetings Mr. Marley, what can I do to make your day just a little bit brighter?" No answer. "Mr. Marley?" asked Caspian. "Are you there, sir?"

Finally Michael responded. "How long are you three planning to keep this up? It was mildly amusing the first dozen times, but now——"

"You hated it since inception," interrupted Caspian with a grin.

"Yeah, I did," agreed Michael. "So, when will you guys stop?"

"I'm thinking pretty much never," said Caspian. "You might be some eighty-year old geezer calling one of us up on our translucent hand terminals from The Expanse, and it will still be playing a *Three Little Birds* ringtone."

"Hopefully that will be considered a hate crime by then," responded Michael flatly.

Caspian nodded to himself. "Given current trendlines, I think that's entirely possible. Now, why are you calling? Did you need me to pick up something for tonight's campaign?"

"Kinda," replied Michael.

"Beer?" asked Caspian.

"No…Sara."

"Sara? Does she have the beer?"

Michael sighed. "Are you trying to have me kill you when you arrive, Cas? No, Sara does not have the beer. I have the beer. Jen is bringing some kind of bourbon she made me listen to her explain about for ten minutes, and Dave is bringing more beer."

"Huh," grunted Caspian, then glanced at the large wooden box resting on his passenger seat. "Well, I've got all the D&D stuff. Dice, Dungeon Master privacy screens, graph paper, the works. No figurines though. Dave said he was bringing those. You know painting little statues is just too nerdy for me."

"I didn't ask about any of that," huffed Michael. "I asked for you to pick up Sara."

"You were serious about that?"

"Yes. Why would I joke about giving my cousin a ride, Cas?"

Caspian shrugged. "Dunno. Where is she and why does she need a ride?"

"She's at Antoine's and her car is in the shop."

"Oh, does she need me to drop her off somewhere? If so, I'm going to be late, and I don't need Jenny giving me shit for—"

Caspian could almost see Michael's pinched up face as he interrupted. "No, she doesn't need to be dropped off anywhere. She's coming home, Cas. She's playing with us."

"Really?"

"Dude, we talked about this. That's why I'm DMing, so you can teach her. Obviously Jen and Dave would be horrible teachers."

"Obviously," agreed Caspian.

"And I'm not good at teaching family. I get snippy, which just leaves you."

"Okay, I'll get her, but I think forcing her to play is a big mistake."

"Who said anything about forcing her. She's been on my ass about it for the past two weeks. She wants to play. She's worked out her character's whole backstory. I read it last night."

"Really," said Caspian again, clearly surprised. "Was it any good?"

"Surprisingly good, actually."

"What's she going to play?" asked Caspian.

"Not my secret to share," laughed his friend. "Ask her when you pick her up. Do you have her number?"

"Nope."

"Okay, I'll text it to you. Just give her a five minute warning."

"Will do," said Caspian, then disconnected the call.

Several minutes later, Caspian pulled into the rear load-in area for Antoine's restaurant. He eyed all the warning and tow-away signs nervously, but pulled up to one of the bays. Two burly men wearing stained chef's uniforms were standing near a door smoking. When it became clear that Caspian intended to park, both men began shaking their heads, and making shooing gestures. He rolled down the passenger window and was about to yell to them, but one of the men beat him to it. "You can't park here," said the man, in a thick creole accent. The other man nodded, then gestured toward the restaurant's front entrance.

"I'm not staying," said Caspian. "I just need to pick somebody up."

"Pick them up from there," said the first man, then he, too, started pointing toward the front. Caspian sighed, and was about to put his car back into gear when the back door slammed open. Both men immediately turned toward the sound, and their entire demeanor changed. They threw down their cigarettes, ground them into the cement with their dark soled shoes, and moved toward the door. One man held it open, while the other reached for three of the trays that the person exiting had been balancing.

Sara smiled at them both, then caught sight of Caspian, and waved. The man holding the trays followed Sara's sightline, and asked her something. She nodded, then pointed to Caspian's car. The two of them descended a flight of stairs that joined the Antoine's main floor with the load-in area below. Caspian jumped out of his car, popped the trunk, then made his way to the passenger side.

"Sara, where would you like me to put these?" asked the man. He eyed Caspian, then the open trunk. "You wouldn't let him put our food in that... that trunk. It could spill. I could come with you, and—"

Sara smiled at him. "It's okay Léandre, I'm sure it will be fine."

Caspian saw the young man's growing distress, and said, "Hey, no problem. I can smell something delicious from here. I don't want anything spilling ither." He opened the passenger door. "Here, I needed to move this stuff anyway. I'll stick this box in the trunk, then we can figure out where best to put the food."

"I'll just hold them on my lap," offered Sara.

Léandre shook his head. "No Chef, that will not do. Several of the trays are far too warm." Her smile broadened, causing both dimples to form. "I'll put the hot ones in the seat well, Léandre, and keep the salad and appetizers on my lap." He looked uncertain, and she chuckled, "Will that be acceptable?"

Léandre's eyes widened. "Chef, I'm sorry. I didn't mean to presume. Of course, you know these dishes far better than me. I'll put them wherever you think best." He glared at Caspian who shot a confused look toward Sara. She gave him a subtle shake of the head, then patted Léandre's shoulder. "You were just being concerned, not presumptuous. It's fine." Caspian pretended to ignore their exchange as he quickly moved his box of D&D items into the trunk. He gave it a quick slam then started back toward the two of them. Léandre shook his head as Caspian approached. "I have everything under control, driver. You can get back in your car, now."

"Uh…okay," stammered Caspian. He saw Sara bite her lip in a clear effort to keep from laughing. By the time he had settled himself back into the driver's seat, three of the trays had been gently stowed in the passenger seat well, where Sara kept them in place with her feet. She reached out, accepted the remaining trays, and set them on her lap.

"Is there anything else I can do for you, Chef?" asked Léandre.

Sara shook her head but motioned to the other man who had remained near the rear entrance. Immediately he moved toward them, almost at a sprint. *What the hell is going on with these guys,* thought Caspian, but decided that discretion and silence were definitely the better part of valor, at least for the moment.

Sara extended both her hands through the open car window. The two men stared at them for a moment. She make a gripping motion, then accepted their hands in hers. "Léandre…Vincent…you both were magnificent today." The two men glanced at each other, then beamed. "I'm serious," she added. "Now, listen." They leaned close. "Vincent, I want you to make twice as much reduction sauce as you did over lunch. Tell the waitstaff to offer each diner the option of an additional ramekin of the sauce with their lamb. I assure you, most will accept. The servers will love you for the extra tips, and you will be called to numerous tables to accept the compliments of happy patrons. Léandre, you have truly become the master of the soufflé." He smiled shyly and inclined his head. "But," she added, "such perfection takes time, which you will not have tonight, trust me. Please instruct all the servers to ask each patron to consider the soufflé *while* they are ordering drinks or appetizers. Otherwise, they will need to wait if they request a soufflé after their entrees. That will cause the tables to turn more slowly, and…" she pointed, "the servers will *not* be nearly as happy about such a thing. Understand?"

"Yes, Chef," the two men said together, then Léandre tapped the roof of Caspian's car several times. "You may leave, but drive carefully. You carry precious cargo." He grinned at Sara. "And that is in addition to the wonderful food."

Caspian slipped the car into gear and slowly backed out as gravel cracked beneath his tires. Once they made it out onto open road, he looked over at Sara. "Okay, what just happened? Are they bewitched or something?"

She laughed. "Or something."

"No, I'm serious. They were completely besotted with you."

Sara turned to face him, then thickened her accent. "Do you not think my beauty is enough to besot a man, Mr. Lewis. What of my talent? Are not my beauty and talent enough? Do you accuse me of witchcraft, sir? Voodoo perhaps?"

"Oh dear God," laughed Caspian. "You may not look much like Michael, but holy cow, do you have his warped sense of humor."

Sara leaned back in her chair, voice returning to normal. "They are my students, well of a kind. Antoine's is one of my clients. I was hired to improve relations between the front and back of house, while also increasing per table revenue by at least twenty percent."

"Wow," said Caspian, "that sounds like a pretty impressive mandate."

"Didn't Michael tell you that's why I came to the States, to start my company?"

"He might have, but I only listen to thirty-five percent of what your cousin says. More than that, and I start to get migraines."

He looked over at her and she smiled. "You two, are like brothers…always being mean to each other. Men are so strange."

"Anyway," continued Caspian, "I knew you were a chef and wanted to start a business State-side after having been here last year. I never asked you about that, by-the-way. Michael said you had some medical stuff going on back then. Feel free to tell me to piss off for being nosey, but is everything okay?"

"Piss off," said Sara. Caspian swallowed, and she started laughing. "I'm just kidding. It was no big deal, more annoying than anything else."

"It didn't seem like nothing," said Caspian.

"Well, it was very uncomfortable, and could have become serious. Severe allergies. They flew me to Austin because I was having a hard time breathing."

"And that's nothing," chuckled Caspian. "I'm no doctor, but I've heard breathing is pretty important to, you know, staying alive."

"I've heard that too," agreed Sara, her voice deadpan. "But, as it turns out, I was allergic to Jamaica, so here I am."

Caspian frowned while keeping his eyes on the road. "How can someone be allergic to an entire island?"

He saw her shrug in his peripheral vision. "Pollen, spores, fungus, who knows. The folks in Austin said I should try a change in geography, because I didn't have one attack the entire time I was in Texas."

"And you didn't want to stay in Austin?"

Sara tilted her head forward, grabbed a handful of her long braids, and held them out toward Caspian. His eyes flicked right. "Do you see this hair? I've worked really hard to grow it, take care of it, and braid it." She shook her head. "It would not look good in a stetson."

Caspian started laughing. "I'm not sure *everyone* is required to wear a cowboy hat in Texas."

"I don't know," she replied. "It sure felt that way. Besides, whenever Michael comes home he always talks about how much he loves New Orleans and is never going to leave it. He calls it America's aging courtesan. I thought that was an elegant description, so decided to stake my claim to a small part of her."

"Michael did not come up with that," murmured Caspian.

"What?" she asked.

"The aging courtesan moniker. I bet Michael said he made that up."

Sara laughed. "Let's just say he *highly* implied it."

"Yeah, well he's *highly* filled with bullshit. That term was coined by William Faulkner." She shook her head. "He was an artist and poet from about a hundred years ago, did a bunch of New Orleans sketches. He said *New Orleans is that aging courtesan who shuns the sunlight, yet brings with her the elegance of a bygone era.*"

"Mmm," sighed Sara, "that description sounds as elegant as the city Faulkner was describing. My cousin's overt plagiarism aside, I think I'll keep using it." A brief silence settle between them, then Sara exclaimed "Oh my gosh." Caspian eyes darted around and his foot immediately tapped the brake. Relief washed over him as she said, "I'm so rude. Thanks for giving me a ride, Caspian. Did Michael tell you my car is in the shop?"

He took a deep breath, then slowly let it out. "Not a problem at all, and yeah, he mentioned it. By-the-way, you can call me Cas if you want. Pretty much the only people who call me Caspian are work folks." He paused. "Also Jenny and my parents, but only if she's mad at me or when I'm in trouble, respectively."

Sara reached over and gave Caspian's arm a quick pat. "Cas it is, well, unless you're in trouble, then I reserve the right to call you Caspian."

He laughed. "Fair enough. I'll do my best to stay out of your bad graces."

She smiled at him. "A wise decision, Mr. Lewis. Michael did say you were a clever one."

"Really?"

"Yes, but he swore me to secrecy."

"Remind me not to share any secrets with you," snickered Caspian.

She waved a hand dismissively, then stifled a yawn. "I'm actually great at keeping secrets. I'm also great at knowing secrets that people actually want told." She gave Caspian a wink. "Mikey thinks a lot of you, Cas. Of course he can't just tell you that, because, as I mentioned a few minutes ago, men are strange."

Chapter 25

A NEW CAMPAIGN

Michael opened the door and frowned at Caspian. "What took you so long? I could have gotten her myself at this rate. Even Jen is here."

Before Caspian could respond, Sara nudged him to the left with her trays. She shoved them against Michael's chest where he reflexively took the stack from her. Sara pointed at him. "Mikey, don't start. This was not Caspian's fault. I got delayed by a couple of the boys at work. Besides which, I'm providing take out from Antoine's that would easily be worth over five hundred dollars, assuming of course, Antoine's lowered itself to do take out, which they wouldn't." She pushed past him and into the foyer. "So, as your mother, my aunty, would say, *you can take that attitude and seal it in a bottle.*"

Caspian grinned. "Guess she told you...Mikey."

"Shut up and get inside," growled his friend. Caspian did.

Jennifer and David walked up to Caspian and each gave him a hug. "You're late," quipped Jennifer.

"Dont' start on me, Michael already tried to give me crap about it," said Caspian.

She laughed. "Give you crap? Oh no, no, no no. This isn't me giving you crap, Cas. This is me thanking you. I only got here about ten minutes ago. I was all set to receive gale force Jamaican blowback from our dearest friend

171

Michael, but he just said...," she pitched down her voice. *"Hey Jen. You can head up to the attic. I'm still waiting on Cas and my cousin."* Jennifer grinned. "That's all he said. It was glorious. I couldn't be late, because you were later. Anyway, I just came up here, poured the nerd and me a dram of bourbon and toasted your tardiness."

Caspian sighed. "Well, thanks for not making it worse by throwing me under the bus."

She laughed again. "Are you kidding? I totally threw you under the bus. I told Michael it was shameful for you to disrespect our first D&D game in years like this, and that I hoped he would be more understanding if I were ever late in the future...because I, at least, would have a good reason."

David shook his head. "And you wonder why you have a hard time keeping men around?"

Jennifer turned to David, reached up and gently pressed his cheeks until his lips puffed out. "Davey, Davey, Davey, what you don't know about women could fill volumes. Let me explain something to you. I do *not* have a hard time keeping men around. I have a hard time finding men *worth* keeping around. There's a huge difference."

Caspian shrugged. "I dunno, Jenny. If the only common denominator between all these failed men and you, is you, then maybe—"

"You are a laugh riot, Cas," interrupted Jennifer, "but you are also wrong. The common denominator between all these, as you say, failed men is that they aren't men at all. They are boys."

"Who are boys?" asked Sara. They all turned to her. She cringed slightly. "Oh, I'm sorry. I just finished setting up the food on Mikey's nifty buffet table, and wanted to tell you guys it's ready. I didn't mean to eavesdrop." She sighed. "I'm always just inserting myself into conversations. I really am sorry."

Jennifer slipped her arm around the younger woman, and pulled her close. "You are always welcome in any conversation, Sara. You're one of our merry, if slightly dysfunctional, band of misfit toys."

Sara smiled. "Merry, dysfunction, *and,* misfit, that *does* sound like me. Thanks for welcoming me aboard. Come, let me show you the food I had *my boys* cook for us while you tell me about *your boys.*" Sara glanced at Caspian and David, then asked, "Are they the boys?"

The two women circled around the large gaming table where Michael continued fussing with his dungeon master's set up. "No," replied Jennifer. "Fortunately or unfortunately, neither Cas or Dave suffer from the Peter Pan syndrome which has so cursed my dating life. I say fortunately because they are both actually men, not boys. Granted, Dave is a nerd-man, but he is a man. They both have jobs. They both have goals and aspirations that extend beyond ranking up on Call of Duty. For that matter, Michael does, too," she gestured to the gaming table, "despite his obvious obsession with his DM blinder boards."

"I know," said Sara, shaking her head. "I've never seen him like this, it's kinda fun. He's always the oh-so-cool one who gets all our State-side distribution channels running like clockwork. Who knew that beneath all that suave business-stuff lurked the heart of a wizard."

"I can hear you," grumbled Michael, "and I am *not* a wizard. I'm a dungeon master. Cas, I thought you were going to teach her?"

"I will," Caspian huffed. "Chill. We haven't even started yet."

Sara ignored the exchange, then asked, "So, I get why it's fortunate they aren't Peter Pans, but why is it unfortunate?"

Jennifer tilted her head toward the younger woman. "Because, my dear Sara, Caspian, David, and your cousin are tangible proof that real men do, in fact, exist, and thus I must continue my quest to find them."

Sara barked a laugh. "I get it. If there was no hope, you could just move on with your life...as a nun right?"

It was Jennifer's turn to laugh. "Did Michael tell you I said that? No, that was a joke. No self-respecting order would have me. I lack both discipline and commitment."

"And punctuality," added David.

"And punctuality," grumbled Jennifer. "Why, thank you Dave. Anyway, now you know the highlights of my ill-fated love life. You'll have to share yours with me over coffee sometime soon."

Sara shrugged. "Sounds like fun, but it will be an espresso, because I'm not much of a dater. Anyway, that's a story for another time. Let me give you a quick rundown on the food, then I'd really like to change."

"Don't change, Sara," yelled David, causing her to jump slightly.

"Oh gawd," murmured Jennifer.

"Stay just the way you are!" said both Caspian and Michael using the same deadpan inflection David had used.

Sara locked eyes with Jennifer. "What just happened?"

"Ignore them. It's something that Cas' dad does with all his kids. Every time one of them says something like, *hey, I'm heading upstairs to change,* he yells out—"

Sara chuckled. "I get it. So, these three may not be Peter Pans, but they do copy dad-jokes."

Jennifer nodded. "Welcome to 2021, Sara. It's slim pickings. Go on now. You run and get into something more comfortable. The food smells fantastic and you can give us your professional chef's description after you've changed."

"You sure?" she asked.

"Absolutely," added Caspian. "I'm super hungry and normally eat stuff without knowing what's in it. I think we're good, Sara."

"You don't have to tell me twice," she said, then headed for the door. Sara paused, turned back, and asked. "I don't have to wear a costume or anything do I?"

Jennifer shook her head. "Nope, just put on your most comfy clothes and hurry back because it looks like your cousin has finally figured out how to block our view of all his tables, charts, and dice."

Sara gave a general thumbs up to the room, then disappeared out the door.

Michael looked up and peered over the top edge of his intricately carved dungeon master's screen. Sara felt his eyes boring into her as she entered the room. She stopped, frowned at him, and said, "What now?"

"Nothing, Cuz," he murmured.

"That's his disappointed voice," said Jennifer.

"Oh, I recognize it," sighed Sara. She flashed a grin toward the other woman. "I grew up hearing that voice, until finally Cousin Mikey, flew away State-side to take over all of our sales and distributions. Gloriously peaceful days followed." Sara glowered at him. "So, what did I do to deserve *the voice* this time?"

"Well, since it is your first time playing with us, I thought you might make at least some effort to look nice."

Sara's eyes narrowed. "Oh boy," said Jennifer and David at the same time. Caspian just shook his head.

"What exactly is the matter with the way I look?" asked Sara in a tone so cold that they could almost see ice crystals form in the air.

Michael waved a hand in her direction. "You're in pajamas." He craned his neck. "And what are those things on your feet?"

"Slippers," she replied flatly, then added, "Spongebob slippers. Do you have a problem with Spongebob, Mikey?" He opened his mouth to respond, but

Sara pointed at him. "I asked if I had to dress up, and Jen said, *no it's super casual.*"

"Well she probably thought you meant dress up as, you know, an elf or something." Sara shook her head at her cousin and bit the corner of one lip. "Fine," she murmured, "I'll go change...again." She started to turn toward the door.

"Hey," yelled Caspian. He caught her eye and gave her a wink. "Don't change, Sara..."

"Stay just the way you are," came the responsive chorus, including Michael.

She stared at Caspian with uncertain eyes. He jumped up from his chair, then closed the distance between them. He put a friendly arm around Sara, and began guiding her across the large attic space to where the trays of food were laid out. She resisted at first, but Caspian leaned close, and whispered, "In the past, it doesn't seem like you took much of what Michael said very seriously, I recommend you not start now." Instantly her entire body language softened and her face broke into a grin. "There we go," laughed Caspian. "I'm telling you, Sara, if I had dimples like yours, I'd be flashing them *all* time. You should never frown, your face just isn't built for it."

"Thanks, Cas. Jen's right, you are sweet."

He shook his head in mock seriousness, "That's just a nasty rumor she made up. Please don't perpetuate it." He made an expansive gesture toward the food trays. "And now, lady Sara, would you be so kind as to explain the bountiful repast you provided."

She arched an eyebrow. "You haven't eaten yet? Please tell me all of you weren't waiting for me. Everything was hot and perfect when—"

"Relax," said Caspian as he began peeling back the tray's foil coverings. "We all ate, we just aren't entirely sure *what* we ate. Everything was amazing, and I, for one, am about to grab seconds. However, since we were all debating exactly what it was we enjoyed so much, I thought you could fill us in."

"All right," she said, rewarding him with another grin, "If you insist, Prince Caspian." Sara immediately shifted into chef presentation mode. "To begin we have a wonderful Creole Andouille Au Gratin with seared local Manda sausage, complemented with Antoine's creole sauce and a broiled 3-cheese topping."

"I already had two helpings of that," whispered Caspian.

"That's too bad, sir because there is enough cream in two servings to cause a coronary within a week. I suggest you get your affairs in order. Moving on, next we have a Deconstructed Roquefort Salad. Crisp iceberg blocks, smoked bacon crumbles, heirloom cherry tomatoes, chives, and a dusting of spiced pecans. All that complemented with our house Roquefort dressing."

"That, too, was amazing," said Caspian, "but I don't get the name. Why deconstructed?"

"Well," snickered Sara, "prior to my consulting with them, it was simply called Roquefort Salad, price eight dollars. Now, it is a Deconstructed Roquefort Salad, priced at ten." Caspian's mouth dropped open. She nodded. "Yes, Mr. Lewis, a twenty-five percent increase which our patrons happily pay for the privilege of enjoying a deconstructed salad rather than a mundane one."

Caspian raised his voice loud enough for everyone to hear. "Finally, someone who understands the true value of consulting, unlike you buffoons. Pray continue, Sara."

"Of course," she replied while gesturing to the third tray. "The dinner entree, which everyone seemed to hate..."

"Totally," interrupted Caspian, "which is why there is just one piece left and David has a broken arm because he tried to eat it."

She laughed. "Since it is Friday, and I know Jennifer, you, and I are all practicing Catholics, I opted for fish."

"Michael's Catholic, too," said Caspian.

"He's rather lapsed," she whispered back.

"Jenny and I are kinda lapsed, too," Caspian added.

"Trust me, not as lapsed as Mikey," snickered Sara while she placed the fish on her plate next to the portions of salad and potatoes that she'd served up moments before. She pointed at the fish. "This is Pompano Pontchatrain, perhaps my favorite fish dish at Antoine's."

"Pompano," sighed Caspian, then turned and called out to his friends. "Pompano....we all got it wrong."

Jennifer shrugged. "I'm a peasant, Cas. I just knew it wasn't Cod, and if it's not lox, David is completely lost."

"Well," continued Sara, "It is nothing like either lox or cod. It's a delicately grilled pompano filet accompanied with butter poached jumbo lump crabmeat, white wine sauce, onion rice, and seasonal vegetables." Sara pointed at the last tray which remained covered. "No one peeked?" she asked.

"No, we actually felt bad enough having scarfed down all that amazing food without you," said David. "The least we could do was wait for you to unveil the dessert."

"You shouldn't feel bad," said Sara. "I see and eat this stuff all week long. Do you guys want dessert now or after we play?"

"Cuz, we will be playing for hours, so it won't be after," said Michael.

"But," interjected Caspian, "some of us are about to have second dinner so will not have room for dessert now. How about we just plan on an intermission? Is that all right with you, dungeon master?" Michael gave a thumb's up. "So, what's in the tray?" asked Caspian as he raised his eyebrows several times.

"Only my favorite dessert that doesn't include chocolate. Chocolate is cheating and I wanted to impress my new friend group without cheating." She lifted one corner of the tray's covering foil, then wafted the air toward Caspian with her other hand. Sara watched his nose flare as he took in the scents. "Any ideas?" she asked.

"Smells like rum and cinnamon."

Sara nodded, then resealed the foil. "You have a good nose, sir. That is Antoine's bread pudding. Its base is traditional Leidenheimer french bread that is drenched in a combination of eggs, cream, cinnamon, vanilla, and buttered rum." She placed a hand on Caspian's chest and affected a sad expression. "Alas, if you eat this after also having two portions of the Au Gratin, I fear you might expire before the night is over."

"What a way to go," laughed Caspian then turned toward his friends. "Ladies and Gentlemen, I give you Chef Sara Edwards, the founder of the feast. What say you?"

Everyone began pounding the table enthusiastically and cheering with poorly affected British accents.

Caspian bowed with a flourish toward two of the chairs. "I have been charged with your education this evening, Lady Sara, assuming you will have me."

She inclined her head seriously, "I will, sir, and what will be our first lesson?"

Caspian smiled at her. "Why Lady Sara, we must determine what race you are."

Chapter 26

THE TOMB OF HORRORS, DAY ONE

Sara tilted up her face and pretended to stare at the ceiling for several seconds. "I think," she began, "after hearing all my options, and after careful consideration, that I will be..." She paused, then scanned the table. Everyone leaned forward slightly in anticipation of her answer. "A wood elf rogue," declared Sara. Her brow immediately furrowed at the room's reaction, or lack thereof. Jennifer and David sat expressionless as if they had suddenly been frozen in place. Michael stared at her, blinked, then said, "Uh, what about playing a dark elf?"

"You play a dark elf, Mikey. Why do I have to play one too?" asked Sarah. "Is it because we're from Jamaica? Am I unfairly appropriating wood elf culture, Cousin?" She grinned, but it fell away almost immediately, shifting to confusion. "Did I say something wrong?" she asked.

"No," answered Caspian, "it's a great choice. You wanted to play someone sneaky and stealthy. Rogues are most certainly that. As for the race, elves definitely make excellent rogues, no argument there either."

"But why a wood elf?" asked Jennifer.

"Yeah," interjected David, "I rarely agree with your cousin, but dark elves have way better night vision."

Sara's shoulders sagged slightly under their additional scrutiny. "Well," she said, "I had read up on all the races earlier today, but didn't get to the classes. Once I decided on being a rogue, I knew I also wanted to be an elf. The wood elves have kinda coppery skin, and according to the book, can also have hazel eyes." She held up one arm. "So, it's a stretch to call this coppery, but my eyes are definitely hazel, and I'm the only one in our whole family who has hazel eyes. Also...wood elves live for hundreds of years, and I'd like to live a long time, too. They love exploration and adventure. That's me. Finally, they are described as slender *and* graceful."

"No one has ever called you graceful," snickered Michael.

"You shut up now, Mikey," she snapped, then pointed at him. "No one ever called you slender until you left home, or shall I pull up of a few of those chunky-Mikey pictures that are likely buried in my phone somewhere?" Sara took a deep breath. "Clearly, you guys don't want me to be a wood elf, so I'll —"

"You'll be exactly the race and class you chose, Sara," said Caspian. He gave his three friends a pointed look. "It's fine." They all nodded, and Caspian turned to Sara. He saw her continued hesitancy, shot her a smile, then said, "So, you are a level 1, wood elf rogue. Have you come up with a name? Names given freely, have power, you know."

Her concerns seemed to evaporate into enthusiasm. "I came up with the name first. Are you ready?"

Caspian rubbed his hands together, "Hit me."

"Okay...I'm so jazzed about this name. Her name is, Valdania Shannara. Pretty good, right?"

Caspian laughed. "It's a solid name, if a bit plagiaristic."

"It is not plagiaristic," scoffed Jennifer. "It's an homage, right Sara?"

The younger woman nodded. "I loved those Shannara stories growing up. I must have read the first trilogy at least five times."

Caspian clapped his hands together. "Dungeon Master, attend to your players. We have an announcement to make."

Michael gave him a solemn nod. "Your master hears you, Tholem of Surrealia. What say you?"

"Our noble band seeks to welcome a new misfit among our ranks. Where we go, she will go. Where we lodge, she will lodge. Our people will be her people, and our gods will be her gods. Master, please write in the scroll of life that this day, Valdania Shannara, wood elf Rogue, has joined the Band of Misfit Toys."

"Do all current members of the band agree with this proclamation?" asked Michael.

"We do," replied both Jennifer and David.

Michael turned to his cousin, who seemed to be vibrating in anticipation of what, she did not know. "Valdania Shannara, you have been given a solemn invitation by Tholem of Surrealia. You heard his expectations of you. Are you prepared to pledge to them your life, your fortunes, and your sacred honor?"

Sara looked around the table. David and Caspian both stared back with serious expressions. Jennifer's lips quirked up, and she gave an almost imperceptible nod. Sara squared her shoulders, then lifted her chin, and said in a clear voice, "I, Valdania Shannara, wood elf rogue of the mysterious Jamaicamahn island, accept this invitation without reservation."

Laughter, woots and cheers erupted from everyone but Michael. After allowing a few moments of celebration, he intoned, "Very well, Valdania. You are now bound in this life and the next to those of your fellows. You join at a perilous time, for the Band of Misfit Toys has just discovered..." He paused for effect, then boomed, "A Tomb of Horrors!"

"What's in there?" asked Jennifer as Sara held up a small pitcher.

"Creamy heaven, that's what. Now lift your plate. I have to drizzle it over the bread pudding just right."

"Only a little," cautioned Jennifer, "I'm going to be thirty and I don't need your devil-sauce permanently attached to my thighs."

Sara began drizzling, but said, "Thirty? When will you be thirty?"

"Someday," snickered Jennifer, then tried to pull her plate away. "Stop, with the cream already." She slid one finger across the bread pudding and took a lick. Sara arched an eyebrow. "Okay," said Jennifer, "maybe just a tiny bit more. I'll run an extra mile tomorrow."

"Good call," whispered Sara, then looked around. David and Caspian had both returned to the gaming table where they chatted in-between bites of bread pudding. Michael had scarfed his down in several giant mouthfuls, and now hunched behind his dungeon master screens, pouring over various maps. "Uh, Jenny, can I ask you something?"

"Hmm...sure...always." She saw Sara cast another furtive glance toward the gaming table, and asked, "What is it?"

Sara set down the pitcher of cream, then leaned close. "What the heck was going on with my character's race and class? You guys stared at me like you'd seen a ghost. I let it drop because—" She broke off a second, eyes widening. "That's the look. You're giving me the same look, right now. What is that look about?"

Jennifer set down her plate next to the serving trays and moved so her back was to the gaming table and she completely obscured the smaller woman from view. "I'll tell you," replied Jennifer softly, "but you cannot change what you've done, and you cannot freak out, okay?"

"Well, now I'm definitely going to freak out," hissed Sara. "What did I do?"

Jennifer reached a clandestine hand down and took one of Sara's in her own. "You didn't do anything. There's no way you could have known without one of us having told you, and why would we? I mean what are the odds?"

"Odds of what, Jenny?" asked Sara.

The other woman let out a breath. "Odds that you would choose the exact character race and class that Elizabeth played."

Sara held a hand up to her mouth and her eyes immediately began to fill. She tried to look around Jennifer. "Don't look at him," whispered Jennifer, "and do not freak out."

"I'm so stupid," said Sara. "The looks, the questions, everything you guys were saying. Oh my God, I am too dumb to live."

"Not all of us were saying it, and you are not dumb at all. The most important person, in this particular regard, is Caspian, and what did *he* say?"

"He was just being nice," murmured Sara.

Jennifer shook her head. "Let me tell you something about Caspian Lewis. He *is* nice. He's probably the nicest guy I know, but he *never* and I mean *never*, says something he doesn't believe just to be...*nice*. If he said you made a good choice, he believed it. That's why I gave you the nod. It's also why you cannot let him see you're upset. This is a big deal, Sara. It's also one heck of a compliment if you ask me. We don't just invite anyone to play with us, but if we did invite someone and they wanted to play that combination, I guarantee you Caspian would have vetoed it." Jennifer lowered her voice even further. "He didn't veto it though, did he? In fact, he vetoed our attempted veto. Quite frankly that says a lot about you, and, well, I think it's a really good sign."

"So, don't screw it up?" asked Sara with a smile.

"Exactly, see, you can catch subtext when you aren't all excited about becoming a wood elf rogue."

Sara barked a laugh, then covered her mouth.

"Hey, are you guys going to eat bread pudding all night, or are we going to play?" yelled Michael. "I want to read the campaign's prologue and get you guys through at least one encounter before we call it for the night."

"Coming, Dad," snarked Jennifer, then gave Sara a wink as they headed toward the gaming table.

Michael held up his hands. "OOC, this campaign is an original Gary Gygax S1 module. I've updated it for—" Sara raised her hand. "How could you have a question already, Sar? Also, this isn't school. You don't need to raise your hand."

"Fine," huffed Sara, "I won't, but your first sentence used something I'd never heard of. What does—"

"OOC means Out Of Character," offered Caspian. "We use it whenever one of us wants to talk real-world stuff."

"Yeah," said David, "like if I wanted to bring up how things were going at work. I'd say *OOC* then wait for everyone to give me a nod, then I'd follow up with something like, *I'm going to use that last fight as a model for a mission in Mass Effect 4.*"

Sara nodded. "Okay, I get it, but Michael didn't wait for us to nod. He just plowed ahead."

"Dungeon masters don't have to wait," said Jennifer. "They set the context for an entire campaign, so can break it as they like."

"But we don't do it willy nilly," added Michael, "because any decent DM creates an immersive experience. Now, may I continue?" He didn't wait for a response, but said, "This module is also the one that was referenced in *Ready Player One*, the book, not the movie. The movie sucked. Anyway, it's been out of print for decades, but *I* found a copy." He held up a finger. "I caution you to *not* rely on anything from Ernie Cline's book during this campaign. I've changed things around. There may, or may not, be a Lich in this tomb, but if there is, he won't be playing Joust. If by some miracle one of you have actually played the Tomb of Horrors before, rest assured, I have populated this dungeon with a *lot* more monsters than in the original module. Everyone clear, because I know Caspian has listened to that audiobook a dozen times. Don't let him walk you guys off a proverbial cliff because he thinks he knows something."

Michael pointed at him. "You know nothing, Caspian Lewis. Okay, end of OOC. Here we go."

Michael glanced down, and clearly began reading from something obscured behind his DM screens. "There has long been tales told of a labyrinithine crypt located somewhere under a lost and lonely hill of grim aspect. It is rumored to be filled with terrible traps, and not a few strange and ferocious monsters that slaver at the prospect of slaying the unwary. If legends are to be believed, the tomb also contains rich treasures, both mundane and magical." Michael looked up, shook his head in warning, and gave his voice a menacing tone. "Know this brave adventurers, in addition to the aforementioned guardians, there is said to be a lich who still wards this, his final haunt. No one has ever found Acererak's crypt, or if they have, none have lived to tell the tale. Only the bravest, strongest, and most well prepared parties should even consider the attempt. My question to you who comprise the Band of Misfit Toys is this, are you such a party?"

Caspian slammed his fist onto the table, but it was so sturdily built that their drink glasses barely jumped in their holders. Sara, did jump, then grinned when Caspian, Jennifer, and David all cheered, "We are!" She was still smiling when silence descended, and four pairs of eyes bored in to her expectantly. "Oh," she said, then pitched her voice down slightly, "I mean, Oh-of-course, we are such a party. What a silly question to even have asked. No creatures above the earth or within a tomb are a match for my blades. No traps can remain hidden from my sight, and no locks can withstand my deft touch." She raised her hand brandishing an invisible dagger. "Acererack will fall to the Band of Misfit Toys, and all his treasure will be mine!"

Jennifer's eyes danced, and she made several quiet claps toward Sara. "Perhaps you misspoke Valdania Shannara," boomed Caspian. "Or do the ways of those from your island differ so greatly from those of this land. Perhaps you could clarify what you meant by saying all *his treasure will be yours?*"

Sara showed her teeth. "Of course, Tholem, forgive me for my poor turn of phrase. I should have said, Acererack will fall to the Band of Misfit Toys, and all his treasure will be *ours!*"

Caspian narrowed his eyes at her, and Sara leaned back in her chair, interlacing her hands behind her head in affected nonchalance. "I don't know if I can trust you, Valdania," said Caspian.

"Oh, I know," replied Sara. She put both elbows on the table, then rested her chin in the palm of her hands, and locked eyes with Caspian. "You can't." She smiled causing her dimples to appear.

"A rogue after my own heart," he laughed.   She shrugged, and neither of them noticed the silent looks shared between Jennifer, David, and Michael.

Chapter 27

DECRYPTION

David Rushing lay on his couch, eyes closed, as the sounds of Dumbledore's study flowed from his television's sound bar and throughout his living room. He drifted in and out of sleep, enjoying what David told himself was a well deserved nap. He was only vaguely aware of the Harry Potter ASMR YouTube channel, with its soft rustling of papers or occasional fireplace pops. *Ah, the benefits of working from home*, he thought lazily. After their first *Tomb of Horrors* D&D night, David spent twelve hours on Saturday and fourteen hours on Sunday, working through his team's Mass Effect 4, development stories. Consequently, his team had at least three days worth of backlogged work, which meant David had three days to do with what he wanted. At the moment, that meant snoozing on his couch listening to Dumbledore's study.

Several minutes later, his situation changed, when a woman's voice began speaking with a distinctively Scottish brogue. *Hello, David, are you there?*

He opened one eye. "Hi Shannon, what's up?"

Two things are up, David. One is a joke. Would you like to hear a joke? Yes or No.

He interlaced his hands behind his head, and smiled. David had recently created a custom Alexa skill that integrated all of his Echo devices with the rudimentary *Shannon* AI that continually ran on his Mac Pro. One of the new subroutines he added was for her to offer jokes at random intervals. This was the first time that subroutine had activated. All things being equal, David thought this was pretty darn cool. "Yes, Shannon, I would like to hear a joke."

Knock Knock, said the AI.

"Oooo, a knock-knock, joke," said David.

I'm sorry, replied Shannon, *that is an incorrect response. The correct response is who's there. Would you like to try again?*

"Yes, sorry, Shannon."

That is all right, David. I will try again. Knock Knock.

"Who's there?" he asked.

Hatch.

David gave a low chuckle. "Hatch who?"

Bless you! Replied the AI.

"Hey, that one wasn't bad at all," laughed David. "Okay, Shannon, what else is up."

The RushingViolence algorithm successfully generated a private key that decrypted file, Elizabeth_Winters002.

David bolted upright. "Holy crap, are you kidding me right now?"

I'm sorry David, replied the AI, *I am not kidding you right now. I have already told you a joke. Would you like me to—*

"Shannon—cancel." David grabbed the remote from his coffee table, pressed the voice activation button, and said, "Initiate group FaceTime to fellowship-of-the-ring." Dumbledore's study vanished from the TV, and was replaced moments later by three squares, each of which contained a face. Caspian, Jennifer, and Michael stared at David from the large screen. He offered an exaggerated thumb's up gesture. "RushingViolence remains undefeated. Are you guys ready for another road trip?"

"Wait," said Jennifer, "before you open the file, I want to ask you guys something. I was thinking about this all weekend."

Caspian furrowed his brow. "Why did you stew over whatever it was for two days?"

"I'm more concerned that Jennifer has been *thinking* for two days," snickered Michael.

"Shad-up, Mikey," she lilted. "As for why I held my tongue, simple, I expected Dave to fail."

"Never bet against RushingViolence," yelled David, then lifted both his arms and hopped around his living room in a decidedly Rocky'esque fashion. "Undefeated!"

"Oh my God," sighed Jennifer, "this just proves my point. Guys, can we invite Sara into our little fellowship...pleassse? I hate being the only girl, and I'm really afraid I might start growing facial hair from..." she gestured to David's still hopping form, "...all the unbound testosterone."

Michael shrugged. "I don't care. It's fine with me if she joins."

David lowered his arms long enough to stare into the TV's camera, nod his head, and say, "I think it would be great. She's awesome. I've never seen someone take to D&D so well before."

"Absolutely not," said Caspian in a tone that brought everyone up short. He felt their eyes on him as his three friends each focused on their respective cameras. "Don't look at me that way," he grumbled. "I'm exercising my veto authority on this one."

"Veto authority?" asked Michael. "Did I miss a memo or something? Cas, your veto power is very narrow, just like the rest of ours. Our fellowship of the ring stuff is not, in any way, D&D related."

David and Jennifer both nodded their heads in agreement. "I'm extending my veto authority," said Caspian flatly. "Listen you doorknobs, I think you have lost sight of something." He didn't wait for them to respond. "We're committing felonies at the request of my dead fiancé."

"I haven't committed anything," said Michael, then pointed at his camera. "David did."

"Accessory before, during, and after the fact, bitches," yelled David, then resumed hopping.

Michael frowned. "Is that a thing?"

"Oh yeah it's a thing," chuckled Jennifer, "and we're tits deep in that thing."

"Whatever," sighed Michael, "my cuz can keep a secret. She wouldn't tell anyone."

"Not going to happen," said Caspian. "Felonies aside, we're still doing all of this based on Lizzie coming to me in a dream and to Whittaker having those weird visions."

Jennifer looked confused. "What are you saying, Cas? You can't possibly start doubting now."

He shook his head. "Oh hell no, I'm completely convinced Lizzie is somehow communicating with us. That's why I'm not going to let any of you screw things up. I'm the one who had the dream. She said I needed to go on this quest with you three, not you three and Sara. I like Sara. She's adorable, and Dave's right, she's also an awesome D&D player. I can't wait to play with her again. I also hope she brings us more food, which is beside the point. Finally, I hope she becomes a regular member of our friend group. I hope all of those things, but remember what I told you guys. Lizzie said, if I do this properly, I will get to see her in the waking world." He shook his head. "No, I'm not risking it." Caspian made a gripping motion with his right hand and pretended to slam it down on something. "Veto!"

Everyone remained silent for several seconds, then his friends all nodded. "Sorry, Cas," said Jennifer. "You're right, of course."

"Yeah, I'm sorry, too," offered Michael.

David shook his head at his TV's camera. "I told you guys that Cas should have a veto about this, but you two fought me every inch of the way. I'm glad you're finally seeing reason." He made a fist pump toward his camera. "Veto deployed!"

Jennifer shook her head. "Shut-up Dave, you did not object at all. Now, open the file."

David's eyes scanned the PDF on his laptop. "Well, now I understand the extra encryption."

"Why," asked Caspian.

"She's a minor. Mary Foster, age 17 of Rock Springs Wyoming. Hey, Cas, she has the same first name as Elizabeth's mom." His eyes widened. "Do you think that means something?"

"I don't know, Dave," replied Caspian sarcastically, "This is my first paranormal experience."

"Yeah, you're right, it probably doesn't. Rock Springs. Rock Springs. Why does that sound familiar? Wait, is that the town from *Blazing Saddles*? Boy, there's a movie you couldn't make today because—"

"No, that was Rock Ridge," interrupted Caspian. "Rock Springs is one of the largest Wyoming cities, and by largest, I mean far less than what fits in the SuperDome. Guys, not a lot of people live in Wyoming. I went to Cheyenne once for a consulting gig. It's the State capital and New Orleans is about seven times bigger."

"Well, it looks like we're going to Wyoming," said Jennifer. "I just pulled it up on the Interwebs. Ooo, they wear hats there. I'm going to get a hat, and some boots, and...oh wow, guys, did you know Wyoming has mountains."

"Yes, Jenny, I believe they just added them last week," snarked Caspian.

She pointed at her camera. "You can stow that attitude, mister. I didn't know. I'm a native NOLA gal, we don't associate with y'all yankees unless we have to."

"Jen, Wyoming didn't even exist during the civil war," began David, "and if it did, I don't think it would have aligned with the North. The feds actually designate Wyoming as part of the West, not even the Northwest."

Jennifer flared her nose. "Dave, didn't one of us ask you to poop out that encyclopedia you ate?"

"That was me," offered Michael. "Clearly, he's constipated, which is surprising given how much fiber must be in an encyclopedia."

"Did you quote endless facts on your..." Jennifer made air quotes, "*date*, this past weekend."

David mirrored the motion. "My *date*, actually went really well. She's very sweet, unlike a certain harpy-shrew who will remain nameless. And, no, I did not quote endless facts. I took Caspian's advice. I listened. In fact, I may have only said about five words the whole night."

Jennifer nodded. "I'm impressed. I bet she liked that."

"Actually, it was very strange. After dinner, she suggested we go for coffee and beignets at Cafe Du Monde."

"That means she liked you," laughed Jennifer.

"Which is why he found it strange," interjected Michael.

"No, stop, I'm being serious," said David. "So after dessert, we were saying goodnight in the parking lot, and she told me that I was a really great conversationalist. That's what I found strange. Like I said, I barely uttered a word the whole night."

Jennifer shrugged. "Girls like that. Listening *is* conversation for us." She pointed at her camera. "Caspian has been well trained. Some gal is going to be very lucky to have you someday. It'll be like taking in a potty trained dog from rescue. She'll get all the loving without the mess."

Caspian sighed, "I'm not convinced there will be another gal for me, Jenny, but I am completely sure that neither Michael, David, or I could have gotten away with that metaphor."

Jennifer showed her teeth. "Girl privilege. Now, when are we going to Wyoming? I can't wait to meet this Mary Foster. Do you think she's had visions, too?"

"I'm booked solid for the next two weeks," said Michael. "I'm covering eight states in ten days. A whole bunch of our distribution contracts are up and I have to make sure they get renewed. I'm good from the middle of April on though."

"I can go whenever," said David.

"Obviously, I can only go on weekends until school's out in May," said Jennifer. She saw everyone's expression, and held up a hand. "Okay, I could probably take off another Friday, but no more than that."

"What about you, Cas?" asked Michael.

"Middle of April works for me. McKinsey doesn't much care where I am as long as I get my work done, but, guys, this cannot be like it was with Whittaker." He saw their blank expressions. "This Mary Foster, is a kid. According to Dave, she's seventeen. We can't just walk up to her and go, *Hey, we're four ghost hunting ghouls from New Orleans, and we've committed multiple felonies to find out that you're breathing with someone else's lungs in your chest.*"

Michael pursed his lips. "Yeah, I can see how that might be bad. So, what do we do?"

"Parents," said Jennifer. "We need to talk with her parents when she's not around. That means we definitely should do it before school gets out. Dave, can you find out what her parents do for a living? Maybe they are still working from home because of the pandemic. That would make things easier."

David affected a salute toward his camera, and laughed. "That's a piece of cake compared to what you guys have been asking of me. By-the-way, are we playing D&D again next Friday?"

"Pffft...yeah," huffed Michael. "We're playing every Friday unless one of us is out of town or we're on a LizzieQuest mission."

"Okay, don't get pissy," said David. "I was just checking. I'll have all the parental info for you guys by Friday then."

Caspian nodded. "That sounds good, but..." he raised a finger, "do *not* bring any of this up in front of Sara. Maybe we could meet a few minutes before and —"

"No, you are picking her up from whatever restaurant she's working at that day," said Michael.

"I am?" Caspian asked, then frowned, "Why am I picking her up again? Isn't her car fixed yet?"

"Do I look like Sara's mechanic, Cas? No I do not, and therefore I have no idea whether her car is working or not. What I do know is that she asked me if you would give her a ride, and it's the least you can do in order for us to secure another amazing dinner. Don't screw this up for the rest of us."

"Okay, okay, I'll give her a ride, sheesh," grumbled Caspian.

"Good," said Michael, "Sara gets up around six in the morning on weekdays. Trust me, she'll be angling for her bed as soon as we're done playing for the night. I'll just tell her we don't need her to help clean up, then we can talk after. Sound good?"

Everyone nodded. "Cool," said David. "Seems like we have a plan. Now I'm going to get back to what I was doing. Say, goodbye, Dave, you are fantastic."

"Goodbye Dave, you are fantastic," came the chorus.

He smiled as the three windows went blank, then picked up the remote, and thumbed the voice activation. "Play Dumbledore's Study ASMR." Less than a minute later, David Rushing was, once again, dozing on his couch.

Chapter 28

THE TOMB OF HORRORS, DAY TWO

"A rodent of unusual size leaps out from the crypt alcove Tholem was investigating," began Michael. "The ROUS bares its teeth at him. Foam drips from its mouth. It's rabid. If it even scratches him, Tholem will have to save versus poison or become infected. Meanwhile—"

"Am I within backstabbing distance?" asked Sara earnestly.

Her cousin frowned at her, increased the volume of his voice, and said, "Meanwhile…OOC David pay attention or your character is likely to die. You don't want Harg to die, do you?"

David talked around a chunk of fried cheese curd he had just popped in his mouth. "Wha? How is Harg going to die? He's just standing there. Michael, do not try and kill off my favorite Orc fighter just because he rolled a nat-twenty on that last encounter."

Michael ignored him. "As I'm sure all of *you* recall, Harg decided to lean causally against the tunnel wall while Tholem and Valdania poked through that pile of bones for coin. Well, it turns out that Harg isn't very perceptive."

"Uh oh," said Jennifer, then shook her head at David. "I told you not to touch stuff, didn't I…Harg. You are always putting your beefy green hands on stuff you aren't supposed to. Now something bad's going to happen, and *I'm* going to have to fix it."

195

"Good luck with that," muttered Michael under his breath, then raised his voice. "One of the bricks Harg leaned against shifts slightly and the floor beneath him begins to give way."

"Wait a minute," sputtered David, "Our Cleric warned me not to touch stuff. When I touched the wall, anyway, she would have done a perception check."

"She did," said Michael flatly, "and she failed it."

"What?" cried Jennifer, "Samara Mournforge does *not* fail perception checks. I'm wearing a cloak of perception for God's sake."

Michael sighed, then lifted a red twenty-sided die from behind his screen. He tilted it toward Jennifer, displaying a white number one, set against the die's crimson background. Caspian laughed. "I guess that nat-one makes up for Dave's previous nat-twenty." He winked at David. "Sorry, brotha, looks like Harg is going to fall into some kind of pit."

Michael arched an eyebrow at his players. "That depends on Sara, I mean Valdania."

Sara perked up. "What, I'm a rogue not a doctor, what the heck am I going to do. Besides, I hate orcs and barely tolerate Harg. He smells. He's rude, and...he smells."

Caspian fake whispered, "You said *he smells* twice."

"Because," Sara replied, "he smells two times as bad as a normal orc, which is pretty bad." She made a show of blinking several times. "The stench makes my eyes water."

Caspian and Jennifer both nodded in agreement as Michael valiantly tried to soldier on with his narration. "As I was saying, Harg's fate depends largely on you, Valdania, as does the fate of Tholem. Your rogue's senses detected the trap a split second prior to Harg tripping it. You have time to perform one action. You can either backstab the rodent of unusual size *or* you can try and push Harg to safety."

"This is complete bullshit," grumbled David.

"I know," agreed Jennifer, "like that copper-toned wood elf wench would have better perceptions than me." She snorted. "I think not."

"That wasn't my point, Jen, and you know it," said David.

"What if I use my rapid movement ability toward Harg, *and* throw a previously empowered dagger at the, what did you call the rat?"

"A Rodent of Unusual Size, or ROUS," replied her cousin.

Caspian leaned toward Sara and whispered in her ear. "He stole that from *The Princess Bride*."

She giggled, then tilted her head away. "I *knew* I heard that name before. Stop, that tickles. We wood elves have very sensitive ears, you know." She focused on Michael. "So, can I do that, push Harg out of the way and perform a distance backstab on the ROUS?"

"No," he replied flatly. "Your backstab only works as a melee attack, besides I told you already, you have one action, not two." Michael grinned at her, then set a small plastic hourglass in front of his DM screen. The sand began to quickly run from the top half and into the bottom. "Tick-tock, Valdania," he said with a wink. "You can save the Orc or you can save the Human, but you can't save both." Michael eyed the timer, "Of course, you could lose both if you don't decide before the last grain falls."

"Tholem has great saves against poison," pleaded David. "Harg is just a baby. He's only been on one other campaign. He's too young to die."

David clasped his hands together in supplication, but Sara just shook her head. "Sorry, Dave. Despite Harg's, bad hygiene and generally boorish nature, I've grown rather fond of him." She glanced at Caspian. "However, Tholem's charisma is off the charts. In addition, he's being attacked by rats from one of the best movies of all time." Sara gave a nod to Michael, then said, "Valdania sees the rodent of unusual size, and refuses to let it take down Tholem like it did her first love, Wesley, the farm boy. She whirls around, then plunges her dagger between the vermin's shoulder blades."

Everyone but David gave her nods of approval as Sara scooped up her dice and tossed them. "Wooo!" shouted Jennifer, "that is one dead rat. No way it survives once the backstab adjustment is added."

They heard Michael tapping on his iPhone screen as he entered the damage in to his DM app. He looked up, inclined his head to Sara, and said, "Valdania strikes true. Her blade passed easily between the ROUS's shoulder blades and into its heart, killing the massive rat instantly. It had no chance to even give Caspian a death blow attack."

Caspian said, "Tholem turns around, unaware of how much danger he was in, sees the rat's still twitching corpse, and realizes how close to death he just came. He gives a grateful smile to Valdania and—"

"Harg falls through the floor," yelled Michael, interrupting whatever Tholem was about to tell Valdania. "As the tunnel's rough hewn floor tiles give way beneath him, Harg desperately grabs for any purchase whatsoever. He lets out a rather pathetic cry, almost like that of a child." David shook his head as Michael continued with a self-satisfied smile. "Harg's last thoughts as he disappeared from sight were probably something like, *I really should have paid attention to that small, but very wise, voice that kept telling me not to touch or lean on things in the Tomb of Horrors.* Sadly," continued Michael, "it was too late to listen to the small, but very wise, voice, as Harg looked down to see an array of spikes jutting up from the relatively shallow pit."

"My armor should definitely protect me from a shallow pit, dude," complained David.

Michael pretended not to hear. "However, Harg's amour and thick Orc skin has a chance of protecting him since the pit is relatively shallow. All armor has its weak points, and Harg's is no different." Michael gave his friend the most evil of grins. "A spike has found its way into one such weak point, but which one? Harg groans from the pit's bottom, begging for aid. What do you do?"

"How deep is the pit," sighed Jennifer.

"About eight feet."

"Okay," she said, "Samara jumps into the pit, careful to avoid the spikes, and begins casting healing hands on her stupid Orc friend. What's the injury?"

"The pit spike pierced Harg at the shoulder, knee, or..." Michael paused for effect, "groin."

"Oh for frak's sake," hissed David. "Is this my punishment for not paying attention to your..." he made air quotes, "small, but very wise, voice?"

The two men shared a look, then Michael shrugged, and handed David an emerald colored, six sided, die. "I have no idea what you are talking about, adventurer. Shoulder on one, thigh on two or three, and Harg's family jewels take a beating on either a four or five. Finally, he becomes the world's first Orc eunuch on a six."

"Dave, you better pray for a three or less," laughed Jennifer, "because I'll tell you one thing for certain. Samara is not placing her healing hands on your Orkish junk."

David snatched the die from Michael and angrily tossed it into the dice tray. It rattled against the high sides of the tray then spun on its edge for a second or two. Finally, it came to rest with three pips facing up. David let out a relieved sigh. "Harg has impaled his thigh on a spike, severing an artery," said Michael, "He will bleed to death in six turns without help. Will anyone help him?"

"I will," said Jennifer, then asked, "Has Samara already jumped into the pit?"

"No," replied Michael, "She was about to, but took time to see where Harg was wounded."

Jennifer nodded. "Okay, once again, Samara makes very careful note of all the spikes, then jumps into the pit, and casts healing hands."

Michael nodded. "Samara Mournforge being a cleric of high ideals, leaps in to save the foolish Harg. She places glowing hands to the orc's thigh and, within minutes, Harg is back on his feet." Jennifer, Sara, and David all gave a little cheer. Michael raised a cautionary finger. "However, Harg will walk with a limp for two weeks causing his movement speed to decrease by twenty-five percent. The Orc counts himself lucky for having escaped the pit trap with his manhood."

"I bet he does," snickered Caspian. "For his part, Tholem reaches into the pit and extends one hand to Samara."

"I clasp my hand to his wrist, and he pulls me up," said Jennifer. "I then turn around and offer my hand to Harg, but when he reaches for it, I pull back, and ask if he promises to stop touching things *and* to bathe at least once a week."

"Yes," cheered Sara, "excellent call, Jenny."

"Why thank you," replied Jennifer

"Fine, I accept," grumbled David, "but you should all know that Harg feels very judged right now." He fake sniffled. "Orcs are people too, you know. We have feelings. We are not carved of stone."

Michael tapped his DM gavel against the table. "Annnd, that's a good stopping point for the night. Tholem didn't get rabies, and Harg didn't become a eunuch. All-in-all, I'd say a very—"

"Wait," interrupted Sara. She shot an impish grin in Caspian's direction. "I believe Tholem was in the middle of expressing thanks to fair, but stealthy, Valdania when Harg ruined the moment by nearly castrating himself." Sara put the heels of both palms together and rested her chin there. She affected a longing gaze in Caspian's direction, and continued, "Go on then, Tholem of Surrealia. What do you have to say to the woman who saved you from such a deadly and foul creature?"

Caspian extended a hand toward Sara. "Why fair Valdania," he intoned, "I am at your service. Whatever boon you would have of me, is yours."

"Really?" she asked, her voice rising. "Any boon, without restriction, my... my...my." She traced a finger along the back of Caspian's hand. "I believe I'll take some time to ponder in my heart what boon to ask of you." Her eyes seemed to dance, and she laughed. "I think I might like the feeling of having you in my debt for a while...Tholem."

Several whoops and cat-calls erupted from around the table, with David adding, "From the looks of things, the *service* Valdania might demand, could require a tavern room."

Sara laughed, then pulled away from Caspian, both hands raised in negation. She shook her head, "Valdania is not that kind of wood elf." She locked eyes with Caspian, gave him a wry grin, then said, "She mates for life, and any man foolish enough to throw her over, might just have a dagger thrown at him."

Jennifer clapped her hands together. "You tell him, Valdania." She pointed at Caspian. "Oh, look, she actually made Cas blush."

"Pfft, no she didn't," he sputtered far too forcefully to be believed.

Jennifer wrapped her arms around Sara, squeezed her, then the two rocked back and forth several times. "You totally made him bluh-ush. Do you know how hard it is to make that boy blush? Sara, you are my new hero."

"I didn't blush," muttered Caspian again.

"I completely agree," said Sara with mock seriousness, "the redness in your face could have resulted from anything." She gave him a wink, then added, "Well, as much fun as this is, I have to get up early in the morning because I promised to do a dry-run with Brennan's in prep for their Sunday brunch this weekend. We've really tweaked the menu and they're all freaked out." She stood and frowned at the mostly empty buffet trays and dirty dishes. "I hate leaving you guys with this mess though. Why don't I at least help put the—"

"No, no," interrupted Michael. "The deal was, you bring the food, we clean up, and you most definitely brought the food...again. What time do you need to be up in the morning?"

Sara groaned. "About five-thirty."

Caspian looked at his watch. "It's after midnight. You need to get into bed, and I mean right now."

"Really?" she said smiling, then tilted her head toward Caspian. "Look's like someone is trying to take charge." Sara pouted, then pitched up her voice, "I'm sorry, Mr. Lewis, but like Valdania, I'll not be having some ma-man bustle me off to bed." She placed a hand to her lips. "I mean, after all, what would our friends say?"

Cheers erupted around the table. Sara gave an exaggerated bow, blew a kiss to Caspian as he slowly shook his head, then skipped out of the room.

Michael pointed at him. "Damn if my cousin doesn't have your number." He barked a laugh. "I think my blushing brotha from another mother has met his match in her. Now, come on and let's clean up this mess."

"I didn't blush," said a clearly frustrated Caspian as he picked up his plate.

Jennifer set hers on top of his, and gave him an empathetic nod. "Of course you didn't, pumpkin. We know. It's just the big bad rogue scared you with her sharp daggers. That's what made you get all red."

"I hate every one of you," sighed Caspian, then did his best to ignore the snickers as all four continued cleaning up.

Chapter 29

MARY FOSTER

"Where does this go?" asked Caspian as he lifted up a large monkey pod wood bowl.

Jennifer frowned at him. "How should I know? Cas, just because I have a uterus doesn't mean I know where to put away fancy bowls. You've seen my apartment. The nicest thing I own is the coffee table that Maddison Whittaker talked me into."

"Okay, don't get snippy," said Caspian, "I'll take it down to the kitchen and —"

"No," whispered Michael as he creeped into the attic room, and slowly shut the door with a soft click. "That's a D&D bowl. It stays up here."

"What the hell is a D&D bowl?" chuckled David.

Michael glared at the younger man. "It's a bowl...we use when we're playing D&D." He looked at the pile of dishes and flatware drying beside the attic's wet bar. "Did you guys wash those by hand?"

Michael watched as all three of his friends nodded, then Caspian and Jennifer pointed at David. "You didn't," they said together.

"I handed you the plates. I also put away the D&D books, dice, and such. I helped."

"That wasn't my point," sighed Michael, then moved between Caspian and Jennifer. He reached to the left of the sink, slipped his hand along an indention, and pulled.

Jennifer's nose flared. "What the heck is that?"

"Why, it's a dishwasher, Miss Landry," said Michael.

"I know *what* it is," she grumbled, "When did you get it? Don't even tell me the thing was here all along."

"It definitely wasn't here last time," said Caspian.

Michael sighed in frustration. "Guys, we wanted our campaign space to be self-sufficient right?" Everyone nodded. "Sara said we needed a buffet table, so I bought a buffet table. Jennifer said we needed a bar, so I had a wet bar built. Now, I ask you, what self respecting wet bar doesn't have a dishwasher? The answer is none. So, in response to your question, I just had it installed on Tuesday."

Jennifer shot him a flat look. "Well, thanks for letting us know."

"Sure thing," replied Michael, completely ignoring her sarcasm. "I also hired a carpenter to make places for all the other food related stuff." He pulled out a drawer. "Flatware here." He moved down to open a cabinet. "Bowls, trays and platters here." He gave them both a self-satisfied smile. "By the time we meet for the next game, I'll have this place completely self sufficient. I've even bought warming trays for the buffet table." Michael pointed to the large brick fireplace that took up much of the attic's far wall. "Next week folks from the Mad Hatter come to bring that up to spec. Just wait until we play this winter with a crackling fire."

"That does sound pretty cool," said Jennifer reluctantly.

"Damn straight it does. Anyway, I just checked on my cousin and her room's dark, so I think we're good to move onto the next item of business, Operation LizzieQuest, stage two." Michael reached overhead, opened a cabinet and pulled out a narrow bottle. He tilted it back and forth. "Old Forester 1910 double casked bourbon. LizzieQuest planning requires liquor, am I right?"

Jennifer reached for the bourbon bottle. "You're not wrong, Rastamahn, I'll give you that much." She peered at the lettering. "I've never heard of this. Is it any good?"

Michael looked hurt. "Madam, while nothing is as good as fine Jamaican rum, I do *not* serve inferior bourbon. This one actually has an interesting story. You see, back in 1910, there was a fire that shut down the bottling line. Worse, there was a whole batch of mature whiskey, just waiting to be bottled." Michael's face became a mask of desperation. "Oh no, what to do, right? You couldn't just leave the whiskey in the vat, it would be ruined."

"High crime and misdemeanor for sure," said Caspian. Jennifer nodded.

"Indeed," agreed Michael. "Fortunately, Old Forester *did* have a whole bunch of new, charred oak barrels ready to go for their next batch."

"Ahh," said David as he reached for the bottle Jennifer had been reading. "So, they stored the ready-to-go whiskey in the new barrels. That's why they call it double-barreled."

Michael pointed at David, then touched his own nose. "I rarely say this, but Dave's right. That's exactly what they did. Put that old whiskey in new barrels for another four months until the bottling line was fixed, then they sold it."

"Did Forrester tell anyone?" asked Jennifer curiously.

"Nope, they tried to pass it off as a normal whiskey."

"Which, I'm guessing didn't work," said Caspian.

"Nope again," agreed Michael. "Lots of people noticed." He paused, "and lots of people wanted to know what the master distiller had done to make such an amazing whiskey."

David started laughing, then affected a bad Kentucky accent, "Oh, it t'wasn't a big deal, I just had to burn down the distillery for y'all."

Michael retrieved his bottle, and twisted the cap. The cork pulled free with a pop, then he began filling four Glencairn whiskey glasses, three fingers high. They each accepted one, and clinked as Michael raised his above the wet bar. "To distillery fires and Wyoming road trips," he cheered. "I hereby call to order this meeting of the LizzieQuest fellowship." Michael nodded to David. "You have the floor. Tell us what you've got."

David held up his phone while his friends gathered around. "This room needs a TV," he murmured.

"I'll get right on that," said Michael. "In the meantime, stop whining and tell me what we're looking at."

"Okay," began David, as he pointed at a blue dot within his phone's map app. "This is the Foster's house. Obviously you can see the address. It won't take us long to get from the regional airport to Rock Springs, we likely won't even need to rent a car. Anyway, the dad's name is Henry and the mom is Susan. Henry is a high school biology teacher and Susan is an at-home mom, maybe because of the extra care Mary needed the past couple years."

"Hang on," said Caspian, "extra care for what? We still don't know why Mary was on a donor list."

"Oh," replied David, shaking his head. "I'm stupid. Sorry, just a sec. This really would be easier with a TV. Why don't we just quietly go downstairs and —"

"Are you nuts?" hissed Caspian. "I do not want to risk waking Sara up, and then having to explain why we're looking at illegally obtained organ donor records or why we are stalking seventeen year old girls. We might as well just leave vacation brochures to Epstein island laying on the kitchen counter while we're at it."

"That dude totally didn't kill himself," muttered Jennifer. Everyone stared at her. She raised her hands. "I'm just sayin'...nope not buying it."

"Anyway," huffed Caspian, "we'll muddle along fine with your phone. I'm sure Michael will have this place outfitted with a ten thousand dollar OLED TV by next week, so then you can whine about something else. Now, what's wrong with Mary Foster?"

"She has CF," said David, "or she had it until the transplant." Three pairs of eyes fixed on him blankly.

"Don't make me ask you," grumbled Michael.

"Cystic Fibrosis," said David. "It's incurable, existing treatments aren't all that great, and most people die young, sometimes very young." David swiped at his phone, then pointed at a newspaper headline. *Local teen athlete saved by unlikely transplant.* "To me, this whole newspaper story seemed a HIPAA violation but—"

Jennifer popped David softly on the back of the head. "There's a picture of Mary and her parents just to the right of the copy, doofus. Clearly they gave permission. Didn't you read the article?" David shrugged and she made a sour face at him. "I swear...I love you guys...but sometimes you are so stupid." Both Caspian and Michael began shaking their heads defensively, but she just said, "No, and I'm talking about, literally, *all* men. I think it may have something to do with blood being diverted from brains to penises every morning, but come on, why won't your entire gender read articles, assembly instructions, or ask for directions." She slumped against the wet bar, and sighed. "Sometimes I wish I wasn't as straight as I am."

"Moving on," said David, "despite my penis-induced brain damage, I was able to confirm the high school where Henry teaches is still partially operating with virtual protocols."

"How does *that* help us?" asked Michael, "It just means both he *and* Mary will be home during the day."

David shook his head. "I said partial. Outdoor sports are happening, after normal school hours."

"And that helps us, how?" asked Caspian.

"It helps us," replied David flatly, "because Mary is back to running track. They have practice from four to seven three times a week, Monday, Wednesday, and Friday."

The four friends stood silently for several seconds while they all stared at the smiling newspaper picture of Mary Foster as she sat with her parents on either side. Finally Caspian nodded. "Okay then, when can we make this happen? Jenny, you said you could do a Friday in April, right?"

She nodded. "I need to give my principal a couple week's notice, but yeah, I can make it work."

"What about you guys?" he asked turning from David to Michael.

They both just shrugged. "My time is my own in April," said Michael.

"Yeah, and I can work from any place there's an internet connection," added David.

Caspian slipped out his own phone, and pulled up his calendar. "How about we take an early evening flight out on Thursday the 22nd, then come back on the last flight Friday night."

"It's Wyoming, not Las Vegas," laughed Michael. "Last flight from Nowhere's Ville, Wyoming might be at 6pm. Why don't we just take a flight home on Saturday?"

"Fine with me," replied Caspian.

"It's not fine with me," barked Jennifer. "Have you seen those mountains? If I'm going all the way to Wyoming, I want us to actually see something. Let's come back Sunday afternoon."

"Objections?" asked Caspian. Everyone shook their heads. "Alrighty then. LizzieQuest two is afoot. Who wants to book the flights so we can get adjoining seats?"

They all looked at Michael. He frowned. "Why do *I* have to do it?"

"Because you are the one with all the frequent flyer miles, and every airline on the planet sucks up to you," replied Jennifer sweetly.

"Fine," he grumbled. "I'll do it, but one of you needs to rent the car this time."

"I'll take care of that," said Caspian. "Car rental places like me almost as much as airlines like you." He held up a finger. "One thing though…"

Everyone paused to look at him. "Remember, no one breathes a word of this to Sara. We all just happen to be away for that weekend, capeesh?"

"I don't like lying to her," said Michael. "She's family."

"I'm not thrilled with it either, Cas," said Jennifer.

"I'm perfectly fine with lying," offered David.

Caspian held up both hands. "We are *not* lying. We're just not offering up additional information. If she asks, just give a vague answer." They all looked doubtful, then Caspian added, "I think you guys are becoming too comfortable with how crazy this whole thing is. Let me remind you. The ghost, or whatever, of the woman I love is leading us on a cross-country quest that she said I should keep between the four of us." He saw them all shrink back slightly as his words hit home. Caspian smiled at his friends. "Tell you what, next time Lizzie comes visiting, I'll be sure to ask her if she'd like me to include Michael's young and beautiful cousin in our little adventure, how's that?" Caspian didn't wait for a response. He just flashed his friends an incredulous look, gave them a wave, then headed out the attic's door.

Michael and Jennifer's eyes grew wide, as smiles spread across their faces. "What are you, two, grinning about?" asked David. "Cas just ripped us a new one."

"So oblivious," chuckled Michael, "Please, tell me you aren't the one writing the romance scenes for Mass Effect 4."

David's brow furrowed. "No, of course not. I have writers for that, but what does that have to do—"

Jennifer reached over and squished David's cheeks together until his lips pursed. She kissed his nose, then spun around, grinned, and lilted, "Cas thinks Sara's pretty."

Michael extended his elbow so she could loop her arm in his. They spun in a circle as he joined in. "And I know she likes him."

David's mouth dropped open slightly, then he, too, started grinning. "I think you're right guys. Wow, I didn't see this at all."

Jennifer and Michael stopped, both pointed at him, and said as one, "Because you're oblivious."

Chapter 30

ADORABLY INTRUSIVE

Caspian waved at the Uber driver as she pulled up beside his hotel. He had just settled himself into the back seat, when his phone began vibrating and Michael's face appeared on the screen. Caspian accepted the call, then said, "Hey, give me a second. I just got in my Uber and need to ask the driver something." He noticed how her eyes flicked to the rearview mirror, and quickly set the phone down before Michael could respond. "Hi, it's Sofia, right? Thanks for getting here so fast. I'm late for my flight...again."

She nodded. "Yep, Sofia." The driver glanced at her phone as it rested in its dashboard holster. "And you're Caspian. Well, Caspian, don't feel bad. I'm always late for everything, well, except Uber pick-ups."

Caspian laughed. "I have a friend like that. I'm strangely punctual, except for flights. As much as I've enjoyed my three days in the Golden State, I really want to get home to New Orleans. According to Delta, my flight boards at 7:50 tonight, and the Uber app said something about LAX not allowing ride shares."

The driver sighed. "Yeah, it's some kind of crack down on gig economy folks. I think it has more to do with pick-ups than drop-offs." He could see her face break into a smile even from behind. "Don't worry, Caspian, we've found ways around their little rules. I just take down my Uber light when we get close, then it just looks like I'm dropping off or picking up a friend." Sofia glanced at her navigation display. "Your flight's at 7:50? No problem. I'll get you there with plenty of time to spare." Caspian let out a relieved sigh, then relaxed into the seat. "Uh," began the driver, "don't you have someone waiting for you on your phone?"

"Oh shit," sputtered Caspian, then retrieved the still glowing device from beside him. "Hey, Michael...sorry brotha, I'm brain-dead. I've already put in over forty hours and it's only Wednesday."

Caspian's brow raised as a woman's voice responded. "Oh, poor baby. Do you need a back rub?"

"Sara?" he asked, confused, then stared at the phone's screen. Michael's profile picture stared back.

"The one and only," she laughed, "and you would have known that if you had let me get a word in edgewise before chatting up...Soophhia."

"Very funny, Sar. I think you've been spending too much time as your rogue alter ego. I wasn't chatting up anyone." He paused. "Uh, why are you using Michael's phone?"

"I'm at the Apple store. My phone is in surgery. Battery replacement. Mikey is over by the laptops, and he let me borrow his."

"Why is he looking at laptops? His is less than a year old, what's he doing?" asked Caspian.

After a brief pause, Sara said, "From what I can see, he's drooling."

"Over a laptop?" asked Caspian.

"No," she snickered, "he's drooling over the Apple-girl who clearly isn't buying into whatever bullshit he's selling."

Caspian shook his head as a smile spread across his face. "What approach is the Jamaican Casanova trying?"

"Hmm, oh he's showing her his business card, which I really don't think is going to...wait. She's doing something on her phone. Unbelievable! I think she's texting him her number. I just can't believe this works on people. I'd never give out my number, like that. I've had this number since I was twelve."

"You gave me your number," said Caspian. "How do you know I'm not some consulting Casanova?"

She laughed again. "The only thing Casanova about you, sir, is the first three letters of your name."

"Ouch," he replied.

"No, it's a compliment. No smart girl likes a Casanova. Anyway, aren't you the least bit curious about why I called?"

"Well, now I am," he replied.

"Just now?" she snickered. "I guess I need to work on being more mysterious. Everyone says I'm too much of an open book." She sighed a moment later, then said, "Mikey told me that we won't be having D&D next week because he's going to be out of town."

Caspian's eyes widened. "Really?"

"Yeah, he's flying out on Thursday the 22nd and won't be back until Sunday."

"Really?" repeated Caspian, then grimaced at himself.

"Yes, really, and you'll never guess where he's going...Wyoming of all places. I didn't even think they drank in Wyoming."

Caspian shook his head while whispering, *Michael, you idiot,* under his breath.

"What's that, Cas?" asked Sara. "I didn't catch it."

"Oh, I was just saying that you might be thinking of Utah. Lots of Mormons live there and they don't drink. Well, they don't do lots of other things, too. No caffeine or tobacco either."

"Wow," replied Sara, "there goes my plans for becoming Mormon. I could only manage one of the three."

"I know, right," said Caspian. "You are also too snarky to be a Mormon. Every one of them I've ever met has been ridiculously nice."

"Know a lot of Mormons, do you?" she snickered.

"Don't laugh, I actually do. In fact, my manager on this California gig is Mormon. I also once gave my pants to a Mormon at the Vatican."

Caspian saw the Uber driver's eyes flick toward his reflection in her mirror. He grinned at Sofia, shook his head, then pointed at the phone to indicate the silence he was getting from Sara. After at least another two-seconds, Caspian barely managed to stifle his own laughter as Sara, said, "Now you are just pulling my leg."

"No leg pulling, Miss Edwards," he replied seriously, "I was backpacking in Europe with Dave, Jenny, and Elizabeth. We were at the Vatican, and were coming out of St. Peter's Basilica, when these three guys came up to us. They were wearing shorts and we had on pants. One of them, a ginger they called Opie, asked if we would mind swapping our pants for their shorts so they could go inside."

"You can't go inside wearing shorts?" she asked.

"No, of course you can't," sputtered Caspian. "It's St. Peter's Basilica. What kind of Catholic are you?"

"The Jamaican kind who's never been anywhere accept my Island, Texas, and Louisiana, but you just rub it in, Mr. World Traveler."

ROBERT ROSS

"Sorry, I'm not trying to rub anything in. If it helps, I've never been to Jamaica."

"You are forgiven, sir, please continue with this obviously fabricated adventure."

"It's not fabricated," he said, "I can't make up lies this detailed. For example, you probably know this by now, but Dave doesn't trust anyone. So, he asked the three guys how we knew they wouldn't abscond with our pants, and Opie says, *Dude, we're Mormons.*"

"And that was it?" chuckled Sara.

"Yep, that was it. Next thing we knew, we were swapping pants in a public restroom with two Mormons."

"What about the third one?" she asked.

"What third one?"

"You said there were three of them."

"Oh, yeah, the third guy was already wearing pants."

"Lucky him," she said. "Also, lucky that you and Dave just happened to be the same size as the other two."

Caspian shook his head. "Are you this suspicious of everyone, Miss Edwards, or do I just seem especially untrustworthy? For your information, we were *not* the same size. We looked ridiculous. Dave's shorts came up to his ribcage and my shorts made me look like I was wearing a kilt."

"Nice," she purred, "I do love a man in a kilt. I wish you had pictures. Oh, and for the record, I don't find you untrustworthy, Mr. Lewis. I find you roguishly wily. After all, you *are* the one with a seventeen charisma score."

"And you are the one who actually *is* a rogue," laughed Caspian, "As for your picture desires, they may yet be filled. There is, in fact, photographic evidence of this auspicious event. Jenny took them. If you're an especially good wood elf, I'll show you when I see you next." Caspian paused. "Wait, so you don't know anything about the Vatican, but you know what men in kilts look like?"

"A girl has to have priorities, Cas," she said, "but Mikey wants his phone back, and I haven't even gotten to ask you what I was calling about. Since, we aren't doing D&D next Friday, I thought I'd invite you to Commander's Palace to taste my new dinner menu. What do you think?"

Frak! mouthed Caspian. "Uh, next Friday? Sara, I'd love to, but I'm not going to be in town either."

She let out a dejected sigh. "Oh, well that sucks. Where are you going to be?"

212

Caspian's mind raced a second, then he said, "It's kind of a charity thing. I'm going to meet a female student athlete who fought back from having cystic fibrosis."

"Oh, that's so sweet," said Sara. "Is it some kind of scholarship that your firm does? Are you giving her money for college?"

I am now, thought Caspian, but just smiled and said, "Uh huh, you got it. Anyway," he continued, "I'd love to sample your new menu. Pick any other time and I'm there."

"Okay," she replied, "how about tomorrow night?"

"Tomorrow?"

He could hear the smile in her voice. "You did say, *any* other time, didn't you?"

"I did," he agreed. "Sure, tomorrow works. What time?"

"11:30," she replied.

"That's a bit early for dinner, isn't it?"

"11:30 at night, silly," she said. "I have to do it when the restaurant is closed, and I figured you would prefer 11:30pm rather than 5:00am."

Caspian nodded. "Definitely! I only do one 5:00 a day, and it's not the AM one."

"You're funny," she laughed. "Okay, it's a date. I'll see you tomorrow night."

"You got it, who else is coming?"

"Mikey wants his phone back. Have a safe trip, Cas...bye."

Caspian pulled the phone down, and looked at its black screen. He pursed his lips, then shrugged.

"Girlfriend checking up on you?" asked Sofia.

"Huh? Oh, no, she's just a friend. Actually she's the cousin of a friend."

The driver's eyes locked with his in the rear view mirror. "If you say so. I only heard half the conversation, but that sounded like girlfriend to me."

"I'm not really on the market," said Caspian.

"You already have a girlfriend?" she asked.

"No, but—"

"Then you're on the market. All guys are on the market, at least in my experience."

"Well, I'm not."

"Are you gay?"

Caspian barked a laugh, then tapped his phone. "Sofia, how have you managed to maintain a 4.8 star rating while also listening to people's calls, opining on their dating activities, and asking about sexual orientations?"

She tilted her head back and grinned in her mirror. "I'm adorably intrusive, and people like me."

"Fair enough," sighed Caspian, "but no, not gay." His voice lowered a bit. "I was engaged."

"Oh, shit, I'm sorry," said Sofia. "She broke your heart?"

"You could say that," he replied.

"I'm sorry," the driver said again, "You seem like a really nice guy. I can tell these things. She's going to regret breaking it off. Good men are really hard to find, trust me. I'm definitely *on* the market, and all I can find are snowflake-y boys that would melt in any direct sunlight."

"She didn't break it off, Sofia." Caspian took a deep breath. "She died. Traffic accident."

The driver lifted one hand to her mouth. "Oh no, I'm so stupid. I wasn't thinking and—"

Caspian waved away her comment. "It's okay. You couldn't know." He smiled. "You were just being adorably intrusive."

"Was it recent?" she asked, her voice laced with concern.

"Feels recent, but no. It will be a year next month. May 17th to be exact."

The two drove in silence for several minutes as Sofia navigated the LAX airport departure lanes. Finally, she pulled up next to the Delta drop-off area, then turned to face Caspian. "Do you mind if I make one additional observation?"

He gave her a closed mouth smile. "Sofia, I think you are genetically incapable of doing otherwise."

She pointed at Caspian's phone. "Does the woman who called you for dinner know about your fiancé?"

"Yeah, why do you ask?"

She nodded. "A lot of us are attracted to broken things. It's part and parcel of that whole XX chromosome thing. We'll bind up bird's wings. We'll cuddle a puppy with a limp. We try to mend what is broken." Sofia pointed again. "If you aren't ready to be mended, you need to tell whoever was on the other end of that call. Broken hearts can be catching."

Caspian stared into Sofia's dark brown eyes, then shook his head in wonder. He held up his phone, then made a dramatic show of tapping the fifth star on Uber's rating screen. She smiled at him. "Like I said, adorably intrusive." He reached for the door handle but Sofia extended a hand and tapped his shoulder.

"Caspian, if your fiancé loved you half as much as it's clear you loved her, don't you think she'd want you to mend? Just something to think about."

He gave her a silent nod, then exited the car.

Chapter 31

A VISITOR

Caspian leaned his shoulder against the door to his apartment, and pushed it open. It was dark. "Alexa, set living room to fifty-percent." A second later, soft warm light bloomed. He walked down the short foyer, then turned left into his bedroom, and tossed his suitcase onto the bed. *I'll take care of that later,* he mused to himself, then headed for the kitchen. Caspian swung his leather messenger bag onto the breakfast bar, where it landed with a heavy clunk thanks to the computer and notebooks within. He opened the refrigerator, and what felt like a blast of cold air passed over him. Caspian shivered, pulled out a Belgian ale, then popped its cap off.

"That looks delicious," came a voice from behind him. Caspian froze. "Don't you dare drop that bottle, Cas," said Elizabeth. He felt his grip on the glass tighten to where his knuckles turned white. Caspian turned slowly around, feeling like the victim in every B-horror movie he'd ever seen. Elizabeth sat facing him on one of the three barstools. She smiled at him. "Hi."

"L-Lizzie?" he stammered.

"It's me, Cas. I told you if you sought out my gifts we would be seeing each other." She rolled her eyes. "Let me tell ya, it wasn't an easy thing to arrange. You met with Thomas and Maddison Whittaker, which is why I could come. If you are as successful with Mary Foster and her parents, I'll be able to come again."

Caspian set down his bottle with a shaking hand then nearly sprinted out of the kitchen and around to the breakfast bar. He reached for her, but Elizabeth shook her head and held up both hands. "No, Cas, don't."

He pulled up short. "You said that last time, too. How…why? Are you a —" he paused.

"A ghost?" she asked, then laughed in a way that seemed so natural that Caspian involuntarily pressed a hand against his chest. Elizabeth shook her head again. "No, I'm not a ghost, although ghosts do exist. I found that out."

"You did? How?"

She smiled. "That's a longer story, and I don't have much time. It takes a lot out of me to appear like this. Trust me, the chill you felt earlier, wasn't from the refrigerator. You always were spouting off about how energy can't be created or destroyed, but just changes form." She smiled. "I just made a lot of the heat in this room change forms into…" Elizabeth pointed at herself, "…me. But you can't touch me, at least not now. If you were to try, well, I'm not sure I'd ever be able to come back to you. Cas, it's hard to explain, but I'm kind of in-between places. You see, I have some unfinished business before I completely shuffle off this mortal coil, so to speak."

Caspian sighed. "Lizzie, I miss you so much. You can't even begin to imagine how much I—"

"I don't have to imagine, Cas," she interrupted. "Just because you haven't seen me, doesn't mean I haven't seen you. Quite frankly, you're a mess."

"Thanks," he muttered.

"Don't mention it. The whole pizza box thing, with the roaches, that was just disgusting." She frowned. "I really hated roaches."

He narrowed his eyes at her. "Well, you seem perfectly fine with everything, now. How do I know you're really *my* Lizzie?"

She gave him a sad smile. "You know I'm *me*, Cas, but you're right, I'm not *your* Lizzie anymore. I have to tell you something, and it's going to hurt. I'm sorry for that, but you need to hear it. Caspian, I love you." He opened his mouth to respond, but Elizabeth silenced him with a gesture, then repeated herself. "I love you, but I do *not* miss you."

Caspian took a step back, a look of complete disbelief on his face. "W-what? What do you mean?"

He saw how her eyes were filled with compassion, but also a resolve Caspian recognized well. "I treasure the time we had together. I can even wish that we had more, but that's not what happened. I can't change it, neither can you. However, we both can forge our futures." Elizabeth snickered, "Of course, my

218

immediate future is a bit stranger than yours will likely be. Those ghosts I mentioned before, they are trapped here. They won't let go. It's not good, Cas. I did let go, not of the love, just of the miss, and of the what-could-have-beens. That's why I came to you in the dream you had at the hospital. It was my way of letting go, and, I hoped, would be that for you as well."

"It wasn't," he said flatly.

"I know, and I'm sorry, but it's also why I'm still here. I won't abandon you to a life of regret, Caspian. I love you too much for that. That's why I nudged you toward," she laughed, "LizzieQuest. I love that name. Dave is so cute sometimes." Elizabeth opened her arms. "Oh, Caspian, there is a chance and hope for you to live a life full of joy." She winked at him and affected a man's British accent, then added, "A chance and hope of my procuring, Ebenezer."

Caspian sighed. "I'm not in the mood for movie quotes, Lizzie. I didn't even watch it this year."

She frowned. "I know, and skipping Alastair Sim's *Scrooge* was the least of the dumb things you did Christmas Eve. I was there. I saw you break your mother's heart by walling off yours from your family..." she sighed, "...and mine."

"Yeah," he said, "I've been getting a lot of feedback on that lately."

"Have you?" she asked as a wry smile played about her lips. "You make it sound like one of your consulting reviews. These are my parents, Cas. They love you, and they *do* miss you. Fix it with them, before you go to Wyoming next Thursday."

Caspian gave a derisive snort. "Yeah, you mentioned Mary Foster, so I guess it makes sense you know about Wyoming. Is there anything you don't know?"

"What I don't know could fill entire libraries, Cas, but I also know lots of things I didn't before. I've seen all those to whom my gifts were given, and they have seen me, at least in dreams." Elizabeth closed her eyes and appeared to take a deep breath. "You are on the grandest of adventures, Caspian, and you've only taken the first few steps. I pray you see it to the finish, because if you do, then I'll be able to give you a gift equal in preciousness to the one I gave Thomas Whittaker, Mary Foster, and, well, the last person, too."

Caspian furrowed his brow. "Who's this last person and what did you give him?"

Elizabeth pursed her lips, placed a finger against them, and whispered, "Sorry sweetie...spoilers." Caspian opened his mouth to object, but Elizabeth shook her head. "I tell you three times, no. It's a secret you must unravel for yourself, and that's not even why I'm here tonight."

"Okay," said Caspian, "I'll bite, why are you here, Lizzie? What is so special that you can finally make an appearance?"

"Ignoring your tone, I'll tell you," she said sweetly. "I'm here to encourage you to have a good time tomorrow night."

Caspian pinched up his face in confusion, then tried to retrieve his beer from across the breakfast bar, but it was out of reach. He sighed and was about to push off the barstool, when the bottle slid toward him.

His eyes flicked to Elizabeth. She twitched her wrist again causing the bottle to move another few inches. "I have super powers now. I can move beer bottles with my mind." She shrugged. "It's a pretty niche power, but occasionally comes in handy."

Caspian gave her a weak smile, then extended a slightly trembling hand to retrieve the bottle. He took several long swallows then set it down again. "What are you talking about, what's tomorrow night?"

He was in the middle of taking a third drink when Elizabeth answered with a grin. "Tomorrow night is your date." Caspian spat beer all over the counter, and started coughing. "Sorry," said Elizabeth apologetically, "I'd slap your back, but I'm not allowed to touch you just like you aren't allowed to touch me."

Caspian held up a finger as his coughing fit subsided. "What the hell are you talking about, Lizzie? I do not have a date tomorrow. In fact I'm just going to some kind of tasting with Sar—"

He broke off, eyes going wide. "Yep, it's a date," she said with a grin.

"Not with Sara?" Caspian shook his head vigorously. "We're just friends."

"And where have I heard that before," lilted Elizabeth. "Cas, do you remember Steven Bacardi?"

"From high school?" he asked. She nodded, and Caspian continued. "I haven't thought about Bacardi in years. What does he have to do with—"

"Do you remember how you kept trying to set him up with Jenny?"

"Oh," mumbled Caspian, "that. How was I supposed to know he was—"

"Gay? Because everyone with eyes knew, Cas, and yet you persisted. You're adorable, but you had absolutely no gaydar, everyone said so." She laughed, "especially Steven. Anyway, the only thing worse than your *gaydar* is your *girldar*."

"My *girldar* is just fine, Lizzie," objected Caspian, then paused as she smirked at him. "Fine, what do you mean by *girldar*?"

"Melissa Michaels," she lilted.

"We were *twelve!*" huffed Caspian, "How was I supposed to know she liked me? I just wanted to climb trees."

"I know you did. You were the one who taught me to climb trees," said Elizabeth. "What about Amy Richards or," she locked eyes with him, "what about me?"

"You didn't like me until that asshole Chad threw you over and you got drunk at Pat O'Brien's."

She shook her head. "No *girldar* at all. Cas, do you remember that year the Pearl River flooded?"

"Yeah, what about it?"

"Our house was set in one of the lower lying areas of the neighborhood," replied Elizabeth. "We got totally flooded out."

"Right," agreed Caspian, "You guys stayed with us from Thanksgiving to New Years." He smiled at the memory. "It was awesome."

She returned the expression. "It was. We had turkey together. We wrapped presents together. We watched *It's A Wonderful Life* together."

"I think I fell asleep," snickered Caspian, "It was the first time I'd seen it, and I wasn't the fan then that I am now."

"You did fall asleep, about fifteen minutes in, but I didn't. I watched the whole thing, and I watched you sleeping, too." She sighed, "and at the end of the movie when that little bell rang on the Bailey's Christmas tree, I creeped over to you. I leaned down, and I whispered, *Is this the ear you can't hear on? Caspian Lewis, I'll love you 'til the day I die.*" She shrugged. "And I did, you just didn't catch up for over a decade. See, no *girldar*. Not with Melissa. Not with Amy. Not with me..." Elizabeth tilted her head meaningfully, "and not with Sara."

"It's a group thing, Lizzie. We're all meeting for a food tasting of some kind," countered Caspian.

She gave him a look halfway between amusement and curiosity. "Are you? Who else is going?"

"Well," he began, "all of us, I assume, Dave, Michael, and Jenny."

Elizabeth nodded, but Caspian recognized the patronizing look, as she said, "Did Sara tell you there would be others coming?"

"We didn't discuss it," replied Caspian.

"Well, that's not exactly true," said Elizabeth. "You asked who else was coming, and Sara took that moment to disconnect the call." Elizabeth grinned. "Didn't she?"

Caspian swallowed. "Shit."

"Oh, don't look that way, Cas. She's more terrified about the whole thing than you are." Elizabeth cocked her head, "However, you're rapidly catching up to her. Don't be dumb. You know you like her."

"I never thought about it one way or another," said Caspian defensively. "I'm not—"

"On the market, yes I know. Okay, let me tell you then, since you're obviously too closed off to know for yourself. *You like her.* She's adorable. I mean, honestly, what's not to like? She's smart. She's beautiful. She's independent and headstrong. She's totally your type. *I* like her."

"I don't have a type," he countered.

Elizabeth smirked. "Yes you do. Smart, beautiful, independent, and headstrong. That's your type. I know because I was obviously your type and I am all those things." She paused, "Or I was anyway."

"This is too weird," murmured Caspian, then drained the rest of his beer. "I really hope I'm having a brain aneurism and this is all in my head."

"It's not in your head, but you'll know for sure tomorrow when you and Sara are in a romantic restaurant, all alone, no other friends, and she wears that cute little red number she has, or maybe the black one, honestly she keeps going back and forth on it. Don't worry though, Jenny's going to help her figure it out. I'm hoping for the red. Sara looks great in red."

Caspian suddenly felt himself getting angry and it took him several seconds to figure out why. He slammed his now empty bottle on the counter. "Elizabeth, you were going to be my wife. I don't want to date. I don't want another woman. I want you. I love you."

"Well, you can't have me, Caspian," she replied flatly. "Unlike you, I am decidedly *not* on the market. You're also holding on so tightly to the love we shared because you're broken. You've convinced yourself that if you love again, it will be a betrayal, but that is just utter bullshit." She saw his expression, then shook her head. "Okay, you asked for it. I'm pulling out the Shakespeare." Elizabeth slipped off her stool, took several steps into the living room, then turned around. She clasped her hands together over her chest, then projected as if speaking to an auditorium, "My bounty is as boundless as the sea, my love as deep." She pointed meaningfully at Caspian, then emphasized the next words, "the more I give to thee, the more I have, for both are infinite." Elizabeth saw Caspian slump on his stool. She smiled at him. "How many times did we play that scene together from Romeo and Juliet, first as friends, and then as more than friends. Cas, you know it's true. Love is one of the few things you can't out-give. Truly, the more you give, the more you have. Quite honestly, love is the only thing that has a chance to mend your brokenness and restore your faith in God."

"I'm not broken, and I don't need mending," he replied petulantly, then felt his anger rise again. "I certainly don't need God. In fact, he can either kiss my ass or smite me where I stand. I couldn't care less which."

Elizabeth cocked her head. "Now, that's not something I've seen from you before. Where did all the God-hate come from?"

"You have got to be frakking kidding me," sputtered Caspian. "Where did it come from? It came from 2020, Lizzie. Where was God when this Pandemic wrecked the world? Where was He when that idiot motorcyclist decided to play Evel Knievel during a hurricane?" Caspian pointed at Elizabeth. "Where was He when He let you die? Screw him. I hate Him, and don't want anything to do with Him."

Elizabeth's eyes seemed to fill with tears, and she shook her head sadly. "Oh, Caspian. It's not like that at all, but you just can't see it, now. God didn't do anything to the world or me. We do things to ourselves. It's a broken world, filled with broken people, doing very broken things. Allowing something to happen isn't the same as doing it, but—"

"Doing it or allowing it amounts to the same thing," spat Caspian, "besides, your opinion is invalid, Lizzie or my delusion of Lizzie. You're dead."

"No, my love, I am not dead. Do I look dead?" She didn't wait for an answer. "I am absent from the body, and that is a very different thing from being dead. Truth is, Cas, you are far more dead than I am. As for your hatred of God, well, I think He can take it. After all, the opposite of love isn't hate, it's indifference," she sighed, "and you certainly don't seem indifferent. All that anger you're feeling is tied up in—"

"I'm not broken," he said again, "I don't need mending, and my faith certainly isn't in need of restoration."

"You are, you do, and it does," she replied softly. "Cas, you can still love me. I will always love you. However, the time has come for you to live again as well." She smiled at him. "Now, my broken love, I'll add a more reserved performance from our second favorite play to make a final point." She walked close to him, stared deeply into his eyes, and said, "Close them so you can hear my words without distraction." He continued staring at her. She sighed. "Please, Caspian, close your eyes."

He inhaled deeply, drew his lips to a line, then slowly closed his eyes. Caspian thought he could feel her breath on his ear as she whispered, "My dearest Benedict, serve God, love me, and mend. There I will leave you too, for here comes one in haste."

Caspian's mobile phone began ringing. His eyes flew open. The room was empty. He quickly looked around, but Elizabeth was gone. Caspian swallowed, picked up his phone, and tapped accept. "Hi Mom," he said, while trying to catch his breath. "You must have known I needed to talk with you. Something pretty strange just happened, and I want you and dad to tell me if I'm completely nuts. Sure, I'll wait while you get him."

Jennifer swatted at her phone in an unsuccessful attempt to make it stop vibrating. Finally she rolled to one side of her bed, and pulled it from its charging mat. "Hello?" she groaned.

"Jenny? Jenny, it's Cas."

"I know who you are," she said, then tried to focus on the screen. "Please tell me it's not actually 2:30 in the morning. I have to be up in three hours, and it's Friday so my little hellions will be..." she paused trying to pull the desired term from her sleep dampened mind, then gave up. "Well, they'll be hellions. They can smell weakness, Cas, and I'm weak without sleep. You better be trapped under something heavy or on fire."

"Lizzie just came to see me," he said softly.

Jennifer sighed. "It was a dream, Cas. I'm not saying it wasn't Elizabeth, because we're living out a Twilight Zone episode, but—"

"I haven't been to sleep, Jenny. I tried talking with my parents, but they don't know about all the weird shit that's been going on, and I decided to keep it that way. Then, I tried dealing with it myself, and now I just had to talk with someone who is going to frakking believe me."

Jennifer rubbed at her eyes, then pushed herself into a more upright position. "How do you know it wasn't a dream?"

"Because I was drinking a beer at the time, Jenny. I'm now looking at the empty bottle of said beer, so unless I've taken to sleep-drinking, I was awake."

"Where did you see her?"

"She was sitting on one of my barstools."

Jennifer yawned. "And what did she say?"

"Lots of stuff, Jenny, and I recognize your *Cas is full of shit, let me go back to sleep voice*."

"Good," she replied, "because you likely are and I definitely want to." Jennifer sighed. "I'm going to give you three sentences. Take a moment. Gather your thoughts, then speak three sentences. Once you do, I'll make sense of the whole thing."

Caspian felt himself relax for the first time in hours. This was a game he knew. It was a game he understood. David had invented it, and Jennifer, Elizabeth, and Caspian had all played it together for years. Any complex issue could be understood, any seemingly unsolvable problem could be solved...if you limited your explanation to three sentences. He took a deep breath, and prepared to cheat by using horribly crafted run-on sentences.

"Okay," he began, "Lizzie says I have no *girldar* and that she, Melissa Michaels, and Amy Richards all liked me, but I was as oblivious to that as I was to Steven Bacardi's sexual team choices."

"That's definitely true," said Jennifer, "but you are even more oblivious, than that. I've been madly in love with you for years."

"What!" sputtered Caspian. "Jenny, I—"

"Oh shut up," she said, "I'm yanking your chain for waking me up in the middle of the night. I wouldn't sleep with you if you were the last man on earth." She paused, "Well, maybe if you were the *last* man, but only if there also wasn't any chocolate. Okay, that was sentence one, and I'm not anywhere close to being convinced. Two to go."

"Lizzie says I'm broken, and I've decided that allowing myself to feel anything for another woman would be a betrayal of my love for her, which she then said was complete bullshit."

Jennifer's response came slower this time, her voice more reserved. "Well, that sounds exactly like something Lizzie would tell you. Go on, you have one sentence left."

Caspian took a deep breath then erupted in a torrent of words. "Apparently, I am meeting Sara tomorrow night for dinner, and what I thought was a friendly meeting of all my friends, is, in fact, a date because Sara likes me, and not in a cousin-of-one-of-my-best-friends kinda way, more in the I'm going to wear a slinky red dress kinda way, at least Lizzie hopes it's the red dress because she says Sara looks better in the red one than in the black one." After several seconds, Jennifer realized her mouth was open, and she had stopped breathing. She sat up, rolled out of bed, and began pacing back and forth in her bedroom. Caspian stared at his phone to make sure the connection hadn't dropped. "Jenny, are you there?"

"Yeah, I'm here," she whispered.

"Well, tell me I'm nuts. Tell me there's a big difference between having dreams that encroach on reality and spectral visitations."

Jennifer walked into her bathroom. She shook her head at the reflection she saw there. Her nose was red, and tears streaked her cheeks. She sighed. "There *is* a big difference, Cas." She heard him let out a relieved breath, then said, "but here are my three sentences. You are not nuts, but Sara is totally into you. The rest of us were not invited to what is most certainly a date." She swallowed. "Oh, and Sara is going to be wearing a killer red dress, even though we both thought you'd like the black one better, but every time we put the red one back, it kept falling off its hanger, and tumbling out of the closet."

"Oh shit," murmured Caspian.

"Oh shit is right," said Jennifer. "We are definitely through the looking glass now, Alice." She pointed at her phone. "I know what you are thinking. Don't give me any crap about conspiring against you. It's practically in my job description as your hot, but eternally platonic friend. I know you like Sara, even if you are too dense to know it yourself. My boydar is wicked sharp. Anyway, do *not* let on about this, Cas. Sara was terrified she'd be making a huge mistake pursuing it, and I'm the one who convinced her otherwise."

"Seems your ghostly dress selector also had a hand in it," muttered Caspian, then added, "Don't worry. I'll play dumb. Who knows, maybe Sara will change her mind."

"She won't. If I've learned anything about her in the past few months, once that girl's set a course for herself, I don't think anything will stop her. Remind you of anyone?"

"Yeah," sighed Caspian, "she does at that."

"Well," said Jennifer, "despite the long odds of my getting back to sleep, I do have one piece of good news to offer you."

"Great, what's that?"

Jennifer grinned at her phone. "There's no one better equipped to play dumb on a date he didn't know he was having than you, Caspian Lewis."

Chapter 32

A PRIVATE DINNER

Thunder rumbled across the sky only a split second after yet another flash of lightning. Caspian, peered through the windshield of his car, then slipped his phone from its cradle. *I'm here*, he texted, paused then added, *I didn't want you thinking I was blowing off the tasting. It's raining cats and dogs, and I was hoping for it to let up a bit otherwise I'm going to look like a drowned rat.* He paused a moment,

then added, *Before you ask, no, I didn't bring an umbrella, Sara*

Almost immediately, ellipses started animating within his phone's texting app. Several seconds later he grinned. *So many animal references in one text. Cats, dogs, and rats, oh my. Do you need me to come out with an umbrella? I'd hate for you to melt.*

Caspian could almost hear the slight snark of amusement combined with Sara's omnipresent Jamaican accent. His fingers flew over the screen. *No, I do NOT want you to come out. I'm a big boy, and I will not melt. I just didn't want to embarrass you by looking frightful in front of your workmates...workmates? Chefmates?*

"How does she type that fast on a phone," murmured Caspian, as Sara's next response appeared almost immediately. *I think Chefmate is the brand of an oven isn't it? Anyway, you'll be fine. I'll give you a towel. There's hardly anyone here, just one of my sous chefs and a server who's training on the proposed menu.*

Caspian chewed his lip a moment, then typed, *Okay, I'm coming. Am I the last one to arrive? Should I just knock on the front door?*

No, came the almost immediate response. *Come around back. We aren't eating in the restaurant proper. We're eating at the chef's table. I'll meet you back there.*

"Shit," murmured Caspian, only partly to himself. "What does *no* mean. *No*, don't come to the front. That part is obvious, but what about *no*, I'm not the last one to arrive." He glanced at his watch, then sighed. "I'm only ten minutes late. It's perfectly reasonable that if others were coming they could be later than me. There's absolutely still a chance Sara either changed her mind or this wasn't not some clandestine date in the first plate. So, Sara's no could definitely have implied others were still coming, right?" Caspian stared at his reflection in the rear view mirror, then pointed at it. "*You* are no help at all." He shrugged at himself, then quickly opened his car door, and started sprinting toward the nearest awning.

By hugging the side of the building, Caspian managed to avoid a complete drenching. *Just a partial drenching,* he mused to himself, as he navigated the side alley and rear of the iconic restaurant. Given the large gunmetal gray door's thick metal construction, Caspian raised a fist and was just about to give it a good pounding, when it swung open.

Sara grinned at Caspian's upraised fist, then held up both hands in mock horror. "Oh please, don't hit me, Mr. Lewis. I promise to behave." She winked, "Well, maybe I'll behave." Her smile broadened and she stepped aside. "Come on in. You look like a drowned rat."

Caspian walked through the door, and noted with an odd mixture of relief and disappointment, that Sara wore her chef whites, and not a dress. *Regardless of color,* he added to himself. The two walked into what appeared to be a large storage room. Tall shelves rose up against nearly all the walls. They were filled with everything ranging from dishes to non perishable foods. A huge metal door was set in the middle of the right wall, while a pair of swinging ones led somewhere directly in front of him. Sara saw Caspian's expression, then pointed to the metal door. "That's the walk-in. We won't be eating in there." She pointed to the other door. "...annnd the kitchen is just through there."

"Is that where everyone's eating?" asked Caspian, while trying to ignore his inner monologue's laughter at the question.

Sara shook her head. "No, Christophe and Brandon are going to set up the chef's table in here. Not everything's ready yet, but I can give you the," she made air quotes, "cook's tour of the kitchen, if you like."

"Sure," replied Caspian enthusiastically, "I've never been in a working professional kitchen before, let alone one of the most famous in the city." He gestured to Sara's chef uniform which had at least half-a-dozen bright red stains across the chest. "Industrial accident?" he asked with a laugh.

She looked down and sighed. "Close, a culinary school intern who didn't believe me when I told her the bottle she was opening had been sealed under pressure. I look like a shotgun victim don't I?"

"Little bit," chuckled Caspian.

Sara extended a hand toward the kitchen door. "Don't worry, I won't make you stare at it all through dinner. I'm going to get changed once I'm sure the boys have things under control. Come on, let me introduce you."

Christophe pumped Caspian's hand enthusiastically. "I have been very much looking forward to this meeting," he said in a soft French accent. "When the Chef told me we would be entertaining Caspian, I thought she was, how you say, pulling my leg. Pulling my leg?" he asked again.

"Yep, I believe you got that phrase right, but why did you think she was—"

Christophe chuckled while he repeated the name "Caspian, it sounds like the name of a fairy tale prince or a Russian sea. Since it was unlikely Chef Sara invited the sea to dinner, I figured you must be a prince, no? Did I not say that very thing Brandon?"

The lean African American man with a close cropped vandyke beard smiled indulgently at Christophe. "Yes, I believe you have mentioned your prince theory once or twice…or maybe twenty times."

During this entire exchange, Sara had been bustling throughout the expansive kitchen moving one thing, or tasting something else. Now, she walked up between Brandon and Christophe, put an arm around each, then locked eyes with Caspian. "I call them my opposite boys." She pulled Christophe a bit closer. "He's an effusive, if stereotypically pompous, French sous chef." Sara tilted her head so it rested against Brandon's chest. "And he's my tall, dark, handsome, and reserved sommelier."

"I'm not a sommelier yet," Brandon corrected.

Sara patted his chest. "You will be. That test doesn't stand a chance." She winked at Caspian, "He's being tested on Monday, and that's why *we* will be having all sorts of delicious wines paired with our dinner tonight, isn't that right, Brandon?"

He inclined his head. "If I had more notice on what you were serving, I would have—"

She interrupted him. "How much notice will the Master Sommelier be giving you on Monday?" He sighed and she grinned at him. "That's what I thought. Trust me, Brandon, your test will be easier than tonight, and you're going to do great tonight, or else" A brief lull settled among them. It lasted only a couple seconds, then Sara gave Brandon a wink, and clapped her hands together. "Well, everything looks perfect, so, Christophe, I will leave you to handle the final preparations. *I* am going to change out of these whites that make me look like a murder victim. Brandon, I'm leaving Caspian in your capable hands, would you please set up the chef's table and decant something for us to enjoy before dinner?"

"Of course, Chef," he said. She smiled in response, gave Caspian's arm a squeeze then walked through the kitchen and out a pair of french doors.

"Where do they lead?" asked Caspian.

"To the front of house, of course," said Christophe as if it was the most obvious answer in the world.

"Oh," he replied, then noticed how both men were staring at him. "Uh, do you want some help with that table?" Caspian asked, his voice rising. Christophe and Brandon shook their heads in a disturbingly synchronized fashion. "And why are you, two, looking at me that way?"

"What way is that?" asked Brandon cooly.

"Like I just drove an axe into your friend's head and you're trying to decide whether to call the cops or shoot me."

"He is perceptive," began Christophe, "I will give him that."

Brandon grunted something unintelligible, then gestured to the storage room. "Come on then, you can help me set up the table." Caspian started moving in that direction when the other man gripped his shoulder. "Do not tell the chef that I let you help, understand?"

"Okay," replied a rather confused Caspian, then the two headed into the storeroom, leaving Christophe behind to the sounds of pots scraping and low murmurs in his native French.

Several minutes later, Brandon swiped his hand across the small table's white linen for what must have been the fifth time. He peered at it, adjusted two candle sticks, then lit each. Brandon slowly walked around the table, his eyes never leaving the plates, and silverware. He reached out, moved one knife a fraction of an inch, then nodded.

"Looks good to me," said Caspian. Brandon arched an eyebrow. "Uh, not that I know much about this kind of thing. It's my first time eating in a store room."

"This is *not* a store room," said the other man. Caspian looked around and Brandon sighed. "Well, of course it is a store room, but it is the *chef's table*."

"Sorry," replied Caspian. "I don't know what that means."

Brandon lifted a bottle of wine from among four others that were resting on a nearby shelf. There was a brief flash of silver, then his hands were moving around the bottle's neck. Seconds later a pop sounded. He handed the cork to Caspian. "Do you know what to do with that?"

"Yes," he huffed, "I'm not completely ignorant." Caspian squeezed the moist cork then raised it to his nose. Brandon eyed him appraisingly, then said. "You don't know what your nose should be telling you, correct?"

Caspian gave him a sheepish grin. "I usually just make sure the cork doesn't fall apart, then nod. Honestly, I know a lot more about bourbon than I do wine."

A faint smile played across Brandon's lips. "Unpretentious, well at least that part of your description holds true. Let's see if reports of your honesty are also true."

"Huh? My—"

"What are your intentions with our Sara?"

Caspian swallowed. "I don't have *any* intentions. She just asked us to come taste her new menu."

Brandon made an affected show of looking around the otherwise empty room. He then pointed at the two place settings. "Who is the *us* to whom you refer?"

Caspian sighed. "My three other friends, one of whom is Sara's cousin, and all of whom I may murder myself if they planned all this behind my back." He lowered his voice to a growl. "I already know at least *one* of them was involved."

"You didn't know this was a dinner for two?"

"Not when Sara initially invited me," grumbled Caspian, "but now that I'm reviewing every bloody conversation in my head, she definitely left the guest list exceedingly vague."

"Well, what do you know," chuckled Brandon, "that *does* change things a bit. I thought you might have been a predator after our Sara," his smile broadened, "but now I see the truth of it." He pointed at Caspian. "Creole spiced Harris

Ranch tenderloin is not the only thing on the menu. Apparently, *you* are as well."

Caspian nodded. "So, I assume *the chef* doesn't host many people to her private table."

"Actually, she does. On average, she entertains some VIP once a week… during the times she's here, that is. However, she has *never* hosted a table only for two."

Caspian pursed his lips thoughtfully, then gave Brandon a conspiratorial wink. "Since I am decidedly *not* a VIP, I don't suppose you want to share what I should take from being given this rather unique honor."

A sound came from the kitchen. Brandon cocked his head, then moved to one side of the table. "I'd be happy to share, Caspian. You—"

He broke off as the storeroom door opened. *Oh boy,* thought Caspian, as Elizabeth's words from the previous night came to the fore. Kitchen light framed Sara, giving her an almost golden glow. She smiled at him, then unconsciously lowered a hand to prevent the swinging doors hitting her from behind. "Well," she asked, "I clean up nicely, don't I?" Brandon silently slid one chair out from beneath the table, as Sara walked further into the room. She arched an eyebrow playfully, then fake whispered, "Cat got your tongue, Mr. Lewis?"

He shook his head. "No, more like my eyes. That's, uh, an outstanding dress, Sara."

Her face broke into a wide smile, and she did a slow pirouette. "This old thing? Why, I only wear it when I don't care how I look."

Caspian barked a laugh. "Okay, Violet, nice *It's a Wonderful Life* reference, but also appropriate. You definitely could stop traffic…" he pointed, "in that old thing."

She settled into the offered chair with a whispered word of thanks to Brandon, who deftly placed a napkin in her lap. "I almost didn't wear it," said Sara. "I couldn't decide between this red one and—"

"A black one," said Caspian softly.

Sara smiled with surprise, "That's right. How did you guess that?"

"Oh you know," sputtered Caspian, "every woman has a little black dress, right? That's why it's a trope. The red looks great on you though…definitely the right choice."

Brandon leaned over, dropping a cloth napkin into Caspian's lap, and, as he moved to the side, whispered ever so softly, "As I was saying, you are a very lucky man. Hurt her and I'll hurt you worse."

Chapter 33

TRUTH OR DARE

"Yes, we are really doing this," laughed Sara. She shrugged, "unless you are too scared."

"Oh, please," huffed Caspian, "do you really think that amateur psychology trick is going to work on me?"

She grinned. "Let's find out. Truth or dare?" Caspian just stared at her. "Better hurry, Brandon will be back any second with dessert."

"Dessert," said Caspian, then patted his stomach. "I'm totally stuffed. How many courses did we have, five?"

"Six," she corrected, "but one was sorbet and you haven't had the dessert course yet." Sara leaned forward. "Don't change the subject. Truth...or...dare?"

"Fine," replied Caspian, "truth."

Sara pursed her lips thoughtfully. "What's the first movie that made you cry?"

"Huh, that's a good one. Franco Zeffirelli's *Jesus of Nazareth*. My parents were watching it. I was probably in fifth grade or so, and I liked the Romans." Sara cringed. "I know," said Caspian, "but they had swords and armor, and I was ten. Anyway, the way Zeffirelli directed it, and Robert Powell's performance, it just wrecked ten year old me."

"See, I knew someone sensitive lurked beneath those consulting depths," said Sara. "By the way, have you ever seen Zeffirelli's *Romeo and Juliet*? It's definitely in my top ten movies of all time. I know it's really old, but I don't think anything done since can touch it." Sara broke off a moment, then asked, "Do you know when Zeffirelli's version was made? Wait, I'm talking too much, aren't I?" She sighed. "I'm definitely talking too much, and it's your turn, too. Go on, then."

"You are *not* talking too much, and his Romeo & Juliet is one of my favorite movies, too. You're also right, no one has touched it in..." Caspian glanced up for a second, "fifty-three years. That movie came out in 1968."

"No way," she said.

"Way..." laughed Caspian, then furrowed his brow at Sara. "What?" She just made a *hurry-up* motion with one hand, then leaned forward with both elbows on the table expectantly. "All right," he said, "truth of dare?"

"Truth," replied Sara instantly.

"Well, I was going to ask you to tell me your favorite movie or play, but I think I may already know the answer now." Caspian shook his head in mock chagrin, "...thanks Sara, now I have to figure out something on the fly."

She rolled her eyes at him. "No you don't, because I only said Zeffirelli's *Romeo & Juliet* was in my top ten. I didn't say it was my top one." Sara showed her teeth. "See, I didn't ruin anything, now ask already."

"Okay, fine," he sighed. "What is your favorite movie or play?"

"That's easy, well it's easy if I can give you two."

Caspian shook his head. "Sorry, you only get one."

"I'm going to give you two anyway, because one is a comedy and one is a tragedy so they are very different things." She raised a finger. "But, they are both Shakespeare so, it's really like I'm just answering one."

Caspian laughed. "It's not like you're answering one at all, if you give me two different movies. That's the most convoluted logic I've ever heard. You're the one who wanted us to play this game and now you, Sara Edwards, you are breaking the rules."

"I'm not breaking them, Cas. I am changing them. It's a woman's prerogative to change things. Everyone knows that. Anyway, do you want to hear my answers or not?" He nodded. "Okay. They are plays, not movies, and I'm such a fangirl that I have both memorized. My favorite comedy is *Much Ado about Nothing.* My favorite tragedy is, as you already guessed, *Romeo and Juliet,* even though the first two acts of that play are kind of a comedy, at least in print. Mercutio is a clown and Romeo is kind of an idiot, with all his fawning over Rosaline." Sara stared at Caspian as his smile faded. "Something wrong?" she asked. "Not a Shakespeare fan? But you—"

"Huh, oh, no. I'm sorry, your choices just reminded me of something. Actually, I'm a huge Shakespeare fan, and those are two of my favorite plays as well." His smile returned. "I also happen to agree with your assessment of Romeo. I never really thought about it before. I mean, come on, fifteen minutes before he falls for Juliet the guy was head over heels for Rosaline. On top of that, he swears by something as inconstant as the moon, but Juliet totally calls him on that one. Please, give me a break. You're spot on, he *is* an idiot."

Sara set down her coffee cup and nodded. "I know, right. Juliet should have known better, but that's fourteenth century women for ya. I'd have kicked Romeo to the curb immediately." She shrugged. "He was way too immature, and being pretty can't make up for stupid. In fact, I have a theory that all men are really still just boys until at least thirty. Only after about thirty do you guys become worth anyone's time." She grinned. "How old are you, again?"

"Not thirty," he laughed.

"Then you are on probation," she snickered. "Okay, my turn again. Truth or dare?"

"Truth."

She sighed. "Coward. Okay, what part of a woman's body do you find most attractive?" Caspian opened his mouth to respond, but Sara pointed at him. "You cannot say her mind." He sighed, and she laughed. "I may not have known you of old, Mr. Lewis, but I do think I know you. Now, what part?"

"Fine, boobs. I love boobs," he said.

Sara looked down at her chest, and frowned. "Alas, poor Caspian, your date has not been well endowed. It is to weep."

"I didn't say I liked big boobs," he countered.

She nodded. "Nice save." A sound came from the kitchen causing them both to look toward the door. "Okay, I'll move things along and choose *dare* to your last question."

"Really?" Caspian snickered. "You trust me *that* much."

She inclined her head toward him. "Maybe I'm testing you. What does the under-thirty self-described boob man dare me to do?" Sara pitched up her voice. "I'm entirely in your power."

"Well now, this is interesting," began Caspian. "Sara Edwards, I dare you to…share your greatest fear and overcome it in my presence."

"Wow," she murmured, "I did not see that coming. I think I would have preferred something related to boobs." Sara swallowed. "Well, if I'm completely honest then I'd have to—"

The kitchen door swung inward. Brandon entered the room then held it open for Christophe. The Frenchman held a large rectangular platter on which sat two plates, each with a metal domed cover. He also looked supremely happy with himself. He set the platter in the middle of the table, then took a half step back. Sara's nose flared slightly and she smiled at him. "Christophe, I told you not to bother with that."

He shook his head. "I have no idea to what you could possibly be referring, Chef."

"I can smell the whiskey, the cinnamon and the cream, Christophe. How long did it take you?"

"No time at all," he replied far too quickly to be believed.

Sara's eyes fixed on Brandon. "How long did it take him?"

"The better part of an hour," replied the sommelier.

"Christophe, Christophe," whispered Sara, "thank you, but it really wasn't necessary."

"It is your favorite and it was absolutely necessary. Now, may I?"

"Please do," she replied.

Both Brandon and Christophe stepped forward. Each of the two men set their right hand on one of the domes. They paused for a brief moment, then lifted the lids while speaking as one, "And voilà."

"Wow," murmured Caspian, drawing out the word. "What in the name of all that's holy are these delectable things?"

Sara smirked at him. "I thought you were full."

"I was," he agreed, "and I'm not anymore. Or maybe I still am, but will suffer later."

Christophe gestured to the plate nearest Sara. "This is our Creole Bread Pudding Soufflé. I will finish it at table with warm whiskey cream." The sous chef pointed to the other dessert. "And this is our Piety and Desire Chocolate Coconut Bar. It is dark chocolate and chicory ganache blended with toasted coconut throughout. It is topped with our own Commander's French Truck coffee-coconut cream, toasted almonds, and Ecuadorian cocoa nibs."

"It looks horrible," said Caspian.

Christophe nodded. "I assure you, monsieur, if you were to die in exchange for eating these desserts, you would believe the transaction fair." He gave Caspian a wink, then the two men withdrew.

Caspian picked up his spoon, and was about to dip it into the coconut bar when he said, "Despite what Christophe said, there's no way I'm getting through all this." He pinched up his face. "How bad will it look if we pack some of it to go?"

Sara had already taken her first bite of the soufflé. She rolled her eyes, then tapped her spoon against the plate. "I eat this kind of thing all the time, but Caspian, I have to tell you, Christophe is a damned alchemist. Bottom line, it would look bad if we left the tiniest scrap behind. Honestly though, you shouldn't worry about that. The question isn't whether we take some of it with us, it's whether one of us kills the other so they can eat all of it here."

Caspian laughed. "I'll demonstrate some restraint and let you live." He lifted a spoon full of coconut and chocolate, then moved it toward Sara. She smiled, then leaned forward and opened her mouth slightly to accept the offered dessert.

"Definitely outstanding," she said, "but I have to say I like mine better. Want to try?"

"Hell yes," replied Caspian, then accepted her own offered spoon.

"Oh, wow," he sighed. "You're right. That's better. Of course that's like saying platinum is better than gold. It is, but the other is still bloody gold."

Sara took another bite of soufflé then pointed with her spoon. "Totally agree."

She seemed about to say something else when Caspian interrupted. "You still owe me a dare. Did you think I forgot?"

Sara set down her spoon, then leaned back in her chair. "No, but I hoped you had."

Caspian held up a hand. "I was just kidding. Honestly, don't do anything that makes you—"

"Oh no," she said, "I wouldn't have let you off the hook." She took a deep breath. "Share my greatest fear and overcome it in your presence. Okay, here it goes. My greatest fear is that I'll never find someone who loves me with the same fire I love them." Caspian set down his own spoon and focused on her. "You see, I'm the kind of person who gives her whole self. I've done it once before only to find out that the person to whom I gave my heart was incapable of doing the same."

"Maybe he just wasn't the right guy for you, Sara," said Caspian softly.

She shook her head. "No, you don't understand. He definitely *wasn't* right for me, but that's not what I'm talking about. He's married now and has two kids. I know his wife. She lives back home and we became friends." Sara shrugged. "Neither of them love the other with their whole selves. I'm talking about the kind of love where you don't know where one of you ends and the other begins." She looked down. "That's the only way I know how to love, Caspian. It's all or nothing."

The two sat in silence for several seconds. Finally he said, "Here's what I can tell you. Those people *are* out there." Caspian reached out and gave Sara's hand a squeeze. "I was one of those people."

She nodded. "I know you were...I know you are." Sara bit her lower lip then closed her eyes for moment. "Which brings us to the second part of your dare." She opened her eyes and fixed her gaze on Caspian. "I like you, Caspian. I liked you from the moment I met you. Now, three months later, I like you a lot more." She saw his expression shift, then joined her free hand with the one he still held. "You don't have to freak out. I'm not saying I love you or anything. I'm just saying I like you, but within that like, I see the potential for more."

Caspian let out a ragged breath. "Sara, I don't know if anyone has shared with you about—"

"I know about Elizabeth. I know how much you loved her. It's how I know that you're like me. You didn't hold anything back from her. You shared your whole self."

"And it nearly killed me," he whispered.

"That's the risk we take," she agreed, then said, "I'm not rushing you, Cas. You've endured a tragedy the likes of which I cannot begin to imagine. You may be thinking that you never want to risk that kind of heartbreak again." Sara gripped his hand tightly, and looked directly into his eyes. "I know something about heartbreak, Caspian. I also know that we are never promised tomorrow. All we have is today." Sara leaned forward, kissed him softly on the lips, then withdrew, their eyes remaining locked together. After several seconds, Caspian let out a breath, then leaned forward to return the kiss.

A moment later, they parted. Sara immediately recognized Caspian's expression. She shook her head. "Don't do that. You have betrayed nothing. If you had not loved Elizabeth with your whole heart, then you would not be who you are today." She smiled. "If you were someone else, I would not have wanted to kiss you, and you would not have kissed me back."

Caspian considered this for several seconds, then nodded. He was about to speak when she rested a finger on his lips. "You are who you are, and I will bide my time, because you are worth the wait. The love you hold in your heart for Elizabeth doesn't intimidate me. It doesn't makes me jealous. It just make me know that you are capable of loving with your whole self." She lifted his hands and kissed them. "That's a rare and precious thing."

"Wow," said Caspian, "You really are something."

"So I've been told," chuckled Sara, "and it's not always been a compliment. Still, now you know my greatest fear, and—"

"In sharing it with me, did you overcome it?" he asked.

She lifted a hand then tilted it left and right. "I suppose that depends on whether you ever want to see me again." She swallowed. "Do you?"

Caspian crooked his finger and the two leaned to where they almost were touching again. "I can think of no one alive today that I'd want to see more than you." He saw joy and relief war for dominion on her face, then said, "Besides, I'd be a fool to let someone who cooks like you get away without being absolutely sure, right?"

She laughed. "Are you referring to me or Christophe? He did all the cooking, but I have much nicer boobs."

Chapter 34

THE WINTERS

Caspian sat in his car staring at the Winter's front door. His mind was a whirlwind of interconnected thoughts. One moment he was replaying scenes from the dinner he shared with Sara the night before, the next he heard Elizabeth's voice telling him to *fix it* with respect to her parents. Finally, Caspian closed his eyes. He just sat silently, trying by sheer force of will to find some calm center from which to move. After several minutes, he glanced at his watch, then shook his head. *It's not going to get any easier if you wait another fifteen minutes,* he mused to himself, *and then, you'll have to apologize for being late as well as an inconsiderate asshole.*

He sighed, then looked at the passenger seat. It was empty except for two bottles of wine, that he knew both Roger and Mary liked, and one bouquet of flowers. "Uh, Lizzie," he whispered, "are you around, uh, somewhere? I know you've been watching us, and maybe doing things too. Now would be a really great time for some advice." Caspian waited. Nothing happened. He pursed his lips. "Are you not responding because it's hard for you, or are you mad about what I did with Sara...or are you just not really here."

"I hope you aren't mad about Sara. I didn't do anything, not really. She kissed me, just like you did, after the Chad thing. Well, not just like you. She wasn't drunk, but it was similar. Why are women always kissing me first?" He paused, then murmured, "Jenny must be right, I have no *girldar.*"

Caspian shivered and his breath condensed into a puff of white air, despite the warmth of a Louisiana spring evening. Frost covered his phone as the screen began flashing through his music library to settle on his rather expansive Sinatra collection. The car's speakers crackled to life and his navigation screen illuminated with album art. Sinatra crooned, *Fools rush in where angels fear to tread.*

Caspian stared at the screen, swallowed, then whispered. "Lizzie, is that you…is that your answer to why I'm the kiss'ee and not the kiss'er." He laughed. "Because you all are fools." He laughed again. "So, you're not mad about Sara?"

His phone flashed, and a different album appeared. Once again, Sinatra's voice filled the car, *I must confess what you say is true. I had a rendezvous with somebody new. That's the only one I ever had. Baby, baby, don'cha go 'way mad.*

"Holy shit," murmured Caspian. He picked up his phone and stared at it. "Okay, this is very weird, but also incredibly cool. Lizzie, what the heck do I say to your folks?"

What can I do to prove it to you that I'm sorry, I didn't mean to ever be mean to you. If I didn't care I wouldn't feel like I do.

Caspian slumped in his seat. "Yeah, you're right. I feel like shit, deservedly so. I'll just tell them that. I hope they forgive me."

Take these lovely flowers, or they'll be lonely too. Flowers mean forgiveness. Forgive me, say you do.

He sighed. "You and your mom love flowers, so I figured it was a good move." Caspian rubbed at his chin, then asked, "Should I tell them about you, I mean that you're…" He shook his head. "I don't exactly know what you are, Lizzie? Still, should I tell them what I know?"

Yes, ma'am, we've decided. No ma'am, we ain't gonna hide it. Yes, ma'am, you're invited now.

Caspian arched an eyebrow at his car's entertainment system. "Well, I'm not a ma'am, but I guess you have to make do with what you've got." He stared at the front door again, but this time with more confidence. "Okay, I'm going in, but hey, I hope we could do this again. Can we?"

Wishing on a star never got you far, and so it's time to make a new start.

"A new start. You mean Sara, don't you? Lizzie, I'm not ready." He frowned. "Besides, ugh, apparently you want me to go to Wyoming this Thursday, and meet someone who received your…well you know what she got. Do you have any brilliant advice about that?"

Come fly with me, let's fly, let's fly away

Caspian barked a laugh. "Very funny, but—" He paused, noting that, this time, his expelled breath didn't condense. "Lizzie? Lizzie are you still there?" The screen to his phone dimmed then went black. Caspian's mind went back to something Elizabeth told him when she first appeared in his apartment. He nodded to himself. "Thanks, babe. I know this takes a lot out of you." He glanced up through the car's moon roof, kissed his fingers then pressed them to the glass. "Love you."

Mary and Roger both stared at Caspian with nearly identical expressions. Mary drained her wine glass then held it out to Caspian. He refilled it. She drained it a second time, then extended her hand again. This time she eyed the refilled glass, but didn't drink. "I know it's a lot to take in," Caspian said.

"That's the understatement of the year," murmured Roger, then took a sip from his own glass.

Mary nodded. She reached out to take Caspian's hand in hers. She smiled. "Well, that at least explains why you dropped off the edge of the earth." Her eyes slipped off his, and she said, "We were afraid you didn't ever want to see us again."

Caspian dragged a hand down his face, then shook his head. "Mary, I wish I could hide behind this paranormal stuff, but the truth is, that's all relatively new. I went off the rails, heck, I'm *still* mostly off the rails, but I'm trying to be better. Everyone told me I was being an asshole to you guys and—"

"No, honey you were—" began Mary, but Roger nudged her to silence.

She eyed him, but Roger shook his head, and whispered, "Let him finish, Mary. He's trying to apologize."

Caspian nodded. "Thanks Roger."

The older man mirrored the motion, then said, "For the record, I agree with you, Cas. You were being an asshole." Mary looked horrified as Caspian and her husband stared at each other across the kitchen table. Finally, Caspian's lips curled up slightly and Roger grinned at him. "There, I almost had you."

"Oh no," said Caspian, "you totally had me, because it's true."

Roger shrugged. "Maybe it is, but we all deal with grief differently, Cas. I bought a five thousand dollar gaming computer, regressed to a twenty something, ignored my grieving wife, and played online games until my eyes fell out."

"And I didn't even know I was being ignored," said Mary, "because I went to Mass every morning, then stayed around the church most days until dark."

"All three of us abandoned each other," whispered Roger. "There's plenty of blame to go around, so why cling to it. In many ways, Elizabeth was the sun about which we all orbited. She was warm, and bright, and filled with life. Then she was gone and—"

"We were left cold and in the dark," added Mary. "We all spun off in different directions, trying to fill the hole she left by her passing."

The three sat in a comfortable silence. Finally, Caspian said, "I'm sorry she hasn't been able to connect with you guys. I'm sure she wants to."

Roger waved away his concern. "It's more than enough that she's communicated with you." He shook his head in unconcealed amazement, "I mean, Caspian, this is a miracle. What a gift, she's given you, and through you, us. Our daughter is not dead. She's, what did she call it?"

"Absent from the body. I'm not sure what that means, but—"

"If you would come with me to Mass, you would," snarked Mary gently. "It's a Bible verse." She noticed Caspian's confusion, then sighed. "You don't recognize it at all?"

He shook his head. "God and I aren't on speaking terms right now. We might never be."

Roger pointed at Caspian. "See, it's not just me, Mary."

"I never said you were alone in your thinking, Roger. There's no limit to how many people can be wrong at the same time."

He frowned. "Do you see what I have to put up with? It's *God has a plan*, this, and *He'll work all things to good* that."

"Yeah," said Caspian, "sorry, Mary, I'm not singing from that hymnal. I'm more in the camp of what's the point to being an omnipotent being if you don't bother preventing pointless tragedies."

"Right with you, Cas," sighed Roger. "God takes Lizzie from me, I take me from God. I'm done."

"I'll not be baited into another fight," said Mary as she looked from Roger to Caspian, "by either of you. Believe what you want, but I'll tell you this, when you wrestle with God, all you end up with is a bad hip."

Caspian pinched up his face, confused. "Don't worry about it, Son. She's quoting something again."

Mary rolled her eyes, took a breath, then asked, "So you said you're going to Wyoming this Thursday?"

ONE HEART THAT BEATS FOR TWO

Caspian nodded. "David hacked the donor database again. We got both a name and address. She's a teenager. Her first name is Mary, just like you. Mary Foster. Apparently, according to the Internet, she was some kind of track and field phenom until she got sick."

"Cystic Fibrosis, you said?" asked Roger.

"Yeah, I didn't know much about it until Dave's hackery, then researched it a bunch. Nasty thing. Attacks the lungs. Most folks don't live past thirty."

Mary wiped at her eyes, sniffed, then reached for Roger's hand. "Look at our baby go," she said, "making blind men see, and young girls run like the wind."

Caspian and Roger stared at her, then each other for a moment in silence, then Roger reached for a tissue. He took one look at Caspian's face, handed it to him, then took another for himself. Mary nodded at the two men. "Serves you both right for being such...such men about this whole thing. As Lizzie would say, *There's more things in Heaven and Earth, Horatio—*" she paused, then shifted her gaze expectantly between Caspian and her husband.

"*—than are dreamt of in your philosophy,*" finished the two men.

〜〜〜

David leaned forward from the third row seat of their Uber, "Wait, you and Sara had a date? When the hell did this happen? Why doesn't anyone tell me anything?"

"Get in line for info, Dave," said Jennifer. "Cas was in the middle of answering me. Go on, Caspian."

He shrugged. "There not much more to tell. Roger, Mary, and I hugged it out. Mary was incredibly gracious because, well, she's Mary. On the other hand, Roger agreed I was being an asshole. Mary also thought Roger was being an asshole, so I had some company in that respect."

"How'd they take the whole ghost-Lizzie thing?" asked Michael.

"Surprisingly well," replied Caspian. "Again, Mary did far better than Roger, but then she's not feuding with God like both he and I are."

"That's not going to end well for you," mused Jennifer.

Caspian frowned at her. "What's he gonna do, Jenny, kill my fiancé...again."

She opened her mouth to respond, but Michael cut her off. "I should have sat between you two. Stop already, or I'll have Larry turn this Uber around."

"If you do, you'll miss your flight," said the driver, then added, "not that I'm listening."

"Can we please get back to the Sara thing?" asked David.

"Oh my God," said Michael, "Why is everyone hot for my cousin all of a sudden?"

"What?" sputtered David, "I'm not hot for anyone. No, that's not true. I am hot for someone actually, but it's not Sara. Where did you even get that idea, dude? I'm just trying to grok how Mr. closed-off-bug-filled-pizza-box-man ended up on a date."

"Lizzie," said Caspian and Jennifer together.

"You are frakking kidding me right now," sputtered David, "Lizzie is setting you up with people now?"

"Not people, just Sara," said Caspian.

"I am not okay with this. Nope, not okay," muttered Michael.

Jennifer held up her hands. "Everyone take a step back. Technically, Sara set herself up with Cas. She asked me to help, so I did…a little."

"So then what did Lizzie have to do with it?" asked David.

"I thought it was just a group outing at her restaurant," said Caspian, "Lizzie told me it was a date and that I should go."

"She also picked out Sara's dress," added Jennifer.

"You are frakking kidding me," said David again.

"Nope, I wanted her to wear a black one. Lizzie wanted the red. Red was the better call. Elizabeth always had better fashion sense than me."

By this point David had given up all pretense of letting his seatbelt do its job. He crouched in front of the third row with his arms around the second row head rests. "So, let me get this straight. Elizabeth shows up in Cas' apartment as a full-on apparition to tell him that he should go on a date with Michael's cousin, and then shows up in Sara's room to pick out her dress? Is that what you're telling me?"

Jennifer shook her head. "No, don't be ridiculous, Dave." He seemed to relax slightly, then she added, "Lizzie didn't actually *show up* in Sara's room. How do you think that would have gone over? No, Elizabeth just kept throwing the red dress on the floor every time I told Sara she should wear the black one."

David fell back into his seat, then reattached his seatbelt. "Yeah, that actually changes things…" his voice rose, "not in the least freaking bit."

"What happened on this supposed date, that I, also, didn't know about?" asked Michael. "You guys do realize that, according to my extended family, I'm responsible for Sara's well being." He turned and narrowed his eyes at Caspian. "What did you do?"

"Nothing happened. We had dinner. It was good."

"Oh, do shut up, Caspian Lewis," snickered Jennifer, then clutched both hands to her chest. "They kissed."

"Man, I am not sure I'm cool with this," grumbled Michael. "Caspian is a complete train wreck."

"Dude, I'm literally right here listening to you tell me what a mess I am."

Michael stared at him. "I'm your best friend."

"One of—" corrected David.

"Fine, I'm *one of* your best friends. I should lie to you now? Cas, you *are* a train wreck." Michael pointed at his friend. "Caspian Lewis, I want you to hear me, loud and clear. Less than a year ago, Sara was rushed off to Austin for God knows what. I do *not* need you messing with her head. She's my little cousin, and, no bullshit, I love her to pieces. She is *not* some kind of transitional plaything." Jennifer and David both cringed at the outburst. Michael took a breath. "Okay, that was too far. I'm sorry. I know you don't think of her that way, but—"

"I don't know what to think about anything," said Caspian, "and I don't blame you for looking out for Sara. I *am* a train wreck. I have no idea what I'm doing, but I can promise you that one thing I won't do is hurt her."

Michael relaxed into his seat, apparently mollified. He took another deep breath, then stared at his friend. "Cas, one last thing. I know you. I love you like a brother, and I know you would never knowingly hurt Sara, but two's company and three's a crowd. You, Sara, and Elizabeth...that love triangle is just not going to work."

"I know," Caspian whispered. "I know, and I'll figure it out. I promise."

"Okay," said the Uber driver. "Here we are. Delta drop-off." Larry turned around and gave the four of them a bemused shake-of-the-head. "Hope you all have a safe flight. Just so you know, I'm giving you five stars, because this was *the most* strange-as-shit rideshare I've ever had. Well done, you guys."

Chapter 35

THE BREATH OF LIFE

Jennifer, David, and Caspian waited on the sidewalk while Michael handed the cabdriver a credit card. David shook his head. "You know we've left civilization when your options are a cab or walking."

Caspian frowned at his friend. "I told you there was a rideshare available from both Uber and Lyft. *You* didn't want to wait."

"Actually, I'm the one that didn't want to wait," corrected Jennifer. She saw Caspian's expression, then shrugged. "I'm all for blaming Dave, but fair is fair. This one is on me. We already got a late start, and our best window for catching Mary's parents alone is now…ish."

"Exactly," interjected David. "Besides, in addition to the thirty minute wait both apps projected, I'm telling you, it was the same car." He laughed. "I think this town literally has one person covering both Uber and Lyft." He shook his head. "I couldn't live here, no way."

Jennifer pointed at the distant mountain. "You are a doofus. Look at that. I totally could live here, and everyone has been so nice, especially that gate agent." Her voice lowered slightly, "He was *really* nice."

"Dave, you didn't leave that bucket of ice in the cab did you?" asked Caspian. "I think Jenny's overheating again."

"And I think you're an inconsiderate jerk-face," she replied, "so there."

Michael walked up, took in his friends' expressions, then sighed. "What's going on?"

"Jenny's ovaries are exploding, again," replied David.

"They were not exploding, Dave," said Caspian.

Jennifer nodded to him. "Thank you, Cas, I app—"

He interrupted her. "They were targeting." Caspian held a hand up to his mouth and shifted his voice to have a mechanical cadence. "Red five this is Red Leader. Stay on Target."

David's face lit up. "I can't hold it. I can't hold it," he screamed.

"Stay on target," repeated Caspian, then glanced at Jennifer's darkening expression.

Michael laughed. "Oh, the gate agent, right?"

She made a sour face. "You are all misogynists and I don't know why I spend any time with you."

"Because we're the keepers of the ice bucket," said Michael. He made a show of looking around. "Dave, did you forget the ice bucket? Dude, she could literally melt down. How could you forget the ice bucket?"

"Sorry, I got distracted," David said. "I'm worthless and weak."

Jennifer started walking down the sidewalk and toward the nearest house. She raised one hand and extended a middle finger. "I hate every one of you."

The four friends stood in front of the Foster's front door, clearly unsure of what to do next. "I can't believe you guys didn't plan this far ahead," grumbled Jennifer.

"Hey, I found the girl," said David. "I also found the parents, and the address. That should be more than enough."

"I paid for the cab," offered Michael.

Three pairs of eyes fixed on Caspian. "Don't look at me," he said. "I'm the protagonist of this story. Protagonists don't plan." He waved his arms expansively. "Others in the world plan around them. I blame Jenny. She's the mom."

"Don't even with me right now," she hissed. "If any of you were mine, I'd put you in a basket with a *Claus* necklace and send you to Tanta Kringle."

"Well, I don't think Cas should be in front," said David. "What if Mary has drawn pictures of him, like Whittaker did? If they see Caspian first, the parents might completely freak out."

Caspian nodded. "Good point. Michael, you should be up front. I'll hang behind you."

"I am not going to be up front," he laughed.

"Why not?" asked Jennifer. "You're the oldest."

"I'm also the darkest. Have you noticed how *pale* Wyoming is?" He saw their blank expressions, then pointed. "Now, that's white privilege."

His three friends stared back for a second, caught each other's eye, then said as one, "Shut up!"

He grinned. "It was worth a shot. Still, if we were back home, and it was three of my local friends and one of you. I'd not be putting you up front. Jen should ring the bell."

"What?" she sputtered. "Why me?"

"Women are less threatening," Michael replied. He saw her eyes narrow, then added. "Well, not you specifically, but they don't know you, yet. By the time they realize how dangerous you are, it will be too late and we'll be inside. Now, ring the bell. Cas, you stand behind Dave and me."

"This is so dumb," muttered Jennifer, "I can't believe none of you bone-heads thought this through." She sighed, then reached forward and pressed the doorbell.

Almost immediately a male voice spoke to them. "I was wondering if any of you were ever going to ring the bell. You're right Michael, statistically speaking, women are often considered less threatening. However, from what my little Ring doorbell cam has been showing me over the past five minutes, I think Jennifer may be an outlier."

David peered at the doorbell. "Wow, that must be the pro-model. You can barely see the camera lens. Still, my bad, I probably should have noticed."

"Ya think," growled Caspian. "You're our tech support."

The door opened to reveal a middle-aged man with pale red hair, glasses, and a face full of freckles. A dark haired woman stood beside him. Both wore smiles. Henry Foster started to push open the storm door, then paused a moment as Michael and the others took a couple steps back. The older man held the door open with his left arm, and extended his right hand to Michael, who shook it warmly. "Welcome to Wyoming." He glanced at his wife. "Look, Susan, I think it's a black man. We've never seen one before, have we?"

Jennifer's face split into a wide grin. "Oh, I like these two."

Henry saw Michael's expression shift toward embarrassment, but gave him a quick wink. "I'm just ribbing you. Please, come in. Come in. Mary's not here, but you probably planned it that way. We've been expecting you."

"Yes, please do come in," echoed Susan. The four began filing into the Foster's home, but as Caspian started to pass by, Susan reached out to gently touch his arm. "You're Caspian, right?"

His friends turned toward them, and he nodded, "Yes ma'am."

Susan wrapped her arms around him and squeezed. Caspian tensed at first, then relaxed into the mother's embrace. She pushed back a moment later, and looked up with eyes bright with tears. "I'm so sorry for your loss. I only hope that when you meet our Mary, you will find some solace in what Elizabeth's gift has done for our girl—"

"—and us," added Henry, then slowly shut the door. "Please, come into the living room."

"I'll get us some snacks and drinks," offered Susan. "What would everyone like? Water, coffee, tea—"

"Bourbon," muttered Caspian without thinking, then shook his head. "Sorry, I—"

Henry laughed. "No, that's exactly the same thing I had in mind." The older man lifted his left arm and made a point of looking at a watch that didn't exist. "Well, would you look at the time. It's five o'clock somewhere. Honey, would you bring the Horse Soldier bourbon. I think we have a lot to discuss before we go meet Mary at the track later."

〜⁊⺑⺄〜

Michael shot a meaningful glance Caspian's direction, but his friend just took another sip of bourbon and continued staring off into the middle distance. "It's a lot to take in," said Henry. "We've had months to deal with all this. You four have had, what, ten minutes?"

"Well," began David, "we've already had our share of weirdness, trust me, but what you just described definitely takes things to another level."

"That's for sure," said Michael, then asked, "What exactly did you mean when you said *Mary wrote down our names and showed you our faces?*"

"It happened when Mary breathed out," said Susan, "not all the time of course, and it wasn't all of your faces." She gestured to Caspian. "Just his and," she paused, "Elizabeth's."

"And you said, your daughter breathed out frost? Did I get that right?" asked Jennifer. Both Henry and Susan nodded. Jennifer tapped Caspian's leg. "Cas, care to engage here?"

252

He tilted his glass up, drained the rest of the bourbon, then sighed. "It actually makes sense." He looked at his friends. "So, I left something out when I told you about meeting with Lizzie's parents earlier. She, uh...well, she communicated with me, again."

"What," they all said together as the Fosters shared a look.

"You mean she physically showed up again?" asked David. He turned to Susan. "Mrs. Foster, did Lizzie physically show up to you guys as well?"

Susan shook her head, and was about to respond, when Caspian said, "She communicated, but not in person. Obviously I don't understand any of this, but my guess is it takes a *lot* of effort for her to physically appear. This last time, she just communicated by playing snippets of songs that she knew I had on my iPhone."

David's mouth dropped open. "You mean like Bumblebee did in the transformers movie."

Jennifer smiled. "Lizzie loved that movie."

"Yeah," said Caspian, "I guess it was kind of like that except much more precise and without the radio-station skipping. It was all Sinatra songs, too." He focused on the Fosters, then added, "It got cold in the car just as it happened. I could see my breath. The same thing happened once before, too. She physically appeared that other time, and when she did, it got a whole lot colder."

"That's when she showed up in your apartment, right?" asked Michael.

Caspian nodded. "I think she somehow uses the ambient heat to enable her to communicate or even appear."

Susan nudged her husband. "Show them the video."

He stared at her a second, then said, "We promised Mary to keep it in the family."

"Henry," she replied flatly, "I think they qualify. Please, show them."

He turned, and saw the expectation in all four of their faces, then nodded. Henry reached for the nearby remote and clicked on the television. He navigated to what appeared to be a cloud library filled with home movies, then scrolled down to the last one in the list. "Are you sure you want to see this?" he asked, "because, trust me, there will be no unseeing it." Nods occurred throughout the room. He took a breath. "As you wish."

The thumbnail image disappeared, replaced by a spinning wheel as the streaming app buffered for several seconds. The screen brightened with an image of carpeted floor, as a young woman called out, "Dad, did you hear me. Dad, it's happening again. Get your phone!"

"I have it Mary," came a man's voice, clearly Henry's. "Susan," he yelled. "Susan, come on! It's happening again. I'm going to film it."

"I'm coming. Where are you?" came Susan's distant response.

"Upstairs." The image started jumping as Henry bounded up the stairs.

"Hurry Dad, I'm in my bathroom."

"I'm coming, baby. I'm coming. It's going to be okay. I'm...oh God."

"Dad, you aren't filming me."

"Oh..." The image jumped again, then focused on a girl in her late teens. She had brown hair that fell just below her shoulders, and was staring directly into her bathroom mirror. The camera shook slightly. "It's so cold," said Henry. "Mary, don't be afraid. I'm not going to let anything happen to you."

Mary Foster turned to face her father. Bright green eyes fixed on the camera and her heart shaped face made her look younger than her seventeen years. Mary's lips parted as if she were about to blow her father a kiss. Frosted air puffed from her mouth, and she smiled. "I'm not afraid, Dad. I think I know what's been happening. She's trying to communicate with me, but it's hard for her. I'm not fighting it now, and I think that's helping."

"Mary, who is trying to communicate?"

Instead of answering her father, the young woman turned toward the mirror and breathed. Frost covered the entire surface except where it looked like a finger had traced two words. *I'm Elizabeth.*

"Oh, shit," said David, then slapped a hand over his mouth, as Henry paused the video.

"Are you guys okay?" he asked. "We've watched this dozens of times and have had weeks to come to grips with it. I just figured showing was better than telling, but if you—"

"Play it," said Caspian. "I want to see what she has to say."

"Yeah, we're okay," said Jennifer. Michael nodded as well.

The video started moving again. Mary said, "Hello Elizabeth, I'm Mary."

I know. Hi Mary.

The young woman shot her father a crooked smile. "Yeah, I guess that was kind of dumb of me. Obviously she knows who I am." Mary pursed her lips in thought then asked, "Why are you here?"

Love

"Who do you love, Elizabeth?" she asked.

Caspian Lewis

Caspian felt the weight of everyone's gaze on him. Tears formed in his eyes, but they didn't fall. He smiled at their concern. "I'm good," he said softly. "Keep going."

"Who is Caspian Lewis?" asked Mary. "Is he your friend, boyfriend, husband?"

Yes to two, almost to last

"Oh no," said Mary. She turned to look at her father, then stared back at the mirror. "I'm sorry, but what can I do?"

Run.

"Run?" said Mary in surprise. "Did you know I used to run?"

Run, Mary.

"I can't run," she replied. "I was sick. I'm better now, but I can never run again."

You can.

"No I can't," argued Mary, her voice rising. "My lungs didn't work. I nearly died. You don't know."

I know...C.F. Run, Mary.

Tears had begun streaking the young woman's cheeks. The image jumped as Susan appeared, clearly having pushed Henry to the side. She reached for her daughter. "Enough, Mary. Take my hand. We're leaving this room. We're leaving this house we're—"

"No, Mom! She knows I had C.F. How could she know that? I'm fine. I'll be fine." Mary squared her shoulders, then gripped both sides of her sink, and leaned toward the mirror. "Elizabeth, how do you know I had C.F.?"

Gave you a gift

"A gift, what do you mean. What gift?"

My breath.

"Oh my God," said both elder Fosters together. Mary became very still. She narrowed her eyes at the mirror. "You gave me your breath?" She lifted one hand from the sink and pressed it to her chest. "Did you give me—"

More frost than before puffed from Mary's mouth. Instead of coating the mirror, it swirled, condensed and formed a face, Elizabeth's face. Her lips curved up in a gentle smile and Henry quickly increased the TV's volume. Even at its maximum setting, Elizabeth's words were almost too faint to hear. *I gave you my breath, Mary. Use it well. Run.*

Mary reached up with a finger, but as she touched the image of Elizabeth's face, it shattered into tiny fragments of frost, that quickly melted away. The young woman breathed out several times, but there was no frost. Susan slipped an arm around her daughter, as Mary turned toward the camera. "Daddy?"

Henry's voice cracked in response, "Yes, baby girl, what is it?"

"Will you wake me when you get up tomorrow?"

The image shifted slightly as Henry nodded, then he asked, "Why do you want to get up that early? Your first online class isn't until—"

She interrupted him. "Because we need to do something."

The camera refocused as Henry walked toward his daughter. "What are we going to do in the morning?"

Mary fixed him with a gaze that left little room for doubt or argument. "We're going to run."

"No," said her mother. "You can't."

"It's too soon," added her father, "The doctors all said—"

"I don't care what they said. Fine, tomorrow we'll walk, but by Thanksgiving we jog, and by Christmas we run. I'm going to make the team next year. Now, are you going to help me, or not?"

Henry's camera captured his wife's look of fear, uncertainty, and doubt, but his response conveyed the opposite. "I'm with you baby-girl, by Christmas, we run."

Chapter 36

RUN LIKE THE WIND

A heavy set man in his early forties walked up from the dirt track, and extended a hand to Henry. The two shook hands for several seconds, then Henry said, "Jim, I'd like you to meet some new friends of the family. This is Caspian, Jennifer, Michael, and David. Guys, this is Coach James Rowe."

"Jim," corrected the other man with a smile, "or Coach. I answer to both." His eyes flicked to Mrs. Foster. "Good to see you, too, Susan. Uh, you guys aren't planning to talk with Mary now are you? She's already started her prep-routine, and you know how she gets."

Susan snickered softly. "I definitely know how she gets, Jim, but no, we aren't going to disturb her. In fact, I wanted to see if we could sit over by the press tent because—"

"Mary never looks at the press tent," finished the coach with a smile. "I remember." He focused on Caspian and the others. "You promised her you wouldn't come today, didn't you?"

"We didn't promise," corrected Henry, "although we might have, accidentally, given her that impression. Anyway, a few things have changed, and I just wanted these folks to be able to see Mary run."

"Well," said Jim, drawing out the word, "You certainly don't look like press, but since I'm the one checking everyone's credentials..." he grinned, "I think you can safely hang out there for a bit."

Henry gave the coach a nod. "Thanks, Jim, much appreciated."

They all started to walk toward a roped off area with a white and blue awning that was set near the track's finish line, when the coach said, "Oh, just out of curiosity, which school are you representing?"

"School?" asked David, "We're not—"

"At liberty to say, right now," interrupted Jennifer and flashed the older man a bright smile. She reached up and laid a hand lightly on his shoulder. "You know how it is, don't you, Jim." He smiled at her, and nodded. "I can tell you this, though," Jennifer said in a conspiratorial whisper, "We're from New Orleans, if that gives you any hints."

The coach's eyes widened. "LSU?" Jennifer's face remained even. "Tulane?" Jennifer arched an eyebrow. "I really couldn't say."

"Ohhh, Tulane," murmured the coach, but Jennifer and the others moved on before he could ask anything else.

"That was pretty smooth," said Henry with a laugh.

Michael slapped the older man on the back. "Yep, and given Dave's almost complete inability to catch social cues, it's a good thing we have Jen around. Of course you haven't seen anything, yet. She's a career criminal, out on parole, and we are accountable for her behavior. That's why there's three of us. It takes three to keep her in line."

Jennifer rolled her eyes, then asked Susan, "Why did Mary's coach think we might be college scouts?"

"Because they've been calling for months," replied Susan. "Truth be told, our Mary has been a big story around here for a long time."

"Rock Spring's first Olympian," interjected Henry. They all looked at him. He shrugged. "That's what the local papers kept writing. I said it was too much pressure to put on a teenager, especially one with a dangerous, if managed, medical condition. Still, Mary, seemed to thrive under the spotlight and her doctor said the running was good for her, so I held my peace."

Susan nodded, "But that all changed when she got sick about eighteen months ago. Everything unraveled so quickly that we were left reeling. All the stories shifted in tone toward heartbreak and sympathy. Mary didn't like that at all. She got angry at first, and that wasn't great. But it was when she started to believe all the doom and gloom that things really got bad."

Henry reached over to take his wife's hand. "Yeah, Mary just kind of gave up. Her health deteriorated to the point where her doctors started talking in ways that no parent ever wants to hear." His eyes flicked among Caspian and his friends. "You know, the *enjoy what time you have left together* speeches that doctors give when all hope is lost."

"I can't even imagine," murmured Jennifer.

"Me either," agreed Caspian. "I'm really sorry that—"

Henry shook his head, then turned to fully face Caspian. "No, don't ever say that. I know you just meant to be consoling, but our trials pale in comparison to yours. That's part of why I wanted you to come see this rather than just wait for Mary to join us at home later." Henry pointed to the track where ten young women had begun milling around the starting blocks. "That's the rest of the story. That's why the press is all over a tiny town like Rock Springs. Mary is the miracle runner. The girl who could barely draw breath, but now runs like the wind." He gestured to several members of the press who were spread out doing live shots. "They all praise it as a miracle of modern medicine coupled with a young woman's perseverance. It is that, but Caspian, there's also a hero who's never mentioned in any of those stories. Her role takes nothing away from Mary or her doctors, but without Elizabeth, none of us would be at this track today."

Caspian's eyes drifted toward the starting blocks, but Susan's voice called him back. "It's not just the transplant. It's her as well. It's Elizabeth. After the transplant, Mary could breathe again. She was going to survive, but it was like she had given up on *living* until that first night when her mirror frosted over and words appeared."

"That must have been one heck of a night," murmured David.

Henry shrugged. "We didn't believe her. We both thought Mary was making things up, delusions to allow her to focus on something other than doing what we all knew she was born to do. It wasn't until nearly a month later that Susan saw it happen for herself, and another two weeks after that when we were finally able to capture the video you saw earlier."

Everyone looked up as an announcer's voice filled the small high school stadium. "Runners, take your places."

They all rose and focused on the ten young women who each took their place within a lane. All but one, scanned the crowd, clearly looking for a loved one or supporter. One woman stared down the track as if visualizing an inevitable future only she could see.

Henry chuckled. "So focused. Susan used to get upset because Mary would never look for us in the stands. She would say—"

He broke off suddenly. Mary had set her feet in the blocks, head down, waiting for the starting gun. A moment later, she held a hand to her lips, rubbed her fingers together, then turned to face the press enclosure.

Caspian felt her eyes lock on his own. Mary smiled at him. She touched her right hand to the tip of her chin, then moved it out and toward him.

"What's she doing?" asked Henry.

Caspian's voice caught in his throat. "It's sign language."

"But, Mary doesn't sign," said Susan.

Caspian nodded. "Someone must have showed it to her."

The two parents shared a look, then Henry asked, "Do you know what it means?"

"Yeah," whispered Caspian, "Lizzie taught me. It means, thank you."

A second later, the starting gun fired, and ten women leaped forward.

Mary Foster lunged for the finish line, completely unaware that her three closest competitors were all bunched up, five-seconds behind her. She quickly glanced over her shoulder, then turned, eyes searching for the automated scoreboard. Names began filling the available slots along with their times and positions. Mary lifted both hands as her name appeared at the top of the roster. She bounced several times, turning in a circle, then was swarmed by her fellow athletes. Women who, seconds ago, were competitors, now embraced her. She felt their arms around her, heard their sincere words of well-wishing, and felt the tears begin to build.

More women pressed around her until all ten of them formed a tight pack with Mary at its center. "Okay, okay," yelled one runner. "Make a hole, she's trying to get to her folks. I see them over there. Hey Mary," continued the girl, "looks like your parents brought scouts with them. I'll take the tall, dark haired one if you don't want him. You could slice cheese with those cheekbones."

Mary tensed, then pushed her way free of the other runners. She felt the last few hands slide off her back and shoulders as she stepped forward, eyes scanning the sideline. Immediately she saw her mother smiling at her, then her dad giving an exaggerated thumbs up sign. She started grinning at his expression, then felt her entire body thrum as if charged with electricity, as her eyes met Caspian's own. Mary continued walking toward them, her mind racing. She knew that face. She knew that man. She knew his name.

Henry and Susan saw the change in their daughter's demeanor and stepped to either side of Caspian. Henry caught his eye, then placed a hand behind his back, and gave him a gentle push. Caspian's gaze shifted from Mary's approach to her father. "It's okay," said Henry encouragingly. "It's all been leading to this. Go on, son. We'll hang back with your friends."

Caspian shook his head. "Don't you want to—"

This time it was Susan who spoke. "No, you two should take a moment alone. It's what Mary wanted. Remember, Elizabeth told us this was coming." She laid a hand against Caspian's cheek. "We trust you, and her. Go."

He glanced at his friends who all gave him encouraging nods, then turned back toward the track. Mary had stopped several feet from him. She waited for him to draw near. The two stared at each other for a brief moment. Caspian took a deep breath as Mary's eyes remained fixed on him. He extended a hand. "Hi, I'm—"

She burst into tears, then launched herself at Caspian. Her arms wrapped around him. She squeezed. "I know who you are," she said, voice cracking with emotion. Mary pushed back slightly, and looked up. "She showed me your face."

Caspian shook his head in confusion. "You had visions of me?"

"No, not visions. She *showed* me." Mary cocked her head. "Didn't my parents play the video for you? Elizabeth told me today was the day you were coming. I asked them to play the video so you wouldn't—"

"They played it," said Caspian, and saw her relax.

"But, if they played it, you should know how she showed me what you look like."

Realization dawned on him, and he said, "She formed my face in mist, the way she did her own?" Mary nodded. "Oh," whispered Caspian, "that must have been in a different video, because—"

"No," interrupted Mary, "there is no video. I only had my parents film it once. After that, it seemed, well, wrong to have anyone else watching." The young woman's nose reddened and tears spilled down her cheeks. "She loves you so much, Caspian, so, very much. Darn it, I promised myself I wasn't going to cry. I promised *her*. It's all she asked of me, and I'm messing it up."

"Hey…hey," said Caspian. He placed a finger under Mary's chin and lifted her face toward him. "You aren't messing anything up, and I find it very hard to believe that Lizzie asked you not to cry. She was a crier that one." He smiled as memories filled him. "She cried at movies, at songs, at puppies. She once cried at the end of the Macy's parade because she was so excited for Christmas season."

Mary laughed, then wiped at her eyes. "No, she didn't tell me not to cry, but I am supposed to deliver a message, and I didn't want to do so blubbering like a baby." She sighed. "I guess that ship has sailed, huh?"

"Pretty much," replied Caspian with a smile, "but I've been a blubbering mess for the better part of a year so no judgement from me."

Mary fixed her eyes on Caspian's. "She told me, and that's part of my message for you."

He looked around. "Uh, should we maybe discuss this at your house?"

"No time," replied Mary, as she glanced toward where the setting sun had given the sky an orange hue. "She's moving on, you see. I don't understand it. I don't think she does either, but this is it for Elizabeth and me." Mary got a faraway look in her eyes. "No more misty words on mirrors, or spectral faces for Mary Foster. I can't believe what I'm about to say, because the first time Elizabeth made herself known, it totally freaked me out, but I'm going to miss her." She saw Caspian's expression shift. "Oh God, I'm so dumb. This isn't about me at all. I mean, I barely knew Elizabeth, but you—"

Caspian laid a hand on the young woman's shoulder. "It's okay, she's infectious like that. Besides, as a friend of mine said recently, we're in unchartered waters here, but you looked at the sky just then. Is something about to happen?"

Mary gave a slight nod. "She said after sundown today, she's moving on to the last person who received one of her gifts. I have two messages. One is for you alone. The other is for both you and your friends." Mary's eyes slipped off his and she looked past him to where her parents and the others waited. "I never saw their faces. Is that Michael, Jenny, and Dave?"

"Oh boy," whispered Caspian, "yeah, that's them."

"You have good friends, Cas. Oh, I'm sorry, I mean Caspian. She just called you Cas a lot and I—"

"Again, it's okay, Mary. All my friends call me that, and you certainly qualify."

"Thanks," she said. "Okay. Okay. Give me just a moment. I've learned how to do this pretty quickly, and I know she's out there, waiting for me, which makes it easier." Mary closed her eyes. She rolled her shoulders, then tilted her neck left and right. After several seconds, she began to take deep breaths. One...two...three. As she exhaled the third time, her breath instantly condensed in a cone of frost.

She opened her eyes, and Caspian's own breath caught in his chest. The young woman's eyes had shifted from their previous dark brown to a bright green. She tilted her face up toward him, and he could see a second face superimposed over Mary's own. He knew that face. He loved that face. "Lizzie?"

Her response came as a whispered breath rather than a vocalized word, *Caspian...*

"I'm here. I'm here. Are you okay?"

All is well, came the response.

"Why are you doing this? Why not just come to me like you did the last time?"

Telling is not showing, Caspian You must see the good if there's any hope for your heart to mend. Speaking like this is hard for me. Time is short. My first gift gave sight to an artist who will create countless beauty. My second gift restored breath to an Olympian who will inspire thousands. My third gift will mend in you what is broken, and deliver generations. Caspian...Caspian...my gifts reveal what you have forgotten. All things my love, all things can be worked for good. Mary gestured toward where her parents and the others were clustered. They immediately drew near. Susan clung to her husband. She stared at Elizabeth's visage as it floated over her daughter's face. Mary's voice spoke first. "I'm okay, Mom. I'm here. Don't be afraid. I promised."

Susan nodded. "I know. I'm so proud of you, Mary." Her mother straightened, then asked. "I see you Elizabeth. Can you hear me?"

The whispered frost filled response came immediately. *I hear you.*

Susan struggled to keep her voice strong. "Thank you, Elizabeth. Thank you for my daughter's life."

Elizabeth smiled. *A gift for a gift. Thank you for allowing my breath to give hope to Caspian.* Her gaze shifted first to Michael, then David, and finally rested on Jennifer, whose eyes were bright with unshed tears. *Help him find my last gift. It is the most precious, and remains well hidden. It cannot be found as the others, not with force or guile, but only with surrender. Keep my Caspian from despair. Do not let him give up. Will you promise me?*

"I promise," said Jennifer. She gave up all semblance of control. Her voice shook as tears flowed. "Oh, Lizzie, it's really you."

"I promise," said Michael and David together.

The visage nodded, then looked one last time at Caspian. The air around them grew even colder. As it did so, Elizabeth's image pulled free from Mary. She leaned toward him, lips slightly parted. *Find my gift. In doing so, your heart will be healed and we can share what we missed at our last parting, a final kiss.*

Caspian reached toward her. As he did so, Elizabeth's image wavered, then puffed away into tiny motes of frost. Mary blinked. Her parents immediately moved past Caspian to support her. She took several breaths, then looked from one parent to the other. "She's gone. I can feel it. Mom...Dad...she's completely gone."

"Do you remember any of what just happened?" asked her father.

"I remember everything. I was here the whole time, Dad. I just kept quiet." She turned to face Caspian. "Did you understand Elizabeth's message? Do you have any idea who has her last gift?"

He shook his head. "I don't even know what it is, let alone who received it. Apparently, that's okay, because my friends have been charged with not ever letting me give up." All three nodded. Caspian smiled at them and they drew close. He felt their arms around him. It felt good.

"Cas?" asked Mary. "Can Elizabeth see the future?"

He arched an eyebrow at the young woman. "Interesting question, but I really have no idea."

"Yeah you do," said David. "You just don't want to admit it. She's been telling you what's about to happen, or at least could happen, for months now. The beach, the Woodworker," he gestured to Mary, "the Olympian."

Mary pointed at David. "That's what I mean. Why did she say that? She never referred to me like that before." Mary turned confused eyes on Caspian.

He smiled at her. "David's right, Elizabeth *has* been pointing the way this whole time. As for why she said what she did about you, I think it's pretty clear. Mary Foster, you may not be an Olympian today, but you will be."

Chapter 37

THE TOMB OF HORRORS, DAY THREE

David took a sip of his bloody mary and gave a contented sigh. Jennifer glanced at him. "Enjoying that, are you?"

"I am," he agreed. "Do you know the last time I flew first class?" David didn't wait for a response. "Never!"

In front of him, a bottle of beer appeared over the seat back, and Michael's voice followed a second later, "You're welcome, young Master Rushing."

Jennifer leaned forward. She reached over the seat back in front of her, and mussed Caspian's hair. He twisted in his seat, trying to see what she was up to. "I just wanted to thank you as well," said Jennifer. "There's no way I'd be flying up front on a teacher's salary."

"Pfft," said Caspian, "we covered all this during our cab ride to the airport. The only reason you guys are on this plane at all is because of me. First Thomas Whittaker, then Mary and her folks. Come on, the least I could do was use a few of my frequent flier points to upgrade you." He jabbed Michael with an elbow, "especially after this guy upgraded Dave."

"I just did it for comedic value," laughed Michael. "I figured, Dave would do, or say, something particularly nerd-tastic, and give us all a good laugh. He didn't disappoint."

"Whatever," huffed David. "I wasn't embarrassed at all."

Michael shook his head. "Well you should have been, making the flight attendant come back six times with more Biscoff."

"I like those cookies," said David defensively.

Jennifer patted his leg. "Well, now you have an entire sleeve of them, *and* that flight attendant can actually pay attention to some of his other passengers."

Michael twisted all the way around in his seat so he was facing them. "Speaking of paying attention to things, what's your plan for hacking back into the donor database?"

David cringed. "Sheesh dude, why not just take out an ad in FBI quarterly that says, *Please come arrest us, love Michael, Caspian, Jen, and Dave.*"

"Nobody pays attention to conversations on planes," said Michael, "Isn't that right, Cas?"

"Huh," replied Caspian, "sorry, I wasn't paying attention. What did you say?"

"Nice," laughed Michael, then the two friends fist bumped. "Anyway, back to the hack. When?"

David rubbed at his face for a minute, then said, "I can probably give it a try on Thursday or Friday." He saw Michael's expression, then added, "Hey, Mass Effect waits for no man. I've got to make up for the time I just took off. Judging from the amount of unread work e-mails filling my inbox, shit's on fire, and I certainly don't want to be..." his voice lowered, "...doing *things* while I'm distracted. I need to catch up, clear my plate, actually get a day ahead, *then* I'll, uh, *do the thing we were just talking about.* I should have an update before D&D time next Friday."

"Mmmm, D&D time," murmured Caspian. "I wonder what kind of food Sara's going to bring. My life is so pathetic that her culinary choices are, quite literally, the highlight of my week."

Michael turned to him. "Is that all my cousin is to you, a source of fine catering?"

"Uh, no," he sputtered. "I was just—"

Jennifer immediately piled on. "Yeah, Cas, what's next? Will you be asking Sara to pick up your apartment?"

"No...what?"

David's eyes shifted from Jennifer to Michael, then he quickly added, "He'll probably ask her to get his dry cleaning."

"Oh, I see what you jackasses are doing," said Caspian.

"Dave," sighed Michael, "you ruined it. You went too far, and you ruined it."

"What are you talking about?" asked David defensively, "how is dry cleaning going too far, but cleaning apartments isn't?"

"I didn't say, clean," snarked Jennifer. "I said, pick-up, *clean* would have been a bridge too far, *pick-up* is not cleaning."

David shook his head. "I don't see the difference."

Michael faced forward again, then pushed back his seat. "Well, clearly Cas sees the difference, which is why our little ball busting effort got ruined...by you." He glanced to his right. "Still, Caspian, I'm serious now. Don't take my cousin for granted. She's entirely too nice, and I don't want you taking advantage of that."

"What?" sputtered Caspian. "She brings the food for everyone, not just me."

"Come on," chuckled Michael "it's not just about the food, it's—damn it, Jen, that hurt."

Jennifer glared at him, while holding a rolled up flight magazine. "You had a fly on your head," she growled, then mouthed *stop...idiot*

Michael stared at her in confusion as Jennifer's fingers began flying over her cellphone. A couple seconds later, he felt his own phone vibrate. She nodded at him. Michael lifted his phone from where it had been sitting on the seat tray, eyes scanning the just received text.

Doofus. Do not bust his balls about Sara. You know they like each other. Mess this up, and I kill you.

Michael look up and his eyes quickly shifted from Jennifer, to Caspian, and back again. He gave her a nod just as Caspian noticed the odd silence that had developed. He twisted in his chair, but Jennifer's expression immediately shifted. She gave Caspian a triumphant smile. "I got it. I got the fly. How does a fly end up on a plane, anyway?"

"Probably how flies get anywhere," replied Caspian in confusion. He looked at Michael. "Now, what were you saying about Sara?"

"Well," began Michael, eyes flicking to Jennifer, "You see, um, what I meant was—"

Jennifer leaned forward, shot Michael another glare, then turned her head to smile sweetly at Caspian. "He just doesn't want you to think ill of his cousin, Cas."

"Huh, why would I?"

"Because she's not bringing all that delicious food just to make us happy and fat. She's also using us as a mini focus group, you know, taste testers."

"She is?"

"Of course she is," replied Jennifer then fixed Michael with a baleful gaze. "Isn't that right?"

"Absolutely," he agreed. "We're taste testers."

"Oh, that actually makes a lot of sense. I wondered why she was always pumping me for the kinds of food I like." His brow furrowed. "Michael, why on Earth would I think ill of her for doing that?"

"Because he's an idiot," said Jennifer flatly.

Michael pointed back at her. "Yeah, what she said. I'm an idiot."

Caspian shrugged. "Okay, I'm certainly not going to argue with that, but I am going to try and take a nap." He squirmed in his seat, then wedged a pillow against the window, and closed his eyes.

Michael turned, waggled his phone at Jennifer, then started tapping. Several seconds later, she shook her head as she read the text.

So, what do we do?

She felt her nose flare as she pounded out a response with far more force than was necessary. *It's new. It's fragile. Do nothing. I mean it. I will kill u.*

Michael looked over his shoulder. Jennifer pointed at him, then drew her finger across her throat. *Okay...Okay...*he mouthed, and turned to face forward again.

Jennifer let out an expansive sigh, then noticed David staring at her. "What?" she asked.

"Something is going on, and I don't know what it is, but figured I should keep my mouth shut."

She patted his leg. "That's because you're the smart one, Dave." Jennifer spared a quick glance to confirm Caspian remained curled up against his window. She then leaned close and began whispering to David. "I'll tell you the same thing I just told the Jamaican doofus up there..."

⌒⌒⌒⌒⌒

Michael peered over his dungeon master's screen, and waited. Four pairs of eyes fixed on him as his hands slipped beneath the table to rest on a small control panel with three buttons. He pressed the first one. A loud *boom* sounded throughout the attic. Everyone jumped. Sara and Jennifer both screamed. Michael pressed the second button. Instantly all the lights went out. Caspian felt a hand grip his. It was pitch black, but he knew it had to be Sara since she was seated to his right. A second later, several sconces began to glow with flickering orange light. Caspian saw her staring at him. At first he couldn't make out her expression, then as the light continued to increase, he saw the dimples. "This is so awesome," she whispered, then squeezed his hand again.

"You've entered a small room," intoned Michael. "It's about ten feet by twenty and has a high arched ceiling that extends into gloom."

"I think this is it," said David. "I think we're in that asshole's final crypt. I look around, what do I see?"

"Nothing," replied Michael.

"Bullshit," spat David.

"I pat Harg on the shoulder to comfort him, then examine the room myself," said Sara.

Michael rolled several dice. "Okay, Valdania's infra vision proves to be *much* sharper than Harg's as is her attention to detail. She sees a small depression, a few inches deep and about two feet square in the center of the floor. What do you do?"

"I check for traps, then examine the depression," replied Sara.

"There's a single hole in the middle of the depression."

Jennifer lifted her hand. "I've got the two keys we found earlier."

"What do you want to do with them?" asked Michael.

"I want to put it in the hole," she said, then noticed the smirks around the table. Jennifer shook her head. "I'm a cleric, *and* I'm offended at my party's juvenile behavior."

"You'll get over it," snickered David, then pretended to take something from Jennifer. "Harg asks Samara Mournforge for the first key, then he inserts it into the hole and turns it to the right."

Michael pressed the first button again, and the entire room reverberated from the boom. "There is a magical explosion. Harg is thrown upward and slams against the ceiling some twenty-five feet above you."

"Orcs are sooo dumb," said Sara flatly.

Caspian frowned at her. She shrugged, and he turned to Michael. "Tholem rushes forward to try and catch Harg on the way down."

"Rangers are dumb, too," snarked Sara. "Do you know how much a falling Orc weighs?" but Michael was already rolling several dice.

"Okay, Harg is lucky. He hit the roof with the least important part of his body, his head. He takes fifteen damage. Tholem takes six and the two go sprawling to the floor while both Samara and Valdania laugh at them."

"I do a little dance too," said Sara then began swaying rhythmically as she lilted, "Orcs so stupid, Rangers so dumb, both so boo hoo wah wah wah."

Michael pointed at her. "No rapping. There's no rapping in D&D, Cuz. This is serious shit. You are literally in the crypt of a demi-lich."

Sara lowered her eyes. "Sorry."

"I'm using the second key," said Jennifer. "I put it in the..." she paused, then narrowed her eyes at Caspian who shook his head innocently. She sighed. "Okay, let me rephrase. I take the second key, and insert the second key into what is now, obviously, a *key* hole."

"Nothing happens," said Michael. "Do you do anything with the key?"

"I turn it."

"Which way."

"Careful Samara," warned Caspian, then pitched up his voice, "It's a trap!"

Jennifer grinned. "No it's not, and I remember what was on the map at the beginning. I turn the key to the right, three times."

Michael gave her an appreciative nod, then said, "Everyone feels the floor shift. To the south, the crypt floor begins to rise toward the ceiling."

"Everyone move!" yelled Caspian.

"Don't have to tell me twice," laughed Sara.

"Okay," added David, "we all move to the other side of the room."

Michael slowly raised a hand, then pointed straight ahead. "Set into what used to be the southern wall, you see a door with an inset ring."

"Harg has had enough of this cloak and dagger bullshit," yelled David. "He pushes everyone out of the way, grabs the ring and pulls."

"And we're all dead," sighed Sara.

Michael narrowed his eyes at her, but said, "The door opens to reveal a massive treasure room filled with armor, weapons, gems, potions, and scrolls." Everyone cheered, but he continued speaking over them. "In the far recess of the vault, you also see a skull and some larger bones set amongst dust and scraps of what you can tell used to be fine cloth."

"Harg, do *not* touch those bones," warned Caspian.

"I wouldn't do that," said David.

"Orcs so stupid, Orcs so dumb," whispered Sara, then stopped when Michael glared at her. "Okay," she said, "I'm a thief, so I'm grabbing those gems right now."

Michael smiled. "As soon as Valdania touches the first gem, you all feel a grave evil descend upon the party."

"And we're all dead," snickered Caspian, which earned him the side eye from Sara.

"Not yet," said Michael, "but all the dust you previously saw surrounding the skull and bones begins to swirl. It floats into the air and forms a vaguely humanoid shape. It is the demi-lich, Acererak!"

David smirked at Sara, then wiggled in his seat. "Wood elves so stupid, Wood elves so dumb..."

Michael tapped his booming button. "The next person who raps, for *any* reason, will cause the entire party to be cursed." Everyone exchanged glances, as he continued. "Oh, I have your attention now? Good. The curse will cause each party member to permanently lose two points of charisma."

Sara leaned over and whispered to Caspian, "Can he do that?"

"He's the DM. He can most definitely do it." Caspian gave her a pointed look. "Please don't test him."

Sara pursed her lips, then gently pinched Caspian's cheek. "Of course I won't put him to the test, Tholem. I like you being so pretty." She sighed. "Of course, my charisma is so high, that losing two points would just make me gorgeous rather than drop-dead, wood elf, gorgeous."

"There's still a demi-lich billowing around you people," huffed Michael. "What are you going to do?"

David raised a fist. "Harg pulls out his axe and—"

"No!" yelled everyone else.

"...and uses it to lean against," finished David with a grin.

"Doofus," said Jennifer. "We wait. What is the lich doing?"

"Nothing," replied Michael, "it's just billowing about."

"Wait some more?" asked Caspian.

"I'm all for that," agreed Sara. "In the meantime, Valdania continues loading up her pack with anything sparkly."

Michael frowned, clearly disappointed. "After a couple minutes, Acererak's ghostly form wavers, then returns to the dust from whence it came."

Everyone paused and looked at each other. Michael finally smiled, then nodded to them all. "Did we win?" asked Sara. "We did, didn't we?"

"You won," confirmed Michael, "and thus ends your expedition into the Tomb of Horrors."

Cheers erupted around the table as everyone jumped up. "This was the most fun I've had in forever," enthused Sara, then wrapped her arms around Caspian. She kissed his cheek, "Thanks for being such a sweetheart of a teacher."

He grinned back at her. "My pleasure, Valdania. You've been an outstanding student."

Jennifer caught Michael's eye as he watched them over his dungeon master screen. She nodded in a clear, *I told you*, gesture. A slow smile spread across his face, then he nodded back.

Chapter 38

A WOMAN'S WISDOM

"Are you guys sure you don't mind?" asked Caspian for the third time.

"No, dude, we've already told you, it's not a problem," said David.

Caspian continued to look uncertain. "It's just that I have to be up at 5:30 in the morning to make my stupid flight."

"You should definitely go," said Sara. "It's almost midnight, you're going to be dead in the morning." She frowned. "Why are they making you fly out on a Saturday?"

Caspian slipped a leather satchel over his shoulder, then focused on her. "We're stress testing the AI safety doors at the memory ward. The best time to do it is over the weekend because that's when the assisted living facility gets the most visitors. The doors should open for visitors, but not patients. It also shouldn't open for visitors if a patient is within sprinting distance, not that these folks sprint that much." He saw the look on Sara's face. "I know, it's boring tech stuff. Sorry, we're mostly just fine tuning things."

Sara shook her head. "No, I don't think it's boring at all. I think you're—" her voice caught. "I mean, I think what you're doing is wonderful. It keeps people safe. I just keep people fed."

"Hey now," chastised Caspian as he headed for the door. "Cream of wheat keeps people fed. Sara, what you do is bring people edible joy. I'm never as happy as when I get to eat the tasty things you've dreamt up."

She beamed. "Really?"

273

"Would I lie to you?"

Jennifer stepped in between the two, gripped Caspian with two hands, and spun him around. "You...go. Get home, and get to sleep." She turned to Sara. "The answer to his question, is yes, absolutely, he would definitely lie to you. He's a man."

"So sexist," muttered David.

"Really?" asked Jennifer, "Remember that picture I texted you from this week's PTA meeting?" He gave a hesitant nod. "What do you think of that red and blue striped dress I was wearing?"

"You looked...good," he replied, then turned to his friends. "Didn't she look good?"

"Yep, good," agreed both Caspian and Michael.

"I looked knocked up!" yelled Jennifer.

"That's my cue," said Caspian, then waved and vanished out the attic door.

Jennifer gestured at the two remaining men. "See, liars. Sweet liars, but still, liars."

Sara cringed. "I was in the group text where you shared the pic. You're right, that dress did look horrible on you."

The two women each grabbed a stack of plates, with several pieces of flatware balanced on them. "Where were you when I put the darn thing on?" snickered Jennifer. She turned toward the men. "We'll get these in the dishwasher if you guys take care of all the catering trays." David and Michael both gave thumbs up gestures. Jennifer inclined her head toward the door. "After you, Valdania."

Sara tapped several buttons on the dishwasher, then closed the door. She watched to make sure the cycle started then turned around and hopped up on the granite counter. "Jenny, can I tell you something?"

The other woman looked up from where she had just thrown out a pile of dirty paper napkins. "Sure, what's up?"

"I need some advice."

Jennifer grinned. "I love giving advice. What's the topic?"

Sara closed her eyes a second, and took a deep breath. "I don't want you to freak out or anything, but..." she paused. "I really want to see if this thing I have, well almost have, with Caspian might go somewhere...I don't know... real."

Jennifer immediately lifted a hand to her mouth and widened her eyes in clearly feigned surprise. "Noooo," she exclaimed.

Sara eyed her. "I haven't been that obvious, have I?"

"Oh honey, please," laughed Jennifer. "I could teach a master class in subtle flirting." She pointed at the younger woman, "which you would have *failed* because you are about as subtle as an earthquake."

"I am?" moaned Sara. "How am I?"

Jennifer joined her on the counter, then patted her leg. "Don't worry, the boys were oblivious."

"Were?" she asked, anxiety filling the one word question.

"Yeah, I told them about the dinner, and about the kiss. Not that I needed to, even those oblivios-os would have figured it out after tonight."

"Oh no...please shoot me now."

"Stop," chuckled Jennifer, "they are thrilled. So am I for that matter. Caspian is too stupid to realize that he's only really happy like his old self when he's around you. Anyway, David and Michael know, but Caspian, being a man, seems to still be oblivious to your full intent, though I give you props for doing your best to make it clear."

Sara's eyes widened. "What do you mean? I didn't want to do *anything* obvious tonight. I told him how I felt at dinner last week, then decided to just let things progress naturally, one way or the other."

Jennifer laughed, then tried to imitate Sara's accent, "No, I don't think it's boring at all. I think you're—I mean, I think what you're *doing* is wonderful."

Sara's mouth dropped open. "I didn't actually say that, did I?"

"You did, and then there is the constant touching. Oh, and when we won the Tomb of Horrors, that *completely* spontaneous hug you gave Cas, pure genius."

"It *was* completely spontaneous," she cried.

"I know," agreed Jennifer, "that's why it's genius."

"I'm so bad at this," sighed Sara.

Jennifer shook her head. "No, you're genuine. Cas loves genuine, and, quite frankly, I think he's going to love you, too."

"You think? He doesn't seem to. I think he likes me well enough, and he did kiss me back at dinner...a little, but just the once." She sighed. "That's not what I'm used to getting from men who are interested in me."

"You were expecting a multi-tentacled man-monster who grabs your boob at its first opportunity?"

She laughed. "Well, that has been my past experience more often than not, but no, I wasn't expecting it. He's sweet so I expected something different, but—"

"Maybe a two armed   romantic prince who subtly kissed your neck when you *spontaneously* hugged him?"

Sara flared her nose. "It *was* spontaneous, Jenny." Her shoulders sagged, and she kicked her legs out from the countertop. "But I guess you're right, I was hoping for *some* kind of sign that he's interested." Sara turned to Jennifer, and frowned slightly. "That's the advice I was talking about. I was wondering if I'm barking up the wrong tree, especially after we had dinner?"

Jennifer arched an eyebrow. "We talked about the dinner. It sounded like perfection. Did something bad happen that you didn't tell me about?"

"No, well, I don't think so. I had a great time. Caspian seemed to have a good time, too." Sara gave Jennifer a shy sideways glance. "He didn't say anything to you?"

"No, but Cas isn't one to kiss and tell," replied Jennifer, "especially since you were the one initiating the kissing."

Sara shook her head. "Maybe I shouldn't have done it. It was a very *not-me* thing to do. Maybe I should have waited for him to——"

"Absolutely not!" declared Jennifer. "Caspian reads girl signals like a blind man trying to read Braille books made out of smooth sheets of glass. You did the exact right thing, and, as you told me, he *did* kiss you back."

"I said he kissed me back...a little."

"Sara, if I kissed Caspian over dinner, first, he would have stared at me like I'd grown a second head, and then he would have started spitting like a cat."

Sara shrugged. "I guess you're right, and it's not like I wanted some super-passionate moment in my restaurant's back kitchen, but——"

"But what?"

"I don't know, maybe...well cliches are cliches for a reason. Maybe he's just not that into me."

"Oh he's into you," said Jennifer emphatically. "He definitely wouldn't have kissed you back otherwise. Some guys would, Caspian...no way." Jennifer reached over and patted the younger woman's hand. "I've known him a very long time. Here's the reality I see. He doesn't know just how into you he is, and that is very different than disinterest. Trust me, I've seen it before. Heck, you may not want to hear this, but I saw it with Caspian and——"

"Elizabeth?"

"Yep," confirmed Jennifer, then quickly added, "which is not a bad thing. In fact, it's a very good thing, but you have to be sure about what you're getting yourself into, Sara."

"What do you mean?"

Jennifer sighed. "Okay, right now Cas loves hanging out with you and, as I mentioned, is his most happy self when doing so. Part of that is because he doesn't really know *why* he's so happy around you. That's not going to last. At some point, even having a penis won't be enough to muddle his brain from the truth. He's going to realize he has feelings for you. Heck, I'm sure that's already rattling around in his head after you guys kissed." Jennifer leaned forward. "What kind of a kiss was it?" She saw Sara's confusion. "You said it wasn't super-passionate, but are we talking Star Trek kiss..." Jennifer pressed a hand hard against her lips then rocked her head back and forth.

Sara started laughing. "No, not a Star Trek kiss."

"Okay, then was it a *this is our first date and I don't know how I feel about you* kiss..." Jennifer lifted her hand up again, then gave it a quick peck.

"Nope, not that either," replied Sara, then whispered, "thank God."

"All right," snickered Jennifer, "then it was a solid wedding altar kiss, right?"

Sara furrowed her brow, considering this for several seconds, then nodded. "Yes...yes, I would say that's a good way to put it. So, shouldn't that have been enough for him to realize he has feelings," she shrugged, "or not?"

"I already told you he has feelings for you," said Jennifer, "that's not what you need to be concerned about."

"Then what *do* I need to be concerned about?" she asked.

Jennifer took a deep breath. "Right, what do you need to be concerned about? Well, once Cas accepts how much he's beginning to care for you, he's going to pull away. I guarantee it. He's going to feel guilty, like he's betraying Elizabeth."

Sara began shaking her head. "I told him I wasn't jealous of his memories of Elizabeth. I'm not trying to steal him from her either, but she's——"

"Gone," finished Jennifer, "well, mostly gone." Sara shot her a confused look, but Jennifer waved it away, and tried to pivot the conversation. "Lizzie will never be completely gone. She's his first true love. You have to be prepared for it, and to fight for him when the guilt comes. That guilt will be complete bullshit, but us knowing that won't make it any less real for Caspian. Are you up for that kind of fight?"

The two women sat for several long moments in silence. Finally Sara said. "I lived too much of my life in fear. I promised myself a year ago, I'd never act or not act because I was afraid." She nodded to herself then locked eyes with Jennifer. "I've seen him several times a week for months now. We've talked on the phone. We've talked in his car. We spent an amazing night together at one of my restaurants. Am I being naive and stupid to think that I might already be in love with him?"

Jennifer barked a laugh. "Love, at its best, is a shotgun blast to the head. You aren't naive. You also aren't just now having these feelings. I saw the seeds of them sprouting months ago at our first D&D night." She grinned. "I might even have sprinkled a little water and fertilizer on those seeds here or there." Sara's eyes grew wide. "Oh, don't look at me that way. I love how he is around you." She turned to fully face the younger woman and held out her hands. Sara accepted them. "Okay, close your eyes, and picture him in your mind." Sara closed her eyes. "Good, can you see him?" She nodded. "Ok, now tell me the truth, and answer me without thinking. Do you love Caspian Lewis?"

"Yes," she replied immediately. Sara's eyes flew open, and she sucked in a breath.

"Well, there's your answer," said Jennifer. She squeezed Sara's hands. "Now, you go get him."

Chapter 39

A DARK ANNIVERSERY

"I'm still not sure about this plan, you guys," said Sara, as she slowly drove through the Garden District and toward New Orleans proper. No answer. She glanced at the car's display screen and saw her four-way call remained connected. "Guys? I'm really starting to feel hung out to dry here."

After another long pause, Jennifer's voice came through the speakers. "Sar, here's the deal. We all knew this was going to be a tough week for Caspian. He's been holed up in that apartment for days, and now he's not even answering his phone. You're really our last option before we do something drastic."

"Me heading to Caspian's apartment unannounced seems pretty drastic, at least to me," countered Sara.

"I went there earlier," said Michael. "He told me to piss off, that everything was fine, and that he was going to be on Zoom calls all day."

Sara shifted her eyes to the screen again. "Which all sounds perfectly reasonable, Mikey."

"Yeah," interjected David, "accept I logged into Caspian's Zoom account. He doesn't have any calls today."

She shook her head. "Dave, is the concept of privacy completely a non-starter with you?"

"Don't blame Dave," said Jennifer, "I made him do it. Besides, Caspian's been using the same password since high school, if he wanted his Zoom account to be private, he'd change it."

"Jenny, I love you, but that's complete bullshit and you know it. So, bullshit aside, why am *I* the one driving over there at six o'clock in the evening?"

"Because you're the one who kissed him while wearing a smoking hot red dress and four inch heels," replied Jennifer.

Sara gripped the steering wheel so tight her knuckles began to pale. "Clearly," she growled, "Dave isn't the only one with privacy boundaries. Silly me, I thought my dress and shoe choices were between *us*, Jenny."

"Did you tell her it was a *vault* conversation, Cuz?" asked Michael.

"No, mainly because I don't even know what that means, Mikey."

"Yeah, we probably should have told you about that," said David. "Our little quartet, now quintet, shares pretty much everything, and things have gotten sticky a few times over the years."

"Right," interjected Jennifer, "so we developed a method where everything is open for discussion among the group, unless someone invokes," she paused, "the vault."

Sara had been shaking her head as the explanation unfolded. Now she said, "Let me get this straight, Jenny. Had I told you to, I don't know, *keep this in the vault*, then you wouldn't have—"

"Shared with Dave and Michael that you went Caspian-hunting in a crimson dress and heels that could kill? Of course I wouldn't have," replied Jennifer, "it would have been in the vault."

"Yeah, you never violate the vault," said Michael.

Sara gave a mirthless laugh. "Good to know. I'm at his place and found a parking spot." She pulled down the vanity mirror, stared at her reflection, then switched quickly between pouting and smiling. "This is so dumb," she said. "He probably won't even open the door."

"He will," said Jennifer. "I know he will."

"Fine, if he does, I'm telling him that I plan to kill all three of you, but I'll tell him to keep that little informational nugget...in the vault."

"Yeah, that won't work," said David. "Michael wasn't completely right before. You never violate the vault, *unless* someone is in imminent physical danger. You making homicidal threats, well, that would cause a vault breach."

Sara ground her teeth as she stared daggers at each of her friends' avatar bubbles where they floated on her car's infotainment screen. "After this conversation, assuming Caspian doesn't throw me out on my ear, he and I might just make our own vault in which we plan every one of your murders. Bye now!" She tapped the disconnect button on her steering wheel then, once again, peered at her reflection. "Are you ready for this?" Sara asked herself. "Are you sure, because I have a feeling it might get pretty rough in there." She nodded at the reflection. "Okay, Sara Edwards, let's go get him."

⌒⌒⟅⟆⌒⌒

Sara knocked on the door for the third time. This time, she called out as well. "Caspian, it's Sara." She placed her ear against the door, and thought she heard someone moving around within the apartment. A few seconds later, she saw a shadow pass across the pinprick of light visible in the door's viewfinder.

"Hey Sara, uh, what are you doing here?"

She cocked her head at the small peephole. "Let me in and I'll tell you."

"I don't think that's a good idea," came his muffled reply.

"Why?" she asked with a grin, "are you indecent?" She pretended to peer at the door, "I might *just* be able to make something out in there."

Several coughs came from behind the door. "It's not that, I'm not feeling well. Could be COVID. I don't want to risk getting you sick."

Sara frowned at the door. "I know a fake cough when I hear one, Caspian. I was the queen of fake coughs when I wanted to get out of——" she shivered, then looked around. "Holy cow, Cas, what's with your apartment building's hallway. It's like the AC is throwing out ice cubes. Let me in before I freeze to death in Spring. I'm Jamaican, we freeze easy."

The shadow disappeared from the viewfinder, and Sara chewed on her lip a moment, trying to figure out what to do next. Finally, she sighed, then turned away from the door.

"Careful," said a young woman with blonde hair and a mask. She hopped to the left, just before Sara ran into her. "We almost had a mid-hallway collision," added the woman as her mask shifted in what Sara assumed was a smile.

"I'm sorry," said Sara, gesturing toward the door. "I was just trying to——"

"——talk with Caspian?" asked the woman.

"Yeah," replied Sara, "do you know him?"

"A bit, we *are* in the same building. He may have added his cell number to our building's resident list, do you want me to check?"

Sara shook her head. "No, I've got it. He wasn't picking up so that's why I...oh my gosh, your building is just ridiculous with the AC. I literally think I just saw my breath." Sara looked around again. "I can't even find where it's coming from." She shivered again, "Do you feel that? Aren't you cold?"

The other woman shrugged. "Feels fine to me. You really seem concerned about Caspian. Is something the matter? I could call the super and have him come and make sure everything's okay."

Sara offered a wan smile. "No, I'm sure he's fine. I'm just a worrier, and he's been through a lot."

"Ahh, you must be the new girlfriend. You have that worrying girlfriend look about you." The woman laughed. "Oh, don't be embarrassed, I recognized it from the look I used to give myself in the mirror when worrying about my own boyfriend."

"He's not my boyfriend, but am I that obvious?" asked Sara, then sighed. "You are the second person in the last month to tell me how obvious my emotions are."

"I'd say genuine rather than obvious, but if you want my advice, don't change, Sara. Genuine is good and all too rare these days. Cas is lucky to have you, even if he is hiding out in there under false pretenses." The woman curved around Sara, then turned and opened her arms. "As the bard once wrote, *Sigh no more, ladies. Sigh no more.*" She pointed at the apartment door, then continued speaking with a poetic lilt, *"Men were deceivers ever. One foot in sea and one on shore, to one thing constant never. Then sigh not so, but let them go, and be you blithe and bonny, converting all your sounds of woe into hey nonny, nonny."* The woman spun around. She headed down the hallway, leaving Sara to stare after her dumfounded, as she called out over her shoulder, "Oh, and Sara, why don't you give that door another try? I have a feeling he'll open up. When he does, be sure to tell him *I* said he's a giddy thing."

Sara's eyes flicked to the closed door for a split second, then back again. She blinked, then tilted her head slightly, confused by the, now empty, hallway. "What just happened?" Sara murmured. She took a few steps away from the door and down the hallway, then shook her head. "Tell him he's a *giddy thing*? He's not giddy and you didn't tell me your name, crazy shakespeare quoting woman." Sara walked back to the door. She looked up, once again searching for the elusive air conditioning vent. "Well, at least that's stopped blowing. Okay, one last try."

Sara lifted both hands and patted out the cadence of *shave and a haircut, two bits* against the apartment's metal door. She lowered one hand, rubbed her fingers together, and stared at the condensation on them. A second later, she placed her free hand against the door again. "Now *that's* freezing cold." She shook her head. "I don't get this place, it's like the whole building is going through menopause. It's hot...it's cold..it's—"

She broke off as the door opened. Caspian looked at her with bloodshot eyes. "Caspian," she began, "Jesus, you look terrible."

"Thanks," he muttered, "on the other hand, you look great." She smiled, and he pointed at the dimples. "Now, you look even greater. Michael was right, those are a secret weapon."

"Mikey is a...giddy thing, and apparently so are you or at least that's what your neighbor told me to tell you. Now, are you going to invite me in or— Cas, your face just went three shades paler." Sara slipped an arm around him, then guided him back into the apartment, and toward the living room. "Come on, let's go sit on the couch. You look like you've seen a ghost."

<hr/>

"What's this?" asked Caspian as he accepted the cup Sara held out for him.

"Tea," she replied.

He peered into the cup. "I had tea?"

She laughed. "Yes, you had tea. Now I wonder how old it is, but," she shrugged, "I souped it up, so it'll probably taste fine." He took a sip, then gave an affirming grunt. "You like?" she asked.

"Yeah, it's actually really good. What did you put in it?"

"Nothing special, just a little milk and honey, the way any civilized person would drink tea."

Caspian took another sip. "It really is good, and I'm not a tea person."

Sara took a drink from her own cup, then placed it beside her on the coffee table, where she sat facing Caspian. "If you're not a tea person, then why do you have it?" she asked, with laughter in her voice. Sara looked around. "It does *not* appear like you are one for entertaining, so..."

Caspian locked eyes with her. "The tea was Lizzie's. She loved the stuff, said it made her feel extra British. I just never got around to throwing it out."

The two stared at each other in silence for several seconds, then Sara lifted her cup. "Well, it's a good thing you didn't, because then we wouldn't have had anything to drink." He nodded, but said nothing.

Sara lowered her eyes, and bit her lower lip. She looked up when Caspian touched her knee. He said, "You do that when your nervous."

"Huh, do what?"

"Bite your lip," he replied with a smile. "You bite your lower lip when you are nervous."

"I do?"

"Yeah, and if I'm being honest, which someone *just* suggested that I be, then I'd have to say it's only one of several adorable things you do."

"Oh," sputtered Sara, "um, thanks?" She sighed. "Well, this conversation sure has taken a turn I didn't expect."

"How did you expect it to go?" he asked.

She reached out and took Caspian's hands in her own. "I know what day it is, Cas. Your friends are all worried about you. I'm worried about you. That's why they roped me into coming here."

"You didn't want to?"

She shook her head. "It's not that I didn't want to, it's that I honestly didn't expect you to open the door."

He nodded. "I didn't expect me to, either."

"Really, what made you change your mind?"

Caspian narrowed his eyes at Sara. "Do you really want to know?" She nodded, and he took a deep breath. "Okay, well, this is where you go running back out the front door. I opened it, because Lizzie came to me and told me I was being an idiot."

"Lizzie?" asked Sara.

"Yep," replied Caspian, then watched as Sara let the implication sink in. After several seconds, he said, "You haven't started running yet, are you frozen in shock?"

"No, I'm actually too busy considering how much that statement alters my entire worldview."

He arched an eyebrow. "You believe me?"

Sara met his gaze. "Are you a Sherlock Holmes fan? I love the mini series, *Sherlock*, with Benedict Cumberbatch."

Caspian nodded in both appreciation and recognition. "Yeah, I'm a fan, and I liked those shows, too. I wish they'd make more, but is your point that when you have eliminated the impossible—"

"Whatever remains, however improbable, must be the truth," Sara finished. "Your apartment building isn't freakishly cold for no reason is it?" She watched him shake his head. "Okay, okay," Sara murmured in an effort to self-calm. "And if your building isn't freakishly cold for no reason, then the masked blonde woman who quoted *Much ado about nothing*, at me then vanished when I looked away—"

"was Lizzie," finished Caspian.

"Was…Lizzie," repeated Sara, "who just showed up on the anniversary of her death to, what, give us both pep talks…I should try knocking one more time…you should open up?"

"She's come to me before," he replied softly, "several times, actually."

"Uh huh," whispered Sara, "and why has she been doing that, do you think?" Caspian gestured to the largely unkept apartment. "Because you are still a mess?" asked Sara.

"That's Lizzie's perspective on it," he said with a mirthless chuckle.

"Well, I happen to agree with her, and I can see why you loved her. She's smart."

"Yeah, she's also…gone," added Caspian. He squeezed Sara's hands, then added, "but you're not."

"That's true," she agreed. "I'm sitting right here, in your haunted apartment, surrounded by what I assume is every dirty bowl and plate you own."

Caspian looked at her. "You're not going to run out the door." It wasn't a question, but she shook her head anyway. "Well, then, what are you going to do?"

"*I* am going to go home, draw a hot bath, then soak in my gloriously deep claw foot tub, and ponder today's events in my heart." Sara pursed her lips, then made a show of scanning Caspian's apartment. "However, Mr. Lewis, that was not the right question. What are *we* going to do tomorrow is the right question."

"Okay," he asked, "what are *we* going to do, tomorrow?"

Sara stood, and Caspian rose with her. "We, are going to have a carpet picnic, in this apartment, tomorrow evening."

"What's a carpet picnic?"

Sara smiled. "You will just have to wait and find out, sir. *I* will get my kitchen crew started in the morning, and then come over here with all the necessary ingredients. Shall we say around ten in the morning?"

"Okay, but why so early if this picnic thing isn't until the evening?"

"Really?" asked Sara, then gestured toward the kitchen. "I wouldn't let my worst enemy eat in this apartment, let alone cook in it. It's going to take us at least a couple hours to kill the botulism and bubonic plague you've managed to cultivate over the past few days." She shook her head in wonder. "I saw this kitchen when we FaceTimed last week. I wouldn't say it looked clean, but it also wasn't…" she shook here head, "…this. How have you done this much damage in so short a time?"

285

Caspian gave her a wan smile. "Hard work and dedication?" Sara's expression went flat. "Okay, I don't know how I managed it, but I can get a start on things tonight so by the time you——"

"No, that's not how you can help," interrupted Sara.

"Okay, how can I help?" he asked.

"Leave everything as it is," she began, "because I think I may have just seen something move over there."

"Funny, but I probably deserved that."

"You did," she laughed, then touched his chest with one hand. "Seriously, just get a good night's rest, and..."

"Yes..." he prompted.

Sara rubbed her fingers along Caspian's stubble. "You could stand a shave." She kissed his cheek, made a show of wrinkling her nose, then said, "and you definitely need a shower. You kinda smell."

"Great," muttered Caspian, "now *I* want to run out of the apartment."

Sara shrugged, then headed for the door. "Sorry, my prince, but life is just too short to share with scruffy men who smell. A girl has to have her standards." She stepped into the hallway, then turned when he called after her.

Caspian stood framed in the light from his apartment. He stared at her for a beat, then sighed. "Sara, I...uh..." he let out a breath. "Thanks. You're just who I needed tonight."

She smiled at him. "That's really good to know, but Cas, you need to know something as well." She pointed at him. "You're worth it." Her smile flashed again. "Goodnight, Prince Caspian. See you in the morning."

Chapter 40

CARPET PICNIC

Sara pulled a four-wheeled industrial trolly through the hallway of Caspian's apartment. She stopped at his door, then glanced at her watch. 10:35. "Could be worse," she murmured to herself, "I could be Jenny." She gave the door a couple quick raps, then waited.

After only a few seconds, the door flew open with such force she almost stumbled backward and into her trolly. "Lady Sara," said Caspian, then bowed with a flourish.

She grinned at him. "Oh, you clean up nice."

"Not just clean," he said, then bent toward her.

Sara immediately caught the hint. She leaned forward, lips lightly brushing his cheek, then made an audible sniffing noise. "Ah," she exclaimed, "my foul prince has been transformed into a fragrant one. Your lady approves, good sir, and now—" She broke off noticing how Caspian had spied her trolly.

"What's all that about? It looks like commercial cleaning equipment."

"Does it?" she asked, "well, that's good, because it's commercial cleaning equipment. Well, not all of it. That big brown bag is filled with the ingredients for our carpet picnic...which we're never going to have if I stay in the hallway all day."

"Oh," sputtered Caspian, "sorry, come on in. Let me get your, what is it, a wagon?"

She breezed past him. "Thanks, and it's an industrial kitchen trolly…of my own design. Whenever I work with a new restaurant I always start by teaching them how to clean the kitchen prop—"

Caspian bumped into her with the trolly as she stood in the living room. "Something the matter?" he asked.

She pointed at the coffee table. "What's that?"

He stepped next to her, put his hands on his hips, and stared at the teapot, cups, and small pastry plates. "Well, that's odd, I would have thought a chef of your skill would recognize what that is?"

Sara gave him a playful slap, as she bent down to look through all the items arranged before her. "If you ever wondered, this is why Jenny calls you a doofus."

"I haven't wondered," said Caspian.

She looked up at him. "Where did you get small batch scones, clotted cream, and…" she dipped a pinky in a jar of something red, "Oh my gosh, Cas, that is pomegranate jam." Sara stood to face him again. "How did you know about scones, clotted cream, and pomegranate jam?"

"Michael."

She shook her head. "Try again, Mr. Lewis. Michael doesn't know clotted from cottage cheese."

"True, but he does know your mother's phone number."

Sara chewed on her lip. "You called my mum?"

Caspian moved past her, picked up a cup, and poured it three quarters full of steaming hot tea. He made a point of lifting a small porcelain pitcher, then carefully added a splash of milk. "Who else would know how best to thank her daughter for pulling someone back from a dark abyss?" Caspian dipped a teaspoon into a small jar of sorghum honey, then drizzled it into the teacup, stirred it a few times, and held it out to Sara. She silently accepted it, then took a sip while staring at him over the brim. He smiled at her. "What might bring boundless joy to Sara Edwards, I wondered? Would it be tangible wealth untold, caskets of jewels or coffers of gold? No said mum. Richer than those Sara will always be, for she loves nothing more than scones and tea."

She took another sip. "This is very good tea." Caspian nodded, and she pointed at the pastry plate. "Those are not coffee shop scones. They are house made." Another nod. Sara gestured with her teacup. "You will not make me cry before noon, Caspian Lewis."

"I wouldn't dream of it," he said with a smile. "I would, however, dream of covering one of those house made scones with clotted cream and fresh pomegranate preserves." He inclined his head toward the coffee table. "I'd have presented this to you on a real table, but I promised someone I wouldn't clean up until they showed me how to do it properly. Of course, sitting around the coffee table should be good practice for a carpet picnic, don't you think?"

He extended an arm and Sara settled herself on the floor beside the coffee table. Caspian sat opposite her and started slicing two scones. "So," she said, "you figured out what a carpet picnic is."

"I cheated," he replied, without looking up. "The interwebs told me."

"Did the interwebs also tell you where to find the scones and jam?"

Caspian handed her a plate. "That, lady Sara, will remain my secret, but definitely proved more difficult. Let's just say, I am glad you were a few minutes late."

She took a bite, and rolled her eyes. "Oh my gosh, that is absolutely heaven on a plate, and just what I needed this morning."

He pointed at her. "You're worth it."

Sara chuckled. "Oh, I see what you did there. I told you that last night so, now you're saying it back to me. Very sweet." She took another bite, the held a hand over her mouth, as she asked. "Please tell me you didn't come up with that caskets of gold thing on the fly."

"Oh my gosh no," laughed Caspian, "I shamelessly stole most of it from a Strickland Gillilan poem my mother gave to me when I left for college. It's actually about how lucky someone is to have a mother read to them, which, of course, is true. Still, I always found it hysterical that Mom wanted to send me off with a poem that gave her props."

Sara nodded. "That sounds like something my mum would do. She's amazing, as you could probably already tell, but she also is not shy about letting us kids know about how amazing she is."

When they had both finished their scone and were mostly through a second cup of tea, Caspian tilted his head toward the trolly. "So, what fancy thing awaits us in that brown bag over there?"

She set down her cup as a broad smile spread across her face. "There's absolutely nothing fancy in that bag, because today is not a fancy day. Given the condition of this apartment, today is a working man's day, so we're going to have a working man's dinner." Her eyes seemed to dance with amusement. "I assume that's okay with you, Mr. Lewis."

"Sounds great to me," he replied. "You're talking to the guy who worked his way through college bucking rivets every summer. So, are you going to tell me what it is and how you're going to make it, or is that a surprise, too?"

Sara pushed herself up and stretched. "Nope, not a surprise. It's Jamaican Roti, curried chicken, plantains, and a spring salad. However, I must disabuse you of something, sir. *I* will not be making it. *We* will be."

"Uh oh," snickered Caspian as he rose to join her.

Sara patted his shoulder in mock consolation. "Don't worry, I'll tell you what to do." She looked around. "Assuming we survive the next three hours. Now, where did I put those hazmat suits?"

"So, roti is really just naan," said Caspian.

"No," corrected Sara, "roti is roti. Naan is naan. Roti is much flakier and fluffier. It also requires a roti board, and a deft touch, which you clearly do not have. Stop, you are going to murder that poor dough before it's had a chance to live. Here, let me show you." She moved behind Caspian, slipped her arms around him and placed her hands over his as he faced the counter. "You want to *gently* roll out the dough on the roti board. You aren't trying to beat it into submission…slow and relaxed movements. The dough needs time to get to know the board."

Caspian stopped moving the rolling pin. He glanced over his shoulder. "What are you talking about? It's a piece of wood."

Sara flicked flour at him. "It is a piece of wood like the Pieta is a piece of marble. This roti board has been in my family for over two hundred years. It is filled with fragrant bacteria, and not the kind that nearly killed us both earlier today. No other roti in all the world will taste like what we have tonight. It's special, Caspian. It's one of a kind."

He started rolling again, and felt her breath on his neck as she watched. "How's that?" he asked.

"Much better, you're finally getting in touch with the Jamaican way… slow…relaxed…gentle."

Caspian tilted his head to the side. "Thanks, Chef. I aim to please. Hey, where are you going?"

"You've got that well in hand," she replied. "I have other things to do."

"Like…" he asked.

Sara laughed. "Like browning the chicken, making the curry sauce, caramelizing the plantains, and mixing up my grandpa's infamous pineapple ginger drink." She paused. "Other than that, nothing. What are *you* doing?"

"I am slowly and gently rolling out roti while silently appreciating the multitasking skills of the beautiful woman behind me."

She grunted. "Nice try, Prince Caspian. Once you are done making six of those, please slice up the tomatoes, cucumber, and peppers for the salad, or do you need further instruction?"

Caspian shook his head with unconcealed amusement, "No, Chef, I believe I am capable of turning whole vegetables into sliced ones, but thank you for the offer."

Sara stared at his back for several seconds, a smile playing across her lips, then began moving effortlessly between several pots and pans.

Caspian and Sara sat on a thick blanket, facing each other in the center of his living room. The coffee table that had been there now rested unceremoniously in a far corner. "Wow," Caspian said, setting down his fork. "I am now convinced more than ever that it is impossible for you to make anything other than delicious food."

She sighed. "It's a curse I willingly bear for the good of mankind."

Caspian offered her a seated bow, complete with flourish. "On behalf of all mankind, Saint Sara, we thank thee." He reached for his glass and drained what was left in it. Sara gave him a wry smile. "What?" he asked.

She tilted her head at the drink pitcher. "How many of those have you had?"

He shrugged. "I dunno, a few. Why?"

"No reason," she snickered. "You just seem a bit, I don't know, looser then normal."

Caspian eyed her. "Have you drugged me, Miss Edwards?"

She laughed. "I think you've drugged yourself. I told you there was rum in it. That's why we have water glasses as well. I think maybe you got the two mixed up."

He stared at the pitcher for several seconds, then said, "I didn't really taste a whole lot of rum."

"Because it's overproof," she explained. "It heightens the citrus notes of pineapple, smooths out a bit of the ginger's heat, and generally makes everyone happy. You look pretty happy."

Caspian pursed his lips a moment, then seemed to stare into the middle distance. He nodded, as if confirming an inner thought, then locked eyes with

Sara. After a couple seconds, she broke his gaze, looking down while smiling shyly. "It's strange," he whispered. "I think I forgot what it felt like."

Sara slid a small piece of roti along one side of her plate without looking up. "What's that?" she asked.

He reached out to touch her hand, and waited until she looked up. "Happiness. I honestly think I forgot what that felt like. I mean, there's certainly been times over the past year that I've laughed, so I must have been having fun in those moments, but I was never really happy." Caspian shook his head. "I really do feel happy. Sara, you make me feel happy."

"Or it could be the rum," she joked, then looked away again.

"Don't do that."

"Do what?" she asked.

"Make light of the amazing gift you've given me. Please don't make light of it."

Sara squeezed her eyes closed, and tears seeped beneath the lashes. "Sara Edwards defense mechanism," she whispered. "As our friends are fond of reminding me, I do not hide my emotions well, but I'm also not great at being vulnerable. Caspian, I've had some things in my life that have really knocked me about, and when I came through them, I promised myself three things." She opened her eyes. "I'd speak truth even if others weren't ready to hear it. I'd love like I'd never been hurt, and I'd live like it's heaven on earth. You scared me a second ago, and I reverted back to the girl I was before making those promises to myself. I'm sorry because what you just shared deserved the woman I am now, not the girl I was. So, let me be clear. I fix restaurants, not men. I know you think you're broken, but you're not. You certainly have a few cracks in your foundation. News flash, so do I. Your cracks were mending before I ever met you, and they would continue to mend with, or without, me. Still, I'm glad I help make you happy." She swallowed hard as the tears broke free, and traced their way down her cheeks. "But, now comes the truth that you may not be ready to hear. I love you, Caspian Lewis." Sara sighed as if a weight had been lifted from her. She smiled. "There you have it. I love you... and unlike last night, now I really do want to run for the door."

"Please don't," whispered Caspian.

She lowered her gaze. "I won't, but I want to."

Caspian reached up and gently slid his thumb against both her cheeks to wipe away her tears. "I can't honestly say that I—"

"You don't have to," she interrupted. "I sprung this on you, and yesterday was—"

"Stop," said Caspian. "You didn't let me finish. There are so many pieces of me that were broken, Sara, pieces I thought would never mend." He shifted to move next to her. "But they are mending...because of you." Caspian shook his head, and laid one hand against his chest. "Still, I'm not free of Elizabeth. If I were, she wouldn't keep coming back to me. She's made that part, abundantly clear. I just don't know if it's fair for you to give your whole heart to someone who isn't prepared to do the same. You are an amazing woman, and quite frankly, you deserve better."

Sara leaned forward and gave Caspian a soft kiss. "We are all broken, Cas... that's how the light gets in." He blinked at her, taking in the words, and she smiled. "Hemmingway, not me." The smile faded. "I'm a grown woman. I know my own mind, and quite frankly, I don't need you to tell me what I deserve." She tapped a finger on the hand that he still held over his heart. "Here's what I do need you to tell me. Are you willing to try and see if, together, we can mend your heart?" He considered this for several long moments, then nodded. "Good," she said, "and when we've mended it, will it be mine?"

Caspian took a deep breath, then slowly exhaled. "Sara Edwards, if not yours, then no one's."

Her smile blossomed. She leaned forward, and whispered, "Care to seal that promise with a kiss, my prince?"

Chapter 41

A FORGOTTEN TRIP

Oh my gosh, thought Sara as three different voices all called *Chef, I need you*, at the same time. It was then she noticed a silent fourth person who was about to pour steaming hot cream into a large bowl filled with egg yolks. "No," yelled Sara, "no, Luiz, wait." The young man paused with the pitcher of cream still hovering over his bowl. Sara placed a steadying hand on his, then said, as calmly as she could manage. "I know we're behind. I know everything is rushed, but I need you to remember what you were taught. What's going to happen if you pour that hot cream into the eggs? Will we get a delicious vanilla bean custard or an odd, and rather soupy, vanilla scrambled egg...thing?" She tilted his hand dribbling a small amount of the warm liquid into the eggs, then quickly whisked with her free hand. "Temper Luiz...temper, temper, temper. Always temper." *Before I lose my own temper,* she thought to herself.

Luiz hung his head, and sighed. "Yes, Chef, sorry Chef."

Sara gave him a wink. "It's okay. You don't even want to know how many times I made scrambled egg ice cream."

"Chef!" came a chorus of other, now even more urgent, voices.

Sara turned around, eyes wide as her mind locked in three additional almost-crises, and she immediately triaged which to handle first.

Several minutes later, she felt a tap on her shoulder. Sara turned to see one of the front of house hostesses, Caroline, smiling at her. "Hi Sara, how's it going?" she asked in a tone so chipper that it set Sara's teeth on edge. *Maybe in my next life*, she thought as she did her best to return the other woman's genuine smile.

"It's going," was the best Sara could manage.

"Here," said Caroline, then offered a bottle of water that the hot kitchen had already caused to be covered in a sheen of condensation. Sara immediately accepted it, and ran the ice cold bottle across her face and neck. She twisted off the top, then took several long drinks. "I know how hot the kitchen gets, so when I started back here to pass along the message, I figured I'd grab a cold water from the hostess station." Caroline shook her head, as she stared at the pile of braids, Sara had arranged tightly on her head. "I don't know how you do it. Isn't this heat and humidity murder on your hair?"

"Caroline, you mentioned a message. Is something wrong up front?" asked Sara, then flinched when a crash sounded behind her. Several curses followed. "I'm kinda busy," she added.

"Oh, yeah. A customer wants to talk with you."

Sara shook her head. "Whatever it is, have Andre handle it. People love talking with him."

Caroline gave Sara a wry smile. "I don't think you want me passing *this* guy off to Andre, although Andre might like it."

"Caroline, I'm *in* a relationship and I don't have time for idle chit-chat anyway. Tell whoever he is, to talk with Andre, leave a note, whatever. I don't give a—"

"Caspian."

"What?" sputtered Sara.

"His name. It's Caspian. I remember because it's like the prince from Narnia. He kinda looks like the guy from that movie too, super sharp cheekbones. I thought you might know him since he asked for you, but since you don't, I'm sure as *hell* not wasting him on Andre, I'm going to—"

Sara pointed at the hostess. "No, you aren't. You aren't doing anything." She looked around and saw how the chaos had increased, just during her brief conversation. "Tell him, I'll be out in five minutes." There was another crash and several more curses. She sighed. "Make it ten. Tell Caspian I'll be out in ten."

"Okay," said the hostess with a shrug, "but honestly I'm fine taking care of him my—"

"He's my boyfriend, Caroline," growled Sara. "Do you know what happens when you flirt with the boyfriend of a Chef who totally aced her knife work courses? You lose body parts." She saw the other woman's face blanch, then added, "I'm just kidding. Please go tell him."

Caroline nodded then scurried from the kitchen. One of the sous chefs, who had been standing near enough to overhear the exchange, said, "You didn't sound like you were kidding."

"Can't put anything over on you, Mark," she replied with a grin, then clapped her hands. All the bustle stopped for a brief moment as every pair of eyes focused on Sara. "Listen up. I need to fix everything you greenbeans are messing up in the next ten minutes, then I need you to not mess anything up for five minutes while I have a quick word with someone."

"From the look on your face, I bet that someone is Caspian Lewis," said a french accented voice from the far end of the kitchen.

"Shut up, Christophe," yelled Sara, but her tone held more humor than heat. "So, if you guys love me as much as you profess, do me a solid and help me out on this one." Various spoons, forks, and knives all banged against things in a universal response. Sara's face broke into a wide grin. "Thanks guys, you're the best."

━⟨⟨⟩⟩━

Almost fifteen minutes later, Sara started moving quickly toward the double doors that led into the front of house. At the last moment an arm jutted out in front of her, blocking her path. She turned to see Christophe staring at her. "No," growled Sara, "whatever it is can wait five minutes." She glanced quickly behind her, then added, "Everything's flawless."

Christophe leaned forward, and untied a spattered apron from around Sara's neck, tossed it to the side, then held a gleaming stainless pan up to her face. "Except you," he lilted. "Now, pull the pins out of your hair, and wipe this towel across your face. It's covered with sweat, flour, and," he frowned, "something I don't even recognize." She groaned, but did as Christophe suggested. He nodded at her, and smiled. "Now go see your prince, and don't worry about things. I can keep the children in line for a few minutes. New love only remains new for so long, don't miss a minute of it. He must be here for a reason."

"I look like crap," she groaned, then showed her teeth to the pan. "Do I have anything in my teeth?"

297

"No," he said, then placed his free hand against Sara's back and nudged her toward the doors, "and you're wrong. You look lovely, and only a fool would think otherwise. Is this Prince Caspian of yours a fool?"

"No," she murmured.

"Then go out there and see him, beautiful Sara."

"Fine," she hissed, "but if he makes a face at me, I'm putting you on egg tempering duty for a month."

"Cas?" said Sara softly. Caspian looked up, from a small ante room where the hostess had allowed him to wait. "I told Caroline I'd only be ten minutes and it's been—"

Caspian set down his phone and stood, his face lighting up as he did so. "Wow, look at you."

She cringed. "I know, it gets hot and—"

"You look beautiful, like a marathon runner crossing the tape. Listen, I'm really sorry to bug you at work, but something came up and..." Caspian glanced at his watch, "I only have about two hours before it's too late to fix a previously made, and epically bad, decision. Do you have just a couple minutes to talk?"

"Actually, I have at least five," she replied, and felt the knot in her stomach turn into a soft glow. "Sit down, we can chat for a few. What is this epically bad decision you made, and why do you only have two hours to fix it?"

Caspian gestured to the other chair. Sara rolled her eyes, but sat, then he settled himself as well. "So, I work for McKinsey."

Sara smiled. "I am aware."

"Right," continued Caspian, "and, well, they think I'm pretty good at my job."

"I'm sure you are," she added, humor creeping into her voice.

Caspian smirked at her. "You're making fun of me, aren't you?"

"Just a little. You're acting so adorably awkward, that it might be an actual crime if I didn't tease you a bit."

"Well, if it keeps you out of jail, and with me in Hawaii, I guess I'll take the ribbing," he said with mock chagrin.

Sara's eyes widened in surprise. "How's that?"

Caspian grinned. "I helped McKinsey win this huge deal by doing an RFP response over the holidays last year...pissed off my folks, all our friends, and it was a generally shitty thing to do, but that's not the point. The point is, McKinsey gave me an all expense covered trip to Maui. I didn't pay it any mind at the time, just threw the whole packet in a drawer, because I had no interest in going. Earlier tonight I was looking for something, and came across the award stuff. That's when I realized I had to confirm my intentions by the end of August, which is…" he tapped his watch, "in less than two hours." Caspian reached across the table and took Sara's hands in his own. He gave them a quick squeeze. "These past couple months have been great. I know between your work, and mine, we haven't seen each other as much as we'd have liked, but still…it's been great." He paused, trying to puzzle out Sara's expression. "Uh, well, it's been great for me at least, but maybe—"

She shook her head. "Huh, oh, no Cas. It's been great for me, too. Quality over quantity, I always say." She cringed a little. "Actually, I never say that so I don't know why I just said it…but it's true," she added quickly. "The museums, the carriage ride around Jackson Square, the day trip to Grande Isle, they've all been fantastic. I've loved them, but am still trying to catch up. What did you say? You want to take me to Maui?"

He nodded. "So…you want to go?"

"When?"

"Tomorrow night," he replied.

"What? Cas? There's no way I can arrange for—" Sara narrowed her eyes at him. "You are joking!"

"Yeah, I'm just kidding about it being tomorrow, but only because it will make the real date seem *so* much more reasonable. The hotel reservations are for September 10th through the 16th. Does that give you enough notice to take off for a week?" Caspian's lips curved up as he stared at her. "Do dimples mean yes?"

She laughed, then leaned forward and kissed him. "Dimples mean, heck yes, and I'm going bathing suit shopping. I've never been to Hawaii." Sara straightened up, then did a little wiggle. "This is so exciting…and so sweet. I can't wait to tell Jenny, or did you already tell her?"

"Hell no, I didn't tell her. I didn't know if you would even say yes. There's a big difference between a day trip to Grand Isle, and a week trip to Hawaii. You might not have wanted to deal with me that long."

Sara shook her head. "You are such a dope."

Caspian shrugged. "I did make sure we could get adjoining rooms though." She arched an eyebrow at him. "I didn't want you thinking this was just an expensive way to lure you into bed or something."

"I...wasn't thinking that at all, actually. We could absolutely share a room, Caspian. Most hotels do have two bed options, you know. We're also both self actualized adults, so I imagine we could even share a bed without it leading to things," she blushed, "it shouldn't."

"Yeah, well, speak for yourself, Miss Edwards," began Caspian, "because after your bathing suit comment, I'm pretty sure I'm not nearly that self actualized. I'm getting us two rooms."

She started laughing. "Well, maybe I'll just leave the adjoining door unlocked to test your resolve. I don't know if I can be with a man who has no self control."

Caspian pointed. "And that's why you are Slytherin. Get back, foul temptress, and no speaking parseltongue to me from beneath the door."

Sara was about to respond, when a young hispanic man trotted up. "Uh, Chef, I'm terribly sorry to interrupt, but Christophe said it was okay."

"We're just about done, Luiz," she replied with a smile, "what is it?"

"Well, there was a fire." Sara's eye's grew wide as saucers. "Just a little one," Luiz hastened to add, then gave her a confident nod. "We put it out."

Sara sighed, then turned toward Caspian, but he had already gotten up. She rose to join him, then looked up to meet his eyes. "This was such a nice surprise, Cas. Thanks."

He tapped her nose. "You're welcome, Slytherin," then gave her a quick kiss. He slid past Sara and Luiz, then turned to face them as he continued walking backwards. "I'll give you a ring tomorrow, and show you pictures of the hotel. You're gonna love it."

She waved to him, whispering. "And you."

"Chef?" asked Luiz.

"Yes, let's go, before something else catches on fire."

"No, I was just wondering, what is a...Slytherin? It does not sound like a very girlfriend word."

Sara patted the young man's back as the two headed back to the kitchen. "Not a Harry Potter fan I see. Come on, and I'll explain it to you..."

Chapter 42

ALOHA

The hotel porter tapped Caspian's key card against the door. An indicator flashed red several times, and he tapped it again. Three more red flashes. The young man gave both Caspian and Sara an apologetic smile. He was about to try again, when Caspian asked, "Did you check the room number? It might be for the other one."

"Sir?" asked the porter.

Caspian pointed to the stylized number on the door. "This is 742. What number is on the keycard sleeve?"

The porter focused on a cardboard envelope that had held the keycard. He looked confused. "You're right. This is for 744. I'm sorry, it seems—"

"No," interrupted Caspian with a smile, "it's my bad. We have adjoining rooms, 744 and 742." He glanced at the porter's name tag. "Sorry about that, Sam. Try the other one."

This time the door's indicator flashed green and gave an audible click. Sam pushed the door inward, then pulled their luggage cart in after him. As soon as he'd made enough space, Sara immediately scampered past him. Caspian grinned as she stopped just past the room's kingsized bed, rose up on her toes to peer out a large, floor-to-ceiling window, then spun around. The porter was still facing Caspian so didn't see Sara's jubilant expression. *Oh...my...Gosh* she mouthed silently, then pointed at the window. Caspian's own smile broadened as he nodded to her, acknowledging what must have been an amazing ocean view. "Excuse me, sir," began the porter, "but which luggage should I leave in this room. I mean is it yours or——"

"It's mine," chirped Sara, then began pulling bags off the luggage cart.

The porter reached for one, but Sara was too fast and his hand only gripped air. He shook his head. "Please ma'am, I can get those for you."

She paused, flashed him a smile, then said, "How will you know whose bags are whose, Sam? I've got these, and please don't call me ma'am. It's sweet, but I'm Sara." Her nose crinkled a second later, and she added, "I bet we're about the same age."

The porter turned toward Caspian, who raised a hand, "Don't try calling me sir either. I'm Caspian. My parents don't let folks call them mister and misses, and I'm going to carry on that fine Lewis tradition." He inclined his head to the door that linked room 744 with 742. "How about we just pop that door open, and I'll start getting my stuff organized."

"You better hurry," lilted Sara, her voice muffled as she called out from the bathroom. "I read up on this place while you slept on the plane. *I* am heading to the pool as soon as possible, and *you*, Mr. Lewis had best be ready to escort me." The porter had just opened the two adjoining doors when Sara's head popped out from within the bathroom. "Oh, Sam?"

"Yes, ma—, uh Sara, what can I do for you?"

"I read there's a beach, too. Where is it exactly?"

"There is a beach," he replied. "It's not large, but it is private and is surrounded by rising volcanic formations. I'll mark it on your room's map if you like."

"Thank you, Sam!" she exclaimed, then disappeared again.

Several minutes later, the porter finished showing Caspian all the numerous and luxurious features of his room. "One more thing," began Sam, as he reviewed a checklist on his handheld device. "With respect to the honor bar, please disregard the price list. Apparently your company has agreed to pay for any sundry expenses, so my manager has applied that to both your rooms, even though you are paying for one of them yourself."

"Wow, that's really nice of you guys," said Caspian, "now we can eat expensive macadamia nuts in *both* rooms without a care in the world."

"The wine and spirits are included as well," added Sam. "Housekeeping will replenish anything you use each morning and—"

Sara bounded into the room, stopped, spun once, and opened her arms. "This, is the softest robe I have ever worn in my entire life. I'm going to wear it every time we're in the room." She shot a sideways glance at the porter.

"Security might need to search my bags when we leave, just to make sure I haven't stolen it."

Sam smiled at her. "I'm afraid you can't steal that."

Sara's eyes widened. "Oh, I was just kidding. I wouldn't—"

"No," interrupted the porter, "I mean, you literally can't steal it. The robe is yours, also compliments of the hotel."

Sara wrapped her arms tightly around herself as her mouth dropped open slightly. "Okay, this is definitely the best day ever." She grinned at Caspian, then disappeared back into the other room.

The two men stared after her for a couple seconds, then Sam turned to face Caspian. "She seems quite happy with her accommodations."

"She does at that," agreed Caspian, then extended his hand. "Thanks Sam, you've really gotten us off to a great start."

The porter accepted the handshake and felt several folded bills press into his palm. He inclined his head gratefully. "My pleasure, Caspian. If there is *anything* you need, please don't hesitate to call the front desk, or—" he paused a moment, then leaned over the nearby desk to write on a piece of hotel stationary, "— call my mobile number, and I'll be sure to take special care of you guys."

Caspian shook the porter's hand again. "Thanks, Sam. Really nice of you to offer, we may just take you up on that."

"I hope you do. In the meantime, please enjoy your stay at the Ritz Carlton, Kapalua." Without another word he slipped out the door, and it clicked shut behind him.

Caspian noticed that Sara had closed the door between their rooms when she'd returned to hers this last time. He softly rapped on it with a knuckle, then waited.

"Who is it?" came a voice from within.

Caspian laughed. "Hawaii Five-O, ma'am. We've received a call about a disturbance in your room. Is everything all right in there, ma'am?"

After several seconds of silence, she replied, "Thank God you're here, officer. There's a strange man in my room and I don't know what he wants or what he'll do. Please help me!"

Caspian noticed how the door had become slightly ajar. He snickered to himself as he pushed it open. Sara stood a couple feet away with her thighs pressed up against her bed's footboard. She pointed at Caspian. "There's the strange man, now." She furrowed her brow. "What do you want, strange man?"

Caspian closed the distance between them until scant inches separated him from Sara. He saw her lips quirk up for a moment, then bent into an affected scowl. "I asked you a question, strange-man-in-my-room. What would you have of me?"

Caspian narrowed his eyes at her a moment, considering, then said, "Why, fair lady, I want nothing. I would never profane with my unworthiest hand, this holy shrine." He reached down and took hold of her hand. "My lips, two blushing pilgrims ready stand to smooth that rough touch with a tender kiss."

Sara draped her arms loosely around Caspian's neck, and smiled up at him. "Don't play the Romeo with me, Mr. Lewis. I know how this scene ends, for saints have hands that pilgrims' hands do touch, and palm to palm is holy palmer's kiss."

Caspian barked a laugh. "You weren't kidding, you *do* have the whole play memorized."

She raised her eyebrows several times. "Care to skip ahead, my prince?"

"To where?" he asked, "I only know bits and pieces."

Sara lifted up on her toes to where her lips nearly met Caspian's own, then asked, "Shall I prompt you?" He nodded, and she brushed past his cheek to whisper in his ear. "This is where Romeo says, *Then move not, while my prayer's effect I take...*after which he——"

Caspian held Sara's face gently in his hands. "I think I have it from here." He stared into her eyes for several heartbeats, then kissed her. Sara melted into his embrace, lifting one hand and entangling her fingers in his hair. Caspian pulled back, and whispered, "Thus from my lips, by yours, my sin is purged."

Sara exhaled, all the while shaking her head slowly. "Then have my lips the sin that they have from yours?"

"Sins from my lips?" asked Caspian, "O trespass sweetly provoked. Give me my sin back."

"Nicely done," she said. "It seems you remember more than just bits and——" He kissed her again, this time longer. The world around them seemed to fade away until, finally, Caspian broke the kiss. Sara dropped her arms, hands resting on the bed's footboard. She sighed, "God, I love Shakespeare."

"He is the bomb," agreed Caspian, "but even his words are but wind compared to the beauty of my Jamaican Juliet."

She crooked her finger several times, then gave him a quick peck on the lips when he drew close. "You are such the flatterer, Prince Caspian. If I didn't know you better, I'd say you were trying to seduce me." Sara spun away, then gripped both sides of the white robe she still wore. Her voice lowered, and took on a husky tone. "Is that what you're trying to do, my prince? Are you trying to seduce me?"

"Never," he replied with a grin.

"That's good, because I am pure as the driven snow, and will remain so until," she held out her left hand while humming a tune Caspian immediately recognized.

He burst out laughing. "Wow, from Shakespeare to Beyonce in thirty-seconds, well done, Miss Edwards, well done, indeed."

Sara fell into a deep curtsey, then pulled open her robe. She let it pool around her feet and kicked it onto the bed. Sara gestured to her bathing suit. "So, what do you think? I know it's not a bikini, but I still think it's pretty sexy," She pursed her lips, "don't you?"

Caspian shook his head. "Don't pout at me woman, of course it's sexy. Then again, you'd look sexy in a potato sack. So, should I assume from your current attire, that we will be heading to the pool?"

Sara curtsied again, "We go forth anon, Prince Caspian. Please don thy trunks with alacrity."

"As my lady commands," he chuckled, then headed for the other room to get changed.

Chapter 43

SUNRISE AT HALEAKALA

Caspian rapped again on the door between his and Sara's room, this time louder. He glanced at his watch, two-thirty in the morning. Several seconds later he heard Sara's groggy voice, muffled by the door. "Cas, is that you?"

"Hi," he whispered.

"Uh, hi? What time is it?"

"It's the middle of the night," he replied, "but don't look at your phone. All you need to know is that it's the middle of the night, and someone is going to pick us up for one last adventure."

There was a pause, then Sara said, "I thought we were leaving today."

"We are. We're just not going directly to the airport."

Another long pause.

"Okay, then where are we going?"

"Someplace magical," replied Caspian.

This time her response came quicker. "I can hear the smile in your voice, Mr. Lewis. What have you cooked up, and when exactly *is* our flight home?" She sighed, "Not that I really want to go home. You're sure we can't just live in this hotel, right?"

"Pretty sure, unless you happen to be a multi-millionaire." Caspian paused a second, then said, "Actually, I guess you guys *are* multi-millionaires."

Sara leaned against the door frame and let out a long breath. "Not me, my prince. Alas, the wealth of my kingdom lies in the hands of others." She twisted and placed her mouth near the seam where door met frame. "Where are we going? Tell me!"

"Nope, but we have to meet our ride downstairs in exactly twenty-five minutes. You have that long to get ready, Miss Edwards."

"We've been here a week, Caspian. When has it taken me longer than ten minutes, besides—"

"The luau," he answered faster than Sara could finish her thought, then added, "and now you have twenty-two minutes."

"The luau was special, and *you* certainly seemed to appreciate the results of that extra hour, sir."

"Twenty-one," chuckled Caspian, "and don't worry about the luggage. That's why I had us pack last night. Wear the travel clothes you left out for the flight, and bring your hoodie. It might be chilly. The hotel will make sure everything gets on our flight, which, incidentally, isn't until six this evening." He grinned at the door. "Get a move on, Sara. You now have twenty minutes."

Caspian placed his ear against the door. He heard several rustles, a loud bang, and the faint sound of running water. He walked over to the end table, and picked up the phone. "Hi, this is Caspian Lewis, in 744. We're checking out today. Oh, yeah, it's been fantastic. Everything has been just ridiculously perfect. No, we don't need a late checkout, I'm actually taking my girlfriend on the Haleakala excursion. Right, they are picking us up in front of the hotel about fifteen minutes from now. I was wondering if it would be possible for you to give us a couple blankets and a large carafe of coffee? Yes, that would be perfect. Thank you so much. What? Oh, no I've never been to Haleakala." Caspian laughed. "Yeah, well, I'm glad you think so, but she's pretty fantastic herself. Okay, thanks again. We'll be down shortly. Okay, bye."

Sara sipped her coffee with one hand while her other rested beneath the blanket, fingers intwined with Caspian's own. She looked through the bus's expansive window and out into a clear, star-filled, night sky. A second later, Sara craned her neck to catch sight of something, then turned to Caspian. "Are those clouds? Are we literally driving through clouds now?" He shrugged in mock ignorance, and she flared her nose at him. "Tell me where we're going."

"Nope," he said, shaking his head. "You are just going to have to wait."

"But I don't like waiting," she replied, then pursed her lips.

Caspian immediately used his free hand to shield his eyes. "Down foul temptress. Your dimpled pout attack has been thwarted." He peered through splayed fingers, and smiled. "Apparently I won my saving throw, probably rolled a nat twenty."

Sara turned back to her window, but mumbled, "My dimple pout attack doesn't get a saving throw. It aways hits."

"It used to," he lilted. "I've developed immunity."

Sara set her coffee in the chair's cupholder, then softly tugged Caspian's hand toward her beneath the blanket. He eyed her warily, but despite the bus's dim lighting, he saw a predatory smile slowly spread across her face. Sara inhaled deeply, arched her back, and watched as his eyes traced downward for a split second before snapping back to her own. Caspian shook his head, and was about to say something when Sara leaned forward, lips moving softly along his cheek until they rested next to his ear. "Just how much immunity..." she whispered, then pulled back slightly. "...do you..." she kissed his lips, "...think you..." another quick kiss, "...might have developed?" Sara pressed her lips to Caspian's and, this time, did not draw back for quite a long time. Finally, she broke the kiss, locked eyes with him, and gave him the devil's own grin. "How's that saving throw working for you now...my prince?"

Before Caspian could answer, the bus's intercom came to life with a soft pop. A man's voice spoke a second later using a tone generally reserved for churches, golf tournaments, and movie theaters. "Ladies and gentlemen, we are about five minutes from the top of majestic Mt. Haleakala. Sunrise will be approximately thirty minutes after that. Once we've stopped, I'd like everyone to disembark as quickly and quietly as possible. You will find a concierge table immediately to your right upon leaving the bus. Please help yourself to coffee, champagne, a variety of juices, and pastries. We also have an ample supply of blankets and chairs, should you rather sit than spread out. There will be no artificial light on the mountain, but you'll immediately see a glow on the eastern horizon. Find a nice cozy spot, and prepare yourself for a singularly magical experience. Two last requests. First, no flash photography. Second, please keep all discussions to a minimum, and your voices at a level similar to that which I'm using now. On behalf of all of us at Polynesian Adventures, allow me to welcome you to Sunrise at Haleakala." The intercom gave another soft crackle. Several seconds later, the bus rolled to a stop, dim lights illuminating down the aisle.

Caspian turned and saw the look of anticipation in Sara's eyes. "What have you done, Mr. Lewis?" she asked playfully.

309

He tapped her nose. "Something wonderful, I hope." He gave her a wink, then whispered, "Come fair Juliet, let's go meet the sun."

Sara snuggled closer, her left arm, looped through Caspian's right. She held a large mug of steaming hot chocolate in both hands, having opted for that over the available coffee and champagne.

She glanced left and right, taking in dozens of other couples, their forms shrouded in the predawn light. She turned to her left, and cast a curious eye at Caspian who continued facing straight ahead. Sara crooked her elbow several times to get his attention. He turned. "How did we manage to get this spot, Mr. Lewis?"

He arched an eyebrow. "What do you mean?"

She shook her head. "I know that voice, Cas. That's your *I'm trying to be innocent* voice. You only use it when you are decidedly guilty." She smiled at him. "We have the best seat in the house, so to speak. We're right at the edge of the whole mountain. No one is in front of us." She sighed, "Oh my gosh, this might be the most beautiful thing I've ever seen." Sara's voice trailed off as the horizon continued to gain color. Directly in front of them, the Haleakala mountain ended, but not to open sky. Beyond the cliff's edge lay a carpet of clouds that extended all the way to the horizon. She tilted her head back and watched as stars faded from sight, succumbing to dawn's arrival. Streaks of wispy clouds, once dark, were now shaded with reds, yellows, and orange, even while the thick clouds surrounding Haleakala remained white as snow.

"Here it comes," whispered Caspian, as if his very words might break the spell he felt weaving between them. Beams of golden light burst from the horizon as the Sun's leading crescent broke free. It scattered the remaining twilight and painted the carpet of clouds with every manner of color.

Sara sniffed beside him, and Caspian turned to see a lone tear streaking her left cheek. "Are you okay?" he asked.

She nodded, but didn't turn. "It's so beautiful it actually hurts," came her nearly silent response. Caspian slipped his arm from hers, then reached around Sara's waist to pull her close. He started moving the blanket to better cover them, when he felt her hand touch his cheek. She turned him to face her, then just stared into his eyes. After several seconds, Caspian's lips quirked up and he opened his mouth to speak. Sara shook her head, then placed a finger on his lips. "Don't say anything. Promise me you won't say anything.

Do you promise?" Caspian nodded. Sara glanced quickly to the now mostly risen sun, then back to Caspian. She took a breath, then let it out. "This is the nicest thing anyone has ever done for me, and I love you for it. I love you for your kindness. I love you for your humor. I love you for even being willing to risk your heart again with anyone, let alone me. I don't want this to end, not this moment, not this day, not us, not ever. But if it did, if it all ended tomorrow, I'd call myself the most blessed of women." She placed a soft kiss on his lips, leaned her forehead against his, and whispered, "I love you, my Prince Caspian. I've set you as a seal upon my heart, with a love as strong as death." Her words pierced Caspian like a lance to his heart, and he was about to reply, when she shook her head. "Shhh. You promised. Love is patient. Love is kind, and I will be both."

Without another word, Sara slipped her arm around Caspian's back, pulled herself closer, then rested her head against his chest, as the two silently watched a new day begin.

Chapter 44

A DEEPER MYSTERY

Jennifer had been leaning against her Mini Cooper when Caspian pulled up beside her at David's apartment complex. He got out of his car, eyed her a moment, then asked, "What on Earth are you doing?"

She glowered at him. "I have no idea what you're talking about?"

Caspian pointed at her. "It looked like you were trying to push a parked car."

"Oh, that," sighed Jennifer. "It's just my uterus giving me a Halloween trick, two weeks early. She's pissed and trying to kill me." Jennifer saw Caspian's expression shift, then rolled her eyes. "You know, I find it endlessly amusing that men who spend so much time in pursuit of that bodily area, shrink like wilted violets when any woman dares to mention how things work down there."

"I am not shrinking, Jenny. I'm also not pursuing."

"Well, maybe not mine," scoffed Jennifer then started walking toward David's building.

Caspian fell into step beside her. "Definitely not yours, but also nobody else's."

She stopped and fixed Caspian with a rather baleful gaze. "How long have you and Sara been officially dating?"

"I don't know," replied Caspian, confused, "uh, about five months I guess."

"Almost six," corrected Jennifer, "which reminds me, you should mention something to her about it on your six month anniversary."

"What?" sputtered Caspian.

Jennifer stopped. "Your and Sara's six month anniversary, you need to get her something, or take her somewhere, or at least bring it up for God's sake."

"When did this become a thing?" he asked, "An anniversary is after a year. It's right there in the name *anniversary*, *anni* meaning year."

She sighed. "You are a doofus. Girls like marking time, especially the first year." Jennifer held up three fingers, then waggled them, each in turn. "Three months, six months, one year. You already missed the first one."

"Really? You would expect this?"

"Cas, while I thank my lucky stars none of you boys have any romantic designs on me, sometimes it is a bit disconcerting that you forget..." She leaned toward him. "I *am* a girl, so while I don't *expect* the broader population of knuckle draggers to actually give a shit, yes, I would *like* them to mark such milestones."

"Huh," murmured Caspian, then cocked his head. "When was the last time you were in a relationship for *that* long?"

He saw the look on her face and immediately regretted the question. "Thank you *so* much for reminding me, Caspian. It's been a while. Apparently, the pool of men who are both *actual men* and who don't expect sex before marriage, is about the size of a thimble." She spun around. "We're in Louisiana, Cas, the Catholic capital of the South. Do you know how many of us Catholic girls are fishing in that same tiny thimble." She poked him in the chest. "All of us!"

"Sorry," he murmured as they went through the front door and toward a bank of elevators.

She waved it way. "Don't mind me. Aunt Irma has me in a foul freaking mood. Still, *you* are supposed to be better than the aforementioned knuckle draggers. I know you aren't one of the," she made airquotes, "third-date-sex-insisters, but that's a pretty low bar."

"Jenny, I'm not...I mean, Sara and I haven't——"

She patted his chest while they waited for the elevator. "I know. I'm Sara's best girlfriend. Girls talk. I know everything. As I mentioned, that's the low bar. You're supposed to be better, so you definitely should mark your six month anniversary." She shrugged. "I'm the one who told Sara you were better than most men. It'll reflect badly on me if you ignore the day. Don't make me look bad, Cas."

The elevator doors opened and the two of them entered.   Jennifer immediately closed her eyes and leaned against one of the safety rails. Caspian frowned at her. "Jenny, are you *sure* you're okay?"

"Huh, oh yeah.   I meant to take something before I left the house and forgot.   It's just day two, and that's the worst for me." She saw his blank expression.   "Aunt Irma...remember...from the IT Crowd.   We all watched that episode together?"

"Ohhh," said Caspian, then his eyes widened, "Oh, that.   Um, well, I'm sure Dave has some Motrin, or Tylenol, or——"

"I sure hope he does because day two is when Irma realizes the interior room she's decorated with Winnie the Pooh and Tigger too wallpaper in preparation of Jenny's baby, isn't gonna house a baby this month.   It makes Irma angry." Jennifer extended her hands and made a clawing gesture. "So, she just *rips* all that Winnie the Pooh wallpaper off the walls without regard for just how much it hurts the owner of said room." She paused. "I'm the owner of the room."

Caspian shot her a flat expression   "Yeah, I've caught up now, and it's a good thing you guys have the babies.   If men had to, we'd be extinct in a generation."

"Truer words have never been spoke," chuckled Jennifer.   They walked up to David's apartment door, and she gave it a few good knocks, then turned to Caspian.   "Do you have any idea what bad news Jimmy Neutron was talking about in his text?"

"Nope, he wouldn't say, just that we all needed to come over, he'd explain everything then, but that it wasn't his fault."

Before Jennifer could respond, the door opened.   David frowned from one to the other.   "You're both late.   Come on in."

<hr/>

"Here you go," said David, then handed Jennifer a glass of water and four blue pills.   She immediately popped them all in her mouth then drained half the water.

She sighed, gave David an appreciative smile, and headed out from the kitchen with him only a couple steps behind.   Caspian was enthusiastically tapping the keys of a laptop while Michael leaned close and shouted intermittent encouragement.   Jennifer arched an eyebrow at David.   "I asked

Cas if he wanted to take a look at the latest Mass Effect 4 quest my team completed."

Jennifer frowned at her friend. "Well, now we'll never get his attention." She turned back toward the couch, and pointed. "Just look at him. He's trapped in The Matrix, even though *I'm* the one you just blue pilled." Jennifer grinned. "Get it, blue pilled, because you gave—"

David smirked at her. "Yeah, I get it, Jen."

She punched him on the arm, then pouted. "This is why I don't ever try to speak geek with you guys. I never do it well enough."

David started vigorously shaking his head. "No, no, it was actually pretty good. I'm sorry. I—" He saw her expression turn sly. "You're screwing with me, aren't you?"

"How'd you like the pout?"

"I loved it," he replied dryly.

"I know, right. I totally ripped it off from Sarah, but darn if Michael wasn't spot on about the thing. Girl-pouts are a super weapon." She glanced toward the couch a moment, then added, "I just wish I had her dimples."

Michael's eyes flicked to her for a second. "Yeah, those dimples definitely buff-up the pout-power." He turned back to the laptop screen, but added, "You've got incredible legs though, Jen. Just wear more skirts and by the time a dude gets to the pout, he sure as hell won't be missing any dimples."

Jennifer blinked, then smiled at David. "I have incredible legs?"

"Oh yeah," replied David, "remember that cocktail party Michael threw for his distributors?" She nodded. "You wore some slinky black thing. Half the guys there were picking their eyeballs off the ground. Hell, I was even looking, until I realized those legs were attached to, well, you."

Jennifer's nose flared. "You just ruined it."

"Come on, you're like my big sister." He shook his head. "My brain can't even go there."

"Whatever," she grumbled, then projected her voice toward the couch. "Can you two please put that thing on pause or something so David can tell us what horrible news he just had to share in person?"

Caspian raised a finger. "I'm almost at a save point. Give me two minutes. By the time you sit down, I'll be ready."

Jennifer narrowed her eyes at David, then pointed into the living room. "What's he talking about? The chairs are right there."

"He wasn't really listening to you, Jen. Cas just wanted to say a string of words that would make you leave him alone for two minutes." David patted her shoulder as he walked by, then settled himself into one of the two remaining chairs. He pointed at the other. "Come on, he's almost done. I can tell by the music."

⌒⌒⌒〰⌒⌒

"What do you mean, it's hopeless?" asked Caspian. "You said you had figured a way to mask your *something*, which allowed you to poke around the database for as long as you wanted."

"Not mask...spoof," replied David, "and I've spent the last three months poking around. Everything is redacted, well almost everything. There's also an active FBI investigation, which means if we're smart, we'll stay very clear of the whole thing."

"You said, almost everything. What part of the record wasn't redacted?" asked Michael.

"A name," David replied. "Doctor Miguel Alvarez."

"So, this Dr. Alvarez is somehow connected to Elizabeth's last organ recipient?"

"I think so, at least tangentially. I actually found his name related to the FBI investigation, but that case number was cross-indexed to Lizzie's social security number *and* her medical record. This Alvarez cat is definitely connected to something, not that such info helps us any. He also was subpoenaed, but it got quashed, by what has to be someone pretty high up in the DoJ. I'm telling you, it's a complete dead-end." David lowered his eyes. "I'm sorry, guys. I've put off having this conversation at least three times, but yesterday my last lead ended up going nowhere."

"So, what do we do now?" asked Jennifer.

Caspian shook his head. "I can't just give up. Lizzie said I'd see her seven times if we finished the quest. I've only seen her four, maybe five if you count that peripheral vision thing in Chicago, which I don't."

Jennifer slipped out of her chair and squeezed her way between Michael and Caspian. "Cas, if she told you that, then this is just a hiccup. It'll happen when it's supposed happen."

She saw her words were not having the desired effect, then pressed her elbow into Michael's side. "Uh, yeah, Cas. Lizzie has not been shy about pointing any of us in the direction we needed to go." Jennifer rolled her eyes, turned to Michael and mouthed *Sara*. "Oh," he said as if just remembering something, "besides, don't you have some more urgent business on this side of

317

the veil?" Caspian's brow furrowed. "Dude, really," began Michael, "I will absolutely beat you with a stick...urgent business...my cousin...your girlfriend...the woman who is head over heels for you?"

"Oh, yeah," replied Caspian.

"Oh...yeah?" asked everyone at once.

"No, I didn't mean it that way," sputtered Caspian, then slumped deeper into the couch as the weight of his friends' disapproving stares bore down on him.

Jennifer crossed her arms. "Well, then how did you mean it? I swear, Caspian, if you break this girl's heart, I'm going to break your face. Do you know how lucky you are to have experienced two transformational loves in your life? I've had zero." She motioned to Michael and David.

"Nada," said Michael.

David shook his head. "Zip."

Jennifer pointed at Caspian. "And before you start rattling off our past boyfriends and girlfriends, remember I said *transformational* loves, the kind of love that literally changes you for the better. Now, do you feel that way about Sara, or not?"

"I do," he replied, "but—"

"No man, there are no buts with this kind of thing," said Michael.

Caspian stood up, then walked to the living room window, and turned around. "Normally, I'd agree with you, however, I believe we'd also agree this situation is paranormally unique. I just don't think Lizzie is done with me yet, and it wouldn't be fair for me to—"

"She's not done with you, or you're not done with her?" asked Jennifer. "Look, I'm not trying to create false equivalencies here, but Elizabeth was *my* best friend. We shared everything, and I mean everything. I knew all about the Chadsworth bullshit even before you did, Cas. Now, Sara is my best friend. Do you think I haven't had moments where I feel like I'm, I don't know, cheating on Lizzie? Well, I have. I also know that such thoughts are stupid, selfish, and antithetical to everything Elizabeth Winters was about." Michael and David both nodded in agreement. "My friendship with Sara doesn't diminish the love I had with Lizzie. Cas, it honors it."

Caspian closed his eyes, gave the faintest nod, then whispered, "I know." He opened them a couple seconds later, and his friends saw the unshed tears within. Caspian shrugged. "I just need Lizzie to tell me it's okay to move on. She's told me other things."

Michael stood and put an arm around his friend. "Cas, she literally came back from the dead to tell you to go on a date, then practically picked out Sara's dress."

"No, that was pretty much a literal thing, too," corrected Jennifer.

"And she appeared to Sara, let's not forget about that," offered David.

Caspian shook his head. "That one we don't know for sure. Sara said whoever it was wore a mask. It could have been anyone."

"Oh don't be dumb, Cas," grumbled Jennifer. "You don't do dumb well. How many blonde girls do we know who have green eyes, cause the air temperature to drop by thirty degrees, and vanish in hallways?"

"One," sighed Caspian. He held up both hands. "Okay, okay, stop looking at me that way," he pointed at Michael, "especially you. I've been an excellent boyfriend. I call when I say I'm going to call. I tell her she's beautiful—"

"—because she is," interjected Jennifer

Caspian ignored her. "I tell her she's brilliant—"

"—because she is," repeated Jennifer, this time with a slightly bored lilt to her voice.

"We go on trips. We hang out *all* the time." Caspian's face lit up in apparent victory, "I gave Valdania that vorpal dagger Tholem found."

This brought all three of his friends up short. "Okay," said Jennifer, "I'll give you that one."

"Yeah," agreed David, "that dagger was sweeeet."

"Have you told her you love her?" asked Jennifer. Three pairs of eyes locked on Caspian's own. He said nothing for a moment, and Jennifer immediately filled the void. "Don't you love her?"

"It's not that simple, Jenny," he replied.

"Bullshit, Cas!" said Michael, "There's noting more simple than telling someone you love that you love them."

"She's not pressing me, why the hell are you guys?"

"She's nicer than us," said David, and the other two nodded. "We've also known you longer, so aren't going to give you as much rope as she is."

"People with lots of rope, can end up hanging themselves," said Michael seriously.

"Or having the proverbial female-switch flipped," added Jennifer, then noticed how everyone's attention had shifted to her. "Oh you have got to be kidding me," she laughed. "You don't know about the switch?" She saw their looks of negation, then rubbed her hands together. "Okay, boys, I'm going to give you a pearl of greater price than any Caspian's dad has *ever* trotted out.

Here's the deal. Women...have a switch. We'll put up with a lot of shit from you guys, and often for a long time, but..." she held up a finger. "at some point we will have had enough, and *snap,* a switch gets flipped." Jennifer shrugged. "Then it's too late. You can apologize. You can grovel. You can even write us sonnets, but ninety-nine percent of the time, it's no use, because—"

"Your switch is flipped?" asked Michael. Jennifer nodded.

"That's entirely unfair," complained David. "Everyone deserves a second chance, Jen."

"Your entire gender had its second, third, fourth, and more chances *before* the switch got flipped," countered Jennifer, then shrugged. "I don't make the rules, boys, I'm just imparting wisdom, here." She narrowed her eyes at Caspian. "Ignore it at your peril."

"How long's he got?" asked Michael.

Jennifer made a show of staring at the ceiling for several seconds, then said, "These things are somewhat mysterious, even to other women, however, I'd say you best get your shit straight during the holidays, bub, or..." She gestured as if flicking off an invisible light switch.

"She's spending Thanksgiving and Christmas with my whole family," offered Caspian.

Jennifer pinched up her face. "Okay, that's nice. That's important. That's no substitute for a woman knowing her man loves her completely. Don't wait too long, Caspian, that's all I'm saying. Don't wait too long."

He stared into the middle distance for several moments, then nodded. Caspian's eyes traced from one friend to the other. Finally, a faint smile played across his lips. "Thanks guys, yet another successful intervention. You're completely right, and now I know exactly what I'm going to do."

Chapter 45

HOLIDAY MAGIC

Caspian teetered at the top of a sixteen foot ladder, while extending his hand below and making a grasping motion. A second later he felt something placed there. He stared at the ornate angel. Her gown was white fabric with threads of gold, while both her hands and feet were made of fine porcelain. Caspian hooked one arm around the the top of the ladder and pivoted to his right.

"Don't do that," yelled Sara. "You freak me out when you do that one armed thing. You're not a gorilla. Hold on with both hands for God's sake."

"I'm fine," he soothed. "Mom always said I was part monkey. You should have seen the trees I climbed as a kid."

"I don't want to know," grumbled Sara. "Just put the angel where she belongs and come down...please."

Caspian gestured with the figurine. "Are you *sure* Michael is cool with all this? I moved an end table in his condo once, and he gave me crap about it for months."

Sara hopped off the lowest rung of the ladder, stared at Caspian with a flat expression, then moved her hands to her hips. "This is my house, too, Mr. Lewis. My cousin should thank his lucky stars I'm taking the time to make this glorious home look festive for the holidays." She pointed. "Angel, please."

"Yes ma'am," he said, then reached up and set the angel on the topmost branch of a huge Christmas tree. He looked back at Sara. She tilted her head, frowned, then motioned to her left. Caspian adjusted the angel. This time when he looked, she motioned slightly to her right. He adjusted the figurine again. Sara pursed her lips. "Sara, it's straight." She didn't seem convinced so Caspian took both hands off the ladder then started wobbling from side-to-side. "Whoa…" he exclaimed while pretending to lose his balance.

"Fine!" she yelled. "You've made your point, sir. Come down before you fall and crack your damn-fool head on these beautiful hardwoods." She grinned. "I'd hate for them to get scratched."

Caspian slid backwards down the ladder, then stepped close. She looped her arms loosely around his neck. "Thank you, my prince. You do deserve a reward for spending all day helping me decorate."

Caspian slipped his hands around her waist, then raised his eyebrows. "Really, just what kind of reward were you thinking?" She gave him a quick kiss on the lips, then stepped back, slipping out from between his arms.

"That's it?" asked Caspian. "I've been here since ten o'clock." He glanced at his watch. "It's almost six. I toil under your slave master's verbal whip for an entire day, and all I get is a kiss."

Sara affected disappointed. "There was a time, when a kiss from me would have been enough for you to climb the tallest mountain just to bring me a rare winter rose." She held the back of one hand to her forehead. "Alas, the magic is gone."

"Oh, do shut up, Sar, that wasn't even a satisfying kiss. It was barely a peck." Caspian gave her a mischievous grin. She smiled back, and slowly began retreating toward the parlor entrance while keeping her eyes fixed on him. Caspian stopped, placed a hand on his chest, then slipped into his overacted Shakespearean voice. "O, fair Juliet, would thou leave me so unsatisfied?"

Sara responded without missing a beat. She frowned at him saying, "What satisfaction can thou have tonight?" She arched an eyebrow, then pointed at Caspian. "*I* yet wait for thy love's faithful vow. *I* gave thee mine before thou didst' request it." She shook her head, then pointed at him again. "Yet still I wait beneath New Orleans' constant stars and near roiling sea, for thy tongue to confess what is plain to all, but thee."

Caspian stood in stunned silence as they stared at each other across the expansive parlor. Finally, he said, "Okay, I deserved that. I get your point, and appreciate your patience more than I could ever say."

She nodded seriously at him. "You're worth it, but no one's patience is endless, Caspian, even if she wished it were."

He closed the distance between them, and ran one hand along her braids. "Pretty dumb reference for me to use, huh?"

"Pretty dumb," Sara agreed. "You also broke your own rule. *Never ask a question you don't already know the answer to.*"

"Yeah, I stepped into that one for sure," sighed Caspian, "but it was Harper Lee's Atticus Finch who offered that brilliant advice, not me."

"I know," she replied, "You're just the one who ignored it. So, what's the second thing?" Caspian shook his head in confusion. A moment later, Sara's lips curved up and dimples appeared. "After my verbal trouncing, you said *first of all*, then begged forgivess, which I have granted...temporarily. If there was a *first of all* there has to be a *second of all,* doesn't there?"

"Oh yeah," chuckled Caspian, "I almost forgot. I wanted to know where you got that last part from."

"Which part was that?" she asked innocently.

He frowned at her. "You know which part. The, *yet still I wait beneath New Orleans' constant stars and near roiling sea, for thy tongue to confess what is plain to all, but thee.*"

"Oh, that old thing," she replied with a wink, then turned toward the door, "I just made that up on the fly."

Caspian trailed after her, as Sara made her way into the kitchen, and started pulling various things from the large refrigerator.

"You just made that up?"

"Mmm hmmm," she replied while continuing to assemble various ingredients.

Before Caspian could respond, the slightly muffled sound of a door closing filtered into the kitchen. A couple seconds later, Michael's less muffled, "What the heck...Saaaraaa!" could be heard followed by approaching footfalls.

Michael passed the kitchen entrance, then immediately reappeared. He walked in. "Sara...oh hi Cas...Sara, c'mon, we talked about this. What's with all the Christmas decorations?"

"Don't you like Christmas, Mikey?" asked Sara in her best accusatory tone.

"Huh, of course I like Christmas, but not when it comes before Thanksgiving."

She had already put a variety of ingredients into a huge bowl, but looked up as she started whisking them together. "I'm not going to be around to decorate tomorrow, as you well know."

"Yeah, I know. You and Cas are having Thanksgiving with his folks, so what?"

Sara stopped whisking and placed both hands on her hips. "So, I'll not come home to an undecorated house after what I'm sure will be an enchanting family Thanksgiving dinner."

"But——" began Michael.

Sara held up a finger. "That reminds me, Cas, when should I be ready in the morning?"

"Uh, well, Mom likes everyone to see at least part of the Macy's parade, especially the balloons, so I'd say we should be there no later than ten-thirty."

She resumed whisking. "Sounds good. I'll be ready"

"Okay," said Caspian, drawing out the word, "that sounds like I'm leaving. Am I leaving?"

Sara shrugged. "That depends on whether you want to watch me cook for the next three hours. I'd love for you to stay, but honestly you've been a complete sweetheart helping me with the decorations and——"

"I knew it," said Michael. "I knew she couldn't have done all this in a single day. Christmas before Thanksgiving is bad juju, and you helped her. Et tu, Cas?"

Caspian frowned at his friend. "I'm with Sara on this. Get over your after-Thanksgiving BS and go look around. She's made the place look like a mini Biltmore Estate at Christmas. I was just dumb labor."

"Fine," grumbled Michael, "I'll go look, but I just wish someone had at least told me it was happening."

After he walked out, Caspian tapped the side of Sara's bowl with a knuckle. "You were saying..." She dipped a finger in the bowl, then held it out to Caspian. He opened his mouth. Sara slid her finger along his tongue, waited for him to close, then pulled it out with a pop. "Wow, what's that? It's delicious."

"It's *going* to be a bourbon pecan pie, but I'm using Lyles golden syrup from England rather than sugar. I also told your mother I would be bringing the dressing, so will be starting on that next."

"Mom said you didn't need to bring anything," admonished Caspian.

Sara rolled her eyes. "This is, maybe, the fourth time I'm meeting your parents, Cas. In at least two of the other three times, I was either sweaty, covered in food stains, or both. I want to make a good impression."

Caspian reached over, stopped Sara from whisking, and smiled at her. "My parents don't want you to try and impress them. They are already impressed with you, because I'm impressed with you."

"Well, I want them to love me then, and nothing says love better than a well made pie, and sage sausage infused dressing." She started whisking again with one hand while drizzling in something thick and golden with the other.

"Sara, " he sighed, "it's the same thing. They love you because I…" Her eyes flicked up for a fraction of a second, but Caspian didn't notice as he reached into the bowl, "…feel the same. Wow," he said again, "that's going to be the best tasting pecan pie ever. My dad's totally going to flip for it."

"That's the idea," said Sara, then pulled the bowl away when he reached for it again. She leaned forward, gave him a quick kiss, then said. "You may be my beloved Prince Caspian, but you are also a distraction that I cannot afford right now."

"Okay, Okay," he laughed. "I know when I'm not wanted. I'll see you in the morning, ten o'clock sharp."

"I'll be ready," she said, "Oh, and Caspian—"

"Hmmm?"

Sara eyed on him a moment as if considering something then said, "feeling a thing, isn't the same as saying a thing, and neither are close to proving a thing."

His brow furrowed in confusion. "What? Who are you quoting now?" She just gave him an innocuous smile. "Fine," he snickered, "be mysterious. I'll just look it up when I get home."

She shrugged. "You do that. Let me know what you find."

"You got it," he said with smile. "I'll ring you before I go to bed, okay?"

"Yep," she replied, "but before midnight, okay? I want to get a good night's rest"

Caspian nodded, gave her a quick kiss, then headed for the door. A few seconds later she heard him call out. "I'm going to find that quote, Sar."

"He's going to find what quote?" asked Michael as he reentered the kitchen. "Oh, and I'm a jerk, because the house looks amazing. We absolutely need to host a Christmas party. Now, what quote is Cas going to find?"

"He won't find it," whispered Sara as she continued to work, "because it didn't exist until I just said it a few minutes ago."

Rachel Lewis placed both hands flat against her husband's chest and began pushing him from the kitchen. "This kitchen is too small for you men to be underfoot. Go back on the porch, or watch a show in the living room. We'll be out soon."

Robert pinched up his face in confusion. "You are always giving me crap about how your day is never done and that there's always something more to tidy up or clean. Now I'm trying to help, and you are kicking me out."

"You made the turkey," replied his wife. "You've got the soup simmering. You and Caspian cleared off the table after dinner. You've done your part, now I love you, but get out."

Robert held up both hands. "Okay, okay, I'm going, but I've recorded this exchange for later when you accuse me of not doing things."

Rachel flicked a dish towel at Robert's retreating form, then turned back to the sink. "Did he really record that?" asked Sara.

"No," snickered Rachel, "he's just being a little shit." She picked up another plate from the stack that hadn't fit in their dishwasher.

Sara continued drying hers, then glanced over at Rachel. "But you love him, anyone with eyes can see that."

"Well, of course I love him. He's the love of my life, the lust of my loins, and the guard at my back." Sara stopped wiping, and turned to Rachel, eyes widening. "Oh, I'm sorry," laughed Rachel, "did I shock you?"

Sara smiled back. "I'm unshockable. You should hear some of the tales I have about my extended family, heck, my nuclear family, as well."

"I'd like that," said Rachel. "I'd like to meet them, too."

"Well, you'll probably have to go to Jamaica then. None of them like leaving the island. It's weird to me, but there you have it. Parents are weird, uh, present company excepted."

"Oh no, we're weird too," said Rachel. "Case in point, my daughter's absence from Thanksgiving dinner. She just started dating someone and didn't want to risk *ruining it by introducing him to us too soon.*"

"Really?" asked Sara, "I just love you guys. You're so, well, real."

Rachel handed over another plate. "Some people don't like real, Sara, but I appreciate the compliment. You're real too, which is just part of why Robert and I are so glad you and Caspian are together." Rachel set down her plate and turned to face the younger woman. "You know it goes both ways right?"

Sara shook her head. "I'm sorry, what goes both ways?"

"Recognizing someone who's in love. You said, anyone with eyes can see that I love Robert. Well, a blind man with a sack over his head could see how much you love Caspian." Sara felt heat rising up her neck, but Rachel reached out, took the plate from her hand, and set it on the counter. "Don't be embarrassed. It's an amazing thing to love someone the way you clearly do my son. I hope you know how lucky he is to have you?"

"I guess," said Sara. "It's just—"

"Just what?" prompted Rachel.

Sara sighed. "Sometimes, I'm not sure it's reciprocal, at least not the same way. You know the term unequally yoked, right?"

Rachel started scrubbing some silverware, and nodded. "Caspian's the one who stopped going to Church, not me. I'm quite familiar with both the term and how you're using it, but you're wrong."

Sara turned anxious eyes toward the kitchen's entrance, then asked, "Wrong? How do you mean?"

"Oh you don't need to worry about them coming in, that's why I snarked at Robert. I wanted us to have some alone time. As for what I meant, I'm a mother, Sara. I know my boy. I know when he's in love. I've seen it once before."

"Elizabeth," said Sara quietly.

"Yes," agreed Rachel.

"I once told Caspian that I wasn't jealous of her, that I didn't want to replace her, and I loved how much he loved her. I still mean all those things, but sometimes, it just feels—"

"A bit crowded?" asked Rachel.

"Yeah," said Sara, sniffed, then wiped at her eyes. "I'm sorry. I'm either being stupid, a horrible person, or both. Probably both."

Rachel dropped her handful of silverware into the rinsing side of the sink, then pulled Sara in for a hug. "You are not being either. If he wasn't my son, I'd be calling him stupid in this situation, but he is, so I know better." She took a half step back and smiled at Sara. "He's scared, and not the selfish kind of scared that's all to expected from men his age. This is the deep fear that gets into your bones and lives there. Sara, Caspian only gave his full heart to one person, and she abandoned him." Rachel's words took Sara by surprise, but before she could respond, Caspian's mother said, "Of course, Lizzie didn't *actually* abandon him, but that's what it *feels* like. Death is the ultimate abandonment. Heck, with divorce, you can at least call up your ex, and tell him he's a piece of shit. Caspian doesn't have that, but he does have you."

Sara gave an awkward shrug. "I'm not sure what to do with that statement."

"You might need to kick him in the ass. I know I had to do that with his father. It's not a bad thing, sometimes it just is. I remember being on the balcony of Robert's apartment. It was late. There was no moon, and the stars were so bright. I stood on that deck by myself for quite a while. Finally, he came out and asked me if everything was okay. I turned to him and I said, point blank, *do you love me, and are you going to marry me?*"

Sara's eyes widened, then a grin spread across her face. "What did he say?"

"Well, at first he just stood there looking stupid," laughed Rachel, "but then he said the sweetest thing. "He said, *I love you more today than I did yesterday and less than tomorrow.*" Rachel laughed. "Then he said, *as for marriage, I have stuff planned. Don't mess it up.*"

"What did he have planned?" asked Sara.

"Oh, probably nothing," snickered Rachel, "but you can be sure he started planning after the verbal kick in the ass I gave him." She sighed. "Your situation is a little different though. At some point, Caspian has to fear losing you to the world more than losing you to an untimely death."

"I told him that love was patient and kind," mused Sara. "I told him I would be, too."

Rachel snickered. "Caspian warned us that head of yours is just chockablock full of Shakespeare, but he didn't mention you stored bible verses up there too. Not that he would, given his current feud with God. Still, what you told him is true. Love *is* patient and kind. It's also admirable that you want to take St. Paul's advice to heart." Rachel shrugged. "Then again, St. Paul never had to wrangle a broken man to an altar with the woman he so clearly loves. My advice, go with me on this one rather than St. Paul."

Sara grinned, then gave Rachel a spontaneous hug. "Thank you," she whispered. "Thank you so much for this."

"Don't give it a second thought," replied Rachel, "but I do have one last question. Have you tried writing out the name Sara Lewis on various pieces of paper only to shred them so no-one could see? I did. It's important. I once dated a guy named Hershel Machels. One day, I wrote down *Rachel Machels*, and that was it...no more Hershel."

Sara slipped from the other woman's embrace and stared at her, lips drawn to a line. "Have I done that?" She grinned. "Only a lot!"

Rachel burst out laughing. "Isn't it a good thing our last name isn't something like *Berra?*" She gave Sara's shoulder a gentle squeeze. "Sara Lewis has a very nice ring to it." She shrugged. "You just need to pick up a bell, and beat my son with it until he can hear the same ring."

Chapter 46

MIDNIGHT MASS

"Holy cow, it's cold," chattered Caspian as he and Sara walked briskly across the St. Louis Cathedral's parking lot.

Sara, rubbed a hand along the back of his coat, then gave him a quick kiss on the cheek. "It's not *that* cold. You are just a big baby."

"Sar, they said it could snow. Do you know how cold it has to be to snow?"

She laughed. "Just because it never snows at home, doesn't mean I don't know how water freezes." Sara slipped her arm around Caspian's waist, and squeezed. "How magical will it be if I see my first American snow on Christmas eve? Won't that just be the best thing ever?" Before Caspian could answer she suddenly pointed off to her right. "Oh, look, there is your mom. She's waving us over. I don't see your dad though."

"He's already inside," chuckled Caspian, "guarding Mom's pew like a Catholic Rottweiler. He started doing that when we were kids, and it's been their midnight Mass operandi for over twenty years now."

Rachel Lewis' face lit up as they approached. "Oh Sara, let me look at you a minute. You wore the coat. I knew it would look great on you."

Sara smiled shyly, "It's beautiful, but I thought Christmas presents were for Christmas."

Rachel waved her hand dismissively. "Some are, some aren't, and some *people* snoop around and play with an X-Box present *weeks* before Christmas without their parents knowing about it."

Sara smirked at Caspian. "Did you do that?"

He shook his head, then pointed at his mother. "I've never met this woman before in my life, but it's Christmas, so let's not disrupt her reminiscing about things that absolutely did *not* happen."

Rachel nudged Caspian out of the way, then gave Sara a tight hug. She kissed her cheek, and smiled at the younger woman. "You are a vision of loveliness, Sara. My Caspian was definitely right about red being your color."

Sara blushed, then ran her hand along her coat's white trim. "We all watched *White Christmas* last night at the big house, and I went on and on about the red and white costumes at the end."

Rachel's eyes flicked to Caspian. "He didn't ruin the surprise, did he?"

Sara gave Caspian a playful slap. "No, the silly man made up a ridiculous lie on the spot. He told me it never gets cold enough in New Orleans to wear such things, so no one even sells heavy coats here." She laughed. "Now, look at Mr. Cold in his fancy, but very thin, wool, overcoat."

"Yeah, and Mr. Cold would like to get inside the cathedral before either freezing rain starts or Dad bites the arm off someone who tries to sit too near him." He crooked his arm toward Sara, but Rachel spun him toward the Cathedral's large double doors. "You go on to your father. We still have over thirty minutes before Mass starts, and I haven't had a chance to see Sara since Thanksgiving."

Caspian narrowed his eyes at his mother. "You may not have *seen* her, but you guys talk all the time." He saw his mother's expression shift, and shook his head. "No, don't even try to convince me otherwise. I just want to know what's so important that you need to talk with her right now?"

"Never you mind, Caspian Lewis. Now listen to your mother and...go inside." Her eyebrows rose as she made a shooing motion. "Go..."

He looked to Sara for support but she just smiled, and said, "I love this weather. See you inside." Caspian frowned at both women, gave a resigned sigh, and began heading toward the Cathedral's entrance.

Once he was some distance ahead of them, Rachel and Sara started to slowly follow. "I can't thank you enough," began Rachel. "He never would have come if just his father and I had asked."

"It was a near thing," sighed Sara. "We actually had our first fight about it." Rachel stopped and looked at the younger woman, but Sara just smiled and shook her head. "It was more of a tiff than a fight, really."

Caspian's mother shook her head, clearly disappointed. "Do you mind telling me what happened?"

ONE HEART THAT BEATS FOR TWO

"Not at all. I said we've been dating for over six months, we went to Hawaii together..." Sara paused, "You know we stayed in separate rooms, right?"

"Yes, dear, you deftly slipped that little nugget into previous conversations at least twice before. Both Robert and I got the message, and good for you. Right now I'm more concerned about—"

"Actually, the two rooms were more Caspian's doing," murmured Sara then froze as Rachel smirked at her. "Uh, not that I wanted us to just have one room. Oh, this is coming out all wrong."

"Stop," soothed Rachel, "it's fine. I know what you meant. Now, start again, what did you tell Caspian that got his heathen butt to Mass?"

Sara took a deep breath. "So, after I reminded him how long we'd been together, I just said I was tired of going to Mass by myself, and Christmas was a perfect time for him to stop being an ass about it."

Rachel laughed. "How did that go over?"

"About as well as you might expect, but this time I called him on his bullshit." Sara cringed a little. "Sorry, I—"

"Oh no, I'm sure that's exactly what it was, bullshit. I just don't know which particular pile he may have been shoveling your way."

"The *I'm not going to a Church that worships the God who killed Elizabeth* pile," spat Sara with far more venom than she intended.

Rachel saw how the younger woman tried to maintain her composure, but was on the verge of giving in to the maelstrom of emotions that swirled just beneath the surface. She guided Sara through the Cathedral doors and into an empty preparatory room situated just inside. Rachel fished through her purse, handed Sara a tissue, and offered an encouraging nod. "It's okay. Go on."

Sara blew her nose, then looked up at one corner of the room for several seconds. "I said something mean. I told him, that he needed to stop railing against the world for what he lost, and start appreciating what he had."

Rachel nodded, "Good for you...then what did he say?"

Sara sniffed. "He said he was trying. He said he was getting better, and maybe he is. Maybe I'm just too impatient. You and I talked about this at Thanksgiving. Love is supposed to be patient. It's supposed to be—"

"No," whispered Rachel. "I'm not going to let you turn this around on yourself. You have been both patient and kind. I love my son, more than words can express, and you're right. He *has* gotten better, but he also seems to have, I don't know, plateaued, if that's the right word."

"I guess," agreed Sara, then her eyes began to fill with tears.

331

"What is it, honey?" asked Rachel. "Tell me."

Sara ground her teeth, looked away, then finally met the older woman's eyes. "Why am I not enough? I don't want to be jealous of Elizabeth. That would just be the height of pride and stupidity, now wouldn't it?" Her voice cracked. "But there you have it. I'm jealous of a dead woman. What's worse, I know for a fact she wants Cas and me to be happy together. He just won't listen to anyone, even Elizabeth." Sara saw Rachel's expression shift toward confusion, then said, "I mean, from what everyone's said of her personality, she'd want Caspian to be happy, right?"

"Of course she would," agreed Rachel, "but this isn't about Elizabeth and it's not about you. This is about my son's pride, and the fact that he feels life has wronged him."

"Hasn't it?" asked Sara.

Rachel reached out and took the younger woman's hands in her own. "Of course it has, but who gets through this life without tragedy. You know what life has also brought my son? Life brought him you. Has your life been free of strife and pain, Sara?"

The young woman barked a mirthless laugh. "If you only knew, Rachel. Maybe someday I'll tell you, but then we'll both be blubbering." She sighed. "I don't have a watch. How much time do we have before Mass starts? I'm so sorry that I—"

"Stop, we have ten minutes yet, and you don't need to be sorry for anything. Listen to me, Sara Edwards. We're going to go into Christmas Mass, and we're going to pray for that block-head son of mine that we both love beyond all reason. We're going to pray that God gives him a good flick behind the ears so the scales can fall from his eyes, and he'll see the beautiful miracle that is you. How does that sound?"

Sara pinched her lips together, then dabbed at her eyes. "It sounds wonderful." The two women embraced for several long moments, then Sara stepped back and smiled. "So, if our prayers for Godly smiting work and the scales really do fall from Caspian's eyes, will you let me call you mom?"

"Let you," scoffed Rachel with mock chagrin, "I'd be insulted if you called me anything but."

ONE HEART THAT BEATS FOR TWO

Robert Lewis bumped his son with a shoulder as they left the Cathedral. "For Pete's sake, Caspian, can't you just admit that you enjoyed the Mass? Don't be such a Scrooge."

"It was nice," he admitted with a shrug, then looked up. The clouds were so thick, neither stars nor moon could be seen. "At least it's not raining anymore, but those clouds look like they could open up again any minute. Remember, I don't get here a day early to stake out a pew and glare at people. We had to park on the other side of Royal Street, and I don't want Sara getting caught in a downpour so—"

"How did I get brought into this," she laughed. "I'm fine, and Robert, if your son is too much of a Scrooge to say it, I will. That was the best midnight mass I've ever attended." She grinned. "It was also my only midnight mass, but still. The carols, and the incence, oh, and the candles. Do they always light candles and sing Silent Night at the end? I absolutely started tearing up." She shook her head. "An entire cathedral lit by hundreds of candles while all those voices sang." She wiggled. "It still gives me chills." She wrapped her arms around Robert and gave him a hug. "Thanks for inviting me, even if it was just so we could get Ebenezer here into a church."

Robert Lewis laughed softly, then gently placed his hands on Sara's shoulders and eased her forward. "You are so welcome, but to be clear, we invited you for you." His eyes flicked to Caspian. "That you managed to get Mr. Scrooge to tag along, well, that was icing on the cake."

Caspian shook his head. "Mom, you want to get in on this action? I don't think you've called me the villain of *A Christmas Carol* yet this evening."

Robert and Sara started down the Cathedral's steps with Rachel and Caspian just behind. She gave her son a kiss on the cheek. "Scrooge wasn't a villain, he was a warning to all of us." She tapped Caspian's chest, then whispered. "My sweet boy, please don't wait too long. Sara will thaw this frozen heart of yours, if you'll just let her. Your father and I, your friends, we've all been praying for you to wake up." She squeezed his hand. "We've sent the hounds of heaven after you, Caspian. If you don't pay them heed when they mewl or nuzzle you, those hounds also have teeth, and they're not afraid to use them when necessary."

Caspian slipped his arm around his mother and started following Robert and Sara as they headed toward his parents car. "Thanks ma, I'll keep that in mind, however, I'm pretty sure your hounds of heaven have more important things to do than chase after me."

⌒⌒⌒⌒⌒

Thunder rumbled overhead, and Caspian tapped the roof of his parents car. "Okay, enough with the goodbyes, already. We'll see you guys tomorrow, okay? I want to get Sara home, so *I* can get to my apartment in time for at least *some* sleep."

Sara crouched down and caught Rachel's eye. "Don't give him even the least bit of sympathy," she laughed. "Jenny and Dave are joining us around ten at the big house for presents, but *I'm* the one who's getting up at eight to make breakfast for everyone."

"We all offered," said Caspian defensively.

Sara held up a hand. "Jennifer isn't allowed to prepare any kind of food that doesn't come with microwave instructions on the back, and you boys are restricted to grilling meat on that big green egg thing. I'm not complaining, I'm just saying *you* shouldn't complain."

"Fair enough," snickered Caspian, then the two waved goodbye as Robert and Rachel drove off.

Caspian crooked his arm for Sara, who slipped hers within. "Home, James," she said imperiously, and the two started walking toward the far end of the Cathedral parking lot, where it met the French Quarter's Royal Street. Lightning streaked across the sky in a jagged line, causing everything to appear as if it were midday. Thunder cracked an instant later. Caspian and Sara grinned at each other. "Run?" he asked.

"Definitely," she agreed, and the two began sprinting across the expansive parking lot.

"Told you," yelled Caspian, as rain began streaming down on them. "They're going to find us tomorrow morning as a couple of frozen Christmas statues."

Sara turned to him. "You are such a baby when it comes to the cold. I swear it's like—"

"Hey!" yelled Caspian, and grabbed the hood of Sara's jacket. She rocked back, turned, and fell into his arms. "You almost ran right into the street, Sar, and you tell me I don't pay attention to things."

She lifted her hood back into place, and smiled at him. "You don't pay attention to things, but you do pay attention to me, and I love that." Sara's voice took on a regal tone, "You saved me, Prince Caspian, from…absolutely

334

no oncoming traffic. Still, you are my gallant prince, you have earned a reward." She raised up on her toes and gave him a quick peck on the cheek.

"Some reward," he grumbled, "and there is, too, traffic." He pointed. "Look, there's a car heading this way right—"

A bolt of lightning struck the large sedan just as it drew near. Sparks flew in all directions and its headlights winked out. Caspian could see the driver struggling with the wheel as the car started careening toward them. "Look out," cried Caspian, but Sara seemed frozen in place as she stared at the oncoming car. He leaped forward, grabbing her around the waist, and lifting her off the ground. He had only made it a few feet when a loud crash sounded from behind them. Caspian stumbled to a stop, set her down, and asked. "Are you okay?"

Sara shook her head but, said, "Yeah…uh, yes, I'm fine." She stared at the skid marks and how they had crossed over exactly where the two of them had been standing. "Oh my God," she whispered, then stared up at Caspian. "Oh my God, you just saved my life."

He was about to respond, when Sara's eyes shifted toward the car which had plowed into one of the French Quarter's electrical poles. The entire hood had crumpled to form a rough U-shape around the cement pole. "Oh no," she cried, "that driver must be hurt." As they both sprinted toward the car, Caspian tried to pull his phone from the breast pocket of his coat. It got turned sideways and wouldn't come out. He glanced down for a second, retrieved the phone, then looked up again. His blood ran cold. "Sara!" he screamed. "Stop! Sara!"

She turned toward him, but it was too late. Her forward motion caused her to step off the curb and into a shallow stream of rainwater that ran along it. The moment her foot touched the water, she went rigid and started convulsing. Caspian dropped his phone, and leaped for her, striking her full in the chest with one shoulder. The two of them tumbled into the center of the street and away from where a downed power line had electrified the rainwater.

Caspian stared down at her. "Sara?" She stared through half open eyes, unblinking. He patted her cheek several times. No reaction. Caspian yelled her name, his voice filled with rising panic.

A car door creaked, then slammed, but Caspian was oblivious to it. "Is she all right?" asked a voice, then said, "I'll call 911 and I've got a couple emergency flares."

Neither the other man's words, or the blossoming violet light from the flares registered in Caspian's mind as he lay his fingers against Sara's neck. He thought he felt something, then pressed an ear against her chest. Relief flooded him. *Oh thank God*, he thought as he heard the first beat, and then another.

Bump-bump...bump-bump-bump...bump-bump...bump-bump-bump.

Caspian sat up with a start. He stared down at Sara, eyes wide, as a torrent of emotions coursed through him.

"Ambulance is on the way," said the driver as he crouched next to them. "How's she doing? Is she okay?"

Caspian grunted something, he thought might have been a yes, then pressed his ear against her chest again. The beats had the same cadence, but seemed slower.

Bump-bump......bump-bump-bump......bump-bump......bump-bump-bump.

"That's weird," murmured the man beside Caspian, "I thought they decided we weren't getting snow." His voice rose a second later. "It's making it hard to see the flares. I'm going to be over there making sure you guys are safe. Call me if I can help."

Bump-bump......bump-bump-bump......

Silence.

Caspian pushed himself up, eyes wide with panic, as he searched for the telltale lights of the promised ambulance.

Nothing.

He opened Sara's coat, as half-remembered CPR training flashed through his mind. He pressed the heel of one hand to her chest but the buttons of her shirt were in the way. He began to undo the buttons. One, two, three buttons came undone. Caspian gently slid the fabric aside, leaving Sara's chest exposed except for her bra. He began shaking, tears falling from his eyes, as they saw the thin line of a scar running down her chest. "Oh no," he cried, then looked up again.

Elizabeth looked down at him while large flakes of snow fell all around them. "You've found my last gift Caspian," she said sadly. "I just hope you didn't find it too late." He pressed the heel of one hand to Sara's chest, while using the other to begin compressions. Elizabeth knelt down beside them. "So many people have been praying for you Caspian, including me. We prayed for it to be easy. We prayed for you to accept all that's happened and forge ahead. You refused. Today, both your time and our patience ran out, so we began to pray something else. We prayed for you to wake up by any means necessary." Caspian tilted Sara's head back, pressed his lips to hers, and gave three quick breaths. Elizabeth sighed. "This is what that looks like Caspian."

He began compressions again, but glared at her. "So, I have to lose her, too! Is that what you're telling me?"

"You have sown the wind these past eighteen months, Caspian. Now, I'm afraid, you must reap the whirlwind."

He continued mentally counting compressions, but cried out, "Lizzie, can't you do something for her?"

"I did do something, Cas. I gave her my heart." Elizabeth shook her head. "Why, oh why, didn't you give her yours?"

"Because I was stupid, and was scared, and I acted like a child who clearly didn't deserve either of you!"

Elizabeth smiled. "We all act like children sometimes, Caspian. When I was a child, I spoke like a child, I thought like a child, I reasoned like a child. When I became a woman, I put aside childish things. So did you, Caspian. You've just forgotten, so let me ask you. Are you finally ready to put aside childish things?"

He gave Sara mouth-to-mouth again, then resumed compressions, and looked at Elizabeth. "What are you talking about? I'll do anything. I'll put aside anything. What do I need to put aside? Tell me and I'll do it."

Elizabeth smiled. "Me, Caspian. You need to put aside, me. It's time. No heart can have two masters. One heart can't long beat for two. Tell her. Tell her what you told me." The snow began falling so thickly that Caspian couldn't see anything more than a foot away. The air became bitingly cold. He felt Elizabeth's hands on his. She pulled them away from Sara's chest, and stared into his eyes. "Tell her, Caspian."

He stared down at Sara's still form, as hot tears dripped from his face to fall against her chest. "I love you," he whispered, then looked at Elizabeth. "I'm sorry——"

"No," she said. "You can't be sorry. Love isn't sorry. Love is patient. Love is kind. Love is joy. Love is not sorrow."

He looked down again, took a breath, then said in a steady voice. "I love you. I want to be with you, whether that's for a day, or the rest of my life, and I'll count myself blessed for every one of them. Please, Sara...please don't leave me."

"Now that is a testament of love done right," said Elizabeth. Caspian's eyes followed her as she stood, and golden light began to surround her. It pulsed several times as Elizabeth's body seemed to drink it in. For a moment, there was darkness, then crimson tinged golden light exploded outward from Elizabeth's chest in radiant beams. Sara's entire body became wreathed in it.

Color returned to her cheeks as her body drank in the light the same way Elizabeth's had moments before.

Caspian cast a hopeful glance upward. Elizabeth smiled, then inclined her head toward Sara. "Listen, Caspian, and know that all things can be mended. All things, even the most tragic, can be worked for good, if only we have the faith to let them."

Sara groaned, and Caspian quickly closed her shirt. He wrapped her coat around her, then looked up to the sound of approaching sirens. "Casp—" murmured Sara.

"Shh," he whispered. "I'm here. I love you, and I'll always be here."

The snow stopped falling and Caspian looked up, half expecting Elizabeth to be gone. Her eyes met his, and she held up two fingers. "You'll see me twice more in the waking world." She smiled, then added, "but the next time won't be for you, and the last won't be for quite some time, at least from your perspective. Until then, live well and love even better." She paused, then her face took on the impish expression Caspian knew well. "Oh, and Cas, don't argue with your wife when she wants to name your daughter after me." She shrugged. "It's a fair trade. After all, you have been a *lot* of work."

The sound of Elizabeth's laughter still hung in the air when two EMT's rushed to Sara's side, and nudged Caspian back. He watched as they moved her onto a stretcher, then nodded when one of them asked if he wanted to join her in the ambulance. He looked up at the clearing night sky. For the first time in well over a year, he felt two things that he never expected to feel again...joy in the present, and hope for the future.

Chapter 47

THE HEART THAT BEATS FOR TWO

Michael leaped sideways from the elevator as soon as the doors had barely parted. He looked around in a panic, unsure of which way to turn. A large, white, ICU sign hung directly above him. He started to sprint down the hallway, when Jennifer called out from his left. Michael skidded to a stop, turned, and saw her motioning to him. He ran up to her. "I got here as soon as I heard. What the hell happened? Where's Sara? Is she all right? It was some kind of car accident? Is Caspian hurt, too? Damn it, Jen your voicemail didn't say shit. Why the hell couldn't you—"

Jennifer wrapped her arms around Michael, hugged him, and began speaking in hushed tones. "The doctors told us that Sara is in serious condition. They have her sedated in the ICU. Caspian is fine, at least physically. He and his folks are in the waiting room just behind me. You can join us once I'm done hugging you and you're in a place where you'll not make matters worse." She felt him flinch. "I know Michael, but freaking out in front of Caspian is not going to help."

After several seconds, he nodded against her neck, then took a half step back. He looked past Jennifer and into the sparsely populated ICU waiting room. Caspian sat in one corner, elbows on his knees, and his chin resting in his palms. His parents sat on either side, with Robert slowing rubbing his son's back while Rachel continuously whispered to him. For his part, Caspian seemed oblivious to both. He just stared into the middle distance, occasionally

339

shaking his head at something. Michael's eyes shifted back to Jennifer. He immediately recognized the expression of concern and appraisal he saw there. "I'm okay," he said, then extended his hand. She accepted it, and he pulled her a few feet down the hallway. Michael took a deep, calming breath. He nodded to Jennifer. "Three sentences...go."

Her nose immediately reddened, as she looked up toward the ceiling. Jennifer swallowed. "Cas and Sara were leaving midnight mass when the next bunch of storm cells started coming through. It began to rain, and they ran toward Cas' car which was parked on the far side of Royal. Just as they were about to cross the street, lightning struck an oncoming car, it careened into an electrical pole, and..." Jennifer's voice cracked as the tears she'd been holding back spilled down her cheeks. "...and Sara stepped in a puddle of electrified rainwater, which stopped her heart."

"Oh God," said Michael.

Jennifer squeezed her eyes shut a moment, then let out a shuddering sigh. "Cas did CPR while the driver of the other car called 911. He got her heart going again, but—"

"How long?" interrupted Michael.

Jennifer shrugged. "Just a few minutes I guess. I don't know."

"Well, what does Caspian say?"

Jennifer started crying again. "He hasn't said anything. I think he's in shock. He hasn't said a single word. He was here all alone after the ambulance brought Sara. One of the nurses triggered the emergency contacts on his phone, that's why his parents and I are here. I called you and Dave as soon as I heard." She locked eyes with Michael. "Have you called Sara's parents?"

He nodded. "They're probably in the air by now, and apparently they chartered a plane for that Austin doctor, too. He called me from the airport as he was boarding the private plane my Uncle got for him."

"What's *he* got to do with anything?" asked Jennifer. "Who is this guy?"

"I don't know, Jenny. He told me his name, but I wasn't listening. He just said not to authorize any operations until he arrived."

"Why?" Michael's expression went flat. "I'm sorry," said Jenny, "I'm sorry...I'm sorry."

"No, it's okay," Michael sighed. "It was odd. I did ask him what I *should* do, and he just said to wait. He'd be here in less than two hours. He wouldn't tell me anything else. He said I had to talk with my aunt or uncle."

"Which you can't," said Jennifer, "because they're somewhere over the Atlantic right now."

"Yep, what a complete shit show."

The two stood in silence for a moment, when the ICU floor's elevator gave a half-hearted ding. A second later, David's voice cut through the omnipresent, low-level, hum of the floor's chatter. Jennifer pressed a hand to Michael's chest. "Go see Caspian. I'll take care of Dave. Once I have him up to speed, we'll join you in the waiting room, okay?"

Michael nodded, then raised a hand toward David, who had just caught sight of them. Jennifer started walking away, but Michael grabbed her hand. She turned. "Jenny, I'm sorry I blamed you for—"

Jennifer shook her head. "Nope, nothing to be sorry for. We just love them so..." she huffed out a breath, then wiped at her eyes. "No, I can't do this now. Go to Caspian."

Michael immediately brushed past her along the wall and toward the waiting room. David skidded to a stop, glanced at Michael's retreating form, and asked, "Where is he off to, and what the hell is going on?"

Everyone looked up as a woman wearing a white doctor's coat entered the waiting room. Her eyes quickly scanned the area, then fixed on the corner where Caspian and the others were sitting. She had shoulder length, light brown hair, that was heavily streaked with silver. The doctor crouched down, and smiled, causing creases to form around her eyes and mouth. "Caspian?" she asked.

"Yeah, that's me," he whispered.

Rachel squeezed his arm. "Doctor, that's the first thing he's said since we got here. I—"

She nodded at his mother but also raised a hand to forestall additional comments, as she focused intently on Caspian. "I'm Doctor Robinson and I'm the chief of cardiothoracic surgery here at Tulane Medical Center. First, I want to tell you that Sara is doing well. She's been upgraded to stable condition, but we're keeping her sedated for the time being."

"Why is she sedated? Can I see her?"

Dr. Robinson nodded. "Well, that's why I'm here. Her parents have just landed and are on their way to the hospital. They gave me permission to take you back to speak with me and her personal physician."

Caspian shook his head. "I don't know any—"

"He flew in from Austin?" prompted the doctor.

Michael leaned over. "Hi, I'm Sara's cousin. Caspian didn't know about the other doctor coming in. My aunt and uncle arranged all that."

The doctor nodded as if she were assembling puzzle pieces in her head, then extended a hand to Caspian. "So, can you come with me now? I'll get you in to see Sara, and maybe you can help me with a few..." she paused, "nagging questions I have about your girlfriend's condition."

Caspian nodded, then accepted the doctor's hand, and the two stood up together. He saw the looks of concern from both his parents and friends. Caspian managed a wan smile. "I'm okay, or I will be once I see her."

Doctor Robinson inclined her head to the others. "I'll have him back to you before too long. I promise," then led Caspian out of the waiting room and down the hall.

～⫷⫸～

Doctor Robinson stood beside a large wooden door that led into one of the patient rooms. The name, *S. Edwards*, was written in dry erase marker on a narrow panel to the door's left. She rested her hand on the curved metal latch, but her eyes remained on Caspian. "There are going to be a lot of tubes, and wires, and machines that make noises. It's okay if they make noises and it's okay if they stop making noises. We have things well in hand, okay?" Caspian continued staring blankly at the door. "Okay?" repeated the doctor.

He nodded. "Got it. Noises good. No noises good. Everything's good."

She patted his shoulder. "Close enough. Come on, then."

They walked into the room and Caspian felt his heart rate increase. Sara lay with her eyes closed on an inclined bed. As the doctor had warned, she was also connected to an IV bag and several pieces of monitoring equipment. A man had been bending over her bed when they came in. He turned at the sound of their entry and gave a curt nod to Dr. Robinson. She nodded back and locked the door. The other doctor glanced up to where a red light glowed beneath the room's security camera. "Yes, I know," murmured Dr. Robinson, then slipped a small tablet from her coat pocket. She swiped and tapped for several seconds, then glanced at the security camera. Its activity light flashed three times, then went off. "We're alone, Dr. Alvarez and I promised you five minutes, because if what you told me is true, I owe you that much."

The man smiled, then crossed to where he stood between Dr. Robinson and Caspian. "Doctor..." he began, his voice soft and lightly accented, "Rebecca... if you did not believe me, there would be police in this room rather than this young man." He extended his hand to Caspian. "Hello. I'm Miguel Alvarez, Sara's doctor."

Caspian accepted Alvarez's hand, but shook his head. "She's never mentioned you."

"No," he said with a low chuckle, "she would not have."

"You're the doctor from Austin who helped her last year, right?" Alvarez nodded. "Your name sounds familiar, but—" Caspian shook his head. "I don't know, maybe she did mention you, after all, and I just can't place it."

"Okay," interrupted Robinson, "I normally have a great bedside manner, but throwing my entire career away has me a bit on edge, so, Caspian, forgive me for being indelicate, but why does your girlfriend's heart not match the rest of her?" She pointed to Alvarez. "He says he performed the transplant surgery last year in his Austin thoracic clinic. Problem is, we have no record of there being a heart available at that time. In addition, there's no record of Sara Edwards ever receiving such a non-existent heart."

Alvarez pointed to the stylized green-ribbon pin attached to Dr. Robinson's coat, then pointed to a similar pin on his own. They were almost identical except that where Robinson's was perfectly symmetrical, Dr. Alvarez's pin displayed a purposeful crack down one side. He opened his mouth to speak, but Dr. Robinson cut him off. "No, I want to hear Caspian. Not one word, Doctor, or I tap the little red button on my tablet, and big men with guns haul you away on suspicion of organ trafficking."

Alvarez didn't seem the least bit upset or worried. In fact, he just smiled, then gestured with both hands toward Caspian.

He felt both doctors' eyes on him, and nodded. "I don't know why Sara needed a heart transplant. I didn't even know she had one until last night. We knew she was treated in Austin about a year ago, but no one knew the reason. We didn't ask, and she didn't offer."

"Damnit," cursed Robinson, "so, you can't help verify that Sara's donor heart was legitimately received." She shook her head at the other doctor. "I'm sorry, I've given you the benefit of the—"

"No, I can," interrupted Caspian, "because I know who gifted Sara with the heart."

Rebecca Robinson's mouth parted in surprise, then she narrowed her eyes at Caspian. "How could you know that? Those records are sealed."

"Yeah," sighed Caspian, "they are, but I knew her."

"Who?" asked the doctor.

"The woman who donated her heart. Her name was Elizabeth Winters. She died last year...May 17th."

Dr. Robinson had begun swiping at her tablet again. "What's her social security number?" Caspian rattled off the number from memory. A second later, the doctor's eyes grew wide. She stared at Caspian. "You're...you're listed as next of kin. Were you related to Ms. Winters?"

"Engaged," he said quietly, then moved to stand beside Sara's bed. He took her hand in his. "I'm just going to stand over here for a while. You can keep asking your questions."

Dr. Robinson turned her tablet to face Alvarez, and pointed at the screen. "It says Ms. Winters' heart was rejected—congenital defect."

"Yes," agreed the other, "a defect that in no way affects the heart's function." He paused as Robinson's eyes continued scanning her tablet, then added, "as you are discovering yourself from reading her chart."

She shook her head. "They discarded it."

"Almost," he said, then tapped the pin on his chest, "but we got to it first."

"You're really one of them," she whispered.

He smiled. "Guilty as charged. I suppose we are organ traffickers in the same sense people who sneak bibles in hostile countries are god smugglers."

Dr. Robinson's eyes lost focus for several seconds while she continued staring at her tablet. She looked up, and murmured, "The ethics of what you people do is—"

"Something I struggled with, when, years ago, I stood where you are standing now," interrupted Alvarez. "I asked the same questions that are likely racing through your mind right now."

"Don't presume to know my mind, Doctor," she growled. "You have no idea what I'm thinking."

Miguel smiled at her. "Why does this young woman, get to live when others die? Is it because she comes from a family of means? Is it ethical for the privileged to live while others do not?" He arched an eyebrow. "Ah, I see, perhaps, I do know what your were thinking. Let me ask you a question, Rebecca. Would it be better for Elizabeth Winter's heart to rot, Sara Edwards to die, and hundreds more like her?"

This last took Dr. Robinson aback. "What hundreds more?"

Miguel tapped the stylized organ donation awareness pin on his lapel. "Do you know the last time I charged a patient for an officially sanctioned transplant procedure?" He didn't wait for a response. "Ten years ago, Dr.

Robinson. In those ten years I've performed two unsanctioned transplants, Sara's was the third. All such arrangements are the same. The recipient or their family must fully fund a clinic in perpetuity. Yes, someone like Sara is saved with an otherwise discarded organ that only wealth and privilege can keep hidden from prying eyes. In return, our clinics seek out and serve those who would otherwise fall through the cracks of an imperfect medical safety net. Judge me all you like, doctor, but quite frankly, I sleep very well at night knowing all the hearts that continue to beat because of what I do." He gestured to Sara. "That includes the one gifted by Elizabeth Winters to the young woman laying in your hospital bed."

Dr. Robinson stared at her colleague for several long moments, then just shook her head. "I'm sorry. I haven't seen what you've seen or walked where you've walked. You're right, Miguel, the ethics are cleaner on my side of this room, but Sara's alive on the other side because of you." As she said this, movement caught her attention, and she was about to cross toward Sara, but stopped when Alvarez gently touched her arm. Caspian was leaning over the bed with his ear resting gently on Sara's chest.

"Oh my God," whispered Rebecca.

"Yes," agreed Alvarez.

"Miguel, he can hear it, can't he?"

"Yes, I'm sure he can. The extra beat persisted after transplantation, but Rebecca, it is a good heart. It is a strong heart, and a precious gift."

Dr. Robinson wiped at her eyes, then looked at her damp fingers. She shook her head. "It's been a long time since these dry eyes have shed a tear, and even longer since they were joyful ones."

Miguel sighed. "I know exactly what you mean." He extended an open palm to Rebecca. In it rested a green ribbon pin that exactly matched his own. She stared at it, but made no move to take it from his hand. "It won't bite," whispered Miguel, "and it is not a commitment, just an offer…an opportunity if you will. There's an encrypted NFC chip inside. If you ever decide to join us, just tap it to your personal phone or tablet. We'll take it from there."

She eyed the pin. "And if I don't?"

Miguel smiled. "If you don't, you'll never hear from us again."

"Right," she sighed, "and my life stays the same."

"No, Rebecca, it does not. Ten years ago I thought that, and no one told me the truth. The truth is your life will never be the same, regardless of what you decide to do, or not do, with this pin." Miguel smiled at her. "I'd say I was sorry, but I'm not."

Doctor Rebecca Robinson slowly reached out and took the small pin from his hand. She looked at it, then raised her eyes to meet Miguel's. "This doesn't mean I'm one of you," she said.

"Of course," he replied, but a knowing smile played about his lips.

Rebecca slipped the pin into her coat pocket, and began editing Sara's medical record as she raised her speaking voice. "Looks like our patient is a lucky young woman."

Caspian glanced over. "So, she's going to be okay?"

"Sara's going to be fine," replied Dr. Robinson, then walked over and twisted a knob on one of the IV bags. "That's what was keeping her sedated while I sorted all this out. She'll be awake soon. You should stay so she opens her eyes to a comforting face. After all, your girlfriend tangled with a high-voltage wire, and came out the other side with a strong, healthy heart, that just happens to give its owner an extra beat."

Caspian laid his head against Sara's chest again, smiled, and said, "It's not just strong and healthy. It's magic. It's one heart that beats for two."

Chapter 48

A NEW BEGINNING

Sara's eyes fluttered open. "Caspian?" She blinked, trying to focus in the dim light of her hospital room. "Casp...Mum? Mum, what are you doing here?"

Sara's mother smiled down at her daughter, then slid to sit on the bed next to her. She ran a hand along Sara's forehead, then down her braids, which were splayed about like a curtain along one side of her pillow. "You gave us all a pretty good scare, Sa'sa."

Sara swallowed. "You only call me that when I'm scared, hurt, or—"

"That is not true," corrected her mother gently, "I call you that because it's what you called yourself when you were little. It reminds me of a time when I could fix all your problems with a kind word, a kiss, or perhaps a bit of gauze."

"What can't you fix?" asked Sara, her voice rising. She looked around. "Where's Caspian? I remember a car. I remember its headlights. There was a flash of light, and—" Sara's eyes grew wide with panic and she tried to push herself up. "Caspian...did that car—"

"He's fine," soothed her mother. "He's just over there, my sweet girl. Look. He's talking with your father."

Sara's eyes shifted to where her mother pointed. Through her hospital room's open door she could just see the two men in profile. She relaxed against her pillow, then tensed again a moment later. Sara turned to look again, then groaned. "Oh, no. Father has that face he gets. Mum, I love this man. Please don't let Father scare Caspian away with his sugar cane machete stories. I—"

Gloria Edwards spared a quick glance toward her husband, then chuckled. "Yes, he has frightened off many an unworthy suitor, I'll grant you that. However, no good father would find the man who saved his little girl's life unworthy of her." She saw Sara's confusion and smiled. "Sa'sa, which one of you is in a hospital bed, Caspian or you?"

Sara's mouth opened as if to respond, then she just sighed and shook her head. "You're right. My mind is all fuzzy. What happened? I don't even know what day it is?"

"Why, Sa'sa, it's Christmas day. The doctors had you sedated since last night. To quote your devoted, and I must say, extremely handsome, friend, Caspian, *you picked a fight with about seven-thousand volts of electricity…and lost.*"

"How bad was it?" whispered Sara. "It must have been pretty bad for you and Father to fly here in the middle of the night."

"Sa'sa, the shock stopped your heart." Sara eyes went wide, and she pressed a hand to her chest. Gloria gave her daughter a warm smile, "Of course it's beating. I meant what I said before, Caspian saved your life. He performed CPR on you until an ambulance arrived."

Tears began leaking from the corners of Sara's eyes. "I wasn't checking to see if my heart was beating, mum. I'm not stupid, and—"

"I know," she interrupted, "I was just trying to make you laugh a little, but —"

"I was feeling the scar, mum. I know how CPR works, you can't do it through a coat. Does he know?"

Her mother's brow furrowed in confusion. "Of course he knows, Sa'sa. But, are you telling me that you never shared this with him?"

"Nobody knew," hissed Sara.

"Well, why didn't they know? Your father and I said to keep the truth close, in order to protect Miguel and others like him. We never told you to keep it from your closest friends or," she inclined her head toward Caspian, "the man you love. So, you never told anyone?" Sara shook her head. "Not even Michael?" Another shake. "Oh, Sa'sa, that explains why he sounded so strange on the phone, he would have had no idea why we called Dr. Alvarez." Gloria spared another quick glance toward the door. "Well, those two will notice you're awake any second now. Once they come over, I'll give your father a moment, then spirit him away before his mouth makes even more trouble for you, but Sa'sa, why in heaven's name didn't you tell Caspian?"

"Because I'm broken, mum," she cried. "I wanted him to see me, to love me for me, not because I was a broken thing in need of care."

"You are not broken, Sa'sa, and you might be able to lie to yourself, but you cannot lie to your mother. I've seen all your lies, and know when you speak falsely." Sara opened her mouth to object, but her mother shook her head. "No," she hissed, "I will not hear you on this. You didn't tell the boy because *you* were afraid he might think you broken, and leave. Now, isn't that right?"

Sara pinched her eyes closed, as a soft cry caught in her throat. She opened them, then nodded to her mother, who just shook her head.

"You are lucky I'm still thanking God that you are alive, young lady, or I would give you a tongue lashing you would never forget. As it is, I will just say this. You've done this boy, this man, Caspian, a grave injustice, thinking he wouldn't love you because of your heart. I tell you the truth, Sara Edwards, that kind of thinking does speak to something being broken within you, but it is decidedly *not* your heart."

Sara groaned again, "You're right, mum. I know you're right, but what should I say? What should I do? I don't want to lose him."

"I wish I could tell you," sighed her mother, "but I suggest you start with something completely different than whatever you've been doing. Sa'sa, one may win a man with beauty and guile, but one keeps a man with honesty, humility, and love." A sound came from her right, and Gloria turned to see both her husband and Caspian walking quickly toward them. She leaned down, kissed her daughter's cheek, and whispered, "Honesty, humility, and love, Sa'sa. I have a good feeling about this Caspian. Trust him."

Vincent Edwards glared at his wife. "Gloria, why are you tugging on my arm? I am trying to have a conversation with my daughter."

She returned Vincent's expression, her tone shifting to one he immediately recognized as meaning he had done, or was about to do, something horribly wrong. "True as that might be, Vincent, our daughter *needs* to have a conversation with Caspian, and she needs to have it, *without* an audience. Now, come and get a coffee with your loving wife, before she throttles you."

Caspian watched the two Edwards leave. Gloria turned, just as the door was closing and gave Sara an encouraging smile. "I just love those two," said

Caspian. "They actually remind me of my parents. It's like they can communicate telepathically or something."

"Or something," sighed Sara, as she shifted to make room for Caspian on the bed. She patted the covers, and he moved to sit next to her. "How ya doing... Sa'sa?" Her lips quirked up, and he asked, "Do I get to call you Sa'sa, too, or is it verboten like Mikey is with Michael?"

"You guys call him that plenty," she replied.

"Yeah, but just to annoy him. I think Sa'sa is adorable, but if you don't——"

She shook her head. "No, I don't mind, Cas. In fact, it would make me happy if you did call me that, at least from time-to-time."

"Then I will——" began Caspian, but Sara reached up to lay a hand against his cheek.

"You didn't let me finish," she said. "I'm not sure you're going to want to call me that, because everyone who does, well, they love me."

Caspian looked down, and shook his head. "I'm so sorry. I should have told you before. All my emotions have been caught up in this Gordian knot that was impossible to untie. Fear, guilt, betrayal, more fear, they were all vying to take first place in that labyrinthine mind of mine. Sara, I never thought I'd feel this way again, but when I did, then I thought maybe I was feeling it too soon. Argh," he groaned. "I'm making a hash of things, what I'm trying to say is that I'm sorry I never told you that I loved you, because I——"

"But you did tell me," she said. Caspian furrowed his brow in confusion, as Sara continued. "I remember it now. I was laying on the road. You were giving me CPR, but I felt like I needed to go somewhere. I also felt safe and loved. I was about to leave, when I heard you talking to me." She smiled. "You told you me you loved me, then you looked up at something I couldn't see. That's when I started to feel warm all over. I remember thinking how strange it was that I felt warm because it had begun to snow." Sara paused for a moment, then locked eyes with Caspian. "I think I was dead, Cas. I felt myself drifting away, when a hand gripped my wrist. I thought it was you at first, but when I looked down, you were still doing CPR on my body. That's when I heard a voice, maybe it was an angel, I don't know, but it asked me, *do you want to stay?*" Caspian pinched at his eyes, and began shaking his head. "I know," said Sara, "I know this sounds insane, but isn't that just the way of things. We say we believe in miracles until they actually happen to us, then we think it's a mental disorder?" She slumped against her pillow and slipped her other hand around Caspian's own. "I wanted to stay, Caspian. I told the voice I wanted to stay, and that's when I stopped drifting. I didn't go back to my body or anything. I just stopped getting further away. Then the angel-voice talked to me again. I'll never forget what she said. It's like a riddle in my mind that I can't figure out."

"Tell me," whispered Caspian.

Sara let out a long breath. "The voice said, *Some believe a gift loses value with each giving. They are wrong. The gift that binds us grows stronger and more valuable in the giving. Twice now a heart's been given, once in spirit and once in flesh. Now you have the chance to give it a third time. It will require both trust and love, but the third time pays for all.*"

Sara stared up at Caspian and shook her head. "See, I told you...delusion. *Third time pays for all?* That's from *The Hobbit*. What kind of angel quotes *The Hobbit?*" She slipped her hand from Caspian's, then patted it. "No, don't say anything yet, because, delusion or not, the voice had a point. I've told you that I loved you, Cas, and I meant it with my whole heart, my whole self, like we've talked about."

"I know you did," he replied softly.

"But I didn't tell you my whole truth. It wasn't fair of me, and I'm sorry. The truth is that I may not have long to live, and you should know that."

"What do you mean?" asked Caspian in alarm. "The doctors said you were going to be fine."

"It's my heart, Cas."

"What about it?"

"My heart," she replied, her tone incredulous. "It's not exactly original equipment. Don't play dumb. You saw the scar, and I know they told you. Last year I wasn't in Austin because of depression, or an eating disorder, I was getting a heart transplant...a very illegal heart transplant that my parents arranged. You see, sometimes there are organs that transplant boards think aren't worth the risk of a malpractice suit if the transplant goes bad, so they——"

"I know about Alvarez, too," whispered Caspian.

"Great," snapped Sara, "do you also know that grade-A heart transplants only lasts about ten years? Now, ten years sounded like a lot to me, because when they flew me to Austin, I didn't have ten days, but you may not want to build a life with someone who has an expiration date. And that's with a good heart, mine is a bad heart, Cas. It could fail tomorrow, and I won't accept another one. I've had my second chance. I won't deprive someone of their second chance just so I could get a third."

A smile spread across Caspian's face as he shook his head and laughed softly. "Oh, I do love you Sara Edwards, but you definitely do *not* have a bad heart. As for ten years, wasn't it you who told me that we were never promised tomorrow. Today, you are here with me. Today, you have given me the greatest gift someone could give. You've given me a love so strong and so true, that it's allowed me to return it, with my whole heart, my whole self. Let me tell you something, whether we have ten months, ten years, or ten decades, I promise you, Sa'sa, I will count each of them as an undeserved blessing, because I'll be spending them with you."

Tears filled Sara's eyes and began spilling down her face and onto the pillow. Caspian stroked her cheek, then kissed her. "Now, it's time for me to trade truth for truth, and help you puzzle out the message you were given, because it wasn't from an angel." Sara lay quietly, eyes wide with wonder as Caspian shared all that had transpired since the two had met. When he was done, Sara took his hand and pressed it hard against her chest. He felt the steady rhythm though his fingertips, *Bump-bump...bump-bump-bump...bump-bump...bump-bump-bump.*

Caspian nodded. "*Twice now a heart's been given, once in spirit and once in flesh. Now you have the chance to give it a third time. It will require both trust and love, but the third time pays for all.* Elizabeth gave her heart to me in spirit when she agreed to be my wife. She gave it to you in flesh so you could live. Now, you've given it back in truth and love. In defiance of all powers and principalities, Sara Edwards, you've restored me to life." Caspian kissed her, and whispered, "Elizabeth loved Tolkien, and Bilbo's dad was right, the third time does pay for all."

Chapter 49

AULD LANG SYNE

Sara stared into the crackling fire and sighed. Caspian eyed her. She sighed again. He nudged her, and laughed. "You sound like Link when he pets a horse in those Zelda games. Out with it, woman."

She snuggled closer to him, leaning her head on his shoulder, and said, "It's nothing."

"Sar, when you say *it's nothing*, it's always something. What is it?"

Sara sat up, causing the blanket they'd been sharing to pull free of Caspian. "Oh, sorry," she said, but he just waved away her concern with a *go-on* gesture. "Okay, well, it's just that tonight's New Year's eve, right?"

Caspian made a point of looking at his watch, then nodded. "For another... thirty-nine minutes, yes."

"Okay," she said again, "so, it's New Year's eve, and what are we doing?"

"We're snuggled up under the amazingly beautiful blanket your mother gave you, amidst a sea of pillows, and in front of a crackling fireplace. In addition, the pillows, blankets, and we, are all surrounded by a magnificent nineteenth century mansion-house. What's your point?"

She frowned at him. "Well, when you put it *that* way, I don't have a point, not a valid one anyway."

Caspian laughed. "So, what *was* your point before my hate-facts made it invalid?"

"You are a doofus."

"Don't steal Jenny's terms of endearment, and *that* wasn't your point."

"Fine, my point was that all our friends are out being young, and having fun. I feel bad because if it weren't for me, *we* could be out there, being young, and having fun." Caspian smiled at her. "What?" she asked.

"Two things. First, the firelight makes the hazel of your eyes look almost gold." He chuckled a moment later. "Well, now you ruined it by rolling them at me."

"What's your second point?" she asked.

"Just this. No one wants to be out there, Sara. Everyone wishes they were in here…like us. In fact, the only reason they are out there this year is so when next New Year's eve rolls around, they can be in here…like us." He smirked at her. "Besides…your whole argument is invalid because you were, quite literally, dead in my arms less than a week ago. Recently dead girls do *not* go out on New Year's eve."

Sara pursed her lips, then inclined her head to Caspian, "Ok, Mr. Lewis. I'll give you that one."

He pushed himself up and stretched. "How magnanimous of you, Miss Edwards."

"I know. I'm just a magnanimous kind of girl, but where do you think you're going?"

Caspian pointed to the keeping room's expansive fireplace. "It needs tending."

She shifted among several of the many pillows that were arrayed beneath and around them, then shivered. Caspian bent down, lifted one corner of the thick woolen blanket, and tucked it around Sara's shoulders again. She grabbed hold of the blanket from within, and drew her arms close. "See," he said, "the fire needs tending."

"No, it doesn't," she laughed. "It's just cold outside and the house breathes more when it's cold."

"Breathes?" he asked. "Is that *Michael* for the old place is drafty? Hey, speaking of drafty, do you remember that scene from *It's a Wonderful Life* where George and Mary threw rocks at the old Granville house?"

Sara gave him a flat stare. "We just watched it last night, Cas, *and* that was the scene where the girl…"

"Donna Reed," interjected Caspian.

"Okay," sighed Sara, "That was the scene where *Donna Reed was* supposedly naked in the bushes, and you kept asking me what I thought she was really wearing." Sara lowered her voice and tried to copy Caspian's American accent.

"It's not *important,* Sar, I'm just curious. You don't think she was *really* naked in those bushes do you?" She smiled but shook her head. "Where are you going with this?"

Caspian put his hands on his hips, and affected a poor Jimmy Stewart imitation, "No, Sara...Sara you don't understand, see. You make a wish and then you try to break some glass, and you've got to be a pretty good shot nowadays too."

He stared at her expectantly, but Sara frowned, and said, "Look, I memorize Shakespeare not whoever made *It's a Wonderful Life.*"

Caspian sighed. "Frank Capra. Okay, I'll play both parts." He pitched up his voice. "Oh no, Caspian, don't. It's full of romance, that old place. I'd like to live in it."

He shifted back to Stewart. "That old place?"

"Uh huh."

"Sa-Sara, I wouldn't live in it as a ghost." Caspian opened his arms and smiled at her.

"Um, is this when I clap?" she asked, "or is it when you explain the meaning you hid so cleverly in your performance that no human being could possibly have sussed it out?"

Caspian bent down, kissed her nose, then tapped it. "Your nose is cold, which is good for huskies, not good for beautiful Jamaican women. This house doesn't breathe. It's old and drafty just like the old Granville place, from *Wonderful Life.* In short, I'm not listening to you, and I'm going to put more wood on the fire."

Sara reached for him but missed. "I think you just wanted to pretend you were George Bailey. I also think, Caspian Lewis, that you are going to burn down a two hundred year old house. The fire does not need—" A loud clunk came from the fireplace, "—more wood," she finished.

Flames licked up the dry hickory causing crackles and a rich, sweet, smell to fill the room. Caspian watched as the wave of increased heat reached Sara and she wiggled her shoulders beneath the blanket. He smirked at her. "Didn't need more wood, eh?"

"Shut up and come over here," she said, and lifted up one corner of the blanket. Caspian quickly snuggled in beside her. They sat in a comfortable silence for quite some time, just enjoying the closeness of each other's company. Finally, Sara broke the silence. "So, you wouldn't want to live here?"

"Where?"

"Here," she repeated.

"Here...here, as in this particular house?" Sara fixed Caspian with a stare that could stop clocks. "Okay," he laughed, "I'm just playing with you. Of course, I'd live here. It's a gorgeous nineteenth century house in the Garden District." He stretched. "I'd want to rename it to *The Old Granville Place* of course."

"Of course," she agreed. "So, you just wouldn't live here if you were a ghost?"

"Right, if I were a ghost, I'd probably live in Scotland. I hear that's the place to go, if you're a ghost." He saw Sara start to stare into the middle distance, and gave her a gentle nudge. "Why all this talk about houses and who's living where?"

She shook her head. "I was just projecting into the future...you know me... project, project, project. I tell others to live in the now, but I'm still a work in progress." She pursed her lips, then said, "Michael agreed to set up the family's whole west coast distribution network next year." Caspian gave her a non-committal shrug. "Didn't he tell you about it?" she asked.

"Sar...he said something about California and rum, but I was juggling hospital administrators, nurses, and doctors at the time, so wasn't really paying attention."

"Well, he's going to be living there for at least six months starting this spring."

"Really?"

"Yes, really, and, well, I don't like the idea of being in this big old house alone. Now, don't make fun of me, Caspian. I'm serious. You've never slept here all night. I love this house, but sometimes, especially in the warm months, it makes noises at night. It's woken me up at two or three in the morning, creaking."

"It creaked?" he asked. She nodded. "I thought you said it breathed." Sara's nose flared. "Okay, okay. I won't tease you anymore. Look, it's just the wood contracting as it cools."

Sara tapped her head. "I know what it is, Caspian, but men have to be good for something. Up until this point, Michael has been good for making me feel safe. I've had to wake him up at three in the morning on several occasions to make sure the creaking is just creaking and not a murderer in my house!"

"I think I see where you're going with this now," said Caspian. "You want me to stay here while Michael's in California, is that it?"

She nodded. "I already discussed it with Michael. He's fine with you taking his room. I was going to talk with you about it on Christmas, but—" she let the words hang in the air for a moment then said, "So, what do you think?"

"Sorry, no."

She blinked. "That's it. Just, *sorry, no?* That's all I get?"

"Look, Sara, I am willing to be on speed dial, but I promised myself no living with someone."

"I'm not just *someone*, Caspian—"

"Right, you are the sexy, beautiful, strong, intelligent woman that I love... and who I should not be within arms length of in the middle of the night."

She frowned at him. "I'll lock my door."

"What if you're taking a late night shower? The house could choose that precise moment to...I don't know...breathe wrong, and you come running out in a towel, or less." Caspian pointed at her. "You're the sucker for romantic comedies, not me. What happens if you run out of the shower in a towel or less? Us in a tangle of limbs on the floor, that's what happens." Sara opened her mouth to respond, but Caspian tilted his watch toward her. It had begun to chime. "Can we pick this up in five minutes? This is your first American new year, and I don't want you to miss it." She nodded, and Caspian gave her a wink. "Okay, be right back." He raced out of the keeping room. Several seconds later a crash sounded from the kitchen. Sara cringed. "It's okay. I'm okay. It was just something of Michael's. No big deal." Caspian skidded back into the room, and set a bottle of Veuve Clicquot on the floor beside her along with two champagne flutes.

Sara picked up the bottle and whistled. "La Grande Dame Yayoi Kusama, 2012. Cas, this is a five-hundred dollar bottle of champagne. What were you thinking?"

He looked over his shoulder as he quickly swiped across an iPad. "Huh, oh, right now I'm thinking that Michael should have put a TV in this room so we don't have to watch the ball drop on an iPad."

"That was me, not him," she replied. "I asked for one common room that had zero technology. This is that room." He turned to find her twisting a thin metal band that surrounded the bottle's cork.

"Hey, what are you doing?"

"Removing the muselet?" she said. "What does it look like I'm doing?"

He took the bottle from her, and continued twisting. "What's a muselet?"

"It's what you just pulled off the cork," she replied with a laugh, then shook her head. "People like you should *not* buy five-hundred dollar bottles of champagne."

"Very funny, *Chef Edwards,* but it only costs that much in one of your fancy restaurants." Caspian gave her a self-satisfied smile. "This is a once-in-a-lifetime occasion, *and* I got it for half that." He put two thumbs under the cork and pushed. It flew into the air with a loud *pop* along with a small fountain of foaming champagne. Sara's eyes went wide in horror. Caspian tilted the bottle toward her, then paused. "What?"

"Nothing," she replied. "I think I might just have had a small stroke, that's all."

"Fine, I'm a peasant. You can teach me the proper way to open champagne next year." He quickly filled the two flutes, then settled himself beside her. Caspian and Sara watched as a large crystalline ball slowly descended in Times Square. People began cheering on the small screen, and they heard the distant sound of fireworks going off throughout the Garden District. Caspian clinked his glass against Sara's. They both took sips, and he leaned in for a kiss. "Happy new year, Sa'sa."

She smiled at him. "Happy new year, Prince Caspian."

He kissed her again. "I love you."

Sara stared at him for several seconds, then said, "I love you, too…so much." She shot him an impish smile. "Now, about this Spring—"

"No, no, no," laughed Caspian. "I have a present for you, then you can harangue me about living arrangements, I promise."

"You promise?" she asked.

"I promise," Caspian said again.

"Okay, but I didn't get you anything. I didn't even know people exchanged gifts on New Year's eve. Is this an American thing?"

Caspian got up and walked over to the fireplace, tossed on another log, then moved to a nearby cabinet. He bent down, unlatched it, and removed a medium-sized box, all wrapped in reds and greens. "No, it's not *an American thing*. This is your Christmas present, or it was. We kinda spent the first four days of Christmas in the hospital, and the next two with your parents doting on you, not that I blame them one bit. So, you get your present on the eighth day of Christmas."

She grinned at him. "There better not be eight maids a milking in that box. I'm not a jealous woman, but I do have my limits, sir."

ONE HEART THAT BEATS FOR TWO

"I promise," snickered Caspian, "no maids a milking, but I was able to make a few adjustments to your present from what I had been planning." He set down the box. "Go on, open it." Sara slipped her arms out from beneath the blanket and reached for the box. Caspian stopped her, and pointed at the bow set in its top. "Just pull that as if you were Christophe revealing a decadent dessert." Sara's eyes flashed with amusement, and she extended her hand again. In one fluid motion she lifted the box lid. "And voilà," cheered Caspian.

Sara peered at the two figurines that stood before her. She crinkled her nose, leaned close, then her mouth dropped open. "Are those, us?" Caspian grinned. She looked again. "Those are our D&D characters!" Sara exclaimed. She held both hands to her face. "Oh my gosh, that is amazing, Cas. Look at them. They're so detailed. Even the base they are standing on is cute." She traced her finger along the raised golden script, while reading it. "Valdania Shannara and Tholem of Surrealia, an epic campaign." Her eyebrows raised. "It says *beginning March, 2022.* How are we going to do a campaign without Michael…via Zoom?"

Caspian shrugged. "We'll figure something out. So, do you like them?"

"I love them!" Sara shot him a crooked smile. "Valdania is looking pretty hot in those rogue leathers of hers."

"Valdania *is* hot," agreed Caspian.

"Mmmm," intoned Sara, "Tholem's not looking too shabby either. Check out his arms."

Caspian lifted one of his, and flexed. "Yeah, well, I took some liberties."

"Can I hold them?" she asked. "I mean, are they fragile?"

"Nope, they are legit action figures. Go ahead, pick her up."

Sara lifted the wood elf doll and turned it around in her hands. "Oh, look," she laughed. "Valdania even has the rogue's pack of holding she found in the Tomb of Horrors."

"Yeah," said Caspian, "and she probably took all the loot, too, despite promising Tholem otherwise."

"Valdania would *never* do that," murmured Sara as she continued staring at the doll.

Caspian shook his head. "I dunno, she *is* a rogue." He bent down, and reached into the doll's pouch, then grunted. "Yep, just as I thought, she's been holding out on poor, trusting Tholem."

Sara looked up. "What are you talking ab——" She broke off as Caspian held a ring between two fingers, "Cas?"

He knelt down beside her. "I love you, Sara. You've become a part of me so precious that I have no idea where I end and you begin. Living the rest of my life with you, Sara Edwards, that would be the most epic of campaigns. Will you marry me?"

She swallowed. Tears filled her eyes, and she glanced back to the display stand. "Epic campaign beginning March 2022?" She sniffed. "You knew about Michael having to stay in California, didn't you?" Caspian nodded. "So, my cousin knew all about this?"

"I talked to him about it the day after Christmas, then I talked with your Dad."

Sara nipped at the corner of her lip. "You talked with my Father?"

"Of course I did. You don't ask a man's daughter to marry you without first asking for her father's blessing, but you haven't answered me. Will you?"

Sara let out a breath as more tears fell. "Of course I will, you ridiculous doofus."

"Hand please," said Caspian, then slipped the heart shaped diamond ring on her finger.

Sara watched as the firelight reflected off both the center stone and a ruby set on either side. "Ohh," she said, looking up, then pointed at the diamond. "One heart..." her finger moved to touch the rubies, "...that beats for two." Sara wrapped her arms around Caspian. "I..." she kissed him, then pulled back a second later. "Love..." another kiss. "You..."

The air condensed to frost as she spoke this last, and the fire began to gutter. They turned to find Elizabeth wreathed in silver light and smiling at them. Caspian saw Sara's face, and whispered, "You can see her?"

"Of course she can see me," laughed Elizabeth, "You are one flesh after all, or will be soon enough. I'm leaving, but wanted to see you both before I went." She focused on Sara, inclined her head, and whispered, "Thank you."

"Thank me? I—"

"Yes," said Elizabeth. "Thank you for making such good use of my gift. Thank you for restoring my Caspian...*your* Caspian, to life."

Sara shook her head. "I don't know what to say."

"You don't need to say anything, because what you've done speaks louder than any words could ever do." Elizabeth drew near, then knelt in front of Caspian. "And thank you, my love. Thank you for all that we shared in this life." She tilted her head toward Sara. "Thank you for embracing the gift of which she's made such good use." The air grew colder still, and frost formed on the keeping room's windows. Elizabeth reached for Sara and hugged her. "Love him well."

Sara squeezed tightly, "I promise."

Elizabeth nodded to her, then moved to embrace Caspian. "Love her well." She felt him tremble in her arms, as he repeated the words Sara spoke just moments before. Elizabeth slipped from his embrace though Caspian hadn't released her. She became less substantial, taking several steps back from them. Elizabeth held up both hands. "This was number six, and I promised seven. You both will see me once more, but not for many years." She smiled. "Time is different where I am, well, all things are different here." She shook her head at Caspian's confusion. "I've told you, I'm absent from the body. Why don't you look it up?" Elizabeth winked at Sara. "You're the wife. Make sure he looks it up. Don't let him become a pig-headed old Ebenezer who ends up seeking forgiveness for having no eyes to see with or ears to hear with." She looked from one to the other, and smiled. "I love you both." Flames rose within the hearth, sending out waves of heat, and Elizabeth faded from view.

Chapter 50

A FINE SPRING DAY

"Sara, stop fidgeting or your veil is going to be crooked." Jennifer shot an imploring look toward Gloria. "Would you please tell your daughter to stop fidgeting?"

The older woman nodded. "Sa'sa, stop fidgeting. Brides are calm as still water. They do not sway and bend like sugarcane in a storm."

Sara became rigid. "Sorry, mum."

Jennifer tried to move her friend's arm, then grumbled, "Now, she's a statue...Gloria..."

Sara's mother stood in front of her daughter. The two locked eyes. "What is it Sa'sa? Are you nervous? It's perfectly natural to be nervous. You just shouldn't look nervous. Men don't like nervous brides. Remember, they believe everything is about them. Caspian will think you're having second thoughts."

"I'm not having second thoughts, mum. I love him and can't wait to be married. I was just thinking of Caroline's wedding, and wished I had thought of something, that's all."

"Who's Caroline?" asked Jennifer while staring over Sara's shoulder at their reflection in a floor length mirror.

"A friend from back home. We went to school together. She was married about three years ago, and it was one of the most beautiful nuptial masses and receptions I'd ever seen, especially when they drove away together."

"Ahh," said Gloria with newfound understanding, "The Salve Regina, that certainly was something to behold."

"I know the Salve Regina," said Jennifer. Sara's eyes met hers in the mirror. "Don't look at me that way, I'm not *that* lapsed, and I'm getting better. Anyway, our Catholic high school made us take Latin and—"

"Made you?" asked Gloria, her tone disapproving.

Jennifer slumped. "Our Catholic high school *gave us the opportunity* to take latin..." Gloria nodded as Jennifer continued, "...and we ended each class by singing the Salve Regina. I love that prayer, especially in latin."

Sara caught her friend's eye in the mirror, and said, "I didn't know you could sing, Jenny. Why haven't I ever heard you sing?"

Jennifer laughed "Because you've never taken a shower with me. I'm really self conscious about it. Cas and Dave try to trick me into singing in public, but I always escape their ill-formed plots." She stood back, and cocked her head while staring appraisingly at Sara. "I think we're done."

Gloria nodded. "I agree. You are beautiful Sa'sa, a pristine white flower, just ready to be plucked by her one true love."

"Mother...don't," grumbled Sara.

Jennifer snickered, then snapped her tongue against the roof of her mouth, and said, "Puh'lucked." Sara glared at her. "What?" asked Jennifer innocently, "I just repeated what your mom said. So, tell me about this Salve Regina thing. Did they sing it at the Mass?"

Sara shook her head. "No, after the reception. Caroline and her new husband, Roje, were running toward their car, and just as they reached it, all Roje's groomsmen began to spontaneously sing the Salve Regina. It was amazing. They drove off to the strains of Hail Holy Queen. It was like angels were singing them on their way." Sara sighed. "I should have thought of that."

Jennifer shrugged. "I wouldn't be thinking about angels while *I* was driving away with my shiny new husband, I'll tell you that for sure." She pointed at Sara. "And you can also be confident that Cas' reptilian brain will be much more focused on the aforementioned *plucking* than any songs being sung."

Sara eyes flicked to her mother, "Thanks mum, now this is what I'm going to be hearing from Jenny for the next...forever."

"You are lucky to have such friends, Sa'sa, and—" all three women looked at the clock as music began playing through the small New Orleans chapel.

Jennifer moved to lower Sara's veil. She grinned at her friend. "Here comes the bride..."

"Well, we did it," said David as he raised a glass of wine. Jennifer and Michael clinked glasses with him, then all three looked out over the dance floor. Caspian and Sara slowly moved to the strains of Rachmaninoff's Rhapsody on a Theme. He said something that made her laugh, and she gave him a quick kiss.

"So, what did you guys give Mr. and Mrs. Lewis as a wedding gift?" asked David. "I didn't realize that Sara had set up a registry until it was too late."

Jennifer gave her friend an incredulous look. "What do you mean, *you didn't realize?* Is this your first wedding or something, Dave?"

He shrugged. "Actually, yes."

"Well, pretty much everyone has a registry," she sighed. "What did you get them?"

"An Xbox." David saw his friends' expressions and hastened to add, "I also got them three years of GamePass, so they can..." his voice started to trail off as Jennifer shook her head at him, "...play games together," he finished.

Michael slapped his friend on the back and pointed at the newlyweds. "Dave, look at those two. There is a years worth of sexual tension packed in that tiny area of the dance floor. Those two will not be playing *any* video games for quite some time. Trust me."

"*I* got them a KitchenAid mixer," said Jennifer proudly. "Of course, I also cheated because I helped Sara set up the registry so bought it for her before anyone else even had access to it." Both men stared at her uncomprehendingly. "The KitchenAid mixer is the pinnacle of registry gifts," she declared. "It lasts forever. It makes delicious things. It's so simple to use, even a man can operate it." Jennifer held up a finger. "Most importantly, with every use Sara will be reminded just how much she is loved...by me. In short, I've won the registry war, bitches." Michael made a point of silently looking away, but Jennifer narrowed her eyes at him, and said, "Why are you doing that?" Her tone became slightly accusatory. "Michael Thomson, what did you get them?"

He held up both hands. "It wasn't me, not really. Honestly, it was more of a family gift." Jennifer just fixed him with a flat stare. "Okay, fine," sighed Michael, "we gave them the house."

Jennifer's eyes flicked to David who had begun to grin like an idiot. "Shut up, Dave," she growled.

His smile only broadened as he laughed. "I didn't say anything, Jen, but you should be happy. Now they have a place to put that mixer."

Michael put one arm around each of his friends. "Stop, you two or I'm going to turn this car around." He inclined his head toward Jennifer. "You still won the registry war, Jen. I'm going to be in Cali for at least six months, and the last thing Cas and Sara need when I get back is a roommate. I only bought the haunted mansion to make her feel comfy, anyway. You know me, the Garden District is nice, but I'm much more of a city guy." He paused, then pointed at the dance floor. "The more important question is not what gifts did each of us give, but which one of us will be next."

"It better be me," sighed Jennifer. "Last night I dreamed my ovaries became self-aware. Guys, they threatened me." She shook her head. "It's not a good thing when your own body parts threaten you with violence."

"What about that guy?" asked David, pointing.

Jennifer looked in the direction he indicated. "The photographer?"

David nodded. "Yeah, what's wrong with him?"

"Absolutely nothing," she replied. "Which means, he either lives with his parents, is gay, or killed someone before heading here to take pictures."

"So cynical," laughed Michael. "He's none of those things."

Jennifer stared incredulously at her friend. "And how do you know *that?*"

"Because *I* hired him," snarked Michael. "His name is Matthew Summers, and he served two tours in Afghanistan. He doesn't live with his parents, may well have killed somebody, but definitely isn't gay."

Jennifer tilted her head. "Then he has a girlfriend."

"Nope," said Michael.

David started laughing. "Did you stock the pond for our Jenny?"

"Nothing that overt," replied Michael. "He and some of his buddies have started a small distillery, and I've agreed to distribute their bourbon. He's just doing the photography stuff on weekends to help make ends meet. Their first batch still has a year to go before I can sell it, but it's going to be really good stuff. Anyway, I try to help vets whenever I can, and this guy has got it going on." Michael glanced at Jennifer. "You should probably stay clear of him."

"Why?"

"I just told you," snickered Michael. "I like him, and try to help vets whenever I can."

Jennifer made a face. "Very funny, Mikey."

Several woots came from among the guests, and the three friends looked up in time to see Caspian triumphantly brandishing a light blue garter in his right hand.

"He's such a doofus," laughed Jennifer. "Look at him holding that thing, like he's Arthur pulling Excalibur from the stone." A few seconds later Sara stood and waved a bouquet of flowers in front of herself. More cheers erupted from the guests. Jennifer felt her friends' eyes on her. "Stop, you guys. I'm not going up there."

"Oh you're going," they said, then pointed to where half-a-dozen young women had already gathered behind Sara.

Michael stood, and made a point of pulling Jennifer's chair away from the table, then Dave yelled, "Sara, don't do anything yet. Jenny's coming!"

"I hate you guys with the heat of a thousand suns," she growled as she made her way to the dance floor.

Sara pretended to throw her bouquet, then spun around to grin at the assembled women. "Who wants this?" she yelled. Cheers and hands went up. "Okay, you better be ready to fight for it then." Sara, once again, turned her back to the women. She looked up. Caspian smiled at her from the other side of the dance floor. He tilted his head to the left. Sara pivoted slightly in that direction. Another tilt, and she moved again. He winked at her. "Here it comes!" yelled Sara. She threw the bouquet. It arced high into the air and eight women all reached toward the tumbling flowers.

A mixture of women's disappointed groans and audience cheers flowed through the reception hall. Jennifer wobbled slightly as she landed, having forgotten to remove her heels before heading to the dance floor. She stared at the bouquet of flowers, then mouthed, *you cheated*, to Sara, who affected an expression so innocent that it caused Jennifer to burst out laughing. She took a step, and the heel of her right shoe gave way. Jennifer flailed her arms in a hopeless attempt to keep her balance. The room spun as she fell, then everything steadied.

Jennifer found herself staring into a pair of bright blue eyes. "Are you okay?" asked the photographer.

"Uh..." stammered Jennifer

"Hey look out," yelled a guest, "you're holding a woman who just caught the bouquet."

"Yeah Matt," came another voice, this one she recognized as being Michael's, "better let go quick before you catch fire."

"Might want to listen to them," snickered Jennifer.

Matthew laughed while helping her back to her feet. "I'm a Marine. I've been in real fire fights. I think I'll take my chances, Miss——"

"Jennifer, uh, I mean Landry...no, it's Jenny...ugh," she shook her head, "and this is why I have to leap for bouquets at weddings, because I clearly cannot speak."

"Hi Jenny, I'm Matthew, uh I mean Summers...no, it's Matt." He grinned at her and extended his hand. "Nice to meet you."

"Nice to meet you, too," she replied, then turned slightly to her left so that Matthew's back was more fully facing away from the tables. Over his shoulder she watched as Michael and David fist pumped and high-fived each other. Matthew saw her eyes shift and turned, but the two men appeared to simply be engaged in normal conversation.

"Such doofuses," she whispered to herself.

Matthew turn back around to face her. "I'm sorry, what?"

Jennifer smiled. "Nothing."

Matthew nodded. "So, you're okay?"

"Right as rain," she replied, then slipped off both shoes. "I'm pretty sure I can manage to not fall off my own feet."

Matthew saw several servers begin to move a table that led to the reception hall's side exit. He gestured to it. "I've got to get out there to take pictures of the bride and groom as they leave." Jennifer nodded. "But, will you be around for a bit after? I'm not the best at meeting people in general, let alone beautiful women, so——"

"Yeah, sure," said Jennifer, "don't feel bad, I'm kinda the same way."

"You aren't good at meeting beautiful women?" he asked with a grin.

"Horrible at it," she laughed.

Matthew headed for the side exit, but called over his shoulder. "See Jenny, we already have something in common."

David and Michael walked up several seconds later. "Sooo," crooned Michael, "what did he say?"

Jennifer eyed them both. "He said I was beautiful, which means he's definitely some kind of murderer, but honestly, I think I'm okay with it."

Her friends both laughed, then David said, "We better get out there or we're gonna miss them leaving."

Jennifer's eyes went wide. "Oh shit!" She dropped her shoes and sprinted for the door.

"What's up with her?" asked Michael.

"Maybe she's afraid that soldier dude is going to escape," chuckled David.

ONE HEART THAT BEATS FOR TWO

Sara and Caspian ran hand-in-hand down a narrow flagstone path, and toward the idling limousine. A driver stood holding the door open for them. Caspian stepped aside to let Sara enter first. She had just bent down when a voice cut through the well wishing cheers. Sara turned, eyes sweeping the small crowd until they found its source. Everyone had fallen silent. The night was still except for Jennifer's voice and the soft clicks of Matthew's camera. Sara's eyes met those of her friend, and they shared a knowing smile. She reached for Caspian's hand. The two stood with rapt attention as Jennifer sang them on their way.

> Salve, Regina,
> Mater misericordiæ,
> vita, dulcedo,
> et spes nostra, salve.
> Ad te clamamus,
> exsules, filii Hevæ,
> Ad te suspiramus,
> gementes et flentes
> in hac lacrimarum valle.
> Eia, ergo, advocata nostra,
> illos tuos misericordes oculos
> ad nos converte.
> Et Jesum, benedictum fructum ventris tui,
> nobis post hoc exsilium ostende.
> O clemens,
> O pia,
> O dulcis,
> Virgo Maria.

Chapter 51

EPILOGUE

C aspian stopped speaking, and set his bottle of water on the lectern. He smiled knowingly at the sea of faces, nearly all of which were streaked with tears. "So, Sara and I were sent on our way to the strains of Salve Regina. I had forgotten how well Jennifer could sing. She never liked to do it, and really hated being the center of attention. Still, she loved us more, so she sang that beautiful prayer." Caspian chuckled to himself, "Then, she padded back into the reception hall with that strong armed, square jawed, as she would say, *maman,* and that was it for Jenny. Or, as her students would later call her, Mrs. Summers."

"That was fifty-seven years ago," said Caspian, then motioned for Sara to join him on the stage. She shook her head. He motioned more insistently. Several people rose from their chairs and began softly clapping. Caspian saw her expression turn toward resignation, and she slowly made her way toward him. One of his students extended a hand as she drew near, helping her navigate the narrow stairs. When she finally stood next to him, Caspian leaned over and kissed her cheek. "You might recall, what Sara told me in that first day in the hospital. She was right, the average heart transplant does last about ten years, but then we're not talking about your average heart are we, Sa'sa?"

"No, we aren't," replied Sara.

"They can't hear you, honey. You have to speak up," said Caspian.

Sara gave him a reluctant nod, then stared out from the stage. She raised her voice. "No, we aren't." Caspian opened his mouth to speak, but Sara patted his arm. "I think you've talked enough, and since I knew you were going to do this to me, I decided to do something to you, too."

The audience made a collective *Woooo* sound.

Sara smiled. "Would you like to see what I've cooked up for Dr. Lewis?"

"Yes!" came the chorus.

Caspian shook his head then pointed at his students with feigned anger. "Et tu Brutus...all of you." They laughed, then fell silent as Sara slipped a hand terminal from her clutch purse. She tapped on it for several seconds, then looked back at the audience. "He made all of you cry, didn't he?"

"Yes..." they yelled.

"Don't you think it's only fair I make him cry a little?"

The room cheered.

"Sa'sa, what have you—" Caspian broke off as the auditorium door opened. His eyes immediately began to glisten. A woman in her middle years stepped into the room, and made her way to the stage. Caspian nodded as tears streaked his cheeks. "Well, played," he whispered, "Well played, indeed. Congratulations, you are the meanest wife, ever."

She smiled. "I learned from the best."

"Hi Daddy," said the woman as the two embraced. She turned to face the silent audience. "My mother told me what *he* planned to do tonight, so we plotted against him, as all good wives and daughters should. My name is Elizabeth Lewis, but my friends call me Lizzie. I was named for another Elizabeth, and it is because of her love and selflessness that my mother is standing here today. It's also why, my kids Jennifer, David, and Michael are right now at my father's house with their own children. Generations exist because of one woman and the love she had for my fath—" Lizzie paused, looked at her parents, then spoke again, "Father."

Frost formed in the air, and a collective gasp escaped from over two-hundred mouths, each of which produced its own small cloud.

Elizabeth Winters looked around the room, then smiled at Caspian, Sara, and Lizzie. She hadn't changed, but remained just as Caspian described. Her long blonde hair moved around her face as if caught in a gentle breeze. Bright green eyes, again, scanned the audience, then she walked to Caspian. Their eyes met, and her smile broadened as she leaned over to kiss his cheek. Caspian reached up, touching the place where her lips had brushed his skin. It felt warm. Elizabeth looked from Caspian to Sara while she spoke. "Seven times I promised, and seven times I've come. Four times for you, twice for you both, and now..." she focused outward, "once for posterity." Elizabeth stepped forward until she reached the leading edge of the stage. "All things," she began, "all things, even the most tragic, can be worked together for good if only our hearts are not hardened to the possibility. Take what you've seen here today, and hold it in your own hearts. Love freely and completely. Never let pride or jealousy take root, for only they have the power to strangle love."

Elizabeth turned to face the three Lewises. "You have set me as a seal upon your heart, as a seal upon your arm; for love is strong as death. Jealousy is cruel as the grave. The coals thereof are coals of fire, which has a most vehement flame."

Caspian and Sara nodded, and Elizabeth began to fade from view. Her voice became whisper soft, yet all in attendance claimed to have heard her final words. "Hold close this story of my Caspian, his Sara, and our one heart that beat for two."

The end of One Heart That Beats for Two

AUTHOR'S NOTE

I hope you have enjoyed *One Heart that Beats for Two*. If you're a reader or listener of either my Fantasy or Science Fiction novels, I think you will likely find this author's note as different from previous notes as *One Heart* is from *Sentinels* or *Paradigm*.

I think it should go without saying, that there will be spoilers ahead. However, so great are the spoilers within this author's note, that I wanted to call it out specifically. In short, if you haven't read this story to completion, please, stop.

Okay, so if you are still here, that means you've finished the book, and are now looking for some of my musings or, perhaps, a bit of backstory. I'm going to serve up a little of both this time around, with topics that include:

- Why Did I Write This Book
- Why This Book Scared Me
- The Concept of Triumph from Tragedy

However, before we get to those topics, I first have to give a shout-out to my patrons.

As anyone who's read, or listened, to my author's notes should know by now, I have a Patreon page listed under my full name, Robert W. Ross, and there are currently fifteen tiers of support starting as low as one dollar. A reader recently asked me why I included tiers at $1, $2, and $3, when most Patreons start at $5. It's simple really, I resisted even having a Patreon for a long time, until both fellow authors and readers convinced me of the error of my ways. As it turns out, there are a lot of benefits to having conversations behind a paywall. Most of those benefits have nothing to do with money. Given that, I wanted to make sure that anyone who sought me out for those kind of semi-private conversations wouldn't be put off because of a high barrier to entry. To be clear, I'm not knocking anyone who's Patreon starts at $5 or $500, that's just not what *I* wanted to do.

For the most part, I like to think we have a fair exchange of value. Each of you spend hard earned money to buy my books, e-books, or audiobooks. In return, I hope you get stories that both entertain and provoke thought. When

I'm especially fortunate, one of you takes the time to write a review. I simply cannot overstate how important those reviews are, so a special thanks to all of you who've taken the time to write them.

Over the years, my Patreon has evolved, slowly becoming a small, but close knit, community. Part of that evolution has included the addition of new support tiers along with associated goodies ranging from signed artwork to named characters being added to a story.

Starting with the Jarvis' Secret Agent tier, I promised to add such supporters' names to each author's note along with providing them a number of other goodies. So, without further adieu, I'd like to give a big shout-out to Keith Criswell, Mike Giallanza, Leslie Mott, Jerry Nelson, Daniel Seif, and Garrett Zeien. Thank you, Keith, Mike, Mott (she goes by Mott), Jerry, Daniel, and Garrett.

And now, back to the topics...

Why Did I Write This Book
Well, I'll start by saying that I didn't plan to write it. Once the idea for *One Heart*, had solidified, I moved from not planning, to actively resisting the writing of it. Ultimately, the story became a splinter in my mind, driving me mad (h/t to *The Matrix's* Morpheus). Eventually, as much as we might want to ignore such splinters, they often get the best of us to the point where we just have to dig them out. For an author, that means writing the darn story, so that's what I did.

Let me take a step back and explain how all this happened. Several years ago, maybe around 2018 or 2019, I was deep into the *Sentinels of Creation* series and just starting to concept *Paradigm 2045,* when I woke up with the entire plot to *One Heart* in my head.

Now, and this is important, nothing like that has ever happened to me before, or since. I know authors who get most of their ideas from dreams. That's not me, unless you count daydreams, which I don't, because dream-dreams are very different. Anyway, I woke up with this plot stuck in my head, and I was *not* happy about it.

I said to myself, "Self, why don't you just vomit this plot into your Mac's Notes app and be done with it? That should make it go away." So, that's what I did. As you probably guessed by now, the story didn't go away. Then I said to myself, "Self, maybe this story sucks. If so, then I should shoot it and put it out of its misery." This seemed like an excellent idea to me, so I printed off the ten page outline I had vomited earlier, and gave it to my daughter. She's a hopeless romantic, and I thought would surely put a stake in the heart of...eh...*One Heart*. About an hour later, she comes padding downstairs. Her eyes were puffy and red. She handed me the pages, and said the worst thing she could have said to me. "Dad <sniffles>, this is sooo good. You *have* to write this story. Promise me you'll write this story."

Well, crap, not what I was expecting. Of course then I did something that was both unthinkable and obvious when faced with one's puffy-eyed daughter, I promised her I would write the bloody story. Clever me though, I didn't say when I'd write it. No, I did not.

Which brings us to today, or more accurately, three months prior to today, July 7th, 2021. That was the day, I gave in, and started writing *One Heart that Beats for Two* in earnest. I had finished the last *Sentinels* book, *A Final Sacrifice,* two months early and sent it off to beta folks. I had run out of excuses, and, of course, there was the aforementioned splinter in my mind driving me mad. Three months to the day later, I'm tapping out this author's note having just put the last period on the last word of *One Heart's* epilogue.

And that, as Paul Harvey used to say, is the rest of the story.

Why This Book Scared Me

The short answer is I was afraid writing this book was preparing me to endure some awful tragedy. Now, to be clear, my personal worldview doesn't include a powerful and vindictive force out to ruin my life. To the contrary, if you recall from a previous author's note, I joked that much of the spiritual world is hidden from our eyes and must be taken on faith. However, we've been given two very tangible gifts as proof there is, indeed, a God who loves us and wants us to be happy. What are those very tangible gifts? Dogs and Beer!

Okay, so in the face of both dogs and beer, why did *One Heart* scare me? Simple, the story has, at its core, the concept that even out of the deepest, darkest tragedy, new light and life can bloom. Well, that's easy to say, Robert, has your life been marked with the deepest and darkest tragedy? That's the question I asked myself while writing this book. Was I even qualified to tell Caspian, Elizabeth, and Sara's story? I didn't think so, and if that was the case, I knew I didn't want to become qualified.

Ultimately though, writing this book brought two things into focus. First of all, none of us are getting out of this life alive. Physical death is the one thing everyone on this pale blue marble has in common. Ultimately, we all end up there eventually. Second, few of us will exit the stage without some challenge or tragedy having marked their life. The breadth and depth of those challenges or tragedies will be different for each of us. Likewise, our reaction to them. I don't share intimate details of my family life in this forum, but I have made no secret that I am the father to someone with special needs. At times it has been tragically painful, but also there have been moments of transcendent joy. One of my best friends lost his wife of only a couple years to cervical cancer, leaving him as a single father to a very young girl, my goddaughter. I've lost friends and family to cancer, and deal with others who suffer with chronic daily pain. In short, we all have our crosses to bear, and I think that's part of what *One Heart* had to teach me. Elizabeth said it just before leaving that last time, *"All things, even the most tragic, can be worked toward good if only our hearts are not hardened to the possibility. Take what you've seen here today, and hold it in your own hearts. Love freely and completely. Never let pride or jealousy take root, for only they can strangle love."*

I've certainly not lived up to those words at many points in my life. Perhaps, you've felt the same. Ultimately, I think if there's a deeper message to this story, that must be it, *All things can be worked toward good if only our hearts are not hardened to the possibility.*

Do I want to be tested any more than I already have been? Oh, heck no. However, one of you reading these words might have experienced a tragic loss the likes of which I cannot imagine. You may also be orders of magnitude stronger of will and heart than me. Perhaps, this story holds a special meaning for you. Perhaps, the path trod by Caspian, Elizabeth and Sara will help you on your own heroic journey to a brighter day. If so, I am incredibly honored, humbled, and grateful for having played even the smallest part in such a healing.

As with most books, we all take different things from within their pages. I hope each of you found something of value from *One Heart that Beats for Two*, whether that be poignant truth or romantic escapism.

The Concept of Triumph from Tragedy

A couple years ago, I received an interesting review that focused on tropes. The reviewer mentioned that I "leveraged some tropes while crushing others."

I had never thought about it before, but they were spot on. Some tropes need to die ignominious deaths. One example, among many, is where the male super hero's power is quickened by the horribly tragic death of a two-dimensional female love interest. Die horrible trope…dieeee!

ONE HEART THAT BEATS FOR TWO

By contrast, triumph born of tragedy is, at least in my opinion, a noble trope that we should see more of, not less. Then again, I may just be biased because triumph from tragedy is the trope equivalent to love's highest form, Agape. If you've read either my *Sentinels of Creation* or *Paradigm 2045* series, you probably have noticed that agape plays a prominent role in both.

That said, it's never played as central a role as it does within *One Heart that Beats for Two.* There are few things more universally tragic than young love cut short. We need look no further than Shakespeare's *Romeo & Juliet,* which has endured for well over four hundred years and inspired countless interpretations. Romeo & Juliet's tragedy extends beyond the death of young love, because there is no redemptive triumph. Shakespeare's star crossed lovers have little in common with either Elizabeth or Sara, who both epitomize the patient and kind qualities many of us hope to emulate. Of course, that's the genius of Shakespeare. He seamlessly blends all the most tragic elements of young love into the perfect package, leaving his readers with the ultimate cautionary tale. *One Heart* is not a cautionary tale. Rather, it is a romantic story that, I hope, reflects our idealized view of how triumph can grow from the ashes of tragedy.

Well, that's it, another novel and author's note in the can. Again, I hope you enjoyed *One Heart that Beats for Two.* As always, I will endeavor to do right by both you and the wonderful characters who inhabit all the worlds you've so graciously taken the time to enter. As always, please feel free to contact me on Facebook, Instagram, or at Spartamac.com.

AUTHOR'S BIO

Robert W. Ross is the author of the best selling *Sentinels of Creation* and *Paradigm 2045* print and audiobook series. With *One Heart that Beats for Two*, Robert branches out from sci-fi and fantasy and into the realm of paranormal romance.

He has both a passion for pop culture and a loathing to discuss himself in the third person. However, Robert's wife convinced him that anyone who took the time to read his books, or listen to his audiobooks, might want to know a little about the person who made them.

To that end, Robert's influences include authors such as Robert A. Heinlein, Philip Jose Farmer, and Brandon Sanderson. He has a deep and abiding love for all things Star Trek, Doctor Who, and Sponge Bob. While Robert can often make obscure TV, Book, and Movie references, he sadly any of his characters' genetic enhancements. To the contrary, he is quite sure the brain space taken up by all that trivia is directly responsible for him lacking any sense of direction.

In addition to his work as an author, Robert has led the Artificial Intelligence and Experience Design efforts for a number of Fortune 100 companies. He is also a keynote speaker and guest-lecturer at both Georgia Tech and Kennesaw State University.

In both interviews and reviews, Robert's unique blend of pop-culture, alternate history, near future science fiction, magical systems, and strong female characters have been highlighted as key factors in his series' success.

While Robert's first series, *Sentinels of Creation*, was written as contemporary fantasy, his second series, *Paradigm 2045*, leverages the hard science side of his experiences. Now, *One Heart that Beats for Two*, joins *Sentinels* and *Paradigm* in weaving the humor and character banter which are hallmarks of Robert's writing style.

Outside of his teaching and writing commitments, Robert enjoys helping to facilitate the collaboration between authors, cover artists, and audiobook voice actors. He is a big believer that such collaboration can make its own magic, causing an already great story to become even greater. For Robert, this magic is the product of his personal collaboration and friendship with narrator, Nick

Podehl and Greek artist, George Patsouras.

Robert lives in Atlanta with his wife, kids, one Siberian husky, and about eleven different Apple products. He is a fierce advocate for children with special needs, their parents, and the local organizations that support both.

Zuri Reyes

64529063R00213